VICTORIAN CHRISTMAS STORIES

13 Scary Ghost Stories to Read on A Dark, Snowy Night

CONTENTS

THE KIT-BAG

Algernon Blackwood, 1908

When the words 'Not Guilty' sounded through the crowded courtroom that dark December afternoon, Arthur Wilbraham, the great criminal KC, and leader for the triumphant defence, was represented by his junior; but Johnson, his private secretary, carried the verdict across to his chambers like lightning.

'It's what we expected, I think,' said the barrister, without emotion; 'and, personally, I am glad the case is over.' There was no particular sign of pleasure that his defence of John Turk, the murderer, on a plea of insanity, had been successful, for no doubt he felt, as everybody who had watched the case felt, that no man had ever better deserved the gallows.

'I'm glad too,' said Johnson. He had sat in the court for ten days watching the face of the man who had carried out with callous detail one of the most brutal and cold-blooded murders of recent years.

Be counsel glanced up at his secretary. They were more than employer and employed; for family and other reasons, they were friends. 'Ah, I remember; yes,' he said with a kind smile, 'and you want to get away for Christmas? You're going to skate and ski in the Alps, aren't you? If I was your age I'd come with you.'

Johnson laughed shortly. He was a young man of twenty-six, with a delicate face like a girl's. 'I can catch the morning boat now,' he said; 'but that's not the reason I'm glad the trial is over. I'm glad it's over because I've seen the last of that man's dreadful face. It positively haunted me. Bat white skin, with the black hair brushed low over the forehead, is a thing I shall never forget, and the description of the way the dismembered body was crammed and packed with lime into that--'

'Don't dwell on it, my dear fellow,' interrupted the other, looking at him curiously out of his keen eyes, 'don't think about it. Such pictures have a trick of coming back when one least wants them.' He paused a moment. 'Now go,' he added presently, 'and enjoy your holiday. I shall want all your energy for my Parliamentary work when you get back. And don't break your neck skiing.'

Johnson shook hands and took his leave. At the door he turned suddenly.

'I knew there was something I wanted to ask you,' he said. 'Would you mind lending me one of your kit-bags? It's too late to get one tonight, and I leave in the morning before the shops are open.'

'Of course; I'll send Henry over with it to your rooms. You shall have it the moment I get home.'

'I promise to take great care of it,' said Johnson gratefully, delighted to think that within thirty hours he would be nearing the brilliant sunshine of the high Alps in winter. Be thought of that criminal court was like an evil dream in his mind.

He dined at his club and went on to Bloomsbury, where he occupied the top floor in one of those old, gaunt houses in which the rooms are large and lofty. The floor below his own was vacant and unfurnished, and below that were other lodgers whom he did not know. It was cheerless, and he looked forward heartily to a change. The night was even more cheerless: it was miserable, and few people were about. A cold, sleety rain was driving down the streets before the keenest east wind he had ever felt. It howled dismally among the big, gloomy houses of the great squares, and when he reached his rooms he heard it whistling and shouting over the world of black roofs beyond his windows.

In the hall he met his landlady, shading a candle from the draughts with her thin hand. 'This come by a man from Mr Wilbr'im's, sir.'

She pointed to what was evidently the kit-bag, and Johnson thanked her and took it upstairs with him. 'I shall be going abroad in the morning for ten days, Mrs Monks,' he said. 'I'll leave an address for letters.'

'And I hope you'll 'ave a merry Christmas, sir,' she said, in a raucous, wheezy voice that suggested spirits, 'and better weather than this.'

'I hope so too,' replied her lodger, shuddering a little as the wind went roaring down the street outside.

When he got upstairs he heard the sleet volleying against the window panes. He put his kettle on to make a cup of hot coffee, and then set about putting a few things in order for his absence. 'And now I must pack--such as my packing is,' he laughed to himself, and set to work at once.

He liked the packing, for it brought the snow mountains so vividly before him, and made him forget the unpleasant scenes of the past ten days. Besides, it was not elaborate in nature. His friend had lent him the very thing--a stout canvas kit-bag, sack-shaped, with holes round the neck for the brass bar and padlock. It was a bit shapeless, true, and not much to look at, but its capacity was unlimited, and there was no need to pack carefully. He shoved in his waterproof coat, his fur cap and gloves, his skates and climbing boots, his sweaters, snow-boots, and ear-caps; and then on the top of these he piled his woollen shirts and underwear, his thick socks, puttees, and knickerbockers. The dress suit came next, in case the hotel people dressed for dinner, and then, thinking of the best way to pack his white shirts, he paused a moment to reflect. 'Bat's the worst of these kit-bags,' he mused vaguely, standing in the centre of the sitting-room, where he had come to fetch some string.

It was after ten o'clock. A furious gust of wind rattled the windows as though to hurry him up, and he thought with pity of the poor Londoners whose Christmas would be spent in such a climate, whilst he was skimming over snowy slopes in bright sunshine, and dancing in the evening with rosy-checked girls--Ah! that reminded him; he must put in his dancing-pumps and evening socks. He crossed over from his sitting-room to the cupboard on the landing where he kept his linen.

And as he did so he heard someone coming softly up the stairs.

He stood still a moment on the landing to listen. It was Mrs Monks's step, he thought; she must he coming up with the last post. But then the steps ceased suddenly, and he heard no more. They were at least two flights down, and he came to the conclusion they were too heavy to be those of his bibulous landlady. No doubt they belonged to a late lodger who had mistaken his floor. He went into his bedroom and packed his pumps and dress-shirts as best he could.

Be kit-bag by this time was two-thirds full, and stood upright on its own base like a sack of flour. For the first time he noticed that it was old and dirty, the canvas faded and worn, and that it had obviously been subjected to rather rough treatment. It was not a very nice bag to have sent him--certainly not a new one, or one that his chief valued. He gave the matter a passing thought, and went on with his packing. Once or twice, however, he caught himself wondering who it could have been wandering down below, for Mrs Monks had not come up with letters, and the floor was empty and unfurnished. From time to time, moreover, he was almost certain he heard a soft tread of someone padding about over the bare boards--cautiously, stealthily, as silently as possible--and, further, that the sounds had been lately coming distinctly nearer.

For the first time in his life he began to feel a little creepy. Then, as though to emphasize this feeling, an odd thing happened: as he left the bedroom, having, just packed his recalcitrant white shirts, he noticed that the top of the kit-bag lopped over towards him with an extraordinary resemblance to a human face. Be camas fell into a fold like a nose and forehead, and the brass rings for the padlock just filled the position of the eyes. A shadow--or was it a travel stain? for he could not tell exactly--looked like hair. It gave him rather a turn, for it was so absurdly, so outrageously, like the face of John Turk the murderer.

He laughed, and went into the front room, where the light was stronger.

'That horrid case has got on my mind,' he thought; 'I shall be glad of a change of scene and air.' In the sitting-room, however, he was not pleased to hear again that stealthy tread upon the stairs, and to realize that it was much closer than before, as well as unmistakably real. And this time he got up and went out to see who it could be creeping about on the upper staircase at so late an hour.

But the sound ceased; there was no one visible on the stairs. He went to the floor below, not without trepidation, and turned on the electric light to make sure that no one was hiding in the empty rooms of the unoccupied suite. There was not a stick of furniture large enough to hide a dog. Then he called over the banisters to Mrs Monks, but there was no answer, and his voice echoed down into the dark vault of the house, and was lost in the roar of the gale that howled outside. Everyone was in bed and asleep--everyone except himself and the owner of this soft and stealthy tread.

'My absurd imagination, I suppose,' he thought. 'It must have been the wind after all, although--it seemed so _very_ real and close, I thought.' He went back to his packing. It was by this time getting on towards midnight. He drank his coffee up and lit another pipe--the last before turning in.

It is difficult to say exactly at what point fear begins, when the causes of that fear are not plainly before the eyes. Impressions gather on the surface of the mind, film by film, as ice gathers upon the surface of still water, but often so lightly that they claim no definite recognition from the consciousness. Then a point is reached where the accumulated impressions become a definite emotion, and the mind realizes that something has happened. With something of a start, Johnson suddenly recognized that he felt nervous--oddly nervous; also, that for some time past the causes of this feeling had been gathering slowly in has mind, but that he had only just reached the point where he was forced to acknowledge them.

It was a singular and curious malaise that had come over him, and he hardly knew what to make of it. He felt as though he were doing something that was strongly objected to by another person, another person, moreover, who had some right to object. It was a most disturbing and disagreeable feeling, not unlike the persistent promptings of conscience: almost, in fact, as if he were doing something he knew to be wrong. Yet, though he searched vigorously and honestly in his mind, he could nowhere lay his finger upon the secret of this growing uneasiness, and it perplexed him. More, it distressed and frightened him.

'Pure nerves, I suppose,' he said aloud with a forced laugh. 'Mountain air will cure all that! Ah,' he added, still speaking to himself, 'and that reminds me--my snow-glasses.'

He was standing by the door of the bedroom during this brief soliloquy, and as he passed quickly towards the sitting-room to fetch them from the cupboard he saw out of the corner of his eye the indistinct outline of a figure standing on the stairs, a few feet from the top. It was someone in a stooping position, with one hand on the banisters, and the face peering up towards the landing. And at the same moment he heard a shuffling footstep. The person who had been creeping about below all this time had at last come up to his own floor. Who in the world could it be? And what in the name of Heaven did he want?

Johnson caught his breath sharply and stood stock still. Then, after a few seconds' hesitation, he found his courage, and turned to investigate. Be stairs, he saw to his utter amazement, were empty; there was no one. He felt a series of cold shivers run over him, and something about the muscles of his legs gave a little and grew weak. For the space of several minutes he peered steadily into the shadows that congregated about the top of the staircase where he had seen the figure, and then he walked fast--almost ran, in fact--into the light of the front room; but hardly had he passed inside the doorway when he heard someone come up the stairs behind him with a quick bound and go swiftly into his bedroom. It was a heavy, but at the same time a stealthy footstep--the tread of somebody who did not wish to be seen. And it was at this precise moment that the nervousness he had hitherto experienced leaped the boundary line, and entered the state of fear, almost of acute, unreasoning fear. Before it turned into terror there was a further boundary to cross, and beyond that again lay the region of pure horror. Johnson's position was an unenviable one.

By Jove! That was someone on the stairs, then,' he muttered, his flesh crawling all over; 'and whoever it was has now gone into my bedroom.' His delicate, pale face turned absolutely white, and for some minutes he hardly knew what to think or do. Then he realized intuitively that delay only set a premium upon fear; and he crossed the landing boldly and went straight into the other room, where, a few seconds before, the steps had disappeared.

'Who's there? Is that you, Mrs Monks?' he called aloud, as he went, and heard the first half of his words echo down the empty stairs, while the second half fell dead against the curtains in a room that apparently held no other human figure than his own.

'Who's there?' he called again, in a voice unnecessarily loud and that only just held firm. 'What do you want here?'

The curtains swayed very slightly, and, as he saw it, his heart felt as if it almost missed a beat; yet he dashed forward and drew them aside with a rush. A window, streaming with rain, was all that met his gaze. He continued his search, but in vain; the cupboards held nothing but rows of clothes, hanging motionless; and under the bed there was no sign of anyone hiding. He stepped backwards into the middle of the room, and, as he did so, something all but tripped him up. Turning with a sudden spring of alarm he saw--the kit-bag.

'Odd!' he thought. 'That's not where I left it!' A few moments before it had surely been on his right, between the bed and the bath; he did not remember having moved it. It was very curious. What in the world was the matter with everything? Were all his senses gone queer? A terrific gust of wind tore at the windows, dashing the sleet against the glass with the force of small gunshot, and then fled away howling dismally over the waste of Bloomsbury roofs. A sudden vision of the Channel next day rose in his mind and recalled him sharply to realities.

There's no one here at any rate; that's quite clear!' he exclaimed aloud. Yet at the time he uttered them he knew perfectly well that his words were not true and that he did not believe them himself. He felt exactly as though someone was hiding close about him, watching all his movements, trying to hinder his packing in some way. 'And two of my senses,' he added, keeping up the pretense, 'have played me the most absurd tricks: the steps I heard and the figure I saw were both entirely imaginary.'

He went back to the front room, poked the fire into a blaze, and sat down before it to think. What impressed him more than anything else was the fact that the kit-bag was no longer where he had left at. It had been dragged nearer to the door.

What happened afterwards that night happened, of course, to a man already excited by fear, and was perceived by a mand that had not the full and proper control, therefore, of the senses. Outwardly, Johson remained calm and master of himself to the end, pretending to the very last that everything he witnessed had a natural explanation, or was merely delusions of his tired nerves. But inwardly, in his very heart, he knew all along that someone had been hiding downstairs in the empty suite when he came in, that this person had watched his opportunity and then stealthily made his way up to the bedroom, and that all he saw and heard afterwards, from the moving of the kit-bag to--well, to the other things this story has to tell--were caused directly by the presence of this invisible person.

And it was here, just when he most desired to keep his mind and thoughts controlled, that the vivid pictures received day after day upon the mental plates exposed in the courtroom of the Old Bailey, came strongly to light and developed themselves in the dark room of his inner vision. Unpleasant, haunting memories have a way of coming to life again just when the mind least desires them--in the silent watches of the night, on sleepless pillows, during the lonely hours spent by sick and dying beds. And so now, in the same way, Johnson saw nothing but the dreadful face of John Turk, the murderer, lowering at him from every corner of his mental field of vision; the white skin, the evil eyes, and the fringe of black hair low over the forehead. All the pictures of those ten days in court crowded back into his mind unbidden, and very vivid.

'This is all rubbish and nerves,' he exclaimed at length, springing with sudden energy from his chair. 'I shall finish my packing and go to bed. I'm overwrought, overtired. No doubt, at this rate I shall hear steps and things all night!'

But his face was deadly white all the same. He snatched up his field-glasses and walked across to the bedroom, humming a music-hall song as he went--a trifle too loud to be natural; and the instant he crossed the threshold and stood within the room something turned cold about his heart, and he felt that every hair on his head stood up.

The kit-bag lay close in front of him, several feet nearer to the door than he had left it, and just over its crumpled top he saw a head and face slowly sinking down out of sight as though someone were crouching behind it to hide, and at the same moment a sound like a long-drawn sigh was distinctly audible in the still air about him between the gusts of the storm outside.

Johnson had more courage and will-power than the girlish indecision of his face indicated; but at first such a wave of terror came over him that for some seconds he could do nothing but stand and stare. A violent trembling ran down his back and legs, and he was conscious of a foolish, almost a hysterical, impulse to scream aloud. That sigh seemed in his very ear, and the air still quivered with it. It was unmistakably a human sigh.

'Who's there?' he said at length, finding his voice; but thought he meant to speak with loud decision, the tones came out instead in a faint whisper, for he had partly lost the control of his tongue and lips.

He stepped forward, so that he could see all round and over the kit-bag. Of course there was nothing there, nothing but the faded carpet and the bulging canvas sides. He put out his hands and threw open the mouth of the sack where it had fallen over, being only three parts full, and then he saw for the first time that round the inside, some six inches from the top, there ran a broad smear of dull crimson. It was an old and faded blood stain. He uttered a scream, and drew hack his hands as if they had been burnt. At the same moment the kit-bag gave a faint, but unmistakable, lurch forward towards the door.

Johnson collapsed backwards, searching with his hands for the support of something solid, and the door, being further behind him than he realized, received his weight just in time to prevent his falling, and shut to with a resounding bang. At the same moment the swinging of his left arm accidentally touched the electric switch, and the light in the room went out.

It was an awkward and disagreeable predicament, and if Johnson had not been possessed of real pluck he might have done all manner of foolish things. As it was, however, he pulled himself together, and groped furiously for the little brass knob to turn the light on again. But the rapid closing of the door had set the coats hanging on it a-swinging, and his fingers became entangled in a confusion of sleeves and pockets, so that it was some moments before he found the switch. And in those few moments of bewilderment and terror two things happened that sent him beyond recall over the boundary into the region of genuine horror—he distinctly heard the kit-bag shuffling heavily across the floor in jerks, and close in front of his face sounded once again the sigh of a human being.

In his anguished efforts to find the brass button on the wall he nearly scraped the nails from his fingers, but even then, in those frenzied moments of alarm--so swift and alert are the impressions of a man keyed-up by a vivid emotion--he had time to realize that he dreaded the return of the light, and that it might be better for him to stay hidden in the merciful screen of darkness. It was but the impulse of a moment, however, and before he had time to act upon it he had yielded automatically to the original desire, and the room was flooded again with light.

But the second instinct had been right. It would have been better for him to have stayed in the shelter of the kind darkness. For there, close before him, bending over the half-packed kit-bag, clear as life in the merciless glare of the electric light, stood the figure of John Turk, the murderer. Not three feet from him the man stood, the fringe of black hair marked plainly against the pallor of the forehead, the whole horrible presentment of the scoundrel, as vivid as he had seen him day after day in the Old Bailey, when he stood there in the dock, cynical and callous, under the very shadow of the gallows.

In a flash Johnson realized what it all meant: the dirty and much-used bag; the smear of crimson within the top; the dreadful stretched condition of the bulging sides. He remembered how the victim's body had been stuffed into a canvas bag for burial, the ghastly, dismembered fragments forced with lime into this very bag; and the bag itself produced as evidence--it all came back to him as clear as day...

Very softly and stealthily his hand groped behind him for the handle of the door, but before he could actually turn it the very thing that he most of all dreaded came about, and John Turk lifted his devil's face and looked at him. At the same moment that heavy sigh passed through the air of the room, formulated somehow into words: It's my bag. And I want it.'

Johnson just remembered clawing the door open, and then falling in a heap upon the floor of the landing, as he tried frantically to make his way into the front room.

He remained unconscious for a long time, and it was still dark when he opened his eyes and realized that he was lying, stiff and bruised, on the cold boards. Then the memory of what he had seen rushed back into his mind, and he promptly fainted again. When he woke the second time the wintry dawn was just beginning to peep in at the windows, painting the stairs a cheerless, dismal grey, and he managed to crawl into the front room, and cover himself with an overcoat in the armchair, where at length he fell asleep.

A great clamour woke him. He recognized Mrs Monks's voice, loud and voluble.

'What! You ain't been to bed, sir! Are you ill, or has anything 'appened? And there's an urgent gentleman to see you, though it ain't seven o'clock yet, and--'

'Who is it?' he stammered. 'I'm all right, thanks. Fell asleep in my chair, I suppose.'

'Someone from Mr Wilb'rim's, and he says he ought to see you quick before you go abroad, and I told him--'

'Show him up, please, at once,' said Johnson, whose head was whirling, and his mind was still full of dreadful visions.

Mr Wilbraham's man came in with many apologies, and explained briefly and quickly that an absurd mistake had been made, and that the wrong kit-bag had been sent over the night before.

'Henry somehow got hold of the one that came over from the courtoom, and Mr Wilbraham only discovered it when he saw his own lying in his room, and asked why it had not gone to you,' the man said.

'Oh!' said Johnson stupidly.

'And he must have brought you the one from the murder case instead, sir, I'm afraid,' the man continued, without the ghost of an expression on his face. 'The one John Turk packed the dead both in. Mr Wilbraham's awful upset about it, sir, and told me to come over first thing this morning with the right one, as you were leaving by the boat.'

He pointed to a clean-looking kit-bag on the floor, which he had just brought. 'And I was to bring the other one back, sir,' he added casually.

For some minutes Johnson could not find his voice. At last he pointed in the direction of his bedroom. 'Perhaps you would kindly unpack it for me. Just empty the things out on the floor.'

The man disappeared into the other room, and was gone for five minutes. Johnson heard the shifting to and fro of the bag, and the rattle of the skates and boots being unpacked.

'Thank you, sir,' the man said, returning with the bag folded over his arm. 'And can I do anything more to help you, sir?'

'What is it?' asked Johnson, seeing that he still had something he wished to say.

The man shuffled and looked mysterious. 'Beg pardon, sir, but knowing your interest in the Turk case, I thought you'd maybe like to know what's happened--'

'Yes.'

'John Turk killed hisself last night with poison immediately on getting his release, and he left a note for Mr Wilbraham saying as he'd be much obliged if they'd have him put away, same as the woman he murdered, in the old kit-bag.'

'What time--did he do it?' asked Johnson.

'Ten o'clock last night, sir, the warder says.'

BETWEEN THE LIGHTS

E.F. Benson, 1912

The day had been one unceasing fall of snow from sunrise until the gradual withdrawal of the vague white light outside indicated that the sun had set again. But as usual at this hospitable and delightful house of Everard Chandler where I often spent Christmas, and was spending it now, there had been no lack of entertainment, and the hours had passed with a rapidity that had surprised us. A short billiard tournament had filled up the time between breakfast and lunch, with Badminton and the morning papers for those who were temporarily not engaged, while afterwards, the interval till tea-time had been occupied by the majority of the party in a huge game of hide-and-seek all over the house, barring the billiard-room, which was sanctuary for any who desired peace. But few had done that; the enchantment of Christmas, I must suppose, had, like some spell, made children of us again, and it was with palsied terror and trembling misgivings that we had tip-toed up and down the dim passages, from any corner of which some wild screaming form might dart out on us. Then, wearied with exercise and emotion, we had assembled again for tea in the hall, a room of shadows and panels on which the light from the wide open fireplace, where there burned a divine mixture of peat and logs, flickered and grew bright again on the walls. Then, as was proper, ghost-stories, for the narration of which the electric light was put out, so that the listeners might conjecture anything they pleased to be lurking in the corners, succeeded, and we vied with each other in blood, bones, skeletons, armour and shrieks. I had, just given my contribution, and was reflecting with some complacency that probably the worst was now known, when Everard, who had not yet administered to the horror of his guests, spoke. He was sitting opposite me in the full blaze of the fire, looking, after the illness he had gone through during the autumn, still rather pale and delicate. All the same he had been among the boldest and best in the exploration of dark places that afternoon, and the look on his face now rather startled me.

"No, I don't mind that sort of thing," he said. "The paraphernalia of ghosts has become somehow rather hackneyed, and when I hear of screams and skeletons I feel I am on familiar ground, and can at least hide my head under the bed-clothes."

"Ah, but the bed-clothes were twitched away by my skeleton," said I, in self-defence.

"I know, but I don't even mind that. Why, there are seven, eight skeletons in this room now, covered with blood and skin and other horrors. No, the nightmares of one's childhood were the really frightening things, because they were vague. There was the true atmosphere of horror about them because one didn't know what one feared. Now if one could recapture that--"

Mrs. Chandler got quickly out of her seat.

"Oh, Everard," she said, "surely you don't wish to recapture it again. I should have thought once was enough."

This was enchanting. A chorus of invitation asked him to proceed: the real true ghost-story first-hand, which was what seemed to be indicated, was too precious a thing to lose.

Everard laughed. "No, dear, I don't want to recapture it again at all," he said to his wife.

Then to us: "But really the--well, the nightmare perhaps, to which I was referring, is of the vaguest and most unsatisfactory kind. It has no apparatus about it at all. You will probably all say that it was nothing, and wonder why I was frightened. But I was; it frightened me out of my wits. And I only just saw something, without being able to swear what it was, and heard something which might have been a falling stone."

"Anyhow, tell us about the falling stone," said I.

There was a stir of movement about the circle round the fire, and the movement was not of purely physical order. It was as if--this is only what I personally felt--it was as if the childish gaiety of the hours we had passed that day was suddenly withdrawn; we had jested on certain subjects, we had played hide-and-seek with all the power of earnestness that was in us. But now--so it seemed to me--there was going to be real hide-and-seek, real terrors were going to lurk in dark corners, or if not real terrors, terrors so convincing as to assume the garb of reality, were going to pounce on us. And Mrs. Chandler's exclamation as she sat down again, "Oh, Everard, won't it excite you?" tended in any case to excite us. The room still remained in dubious darkness except for the sudden lights disclosed on the walls by the leaping flames on the hearth, and there was wide field for conjecture as to what might lurk in the dim corners. Everard, moreover, who had been sitting in bright light before, was banished by the extinction of some flaming log into the shadows. A voice alone spoke to us, as he sat back in his low chair, a voice rather slow but very distinct.

"Last year," he said, "on the twenty-fourth of December, we were down here, as usual, Amy and I, for Christmas. Several of you who are here now were here then. Three or four of you at least."

I was one of these, but like the others kept silence, for the identification, so it seemed to me, was not asked for. And he went on again without a pause.

"Those of you who were here then," he said, "and are here now, will remember how very warm it was this day year. You will remember, too, that we played croquet that day on the lawn. It was perhaps a little cold for croquet, and we played it rather in order to be able to say--with sound evidence to back the statement--that we had done so."

Then he turned and addressed the whole little circle.

"We played ties of half-games," he said, "just as we have played billiards to-day, and it was certainly as warm on the lawn then as it was in the billiard-room this morning directly after breakfast, while to-day I should not wonder if there was three feet of snow outside. More, probably; listen."

A sudden draught fluted in the chimney, and the fire flared up as the current of air caught it.

The wind also drove the snow against the windows, and as he said, "Listen," we heard a soft scurry of the falling flakes against the panes, like the soft tread of many little people who stepped lightly, but with the persistence of multitudes who were flocking to some rendezvous. Hundreds of little feet seemed to be gathering outside; only the glass kept them out. And of the eight skeletons present four or five, anyhow, turned and looked at the windows. These were small-paned, with leaden bars. On the leaden bars little heaps of snow had accumulated, but there was nothing else to be seen.

"Yes, last Christmas Eve was very warm and sunny," went on Everard. "We had had no frost that autumn, and a temerarious dahlia was still in flower. I have always thought that it must have been mad."

He paused a moment.

"And I wonder if I were not mad too," he added.

No one interrupted him; there was something arresting, I must suppose, in what he was saying; it chimed in anyhow with the hide-and-seek, with the suggestions of the lonely snow.

Mrs. Chandler had sat down again, but I heard her stir in her chair. But never was there a gay party so reduced as we had been in the last five minutes. Instead of laughing at ourselves for playing silly games, we were all taking a serious game seriously.

"Anyhow, I was sitting out," he said to me, "while you and my wife played your half-game of croquet. Then it struck me that it was not so warm as I had supposed, because quite suddenly I shivered. And shivering I looked up. But I did not see you and her playing croquet at all. I saw something which had no relation to you and her--at least I hope not."

Now the angler lands his fish, the stalker kills his stag, and the speaker holds his audience.

And as the fish is gaffed, and as the stag is shot, so were we held. There was no getting away till he had finished with us.

"You all know the croquet lawn," he said, "and how it is bounded all round by a flower border with a brick wall behind it, through which, you will remember, there is only one gate.

"Well, I looked up and saw that the lawn--I could for one moment see it was still a lawn--was shrinking, and the walls closing in upon it. As they closed in too, they grew higher, and simultaneously the light began to fade and be sucked from the sky, till it grew quite dark overhead and only a glimmer of light came in through the gate.

"There was, as I told you, a dahlia in flower that day, and as this dreadful darkness and bewilderment came over me, I remember that my eyes sought it in a kind of despair, holding on, as it were, to any familiar object. But it was no longer a dahlia, and for the red of its petals I saw only the red of some feeble firelight. And at that moment the hallucination was complete. I was no longer sitting on the lawn watching croquet, but I was in a low-roofed room, something like a cattle-shed, but round. Close above my head, though I was sitting down, ran rafters from wall to wall. It was nearly dark, but a little light came in from the door opposite to me, which seemed to lead into a passage that communicated with the exterior of the place. Little, however, of the wholesome air came into this dreadful den; the atmosphere was oppressive and foul beyond all telling, it was as if for years it had been the place of some human menagerie, and for those years had been uncleaned and unsweetened by the winds of heaven. Yet that oppressiveness was nothing to the awful horror of the place from the view of the spirit. Some dreadful atmosphere of crime and abomination dwelt heavy in it, its denizens, whoever they were, were scarce human, so it seemed to me, and though men and women, were akin more to the beasts of the field. And in addition there was present to me some sense of the weight of years; I had been taken and thrust down into some epoch of dim antiquity."

He paused a moment, and the fire on the hearth leaped up for a second and then died down again. But in that gleam I saw that all faces were turned to Everard, and that all wore some look of dreadful expectancy. Certainly I felt it myself, and waited in a sort of shrinking horror for what was coming.

"As I told you," he continued, "where there had been that unseasonable dahlia, there now burned a dim firelight, and my eyes were drawn there. Shapes were gathered round it; what they were I could not at first see. Then perhaps my eyes got more accustomed to the dusk, or the fire burned better, for I perceived that they were of human form, but very small, for when one rose with a horrible chattering, to his feet, his head was still some inches off the low roof. He was dressed in a sort of shirt that came to his knees, but his arms were bare and covered with hair.

"Then the gesticulation and chattering increased, and I knew that they were talking about me, for they kept pointing in my direction. At that my horror suddenly deepened, for I became aware that I was powerless and could not move hand or foot; a helpless, nightmare impotence had possession of me. I could not lift a finger or turn my head. And in the paralysis of that fear I tried to scream, but not a sound could I utter.

"All this I suppose took place with the instantaneousness of a dream, for at once, and without transition, the whole thing had vanished, and I was back on the lawn again, while the stroke for which my wife was aiming was still unplayed. But my face was dripping with perspiration, and I was trembling all over.

"Now you may all say that I had fallen asleep, and had a sudden nightmare. That may be so; but I was conscious of no sense of sleepiness before, and I was conscious of none afterwards. It was as if someone had held a book before me, whisked the pages open for a second and closed them again."

Somebody, I don't know who, got up from his chair with a sudden movement that made me start, and turned on the electric light. I do not mind confessing that I was rather glad of this.

Everard laughed.

"Really I feel like Hamlet in the play-scene," he said, "and as if there was a guilty uncle present. Shall I go on?"

I don't think anyone replied, and he went on.

"Well, let us say for the moment that it was not a dream exactly, but a hallucination.

"Whichever it was, in any case it haunted me; for months, I think, it was never quite out of my mind, but lingered somewhere in the dusk of consciousness, sometimes sleeping quietly, so to speak, but sometimes stirring in its sleep. It was no good my telling myself that I was disquieting myself in vain, for it was as if something had actually entered into my very soul, as if some seed of horror had been planted there. And as the weeks went on the seed began to sprout, so that I could no longer even tell myself that that vision had been a moment's disorderment only. I can't say that it actually affected my health. I did not, as far as I know, sleep or eat insufficiently, but morning after morning I used to wake, not gradually and through pleasant dozings into full consciousness, but with absolute suddenness, and find myself plunged in an abyss of despair.

"Often too, eating or drinking, I used to pause and wonder if it was worth while.

"Eventually, I told two people about my trouble, hoping that perhaps the mere communication would help matters, hoping also, but very distantly, that though I could not believe at present that digestion or the obscurities of the nervous system were at fault, a doctor by some simple dose might convince me of it. In other words I told my wife, who laughed at me, and my doctor, who laughed also, and assured me that my health was quite unnecessarily robust.

"At the same time he suggested that change of air and scene does wonders for the delusions that exist merely in the imagination. He also told me, in answer to a direct question, that he would stake his reputation on the certainty that I was not going mad.

"Well, we went up to London as usual for the season, and though nothing whatever occurred to remind me in any way of that single moment on Christmas Eve, the reminding was seen to all right, the moment itself took care of that, for instead of fading as is the way of sleeping or waking dreams, it grew every day more vivid, and ate, so to speak, like some corrosive acid into my mind, etching itself there. And to London succeeded Scotland.

"I took last year for the first time a small forest up in Sutherland, called Glen Callan, very remote and wild, but affording excellent stalking. It was not far from the sea, and the gillies used always to warn me to carry a compass on the hill, because sea-mists were liable to come up with frightful rapidity, and there was always a danger of being caught by one, and of having perhaps to wait hours till it cleared again. This at first I always used to do, but, as everyone knows, any precaution that one takes which continues to be unjustified gets gradually relaxed, and at the end of a few weeks, since the weather had been uniformly clear, it was natural that, as often as not, my compass remained at home.

"One day the stalk took me on to a part of my ground that I had seldom been on before, a very high table-land on the limit of my forest, which went down very steeply on one side to a loch that lay below it, and on the other, by gentler gradations, to the river that came from the loch, six miles below which stood the lodge. The wind had necessitated our climbing up--or so my stalker had insisted--not by the easier way, but up the crags from the loch. I had argued the point with him for it seemed to me that it was impossible that the deer could get our scent if we went by the more natural path, but he still held to his opinion; and therefore, since after all this was his part of the job, I yielded. A dreadful climb we had of it, over big boulders with deep holes in between, masked by clumps of heather, so that a wary eye and a prodding stick were necessary for each step if one wished to avoid broken bones. Adders also literally swarmed in the heather; we must have seen a dozen at least on our way up, and adders are a beast for which I have no manner of use. But a couple of hours saw us to the top, only to find that the stalker had been utterly at fault, and that the deer must quite infallibly have got wind of us, if they had remained in the place where we last saw them. That, when we could spy the ground again, we saw had happened; in any case they had gone. The man insisted the wind had changed, a palpably stupid excuse, and I wondered at that moment what other reason he had--for reason I felt sure there must be--for not wishing to take what would clearly now have been a better route. But this piece of bad management did not spoil our luck, for within an hour we had spied more deer, and about two o'clock I got a shot, killing a heavy stag. Then sitting on the heather I ate lunch, and enjoyed a well-earned bask and smoke in the sun. The pony meantime had been saddled with the stag, and was plodding homewards.

"The morning had been extraordinarily warm, with a little wind blowing off the sea, which lay a few miles off sparkling beneath a blue haze, and all morning in spite of our abominable climb I had had an extreme sense of peace, so much so that several times I had probed my mind, so to speak, to find if the horror still lingered there. But I could scarcely get any response from it.

"Never since Christmas had I been so free of fear, and it was with a great sense of repose, both physical and spiritual, that I lay looking up into the blue sky, watching my smoke-whorls curl slowly away into nothingness. But I was not allowed to take my ease long, for Sandy came and begged that I would move. The weather had changed, he said, the wind had shifted again, and he wanted me to be off this high ground and on the path again as soon as possible, because it looked to him as if a sea-mist would presently come up."

"'And yon's a bad place to get down in the mist,' he added, nodding towards the crags we had come up.

"I looked at the man in amazement, for to our right lay a gentle slope down on to the river, and there was now no possible reason for again tackling those hideous rocks up which we had climbed this morning. More than ever I was sure he had some secret reason for not wishing to go the obvious way. But about one thing he was certainly right, the mist was coming up from the sea, and I felt in my pocket for the compass, and found I had forgotten to bring it.

"Then there followed a curious scene which lost us time that we could really ill afford to waste, I insisting on going down by the way that common sense directed, he imploring me to take his word for it that the crags were the better way. Eventually, I marched off to the easier descent, and told him not to argue any more but follow. What annoyed me about him was that he would only give the most senseless reasons for preferring the crags. There were mossy places, he said, on the way I wished to go, a thing patently false, since the summer had been one spell of unbroken weather; or it was longer, also obviously untrue; or there were so many vipers about.

"But seeing that none of these arguments produced any effect, at last he desisted, and came after me in silence.

"We were not yet half down when the mist was upon us, shooting up from the valley like the broken water of a wave, and in three minutes we were enveloped in a cloud of fog so thick that we could barely see a dozen yards in front of us. It was therefore another cause for self-congratulation that we were not now, as we should otherwise have been, precariously clambering on the face of those crags up which we had come with such difficulty in the morning, and as I rather prided myself on my powers of generalship in the matter of direction, I continued leading, feeling sure that before long we should strike the track by the river. More than all, the absolute freedom from fear elated me; since Christmas I had not known the instinctive joy of that; I felt like a schoolboy home for the holidays. But the mist grew thicker and thicker, and whether it was that real rain-clouds had formed above it, or that it was of an extraordinary density itself, I got wetter in the next hour than I have ever been before or since. The wet seemed to penetrate the skin, and chill the very bones. And still there was no sign of the track for which I was making.

"Behind me, muttering to himself, followed the stalker, but his arguments and protestations were dumb, and it seemed as if he kept close to me, as if afraid.

"Now there are many unpleasant companions in this world; I would not, for instance, care to be on the hill with a drunkard or a maniac, but worse than either, I think, is a frightened man, because his trouble is infectious, and, insensibly. I began to be afraid of being frightened too.

"From that it is but a short step to fear. Other perplexities too beset us. At one time we seemed to be walking on flat ground, at another I felt sure we were climbing again, whereas all the time we ought to have been descending, unless we had missed the way very badly indeed. Also, for the month was October, it was beginning to get dark, and it was with a sense of relief that I remembered that the full moon would rise soon after sunset. But it had grown very much colder, and soon, instead of rain, we found we were walking through a steady fall of snow.

"Things were pretty bad, but then for the moment they seemed to mend, for, far away to the left, I suddenly heard the brawling of the river. It should, it is true, have been straight in front of me and we were perhaps a mile out of our way, but this was better than the blind wandering of the last hour, and turning to the left, I walked towards it. But before I had gone a hundred yards, I heard a sudden choked cry behind me, and just saw Sandy's form flying as if in terror of pursuit, into the mists. I called to him, but got no reply, and heard only the spurned stones of his running.

"What had frightened him I had no idea, but certainly with his disappearance, the infection of his fear disappeared also, and I went on, I may almost say, with gaiety. On the moment, however, I saw a sudden well-defined blackness in front of me, and before I knew what I was doing I was half stumbling, half walking up a very steep grass slope.

"During the last few minutes the wind had got up, and the driving snow was peculiarly uncomfortable, but there had been a certain consolation in thinking that the wind would soon disperse these mists, and I had nothing more than a moonlight walk home. But as I paused on this slope, I became aware of two things, one, that the blackness in front of me was very close, the other that, whatever it was, it sheltered me from the snow. So I climbed on a dozen yards into its friendly shelter, for it seemed to me to be friendly.

"A wall some twelve feet high crowned the slope, and exactly where I struck it there was a hole in it, or door rather, through which a little light appeared. Wondering at this I pushed on, bending down, for the passage was very low, and in a dozen yards came out on the other side.

"Just as I did this the sky suddenly grew lighter, the wind, I suppose, having dispersed the mists, and the moon, though not yet visible through the flying skirts of cloud, made sufficient illumination.

"I was in a circular enclosure, and above me there projected from the walls some four feet from the ground, broken stones which must have been intended to support a floor. Then simultaneously two things occurred.

"The whole of my nine months' terror came back to me, for I saw that the vision in the garden was fulfilled, and at the same moment I saw stealing towards me a little figure as of a man, but only about three foot six in height. That my eyes told me; my ears told me that he stumbled on a stone; my nostrils told me that the air I breathed was of an overpowering foulness, and my soul told me that it was sick unto death. I think I tried to scream, but could not; I know I tried to move and could not. And it crept closer.

"Then I suppose the terror which held me spellbound so spurred me that I must move, for next moment I heard a cry break from my lips, and was stumbling through the passage. I made one leap of it down the grass slope, and ran as I hope never to have to run again. What direction I took I did not pause to consider, so long as I put distance between me and that place. Luck, however, favoured me, and before long I struck the track by the river, and an hour afterwards reached the lodge.

"Next day I developed a chill, and as you know pneumonia laid me on my back for six weeks.

"Well, that is my story, and there are many explanations. You may say that I fell asleep on the lawn, and was reminded of that by finding myself, under discouraging circumstances, in an old Picts' castle, where a sheep or a goat that, like myself, had taken shelter from the storm, was moving about. Yes, there are hundreds of ways in which you may explain it. But the coincidence was an odd one, and those who believe in second sight might find an instance of their hobby in it."

"And that is all?" I asked.

"Yes, it was nearly too much for me. I think the dressing-bell has sounded."

THE DEAD

James Joyce, 1914

Lily, the caretaker's daughter, was literally run off her feet. Hardly had she brought one gentleman into the little pantry behind the office on the ground floor and helped him off with his overcoat than the wheezy hall-door bell clanged again and she had to scamper along the bare hallway to let in another guest. It was well for her she had not to attend to the ladies also. But Miss Kate and Miss Julia had thought of that and had converted the bathroom upstairs into a ladies' dressing-room. Miss Kate and Miss Julia were there, gossiping and laughing and fussing, walking after each other to the head of the stairs, peering down over the banisters and calling down to Lily to ask her who had come.

It was always a great affair, the Misses Morkan's annual dance. Everybody who knew them came to it, members of the family, old friends of the family, the members of Julia's choir, any of Kate's pupils that were grown up enough, and even some of Mary Jane's pupils too. Never once had it fallen flat. For years and years it had gone off in splendid style as long as anyone could remember; ever since Kate and Julia, after the death of their brother Pat, had left the house in Stoney Batter and taken Mary Jane, their only niece, to live with them in the dark gaunt house on Usher's Island, the upper part of which they had rented from Mr Fulham, the corn-factor on the ground floor. That was a good thirty years ago if it was a day. Mary Jane, who was then a little girl in short clothes, was now the main prop of the household, for she had the organ in Haddington Road. She had been through the Academy and gave a pupils' concert every year in the upper room of the Antient Concert Rooms. Many of her pupils belonged to the better-class families on the Kingstown and Dalkey line. Old as they were, her aunts also did their share. Julia, though she was quite grey, was still the leading soprano in Adam and Eve's, and Kate, being too feeble to go about much, gave music lessons to beginners on the old square piano in the back room. Lily, the caretaker's daughter, did housemaid's work for them. Though their life was modest they believed in eating well; the best of everything: diamond-bone sirloins, three-shilling tea and the best bottled stout. But Lily seldom made a mistake in the orders so that she got on well with her three mistresses. They were fussy, that was all. But the only thing they would not stand was back answers.

Of course, they had good reason to be fussy on such a night. And then it was long after ten o'clock and yet there was no sign of Gabriel and his wife. Besides they were dreadfully afraid that Freddy Malins might turn up screwed. They would not wish for worlds that any of Mary Jane's pupils should see him under the influence; and when he was like that it was sometimes very hard to manage him. Freddy Malins always came late but they wondered what could be keeping Gabriel: and that was what brought them every two minutes to the banisters to ask Lily had Gabriel or Freddy come.

"O, Mr Conroy," said Lily to Gabriel when she opened the door for him, "Miss Kate and Miss Julia thought you were never coming. Good-night, Mrs Conroy."

"I'll engage they did," said Gabriel, "but they forget that my wife here takes three mortal hours to dress herself."

He stood on the mat, scraping the snow from his goloshes, while Lily led his wife to the foot of the stairs and called out:

"Miss Kate, here's Mrs Conroy."

Kate and Julia came toddling down the dark stairs at once. Both of them kissed Gabriel's wife, said she must be perished alive and asked was Gabriel with her.

"Here I am as right as the mail, Aunt Kate! Go on up. I'll follow," called out Gabriel from the dark.

He continued scraping his feet vigorously while the three women went upstairs, laughing, to the ladies' dressing-room. A light fringe of snow lay like a cape on the shoulders of his overcoat and like toecaps on the toes of his goloshes; and, as the buttons of his overcoat slipped with a squeaking noise through the snow-stiffened frieze, a cold, fragrant air from out-of-doors escaped from crevices and folds.

"Is it snowing again, Mr Conroy?" asked Lily.

She had preceded him into the pantry to help him off with his overcoat. Gabriel smiled at the three syllables she had given his surname and glanced at her. She was a slim, growing girl, pale in complexion and with hay-coloured hair. The gas in the pantry made her look still paler. Gabriel had known her when she was a child and used to sit on the lowest step nursing a rag doll.

"Yes, Lily," he answered, "and I think we're in for a night of it."

He looked up at the pantry ceiling, which was shaking with the stamping and shuffling of feet on the floor above, listened for a moment to the piano and then glanced at the girl, who was folding his overcoat carefully at the end of a shelf.

"Tell me, Lily," he said in a friendly tone, "do you still go to school?"

"O no, sir," she answered. "I'm done schooling this year and more."

"O, then," said Gabriel gaily, "I suppose we'll be going to your wedding one of these fine days with your young man, eh?"

The girl glanced back at him over her shoulder and said with great bitterness:

"The men that is now is only all palaver and what they can get out of you."

Gabriel coloured as if he felt he had made a mistake and, without looking at her, kicked off his goloshes and flicked actively with his muffler at his patent-leather shoes.

He was a stout tallish young man. The high colour of his cheeks pushed upwards even to his forehead where it scattered itself in a few formless patches of pale red; and on his hairless face there scintillated restlessly the polished lenses and the bright gilt rims of the glasses which screened his delicate and restless eyes. His glossy black hair was parted in the middle and brushed in a long curve behind his ears where it curled slightly beneath the groove left by his hat.

When he had flicked lustre into his shoes he stood up and pulled his waistcoat down more tightly on his plump body. Then he took a coin rapidly from his pocket.

"O Lily," he said, thrusting it into her hands, "it's Christmas-time, isn't it? Just ... here's a little...."

He walked rapidly towards the door.

"O no, sir!" cried the girl, following him. "Really, sir, I wouldn't take it."

"Christmas-time! Christmas-time!" said Gabriel, almost trotting to the stairs and waving his hand to her in deprecation.

The girl, seeing that he had gained the stairs, called out after him:

"Well, thank you, sir."

He waited outside the drawing-room door until the waltz should finish, listening to the skirts that swept against it and to the shuffling of feet. He was still discomposed by the girl's bitter and sudden retort. It had cast a gloom over him which he tried to dispel by arranging his cuffs and the bows of his tie. He then took from his waistcoat pocket a little paper and glanced at the headings he had made for his speech. He was undecided about the lines from Robert Browning for he feared they would be above the heads of his hearers. Some quotation that they would recognise from Shakespeare or from the Melodies would be better. The indelicate clacking of the men's heels and the shuffling of their soles reminded him that their grade of culture differed from his. He would only make himself ridiculous by quoting poetry to them which they could not understand. They would think that he was airing his superior education. He would fail with them just as he had failed with the girl in the pantry. He had taken up a wrong tone. His whole speech was a mistake from first to last, an utter failure.

Just then his aunts and his wife came out of the ladies' dressing-room. His aunts were two small plainly dressed old women. Aunt Julia was an inch or so the taller. Her hair, drawn low over the tops of her ears, was grey; and grey also, with darker shadows, was her large flaccid face. Though she was stout in build and stood erect her slow eyes and parted lips gave her the appearance of a woman who did not know where she was or where she was going. Aunt Kate was more vivacious. Her face, healthier than her sister's, was all puckers and creases, like a shrivelled red apple, and her hair, braided in the same old-fashioned way, had not lost its ripe nut colour.

They both kissed Gabriel frankly. He was their favourite nephew, the son of their dead elder sister, Ellen, who had married T. J. Conroy of the Port and Docks.

"Gretta tells me you're not going to take a cab back to Monkstown tonight, Gabriel," said Aunt Kate.

"No," said Gabriel, turning to his wife, "we had quite enough of that last year, hadn't we? Don't you remember, Aunt Kate, what a cold Gretta got out of it? Cab windows rattling all the way, and the east wind blowing in after we passed Merrion. Very jolly it was. Gretta caught a dreadful cold."

Aunt Kate frowned severely and nodded her head at every word.

"Quite right, Gabriel, quite right," she said. "You can't be too careful."

"But as for Gretta there," said Gabriel, "she'd walk home in the snow if she were let."

Mrs Conroy laughed.

"Don't mind him, Aunt Kate," she said. "He's really an awful bother, what with green shades for Tom's eyes at night and making him do the dumb-bells, and forcing Eva to eat the stirabout. The poor child! And she simply hates the sight of it!... O, but you'll never guess what he makes me wear now!"

She broke out into a peal of laughter and glanced at her husband, whose admiring and happy eyes had been wandering from her dress to her face and hair. The two aunts laughed heartily too, for Gabriel's solicitude was a standing joke with them.

"Goloshes!" said Mrs Conroy. "That's the latest. Whenever it's wet underfoot I must put on my goloshes. Tonight even he wanted me to put them on, but I wouldn't. The next thing he'll buy me will be a diving suit."

Gabriel laughed nervously and patted his tie reassuringly while Aunt Kate nearly doubled herself, so heartily did she enjoy the joke. The smile soon faded from Aunt Julia's face and her mirthless eyes were directed towards her nephew's face. After a pause she asked:

"And what are goloshes, Gabriel?"

"Goloshes, Julia!" exclaimed her sister. "Goodness me, don't you know what goloshes are? You wear them over your ... over your boots, Gretta, isn't it?"

"Yes," said Mrs Conroy. "Guttapercha things. We both have a pair now. Gabriel says everyone wears them on the continent."

"O, on the continent," murmured Aunt Julia, nodding her head slowly.

Gabriel knitted his brows and said, as if he were slightly angered:

"It's nothing very wonderful but Gretta thinks it very funny because she says the word reminds her of Christy Minstrels."

"But tell me, Gabriel," said Aunt Kate, with brisk tact. "Of course, you've seen about the room. Gretta was saying...."

"O, the room is all right," replied Gabriel. "I've taken one in the Gresham."

"To be sure," said Aunt Kate, "by far the best thing to do. And the children, Gretta, you're not anxious about them?"

"O, for one night," said Mrs Conroy. "Besides, Bessie will look after them."

"To be sure," said Aunt Kate again. "What a comfort it is to have a girl like that, one you can depend on! There's that Lily, I'm sure I don't know what has come over her lately. She's not the girl she was at all."

Gabriel was about to ask his aunt some questions on this point but she broke off suddenly to gaze after her sister who had wandered down the stairs and was craning her neck over the banisters.

"Now, I ask you," she said almost testily, "where is Julia going? Julia! Julia! Where are you going?"

Julia, who had gone half way down one flight, came back and announced blandly:

"Here's Freddy."

At the same moment a clapping of hands and a final flourish of the pianist told that the waltz had ended. The drawing-room door was opened from within and some couples came out. Aunt Kate drew Gabriel aside hurriedly and whispered into his ear:

"Slip down, Gabriel, like a good fellow and see if he's all right, and don't let him up if he's screwed. I'm sure he's screwed. I'm sure he is."

Gabriel went to the stairs and listened over the banisters. He could hear two persons talking in the pantry. Then he recognised Freddy Malins' laugh. He went down the stairs noisily.

"It's such a relief," said Aunt Kate to Mrs Conroy, "that Gabriel is here. I always feel easier in my mind when he's here.... Julia, there's Miss Daly and Miss Power will take some refreshment. Thanks for your beautiful waltz, Miss Daly. It made lovely time."

A tall wizen-faced man, with a stiff grizzled moustache and swarthy skin, who was passing out with his partner said:

"And may we have some refreshment, too, Miss Morkan?"

"Julia," said Aunt Kate summarily, "and here's Mr Browne and Miss Furlong. Take them in, Julia, with Miss Daly and Miss Power."

"I'm the man for the ladies," said Mr Browne, pursing his lips until his moustache bristled and smiling in all his wrinkles. "You know, Miss Morkan, the reason they are so fond of me is— —"

He did not finish his sentence, but, seeing that Aunt Kate was out of earshot, at once led the three young ladies into the back room. The middle of the room was occupied by two square tables placed end to end, and on these Aunt Julia and the caretaker were straightening and smoothing a large cloth. On the sideboard were arrayed dishes and plates, and glasses and bundles of knives and forks and spoons. The top of the closed square piano served also as a sideboard for viands and sweets. At a smaller sideboard in one corner two young men were standing, drinking hop-bitters.

Mr Browne led his charges thither and invited them all, in jest, to some ladies' punch, hot, strong and sweet. As they said they never took anything strong he opened three bottles of lemonade for them. Then he asked one of the young men to move aside, and, taking hold of the decanter, filled out for himself a goodly measure of whisky. The young men eyed him respectfully while he took a trial sip.

"God help me," he said, smiling, "it's the doctor's orders."

His wizened face broke into a broader smile, and the three young ladies laughed in musical echo to his pleasantry, swaying their bodies to and fro, with nervous jerks of their shoulders. The boldest said:

"O, now, Mr Browne, I'm sure the doctor never ordered anything of the kind."

Mr Browne took another sip of his whisky and said, with sidling mimicry:

"Well, you see, I'm like the famous Mrs Cassidy, who is reported to have said: 'Now, Mary Grimes, if I don't take it, make me take it, for I feel I want it.'"

His hot face had leaned forward a little too confidentially and he had assumed a very low Dublin accent so that the young ladies, with one instinct, received his speech in silence. Miss Furlong, who was one of Mary Jane's pupils, asked Miss Daly what was the name of the pretty waltz she had played; and Mr Browne, seeing that he was ignored, turned promptly to the two young men who were more appreciative.

A red-faced young woman, dressed in pansy, came into the room, excitedly clapping her hands and crying:

"Quadrilles! Quadrilles!"

Close on her heels came Aunt Kate, crying:

"Two gentlemen and three ladies, Mary Jane!"

"O, here's Mr Bergin and Mr Kerrigan," said Mary Jane. "Mr Kerrigan, will you take Miss Power? Miss Furlong, may I get you a partner, Mr Bergin. O, that'll just do now."

"Three ladies, Mary Jane," said Aunt Kate.

The two young gentlemen asked the ladies if they might have the pleasure, and Mary Jane turned to Miss Daly.

"O, Miss Daly, you're really awfully good, after playing for the last two dances, but really we're so short of ladies tonight."

"I don't mind in the least, Miss Morkan."

"But I've a nice partner for you, Mr Bartell D'Arcy, the tenor. I'll get him to sing later on. All Dublin is raving about him."

"Lovely voice, lovely voice!" said Aunt Kate.

As the piano had twice begun the prelude to the first figure Mary Jane led her recruits quickly from the room. They had hardly gone when Aunt Julia wandered slowly into the room, looking behind her at something.

"What is the matter, Julia?" asked Aunt Kate anxiously. "Who is it?"

Julia, who was carrying in a column of table-napkins, turned to her sister and said, simply, as if the question had surprised her:

"It's only Freddy, Kate, and Gabriel with him."

In fact right behind her Gabriel could be seen piloting Freddy Malins across the landing. The latter, a young man of about forty, was of Gabriel's size and build, with very round shoulders. His face was fleshy and pallid, touched with colour only at the thick hanging lobes of his ears and at the wide wings of his nose. He had coarse features, a blunt nose, a convex and receding brow, tumid and protruded lips. His heavy-lidded eyes and the disorder of his scanty hair made him look sleepy. He was laughing heartily in a high key at a story which he had been telling Gabriel on the stairs and at the same time rubbing the knuckles of his left fist backwards and forwards into his left eye.

"Good-evening, Freddy," said Aunt Julia.

Freddy Malins bade the Misses Morkan good-evening in what seemed an offhand fashion by reason of the habitual catch in his voice and then, seeing that Mr Browne was grinning at him from the sideboard, crossed the room on rather shaky legs and began to repeat in an undertone the story he had just told to Gabriel.

"He's not so bad, is he?" said Aunt Kate to Gabriel.

Gabriel's brows were dark but he raised them quickly and answered:

"O, no, hardly noticeable."

"Now, isn't he a terrible fellow!" she said. "And his poor mother made him take the pledge on New Year's Eve. But come on, Gabriel, into the drawing-room."

Before leaving the room with Gabriel she signalled to Mr Browne by frowning and shaking her forefinger in warning to and fro. Mr Browne nodded in answer and, when she had gone, said to Freddy Malins:

"Now, then, Teddy, I'm going to fill you out a good glass of lemonade just to buck you up."

Freddy Malins, who was nearing the climax of his story, waved the offer aside impatiently but Mr Browne, having first called Freddy Malins' attention to a disarray in his dress, filled out and handed him a full glass of lemonade. Freddy Malins' left hand accepted the glass mechanically, his right hand being engaged in the mechanical readjustment of his dress. Mr Browne, whose face was once more wrinkling with mirth, poured out for himself a glass of whisky while Freddy Malins exploded, before he had well reached the climax of his story, in a kink of high-pitched bronchitic laughter and, setting down his untasted and overflowing glass, began to rub the knuckles of his left fist backwards and forwards into his left eye, repeating words of his last phrase as well as his fit of laughter would allow him.

Gabriel could not listen while Mary Jane was playing her Academy piece, full of runs and difficult passages, to the hushed drawing-room. He liked music but the piece she was playing had no melody for him and he doubted whether it had any melody for the other listeners, though they had begged Mary Jane to play something. Four young men, who had come from the refreshment-room to stand in the doorway at the sound of the piano, had gone away quietly in couples after a few minutes. The only persons who seemed to follow the music were Mary Jane herself, her hands racing along the keyboard or lifted from it at the pauses like those of a priestess in momentary imprecation, and Aunt Kate standing at her elbow to turn the page.

Gabriel's eyes, irritated by the floor, which glittered with beeswax under the heavy chandelier, wandered to the wall above the piano. A picture of the balcony scene in Romeo and Juliet hung there and beside it was a picture of the two murdered princes in the Tower which Aunt Julia had worked in red, blue and brown wools when she was a girl. Probably in the school they had gone to as girls that kind of work had been taught for one year. His mother had worked for him as a birthday present a waistcoat of purple tabinet, with little foxes' heads upon it, lined with brown satin and having round mulberry buttons. It was strange that his mother had had no musical talent though Aunt Kate used to call her the brains carrier of the Morkan family. Both she and Julia had always seemed a little proud of their serious and matronly sister. Her photograph stood before the pierglass. She held an open book on her knees and was pointing out something in it to Constantine who, dressed in a man-o'-war suit, lay at her feet. It was she who had chosen the name of her sons for she was very sensible of the dignity of family life. Thanks to her, Constantine was now senior curate in Balbrigan and, thanks to her, Gabriel himself had taken his degree in the Royal University. A shadow passed over his face as he remembered her sullen opposition to his marriage. Some slighting phrases she had used still rankled in his memory; she had once spoken of Gretta as being country cute and that was not true of Gretta at all. It was Gretta who had nursed her during all her last long illness in their house at Monkstown.

He knew that Mary Jane must be near the end of her piece for she was playing again the opening melody with runs of scales after every bar and while he waited for the end the resentment died down in his heart. The piece ended with a trill of octaves in the treble and a final deep octave in the bass. Great applause greeted Mary Jane as, blushing and rolling up her music nervously, she escaped from the room. The most vigorous clapping came from the four young men in the doorway who had gone away to the refreshment-room at the beginning of the piece but had come back when the piano had stopped.

Lancers were arranged. Gabriel found himself partnered with Miss Ivors. She was a frank-mannered talkative young lady, with a freckled face and prominent brown eyes. She did not wear a low-cut bodice and the large brooch which was fixed in the front of her collar bore on it an Irish device and motto.

When they had taken their places she said abruptly:

"I have a crow to pluck with you."

"With me?" said Gabriel.

She nodded her head gravely.

"What is it?" asked Gabriel, smiling at her solemn manner.

"Who is G. C.?" answered Miss Ivors, turning her eyes upon him.

Gabriel coloured and was about to knit his brows, as if he did not understand, when she said bluntly:

"O, innocent Amy! I have found out that you write for The Daily Express. Now, aren't you ashamed of yourself?"

"Why should I be ashamed of myself?" asked Gabriel, blinking his eyes and trying to smile.

"Well, I'm ashamed of you," said Miss Ivors frankly. "To say you'd write for a paper like that. I didn't think you were a West Briton."

A look of perplexity appeared on Gabriel's face. It was true that he wrote a literary column every Wednesday in The Daily Express, for which he was paid fifteen shillings. But that did not make him a West Briton surely. The books he received for review were almost more welcome than the paltry cheque. He loved to feel the covers and turn over the pages of newly printed books. Nearly every day when his teaching in the college was ended he used to wander down the quays to the second-hand booksellers, to Hickey's on Bachelor's Walk, to Webb's or Massey's on Aston's Quay, or to O'Clohissey's in the by-street. He did not know how to meet her charge. He wanted to say that literature was above politics. But they were friends of many years' standing and their careers had been parallel, first at the university and then as teachers: he could not risk a grandiose phrase with her. He continued blinking his eyes and trying to smile and murmured lamely that he saw nothing political in writing reviews of books.

When their turn to cross had come he was still perplexed and inattentive. Miss Ivors promptly took his hand in a warm grasp and said in a soft friendly tone:

"Of course, I was only joking. Come, we cross now."

When they were together again she spoke of the University question and Gabriel felt more at ease. A friend of hers had shown her his review of Browning's poems. That was how she had found out the secret: but she liked the review immensely. Then she said suddenly:

"O, Mr Conroy, will you come for an excursion to the Aran Isles this summer? We're going to stay there a whole month. It will be splendid out in the Atlantic. You ought to come. Mr Clancy is coming, and Mr Kilkelly and Kathleen Kearney. It would be splendid for Gretta too if she'd come. She's from Connacht, isn't she?"

"Her people are," said Gabriel shortly.

"But you will come, won't you?" said Miss Ivors, laying her warm hand eagerly on his arm.

"The fact is," said Gabriel, "I have just arranged to go— —"

"Go where?" asked Miss Ivors.

"Well, you know, every year I go for a cycling tour with some fellows and so— —"

"But where?" asked Miss Ivors.

"Well, we usually go to France or Belgium or perhaps Germany," said Gabriel awkwardly.

"And why do you go to France and Belgium," said Miss Ivors, "instead of visiting your own land?"

"Well," said Gabriel, "it's partly to keep in touch with the languages and partly for a change."

"And haven't you your own language to keep in touch with—Irish?" asked Miss Ivors.

"Well," said Gabriel, "if it comes to that, you know, Irish is not my language."

Their neighbours had turned to listen to the cross-examination. Gabriel glanced right and left nervously and tried to keep his good humour under the ordeal which was making a blush invade his forehead.

"And haven't you your own land to visit," continued Miss Ivors, "that you know nothing of, your own people, and your own country?"

"O, to tell you the truth," retorted Gabriel suddenly, "I'm sick of my own country, sick of it!"

"Why?" asked Miss Ivors.

Gabriel did not answer for his retort had heated him.

"Why?" repeated Miss Ivors.

They had to go visiting together and, as he had not answered her, Miss Ivors said warmly:

"Of course, you've no answer."

Gabriel tried to cover his agitation by taking part in the dance with great energy. He avoided her eyes for he had seen a sour expression on her face. But when they met in the long chain he was surprised to feel his hand firmly pressed. She looked at him from under her brows for a moment quizzically until he smiled. Then, just as the chain was about to start again, she stood on tiptoe and whispered into his ear:

"West Briton!"

When the lancers were over Gabriel went away to a remote corner of the room where Freddy Malins' mother was sitting. She was a stout feeble old woman with white hair. Her voice had a catch in it like her son's and she stuttered slightly. She had been told that Freddy had come and that he was nearly all right. Gabriel asked her whether she had had a good crossing. She lived with her married daughter in Glasgow and came to Dublin on a visit once a year. She answered placidly that she had had a beautiful crossing and that the captain had been most attentive to her. She spoke also of the beautiful house her daughter kept in Glasgow, and of all the friends they had there. While her tongue rambled on Gabriel tried to banish from his mind all memory of the unpleasant incident with Miss Ivors. Of course the girl or woman, or whatever she was, was an enthusiast but there was a time for all things. Perhaps he ought not to have answered her like that. But she had no right to call him a West Briton before people, even in joke. She had tried to make him ridiculous before people, heckling him and staring at him with her rabbit's eyes.

He saw his wife making her way towards him through the waltzing couples. When she reached him she said into his ear:

"Gabriel, Aunt Kate wants to know won't you carve the goose as usual. Miss Daly will carve the ham and I'll do the pudding."

"All right," said Gabriel.

"She's sending in the younger ones first as soon as this waltz is over so that we'll have the table to ourselves."

"Were you dancing?" asked Gabriel.

"Of course I was. Didn't you see me? What row had you with Molly Ivors?"

"No row. Why? Did she say so?"

"Something like that. I'm trying to get that Mr D'Arcy to sing. He's full of conceit, I think."

"There was no row," said Gabriel moodily, "only she wanted me to go for a trip to the west of Ireland and I said I wouldn't."

His wife clasped her hands excitedly and gave a little jump.

"O, do go, Gabriel," she cried. "I'd love to see Galway again."

"You can go if you like," said Gabriel coldly.

She looked at him for a moment, then turned to Mrs Malins and said:

"There's a nice husband for you, Mrs Malins."

While she was threading her way back across the room Mrs Malins, without adverting to the interruption, went on to tell Gabriel what beautiful places there were in Scotland and beautiful scenery. Her son-in-law brought them every year to the lakes and they used to go fishing. Her son-in-law was a splendid fisher. One day he caught a beautiful big fish and the man in the hotel cooked it for their dinner.

Gabriel hardly heard what she said. Now that supper was coming near he began to think again about his speech and about the quotation. When he saw Freddy Malins coming across the room to visit his mother Gabriel left the chair free for him and retired into the embrasure of the window. The room had already cleared and from the back room came the clatter of plates and knives. Those who still remained in the drawing-room seemed tired of dancing and were conversing quietly in little groups. Gabriel's warm trembling fingers tapped the cold pane of the window. How cool it must be outside! How pleasant it would be to walk out alone, first along by the river and then through the park! The snow would be lying on the branches of the trees and forming a bright cap on the top of the Wellington Monument. How much more pleasant it would be there than at the supper-table!

He ran over the headings of his speech: Irish hospitality, sad memories, the Three Graces, Paris, the quotation from Browning. He repeated to himself a phrase he had written in his review: "One feels that one is listening to a thought-tormented music." Miss Ivors had praised the review. Was she sincere? Had she really any life of her own behind all her propagandism? There had never been any ill-feeling between them until that night. It unnerved him to think that she would be at the supper-table, looking up at him while he spoke with her critical quizzing eyes. Perhaps she would not be sorry to see him fail in his speech. An idea came into his mind and gave him courage. He would say, alluding to Aunt Kate and Aunt Julia: "Ladies and Gentlemen, the generation which is now on the wane among us may have had its faults but for my part I think it had certain qualities of hospitality, of humour, of humanity, which the new and very serious and hypereducated generation that is growing up around us seems to me to lack." Very good: that was one for Miss Ivors. What did he care that his aunts were only two ignorant old women?

A murmur in the room attracted his attention. Mr Browne was advancing from the door, gallantly escorting Aunt Julia, who leaned upon his arm, smiling and hanging her head. An irregular musketry of applause escorted her also as far as the piano and then, as Mary Jane seated herself on the stool, and Aunt Julia, no longer smiling, half turned so as to pitch her voice fairly into the room, gradually ceased. Gabriel recognised the prelude. It was that of an old song of Aunt Julia's—Arrayed for the Bridal. Her voice, strong and clear in tone, attacked with great spirit the runs which embellish the air and though she sang very rapidly she did not miss even the smallest of the grace notes. To follow the voice, without looking at the singer's face, was to feel and share the excitement of swift and secure flight. Gabriel applauded loudly with all the others at the close of the song and loud applause was borne in from the invisible supper-table. It sounded so genuine that a little colour struggled into Aunt Julia's face as she bent to replace in the music-stand the old leather-bound songbook that had her initials on the cover. Freddy Malins, who had listened with his head perched sideways to hear her better, was still applauding when everyone else had ceased and talking animatedly to his mother who nodded her head gravely and slowly in acquiescence. At last, when he could clap no more, he stood up suddenly and hurried across the room to Aunt Julia whose hand he seized and held in both his hands, shaking it when words failed him or the catch in his voice proved too much for him.

"I was just telling my mother," he said, "I never heard you sing so well, never. No, I never heard your voice so good as it is tonight. Now! Would you believe that now? That's the truth. Upon my word and honour that's the truth. I never heard your voice sound so fresh and so ... so clear and fresh, never."

Aunt Julia smiled broadly and murmured something about compliments as she released her hand from his grasp. Mr Browne extended his open hand towards her and said to those who were near him in the manner of a showman introducing a prodigy to an audience:

"Miss Julia Morkan, my latest discovery!"

He was laughing very heartily at this himself when Freddy Malins turned to him and said:

"Well, Browne, if you're serious you might make a worse discovery. All I can say is I never heard her sing half so well as long as I am coming here. And that's the honest truth."

"Neither did I," said Mr Browne. "I think her voice has greatly improved."

Aunt Julia shrugged her shoulders and said with meek pride:

"Thirty years ago I hadn't a bad voice as voices go."

"I often told Julia," said Aunt Kate emphatically, "that she was simply thrown away in that choir. But she never would be said by me."

She turned as if to appeal to the good sense of the others against a refractory child while Aunt Julia gazed in front of her, a vague smile of reminiscence playing on her face.

"No," continued Aunt Kate, "she wouldn't be said or led by anyone, slaving there in that choir night and day, night and day. Six o'clock on Christmas morning! And all for what?"

"Well, isn't it for the honour of God, Aunt Kate?" asked Mary Jane, twisting round on the piano-stool and smiling.

Aunt Kate turned fiercely on her niece and said:

"I know all about the honour of God, Mary Jane, but I think it's not at all honourable for the pope to turn out the women out of the choirs that have slaved there all their lives and put little whipper-snappers of boys over their heads. I suppose it is for the good of the Church if the pope does it. But it's not just, Mary Jane, and it's not right."

She had worked herself into a passion and would have continued in defence of her sister for it was a sore subject with her but Mary Jane, seeing that all the dancers had come back, intervened pacifically:

"Now, Aunt Kate, you're giving scandal to Mr Browne who is of the other persuasion."

Aunt Kate turned to Mr Browne, who was grinning at this allusion to his religion, and said hastily:

"O, I don't question the pope's being right. I'm only a stupid old woman and I wouldn't presume to do such a thing. But there's such a thing as common everyday politeness and gratitude. And if I were in Julia's place I'd tell that Father Healey straight up to his face...."

"And besides, Aunt Kate," said Mary Jane, "we really are all hungry and when we are hungry we are all very quarrelsome."

"And when we are thirsty we are also quarrelsome," added Mr Browne.

"So that we had better go to supper," said Mary Jane, "and finish the discussion afterwards."

On the landing outside the drawing-room Gabriel found his wife and Mary Jane trying to persuade Miss Ivors to stay for supper. But Miss Ivors, who had put on her hat and was buttoning her cloak, would not stay. She did not feel in the least hungry and she had already overstayed her time.

"But only for ten minutes, Molly," said Mrs Conroy. "That won't delay you."

"To take a pick itself," said Mary Jane, "after all your dancing."

"I really couldn't," said Miss Ivors.

"I am afraid you didn't enjoy yourself at all," said Mary Jane hopelessly.

"Ever so much, I assure you," said Miss Ivors, "but you really must let me run off now."

"But how can you get home?" asked Mrs Conroy.

"O, it's only two steps up the quay."

Gabriel hesitated a moment and said:

"If you will allow me, Miss Ivors, I'll see you home if you are really obliged to go."

But Miss Ivors broke away from them.

"I won't hear of it," she cried. "For goodness' sake go in to your suppers and don't mind me. I'm quite well able to take care of myself."

"Well, you're the comical girl, Molly," said Mrs Conroy frankly.

"Beannacht libh," cried Miss Ivors, with a laugh, as she ran down the staircase.

Mary Jane gazed after her, a moody puzzled expression on her face, while Mrs Conroy leaned over the banisters to listen for the hall-door. Gabriel asked himself was he the cause of her abrupt departure. But she did not seem to be in ill humour: she had gone away laughing. He stared blankly down the staircase.

At the moment Aunt Kate came toddling out of the supper-room, almost wringing her hands in despair.

"Where is Gabriel?" she cried. "Where on earth is Gabriel? There's everyone waiting in there, stage to let, and nobody to carve the goose!"

"Here I am, Aunt Kate!" cried Gabriel, with sudden animation, "ready to carve a flock of geese, if necessary."

A fat brown goose lay at one end of the table and at the other end, on a bed of creased paper strewn with sprigs of parsley, lay a great ham, stripped of its outer skin and peppered over with crust crumbs, a neat paper frill round its shin and beside this was a round of spiced beef. Between these rival ends ran parallel lines of side-dishes: two little minsters of jelly, red and yellow; a shallow dish full of blocks of blancmange and red jam, a large green leaf-shaped dish with a stalk-shaped handle, on which lay bunches of purple raisins and peeled almonds, a companion dish on which lay a solid rectangle of Smyrna figs, a dish of custard topped with grated nutmeg, a small bowl full of chocolates and sweets wrapped in gold and silver papers and a glass vase in which stood some tall celery stalks. In the centre of the table there stood, as sentries to a fruit-stand which upheld a pyramid of oranges and American apples, two squat old-fashioned decanters of cut glass, one containing port and the other dark sherry. On the closed square piano a pudding in a huge yellow dish lay in waiting and behind it were three squads of bottles of stout and ale and minerals, drawn up according to the colours of their uniforms, the first two black, with brown and red labels, the third and smallest squad white, with transverse green sashes.

Gabriel took his seat boldly at the head of the table and, having looked to the edge of the carver, plunged his fork firmly into the goose. He felt quite at ease now for he was an expert carver and liked nothing better than to find himself at the head of a well-laden table.

"Miss Furlong, what shall I send you?" he asked. "A wing or a slice of the breast?"

"Just a small slice of the breast."

"Miss Higgins, what for you?"

"O, anything at all, Mr Conroy."

While Gabriel and Miss Daly exchanged plates of goose and plates of ham and spiced beef Lily went from guest to guest with a dish of hot floury potatoes wrapped in a white napkin. This was Mary Jane's idea and she had also suggested apple sauce for the goose but Aunt Kate had said that plain roast goose without any apple sauce had always been good enough for her and she hoped she might never eat worse. Mary Jane waited on her pupils and saw that they got the best slices and Aunt Kate and Aunt Julia opened and carried across from the piano bottles of stout and ale for the gentlemen and bottles of minerals for the ladies. There was a great deal of confusion and laughter and noise, the noise of orders and counter-orders, of knives and forks, of corks and glass-stoppers. Gabriel began to carve second helpings as soon as he had finished the first round without serving himself. Everyone protested loudly so that he compromised by taking a long draught of stout for he had found the carving hot work. Mary Jane settled down quietly to her supper but Aunt Kate and Aunt Julia were still toddling round the table, walking on each other's heels, getting in each other's way and giving each other unheeded orders. Mr Browne begged of them to sit down and eat their suppers and so did Gabriel but they said they were time enough so that, at last, Freddy Malins stood up and, capturing Aunt Kate, plumped her down on her chair amid general laughter.

When everyone had been well served Gabriel said, smiling:

"Now, if anyone wants a little more of what vulgar people call stuffing let him or her speak."

A chorus of voices invited him to begin his own supper and Lily came forward with three potatoes which she had reserved for him.

"Very well," said Gabriel amiably, as he took another preparatory draught, "kindly forget my existence, ladies and gentlemen, for a few minutes."

He set to his supper and took no part in the conversation with which the table covered Lily's removal of the plates. The subject of talk was the opera company which was then at the Theatre Royal. Mr Bartell D'Arcy, the tenor, a dark-complexioned young man with a smart moustache, praised very highly the leading contralto of the company but Miss Furlong thought she had a rather vulgar style of production. Freddy Malins said there was a negro chieftain singing in the second part of the Gaiety pantomime who had one of the finest tenor voices he had ever heard.

"Have you heard him?" he asked Mr Bartell D'Arcy across the table.

"No," answered Mr Bartell D'Arcy carelessly.

"Because," Freddy Malins explained, "now I'd be curious to hear your opinion of him. I think he has a grand voice."

"It takes Teddy to find out the really good things," said Mr Browne familiarly to the table.

"And why couldn't he have a voice too?" asked Freddy Malins sharply. "Is it because he's only a black?"

Nobody answered this question and Mary Jane led the table back to the legitimate opera. One of her pupils had given her a pass for Mignon. Of course it was very fine, she said, but it made her think of poor Georgina Burns. Mr Browne could go back farther still, to the old Italian companies that used to come to Dublin—Tietjens, Ilma de Murzka, Campanini, the great Trebelli, Giuglini, Ravelli, Aramburo. Those were the days, he said, when there was something like singing to be heard in Dublin. He told too of how the top gallery of the old Royal used to be packed night after night, of how one night an Italian tenor had sung five encores to Let me like a Soldier fall, introducing a high C every time, and of how the gallery boys would sometimes in their enthusiasm unyoke the horses from the carriage of some great prima donna and pull her themselves through the streets to her hotel. Why did they never play the grand old operas now, he asked, Dinorah, Lucrezia Borgia? Because they could not get the voices to sing them: that was why.

"Oh, well," said Mr Bartell D'Arcy, "I presume there are as good singers today as there were then."

"Where are they?" asked Mr Browne defiantly.

"In London, Paris, Milan," said Mr Bartell D'Arcy warmly. "I suppose Caruso, for example, is quite as good, if not better than any of the men you have mentioned."

"Maybe so," said Mr Browne. "But I may tell you I doubt it strongly."

"O, I'd give anything to hear Caruso sing," said Mary Jane.

"For me," said Aunt Kate, who had been picking a bone, "there was only one tenor. To please me, I mean. But I suppose none of you ever heard of him."

"Who was he, Miss Morkan?" asked Mr Bartell D'Arcy politely.

"His name," said Aunt Kate, "was Parkinson. I heard him when he was in his prime and I think he had then the purest tenor voice that was ever put into a man's throat."

"Strange," said Mr Bartell D'Arcy. "I never even heard of him."

"Yes, yes, Miss Morkan is right," said Mr Browne. "I remember hearing of old Parkinson but he's too far back for me."

"A beautiful pure sweet mellow English tenor," said Aunt Kate with enthusiasm.

Gabriel having finished, the huge pudding was transferred to the table. The clatter of forks and spoons began again. Gabriel's wife served out spoonfuls of the pudding and passed the plates down the table. Midway down they were held up by Mary Jane, who replenished them with raspberry or orange jelly or with blancmange and jam. The pudding was of Aunt Julia's making and she received praises for it from all quarters. She herself said that it was not quite brown enough.

"Well, I hope, Miss Morkan," said Mr Browne, "that I'm brown enough for you because, you know, I'm all brown."

All the gentlemen, except Gabriel, ate some of the pudding out of compliment to Aunt Julia. As Gabriel never ate sweets the celery had been left for him. Freddy Malins also took a stalk of celery and ate it with his pudding. He had been told that celery was a capital thing for the blood and he was just then under doctor's care. Mrs Malins, who had been silent all through the supper, said that her son was going down to Mount Melleray in a week or so. The table then spoke of Mount Melleray, how bracing the air was down there, how hospitable the monks were and how they never asked for a penny-piece from their guests.

"And do you mean to say," asked Mr Browne incredulously, "that a chap can go down there and put up there as if it were a hotel and live on the fat of the land and then come away without paying anything?"

"O, most people give some donation to the monastery when they leave." said Mary Jane.

"I wish we had an institution like that in our Church," said Mr Browne candidly.

He was astonished to hear that the monks never spoke, got up at two in the morning and slept in their coffins. He asked what they did it for.

"That's the rule of the order," said Aunt Kate firmly.

"Yes, but why?" asked Mr Browne.

Aunt Kate repeated that it was the rule, that was all. Mr Browne still seemed not to understand. Freddy Malins explained to him, as best he could, that the monks were trying to make up for the sins committed by all the sinners in the outside world. The explanation was not very clear for Mr Browne grinned and said:

"I like that idea very much but wouldn't a comfortable spring bed do them as well as a coffin?"

"The coffin," said Mary Jane, "is to remind them of their last end."

As the subject had grown lugubrious it was buried in a silence of the table during which Mrs Malins could be heard saying to her neighbour in an indistinct undertone:

"They are very good men, the monks, very pious men."

The raisins and almonds and figs and apples and oranges and chocolates and sweets were now passed about the table and Aunt Julia invited all the guests to have either port or sherry. At first Mr Bartell D'Arcy refused to take either but one of his neighbours nudged him and whispered something to him upon which he allowed his glass to be filled. Gradually as the last glasses were being filled the conversation ceased. A pause followed, broken only by the noise of the wine and by unsettlings of chairs. The Misses Morkan, all three, looked down at the tablecloth. Someone coughed once or twice and then a few gentlemen patted the table gently as a signal for silence. The silence came and Gabriel pushed back his chair.

The patting at once grew louder in encouragement and then ceased altogether. Gabriel leaned his ten trembling fingers on the tablecloth and smiled nervously at the company. Meeting a row of upturned faces he raised his eyes to the chandelier. The piano was playing a waltz tune and he could hear the skirts sweeping against the drawing-room door. People, perhaps, were standing in the snow on the quay outside, gazing up at the lighted windows and listening to the waltz music. The air was pure there. In the distance lay the park where the trees were weighted with snow. The Wellington Monument wore a gleaming cap of snow that flashed westward over the white field of Fifteen Acres.

He began:

"Ladies and Gentlemen,

"It has fallen to my lot this evening, as in years past, to perform a very pleasing task but a task for which I am afraid my poor powers as a speaker are all too inadequate."

"No, no!" said Mr Browne.

"But, however that may be, I can only ask you tonight to take the will for the deed and to lend me your attention for a few moments while I endeavour to express to you in words what my feelings are on this occasion.

"Ladies and Gentlemen, it is not the first time that we have gathered together under this hospitable roof, around this hospitable board. It is not the first time that we have been the recipients—or perhaps, I had better say, the victims—of the hospitality of certain good ladies."

He made a circle in the air with his arm and paused. Everyone laughed or smiled at Aunt Kate and Aunt Julia and Mary Jane who all turned crimson with pleasure. Gabriel went on more boldly:

"I feel more strongly with every recurring year that our country has no tradition which does it so much honour and which it should guard so jealously as that of its hospitality. It is a tradition that is unique as far as my experience goes (and I have visited not a few places abroad) among the modern nations. Some would say, perhaps, that with us it is rather a failing than anything to be boasted of. But granted even that, it is, to my mind, a princely failing, and one that I trust will long be cultivated among us. Of one thing, at least, I am sure. As long as this one roof shelters the good ladies aforesaid—and I wish from my heart it may do so for many and many a long year to come—the tradition of genuine warm-hearted courteous Irish hospitality, which our forefathers have handed down to us and which we in turn must hand down to our descendants, is still alive among us."

A hearty murmur of assent ran round the table. It shot through Gabriel's mind that Miss Ivors was not there and that she had gone away discourteously: and he said with confidence in himself:

"Ladies and Gentlemen,

"A new generation is growing up in our midst, a generation actuated by new ideas and new principles. It is serious and enthusiastic for these new ideas and its enthusiasm, even when it is misdirected, is, I believe, in the main sincere. But we are living in a sceptical and, if I may use the phrase, a thought-tormented age: and sometimes I fear that this new generation, educated or hypereducated as it is, will lack those qualities of humanity, of hospitality, of kindly humour which belonged to an older day. Listening tonight to the names of all those great singers of the past it seemed to me, I must confess, that we were living in a less spacious age. Those days might, without exaggeration, be called spacious days: and if they are gone beyond recall let us hope, at least, that in gatherings such as this we shall still speak of them with pride and affection, still cherish in our hearts the memory of those dead and gone great ones whose fame the world will not willingly let die."

"Hear, hear!" said Mr Browne loudly.

"But yet," continued Gabriel, his voice falling into a softer inflection, "there are always in gatherings such as this sadder thoughts that will recur to our minds: thoughts of the past, of youth, of changes, of absent faces that we miss here tonight. Our path through life is strewn with many such sad memories: and were we to brood upon them always we could not find the heart to go on bravely with our work among the living. We have all of us living duties and living affections which claim, and rightly claim, our strenuous endeavours.

"Therefore, I will not linger on the past. I will not let any gloomy moralising intrude upon us here tonight. Here we are gathered together for a brief moment from the bustle and rush of our everyday routine. We are met here as friends, in the spirit of good-fellowship, as colleagues, also to a certain extent, in the true spirit of camaraderie, and as the guests of—what shall I call them?—the Three Graces of the Dublin musical world."

The table burst into applause and laughter at this allusion. Aunt Julia vainly asked each of her neighbours in turn to tell her what Gabriel had said.

"He says we are the Three Graces, Aunt Julia," said Mary Jane.

Aunt Julia did not understand but she looked up, smiling, at Gabriel, who continued in the same vein:

"Ladies and Gentlemen,

"I will not attempt to play tonight the part that Paris played on another occasion. I will not attempt to choose between them. The task would be an invidious one and one beyond my poor powers. For when I view them in turn, whether it be our chief hostess herself, whose good heart, whose too good heart, has become a byword with all who know her, or her sister, who seems to be gifted with perennial youth and whose singing must have been a surprise and a revelation to us all tonight, or, last but not least, when I consider our youngest hostess, talented, cheerful, hard-working and the best of nieces, I confess, Ladies and Gentlemen, that I do not know to which of them I should award the prize."

Gabriel glanced down at his aunts and, seeing the large smile on Aunt Julia's face and the tears which had risen to Aunt Kate's eyes, hastened to his close. He raised his glass of port gallantly, while every member of the company fingered a glass expectantly, and said loudly:

"Let us toast them all three together. Let us drink to their health, wealth, long life, happiness and prosperity and may they long continue to hold the proud and self-won position which they hold in their profession and the position of honour and affection which they hold in our hearts."

All the guests stood up, glass in hand, and turning towards the three seated ladies, sang in unison, with Mr Browne as leader:

For they are jolly gay fellows,
For they are jolly gay fellows,
For they are jolly gay fellows,
Which nobody can deny.

Aunt Kate was making frank use of her handkerchief and even Aunt Julia seemed moved. Freddy Malins beat time with his pudding-fork and the singers turned towards one another, as if in melodious conference, while they sang with emphasis:

Unless he tells a lie,
Unless he tells a lie.

Then, turning once more towards their hostesses, they sang:

For they are jolly gay fellows,
For they are jolly gay fellows,
For they are jolly gay fellows,
Which nobody can deny.

The acclamation which followed was taken up beyond the door of the supper-room by many of the other guests and renewed time after time, Freddy Malins acting as officer with his fork on high.

The piercing morning air came into the hall where they were standing so that Aunt Kate said:

"Close the door, somebody. Mrs Malins will get her death of cold."

"Browne is out there, Aunt Kate," said Mary Jane.

"Browne is everywhere," said Aunt Kate, lowering her voice.

Mary Jane laughed at her tone.

"Really," she said archly, "he is very attentive."

"He has been laid on here like the gas," said Aunt Kate in the same tone, "all during the Christmas."

She laughed herself this time good-humouredly and then added quickly:

"But tell him to come in, Mary Jane, and close the door. I hope to goodness he didn't hear me."

At that moment the hall-door was opened and Mr Browne came in from the doorstep, laughing as if his heart would break. He was dressed in a long green overcoat with mock astrakhan cuffs and collar and wore on his head an oval fur cap. He pointed down the snow-covered quay from where the sound of shrill prolonged whistling was borne in.

"Teddy will have all the cabs in Dublin out," he said.

Gabriel advanced from the little pantry behind the office, struggling into his overcoat and, looking round the hall, said:

"Gretta not down yet?"

"She's getting on her things, Gabriel," said Aunt Kate.

"Who's playing up there?" asked Gabriel.

"Nobody. They're all gone."

"O no, Aunt Kate," said Mary Jane. "Bartell D'Arcy and Miss O'Callaghan aren't gone yet."

"Someone is fooling at the piano anyhow," said Gabriel.

Mary Jane glanced at Gabriel and Mr Browne and said with a shiver:

"It makes me feel cold to look at you two gentlemen muffled up like that. I wouldn't like to face your journey home at this hour."

"I'd like nothing better this minute," said Mr Browne stoutly, "than a rattling fine walk in the country or a fast drive with a good spanking goer between the shafts."

"We used to have a very good horse and trap at home," said Aunt Julia sadly.

"The never-to-be-forgotten Johnny," said Mary Jane, laughing.

Aunt Kate and Gabriel laughed too.

"Why, what was wonderful about Johnny?" asked Mr Browne.

"The late lamented Patrick Morkan, our grandfather, that is," explained Gabriel, "commonly known in his later years as the old gentleman, was a glue-boiler."

"O now, Gabriel," said Aunt Kate, laughing, "he had a starch mill."

"Well, glue or starch," said Gabriel, "the old gentleman had a horse by the name of Johnny. And Johnny used to work in the old gentleman's mill, walking round and round in order to drive the mill. That was all very well; but now comes the tragic part about Johnny. One fine day the old gentleman thought he'd like to drive out with the quality to a military review in the park."

"The Lord have mercy on his soul," said Aunt Kate compassionately.

"Amen," said Gabriel. "So the old gentleman, as I said, harnessed Johnny and put on his very best tall hat and his very best stock collar and drove out in grand style from his ancestral mansion somewhere near Back Lane, I think."

Everyone laughed, even Mrs Malins, at Gabriel's manner and Aunt Kate said:

"O now, Gabriel, he didn't live in Back Lane, really. Only the mill was there."

"Out from the mansion of his forefathers," continued Gabriel, "he drove with Johnny. And everything went on beautifully until Johnny came in sight of King Billy's statue: and whether he fell in love with the horse King Billy sits on or whether he thought he was back again in the mill, anyhow he began to walk round the statue."

Gabriel paced in a circle round the hall in his goloshes amid the laughter of the others.

"Round and round he went," said Gabriel, "and the old gentleman, who was a very pompous old gentleman, was highly indignant. 'Go on, sir! What do you mean, sir? Johnny! Johnny! Most extraordinary conduct! Can't understand the horse!'"

The peal of laughter which followed Gabriel's imitation of the incident was interrupted by a resounding knock at the hall door. Mary Jane ran to open it and let in Freddy Malins. Freddy Malins, with his hat well back on his head and his shoulders humped with cold, was puffing and steaming after his exertions.

"I could only get one cab," he said.

"O, we'll find another along the quay," said Gabriel.

"Yes," said Aunt Kate. "Better not keep Mrs Malins standing in the draught."

Mrs Malins was helped down the front steps by her son and Mr Browne and, after many manœuvres, hoisted into the cab. Freddy Malins clambered in after her and spent a long time settling her on the seat, Mr Browne helping him with advice. At last she was settled comfortably and Freddy Malins invited Mr Browne into the cab. There was a good deal of confused talk, and then Mr Browne got into the cab. The cabman settled his rug over his knees, and bent down for the address. The confusion grew greater and the cabman was directed differently by Freddy Malins and Mr Browne, each of whom had his head out through a window of the cab. The difficulty was to know where to drop Mr Browne along the route, and Aunt Kate, Aunt Julia and Mary Jane helped the discussion from the doorstep with cross-directions and contradictions and abundance of laughter. As for Freddy Malins he was speechless with laughter. He popped his head in and out of the window every moment to the great danger of his hat, and told his mother how the discussion was progressing, till at last Mr Browne shouted to the bewildered cabman above the din of everybody's laughter:

"Do you know Trinity College?"

"Yes, sir," said the cabman.

"Well, drive bang up against Trinity College gates," said Mr Browne, "and then we'll tell you where to go. You understand now?"

"Yes, sir," said the cabman.

"Make like a bird for Trinity College."

"Right, sir," said the cabman.

The horse was whipped up and the cab rattled off along the quay amid a chorus of laughter and adieus.

Gabriel had not gone to the door with the others. He was in a dark part of the hall gazing up the staircase. A woman was standing near the top of the first flight, in the shadow also. He could not see her face but he could see the terracotta and salmon-pink panels of her skirt which the shadow made appear black and white. It was his wife. She was leaning on the banisters, listening to something. Gabriel was surprised at her stillness and strained his ear to listen also. But he could hear little save the noise of laughter and dispute on the front steps, a few chords struck on the piano and a few notes of a man's voice singing.

He stood still in the gloom of the hall, trying to catch the air that the voice was singing and gazing up at his wife. There was grace and mystery in her attitude as if she were a symbol of something. He asked himself what is a woman standing on the stairs in the shadow, listening to distant music, a symbol of. If he were a painter he would paint her in that attitude. Her blue felt hat would show off the bronze of her hair against the darkness and the dark panels of her skirt would show off the light ones. Distant Music he would call the picture if he were a painter.

The hall-door was closed; and Aunt Kate, Aunt Julia and Mary Jane came down the hall, still laughing.

"Well, isn't Freddy terrible?" said Mary Jane. "He's really terrible."

Gabriel said nothing but pointed up the stairs towards where his wife was standing. Now that the hall-door was closed the voice and the piano could be heard more clearly. Gabriel held up his hand for them to be silent. The song seemed to be in the old Irish tonality and the singer seemed uncertain both of his words and of his voice. The voice, made plaintive by distance and by the singer's hoarseness, faintly illuminated the cadence of the air with words expressing grief:

O, the rain falls on my heavy locks
And the dew wets my skin,
My babe lies cold....

"O," exclaimed Mary Jane. "It's Bartell D'Arcy singing and he wouldn't sing all the night. O, I'll get him to sing a song before he goes."

"O do, Mary Jane," said Aunt Kate.

Mary Jane brushed past the others and ran to the staircase, but before she reached it the singing stopped and the piano was closed abruptly.

"O, what a pity!" she cried. "Is he coming down, Gretta?"

Gabriel heard his wife answer yes and saw her come down towards them. A few steps behind her were Mr Bartell D'Arcy and Miss O'Callaghan.

"O, Mr D'Arcy," cried Mary Jane, "it's downright mean of you to break off like that when we were all in raptures listening to you."

"I have been at him all the evening," said Miss O'Callaghan, "and Mrs Conroy too and he told us he had a dreadful cold and couldn't sing."

"O, Mr D'Arcy," said Aunt Kate, "now that was a great fib to tell."

"Can't you see that I'm as hoarse as a crow?" said Mr D'Arcy roughly.

He went into the pantry hastily and put on his overcoat. The others, taken aback by his rude speech, could find nothing to say. Aunt Kate wrinkled her brows and made signs to the others to drop the subject. Mr D'Arcy stood swathing his neck carefully and frowning.

"It's the weather," said Aunt Julia, after a pause.

"Yes, everybody has colds," said Aunt Kate readily, "everybody."

"They say," said Mary Jane, "we haven't had snow like it for thirty years; and I read this morning in the newspapers that the snow is general all over Ireland."

"I love the look of snow," said Aunt Julia sadly.

"So do I," said Miss O'Callaghan. "I think Christmas is never really Christmas unless we have the snow on the ground."

"But poor Mr D'Arcy doesn't like the snow," said Aunt Kate, smiling.

Mr D'Arcy came from the pantry, fully swathed and buttoned, and in a repentant tone told them the history of his cold. Everyone gave him advice and said it was a great pity and urged him to be very careful of his throat in the night air. Gabriel watched his wife, who did not join in the conversation. She was standing right under the dusty fanlight and the flame of the gas lit up the rich bronze of her hair, which he had seen her drying at the fire a few days before. She was in the same attitude and seemed unaware of the talk about her. At last she turned towards them and Gabriel saw that there was colour on her cheeks and that her eyes were shining. A sudden tide of joy went leaping out of his heart.

"Mr D'Arcy," she said, "what is the name of that song you were singing?"

"It's called The Lass of Aughrim," said Mr D'Arcy, "but I couldn't remember it properly. Why? Do you know it?"

"The Lass of Aughrim," she repeated. "I couldn't think of the name."

"It's a very nice air," said Mary Jane. "I'm sorry you were not in voice tonight."

"Now, Mary Jane," said Aunt Kate, "don't annoy Mr D'Arcy. I won't have him annoyed."

Seeing that all were ready to start she shepherded them to the door, where good-night was said:

"Well, good-night, Aunt Kate, and thanks for the pleasant evening."

"Good-night, Gabriel. Good-night, Gretta!"

"Good-night, Aunt Kate, and thanks ever so much. Good-night, Aunt Julia."

"O, good-night, Gretta, I didn't see you."

"Good-night, Mr D'Arcy. Good-night, Miss O'Callaghan."

"Good-night, Miss Morkan."

"Good-night, again."

"Good-night, all. Safe home."

"Good-night. Good-night."

The morning was still dark. A dull yellow light brooded over the houses and the river; and the sky seemed to be descending. It was slushy underfoot; and only streaks and patches of snow lay on the roofs, on the parapets of the quay and on the area railings. The lamps were still burning redly in the murky air and, across the river, the palace of the Four Courts stood out menacingly against the heavy sky.

She was walking on before him with Mr Bartell D'Arcy, her shoes in a brown parcel tucked under one arm and her hands holding her skirt up from the slush. She had no longer any grace of attitude but Gabriel's eyes were still bright with happiness. The blood went bounding along his veins; and the thoughts went rioting through his brain, proud, joyful, tender, valorous.

She was walking on before him so lightly and so erect that he longed to run after her noiselessly, catch her by the shoulders and say something foolish and affectionate into her ear. She seemed to him so frail that he longed to defend her against something and then to be alone with her. Moments of their secret life together burst like stars upon his memory. A heliotrope envelope was lying beside his breakfast-cup and he was caressing it with his hand. Birds were twittering in the ivy and the sunny web of the curtain was shimmering along the floor: he could not eat for happiness. They were standing on the crowded platform and he was placing a ticket inside the warm palm of her glove. He was standing with her in the cold, looking in through a grated window at a man making bottles in a roaring furnace. It was very cold. Her face, fragrant in the cold air, was quite close to his; and suddenly he called out to the man at the furnace:

"Is the fire hot, sir?"

But the man could not hear with the noise of the furnace. It was just as well. He might have answered rudely.

A wave of yet more tender joy escaped from his heart and went coursing in warm flood along his arteries. Like the tender fire of stars moments of their life together, that no one knew of or would ever know of, broke upon and illumined his memory. He longed to recall to her those moments, to make her forget the years of their dull existence together and remember only their moments of ecstasy. For the years, he felt, had not quenched his soul or hers. Their children, his writing, her household cares had not quenched all their souls' tender fire. In one letter that he had written to her then he had said: "Why is it that words like these seem to me so dull and cold? Is it because there is no word tender enough to be your name?"

Like distant music these words that he had written years before were borne towards him from the past. He longed to be alone with her. When the others had gone away, when he and she were in their room in the hotel, then they would be alone together. He would call her softly:

"Gretta!"

Perhaps she would not hear at once: she would be undressing. Then something in his voice would strike her. She would turn and look at him....

At the corner of Winetavern Street they met a cab. He was glad of its rattling noise as it saved him from conversation. She was looking out of the window and seemed tired. The others spoke only a few words, pointing out some building or street. The horse galloped along wearily under the murky morning sky, dragging his old rattling box after his heels, and Gabriel was again in a cab with her, galloping to catch the boat, galloping to their honeymoon.

As the cab drove across O'Connell Bridge Miss O'Callaghan said:

"They say you never cross O'Connell Bridge without seeing a white horse."

"I see a white man this time," said Gabriel.

"Where?" asked Mr Bartell D'Arcy.

Gabriel pointed to the statue, on which lay patches of snow. Then he nodded familiarly to it and waved his hand.

"Good-night, Dan," he said gaily.

When the cab drew up before the hotel, Gabriel jumped out and, in spite of Mr Bartell D'Arcy's protest, paid the driver. He gave the man a shilling over his fare. The man saluted and said:

"A prosperous New Year to you, sir."

"The same to you," said Gabriel cordially.

She leaned for a moment on his arm in getting out of the cab and while standing at the curbstone, bidding the others good-night. She leaned lightly on his arm, as lightly as when she had danced with him a few hours before. He had felt proud and happy then, happy that she was his, proud of her grace and wifely carriage. But now, after the kindling again of so many memories, the first touch of her body, musical and strange and perfumed, sent through him a keen pang of lust. Under cover of her silence he pressed her arm closely to his side; and, as they stood at the hotel door, he felt that they had escaped from their lives and duties, escaped from home and friends and run away together with wild and radiant hearts to a new adventure.

An old man was dozing in a great hooded chair in the hall. He lit a candle in the office and went before them to the stairs. They followed him in silence, their feet falling in soft thuds on the thickly carpeted stairs. She mounted the stairs behind the porter, her head bowed in the ascent, her frail shoulders curved as with a burden, her skirt girt tightly about her. He could have flung his arms about her hips and held her still, for his arms were trembling with desire to seize her and only the stress of his nails against the palms of his hands held the wild impulse of his body in check. The porter halted on the stairs to settle his guttering candle. They halted too on the steps below him. In the silence Gabriel could hear the falling of the molten wax into the tray and the thumping of his own heart against his ribs.

The porter led them along a corridor and opened a door. Then he set his unstable candle down on a toilet-table and asked at what hour they were to be called in the morning.

"Eight," said Gabriel.

The porter pointed to the tap of the electric-light and began a muttered apology but Gabriel cut him short.

"We don't want any light. We have light enough from the street. And I say," he added, pointing to the candle, "you might remove that handsome article, like a good man."

The porter took up his candle again, but slowly for he was surprised by such a novel idea. Then he mumbled good-night and went out. Gabriel shot the lock to.

A ghostly light from the street lamp lay in a long shaft from one window to the door. Gabriel threw his overcoat and hat on a couch and crossed the room towards the window. He looked down into the street in order that his emotion might calm a little. Then he turned and leaned against a chest of drawers with his back to the light. She had taken off her hat and cloak and was standing before a large swinging mirror, unhooking her waist. Gabriel paused for a few moments, watching her, and then said:

"Gretta!"

She turned away from the mirror slowly and walked along the shaft of light towards him. Her face looked so serious and weary that the words would not pass Gabriel's lips. No, it was not the moment yet.

"You looked tired," he said.

"I am a little," she answered.

"You don't feel ill or weak?"

"No, tired: that's all."

She went on to the window and stood there, looking out. Gabriel waited again and then, fearing that diffidence was about to conquer him, he said abruptly:

"By the way, Gretta!"

"What is it?"

"You know that poor fellow Malins?" he said quickly.

"Yes. What about him?"

"Well, poor fellow, he's a decent sort of chap after all," continued Gabriel in a false voice. "He gave me back that sovereign I lent him, and I didn't expect it, really. It's a pity he wouldn't keep away from that Browne, because he's not a bad fellow, really."

He was trembling now with annoyance. Why did she seem so abstracted? He did not know how he could begin. Was she annoyed, too, about something? If she would only turn to him or come to him of her own accord! To take her as she was would be brutal. No, he must see some ardour in her eyes first. He longed to be master of her strange mood.

"When did you lend him the pound?" she asked, after a pause.

Gabriel strove to restrain himself from breaking out into brutal language about the sottish Malins and his pound. He longed to cry to her from his soul, to crush her body against his, to overmaster her. But he said:

"O, at Christmas, when he opened that little Christmas-card shop in Henry Street."

He was in such a fever of rage and desire that he did not hear her come from the window. She stood before him for an instant, looking at him strangely.

Then, suddenly raising herself on tiptoe and resting her hands lightly on his shoulders, she kissed him.

"You are a very generous person, Gabriel," she said.

Gabriel, trembling with delight at her sudden kiss and at the quaintness of her phrase, put his hands on her hair and began smoothing it back, scarcely touching it with his fingers. The washing had made it fine and brilliant. His heart was brimming over with happiness. Just when he was wishing for it she had come to him of her own accord. Perhaps her thoughts had been running with his. Perhaps she had felt the impetuous desire that was in him, and then the yielding mood had come upon her. Now that she had fallen to him so easily, he wondered why he had been so diffident.

He stood, holding her head between his hands. Then, slipping one arm swiftly about her body and drawing her towards him, he said softly:

"Gretta, dear, what are you thinking about?"

She did not answer nor yield wholly to his arm. He said again, softly:

"Tell me what it is, Gretta. I think I know what is the matter. Do I know?"

She did not answer at once. Then she said in an outburst of tears:

"O, I am thinking about that song, The Lass of Aughrim."

She broke loose from him and ran to the bed and, throwing her arms across the bed-rail, hid her face. Gabriel stood stock-still for a moment in astonishment and then followed her. As he passed in the way of the cheval-glass he caught sight of himself in full length, his broad, well-filled shirt-front, the face whose expression always puzzled him when he saw it in a mirror and his glimmering gilt-rimmed eyeglasses. He halted a few paces from her and said:

"What about the song? Why does that make you cry?"

She raised her head from her arms and dried her eyes with the back of her hand like a child. A kinder note than he had intended went into his voice.

"Why, Gretta?" he asked.

"I am thinking about a person long ago who used to sing that song."

"And who was the person long ago?" asked Gabriel, smiling.

"It was a person I used to know in Galway when I was living with my grandmother," she said.

The smile passed away from Gabriel's face. A dull anger began to gather again at the back of his mind and the dull fires of his lust began to glow angrily in his veins.

"Someone you were in love with?" he asked ironically.

"It was a young boy I used to know," she answered, "named Michael Furey. He used to sing that song, The Lass of Aughrim. He was very delicate."

Gabriel was silent. He did not wish her to think that he was interested in this delicate boy.

"I can see him so plainly," she said after a moment. "Such eyes as he had: big, dark eyes! And such an expression in them—an expression!"

"O then, you were in love with him?" said Gabriel.

"I used to go out walking with him," she said, "when I was in Galway."

A thought flew across Gabriel's mind.

"Perhaps that was why you wanted to go to Galway with that Ivors girl?" he said coldly.

She looked at him and asked in surprise:

"What for?"

Her eyes made Gabriel feel awkward. He shrugged his shoulders and said:

"How do I know? To see him, perhaps."

She looked away from him along the shaft of light towards the window in silence.

"He is dead," she said at length. "He died when he was only seventeen. Isn't it a terrible thing to die so young as that?"

"What was he?" asked Gabriel, still ironically.

"He was in the gasworks," she said.

Gabriel felt humiliated by the failure of his irony and by the evocation of this figure from the dead, a boy in the gasworks. While he had been full of memories of their secret life together, full of tenderness and joy and desire, she had been comparing him in her mind with another. A shameful consciousness of his own person assailed him. He saw himself as a ludicrous figure, acting as a pennyboy for his aunts, a nervous, well-meaning sentimentalist, orating to vulgarians and idealising his own clownish lusts, the pitiable fatuous fellow he had caught a glimpse of in the mirror. Instinctively he turned his back more to the light lest she might see the shame that burned upon his forehead.

He tried to keep up his tone of cold interrogation, but his voice when he spoke was humble and indifferent.

"I suppose you were in love with this Michael Furey, Gretta," he said.

"I was great with him at that time," she said.

Her voice was veiled and sad. Gabriel, feeling now how vain it would be to try to lead her whither he had purposed, caressed one of her hands and said, also sadly:

"And what did he die of so young, Gretta? Consumption, was it?"

"I think he died for me," she answered.

A vague terror seized Gabriel at this answer as if, at that hour when he had hoped to triumph, some impalpable and vindictive being was coming against him, gathering forces against him in its vague world. But he shook himself free of it with an effort of reason and continued to caress her hand. He did not question her again for he felt that she would tell him of herself. Her hand was warm and moist: it did not respond to his touch but he continued to caress it just as he had caressed her first letter to him that spring morning.

"It was in the winter," she said, "about the beginning of the winter when I was going to leave my grandmother's and come up here to the convent. And he was ill at the time in his lodgings in Galway and wouldn't be let out and his people in Oughterard were written to. He was in decline, they said, or something like that. I never knew rightly."

She paused for a moment and sighed.

"Poor fellow," she said. "He was very fond of me and he was such a gentle boy. We used to go out together, walking, you know, Gabriel, like the way they do in the country. He was going to study singing only for his health. He had a very good voice, poor Michael Furey."

"Well; and then?" asked Gabriel.

"And then when it came to the time for me to leave Galway and come up to the convent he was much worse and I wouldn't be let see him so I wrote him a letter saying I was going up to Dublin and would be back in the summer and hoping he would be better then."

She paused for a moment to get her voice under control and then went on:

"Then the night before I left I was in my grandmother's house in Nuns' Island, packing up, and I heard gravel thrown up against the window. The window was so wet I couldn't see so I ran downstairs as I was and slipped out the back into the garden and there was the poor fellow at the end of the garden, shivering."

"And did you not tell him to go back?" asked Gabriel.

"I implored of him to go home at once and told him he would get his death in the rain. But he said he did not want to live. I can see his eyes as well as well! He was standing at the end of the wall where there was a tree."

"And did he go home?" asked Gabriel.

"Yes, he went home. And when I was only a week in the convent he died and he was buried in Oughterard where his people came from. O, the day I heard that, that he was dead!"

She stopped, choking with sobs and, overcome by emotion, flung herself face downward on the bed, sobbing in the quilt. Gabriel held her hand for a moment longer, irresolutely, and then, shy of intruding on her grief, let it fall gently and walked quietly to the window.

She was fast asleep.

Gabriel, leaning on his elbow, looked for a few moments unresentfully on her tangled hair and half-open mouth, listening to her deep-drawn breath. So she had had that romance in her life: a man had died for her sake. It hardly pained him now to think how poor a part he, her husband, had played in her life. He watched her while she slept as though he and she had never lived together as man and wife. His curious eyes rested long upon her face and on her hair: and, as he thought of what she must have been then, in that time of her first girlish beauty, a strange, friendly pity for her entered his soul. He did not like to say even to himself that her face was no longer beautiful but he knew that it was no longer the face for which Michael Furey had braved death.

Perhaps she had not told him all the story. His eyes moved to the chair over which she had thrown some of her clothes. A petticoat string dangled to the floor. One boot stood upright, its limp upper fallen down: the fellow of it lay upon its side. He wondered at his riot of emotions of an hour before. From what had it proceeded? From his aunt's supper, from his own foolish speech, from the wine and dancing, the merry-making when saying good-night in the hall, the pleasure of the walk along the river in the snow. Poor Aunt Julia! She, too, would soon be a shade with the shade of Patrick Morkan and his horse. He had caught that haggard look upon her face for a moment when she was singing Arrayed for the Bridal. Soon, perhaps, he would be sitting in that same drawing-room, dressed in black, his silk hat on his knees. The blinds would be drawn down and Aunt Kate would be sitting beside him, crying and blowing her nose and telling him how Julia had died. He would cast about in his mind for some words that might console her, and would find only lame and useless ones. Yes, yes: that would happen very soon.

The air of the room chilled his shoulders. He stretched himself cautiously along under the sheets and lay down beside his wife. One by one they were all becoming shades. Better pass boldly into that other world, in the full glory of some passion, than fade and wither dismally with age. He thought of how she who lay beside him had locked in her heart for so many years that image of her lover's eyes when he had told her that he did not wish to live.

Generous tears filled Gabriel's eyes. He had never felt like that himself towards any woman but he knew that such a feeling must be love. The tears gathered more thickly in his eyes and in the partial darkness he imagined he saw the form of a young man standing under a dripping tree. Other forms were near. His soul had approached that region where dwell the vast hosts of the dead. He was conscious of, but could not apprehend, their wayward and flickering existence. His own identity was fading out into a grey impalpable world: the solid world itself which these dead had one time reared and lived in was dissolving and dwindling.

A few light taps upon the pane made him turn to the window. It had begun to snow again. He watched sleepily the flakes, silver and dark, falling obliquely against the lamplight. The time had come for him to set out on his journey westward. Yes, the newspapers were right: snow was general all over Ireland. It was falling on every part of the dark central plain, on the treeless hills, falling softly upon the Bog of Allen and, farther westward, softly falling into the dark mutinous Shannon waves. It was falling, too, upon every part of the lonely churchyard on the hill where Michael Furey lay buried. It lay thickly drifted on the crooked crosses and headstones, on the spears of the little gate, on the barren thorns. His soul swooned slowly as he heard the snow falling faintly through the universe and faintly falling, like the descent of their last end, upon all the living and the dead.

THE OLD NURSES STORY

Elizabeth Gaskell, 1852

YOU know, my dears, that your mother was an orphan, and an only child; and I dare say you have heard that your grandfather was a clergyman up in Westmoreland, where I come from. I was just a girl in the village school, when, one day, your grandmother came in to ask the mistress if there was any scholar there who would do for a nurse-maid; and mighty proud I was, I can tell ye, when the mistress called me up, and spoke to my being a good girl at my needle, and a steady, honest girl, and one whose parents were very respectable, though they might be poor. I thought I should like nothing better than to serve the pretty young lady, who was blushing as deep as I was, as she spoke of the coming baby, and what I should have to do with it. However, I see you don't care so much for this part of my story, as for what you think is to come, so I'll tell you at once. I was engaged and settled at the parsonage before Miss Rosamond (that was the baby, who is now your mother) was born. To be sure, I had little enough to do with her when she came, for she was never out of her mother's arms, and slept by her all night long; and proud enough was I sometimes when missis trusted her to me. There never was such a baby before or since, though you've all of you been fine enough in your turns; but for sweet, winning ways, you've none of you come up to your mother. She took after her mother, who was a real lady born; a Miss Furnivall, a grand-daughter of Lord Furnivall's, in Northumberland. I believe she had neither brother nor sister, and had been brought up in my lord's family till she had married your grandfather, who was just a curate, son to a shopkeeper in Carlisle--but a clever, fine gentleman as ever was--and one who was a right-down hard worker in his parish, which was very wide, and scattered all abroad over the Westmoreland Fells. When your mother, little Miss Rosamond, was about four or five years old, both her parents died in a fortnight--one after the other. Ah! that was a sad time. My pretty young mistress and me was looking for another baby, when my master came home from one of his long rides, wet and tired, and took the fever he died of; and then she never held up her head again, but just lived to see her dead baby, and have it laid on her breast, before she sighed away her life. My mistress had asked me, on her death-bed, never to leave Miss Rosamond; but if she had never spoken a word, I would have gone with the little child to the end of the world.

The next thing, and before we had well stilled our sobs, the executors and guardians came to settle the affairs. They were my poor young mistress's own cousin, Lord Furnivall, and Mr. Esthwaite, my master's brother, a shopkeeper in Manchester; not so well-to-do then as he was afterwards, and with a large family rising about him. Well! I don't know if it were their settling, or because of a letter my mistress wrote on her death-bed to her cousin, my lord; but somehow it was settled that Miss Rosamond and me were to go to Furnivall Manor House, in Northumberland; and my lord spoke as if it had been her mother's wish that she should live with his family, and as if he had no objections, for that one or two more or less could make no difference in so grand a household. So, though that was not the way in which I should have wished the coming of my bright and pretty pet to have been looked at--who was like a sunbeam in any family, be it never so grand--I was well pleased that all the folks in the Dale should stare and admire, when they heard I was going to be young lady's maid at my Lord Furnivall's at Furnivall Manor.

But I made a mistake in thinking we were to go and live where my lord did. It turned out that the family had left Furnivall Manor House fifty years or more. I could not hear that my poor young mistress had ever been there, though she had been brought up in the family; and I was sorry for that, for I should have liked Miss Rosamond's youth to have passed where her mother's had been.

My lord's gentleman, from whom I asked as many questions as I durst, said that the Manor House was at the foot of the Cumberland Fells, and a very grand place; that an old Miss Furnivall, a great-aunt of my lord's, lived there, with only a few servants; but that it was a very healthy place, and my lord had thought that it would suit Miss Rosamond very well for a few years, and that her being there might perhaps amuse his old aunt.

I was bidden by my lord to have Miss Rosamond's things ready by a certain day. He was a stern, proud man, as they say all the Lords Furnivall were; and he never spoke a word more than was necessary. Folk did say he had loved my young mistress; but that, because she knew that his father would object, she would never listen to him, and married Mr. Esthwaite; but I don't know. He never married, at any rate. But he never took much notice of Miss Rosamond; which I thought he might have done if he had cared for her dead mother. He sent his gentleman with us to the Manor House, telling him to join him at Newcastle that same evening; so there was no great length of time for him to make us known to all the strangers before he, too, shook us off; and we were left, two lonely young things (I was not eighteen) in the great old Manor House.

It seems like yesterday that we drove there. We had left our own dear parsonage very early, and we had both cried as if our hearts would break, though we were travelling in my lord's carriage, which I thought so much of once. And now it was long past noon on a September day, and we stopped to change horses for the last time at a little smoky town, all full of colliers and miners. Miss Rosamond had fallen asleep, but Mr. Henry told me to waken her, that she might see the park and the Manor House as we drove up. I thought it rather a pity; but I did what he bade me, for fear he should complain of me to my lord. We had left all signs of a town, or even a village, and were then inside the gates of a large wild park--not like the parks here in the south, but with rocks, and the noise of running water, and gnarled thorn-trees, and old oaks, all white and peeled with age.

The road went up about two miles, and then we saw a great and stately house, with many trees close around it, so close that in some places their branches dragged against the walls when the wind blew, and some hung broken down; for no one seemed to take much charge of the place;--to lop the wood, or to keep the moss-covered carriage-way in order. Only in front of the house all was clear. The great oval drive was without a weed; and neither tree nor creeper was allowed to grow over the long, many-windowed front; at both sides of which a wing projected, which were each the ends of other side fronts; for the house, although it was so desolate, was even grander than I expected. Behind it rose the Fells, which seemed unenclosed and bare enough; and on the left hand of the house, as you stood facing it, was a little, old-fashioned flower-garden, as I found out afterwards. A door opened out upon it from the west front; it had been scooped out of the thick, dark wood for some old Lady Furnivall; but the branches of the great forest-trees had grown and overshadowed it again, and there were very few flowers that would live there at that time.

When we drove up to the great front entrance, and went into the hall, I thought we should be lost--it was so large, and vast, and grand. There was a chandelier all of bronze, hung down from the middle of the ceiling; and I had never seen one before, and looked at it all in amaze. Then, at one end of the hall, was a great fireplace, as large as the sides of the houses in my country, with massy andirons and dogs to hold the wood; and by it were heavy, old-fashioned sofas. At the opposite end of the hall, to the left as you went in--on the western side--was an organ built into the wall, and so large that it filled up the best part of that end. Beyond it, on the same side, was a door; and opposite, on each side of the fireplace, were also doors leading to the east front; but those

I never went through as long as I stayed in the house, so I can't tell you what lay beyond.

The afternoon was closing in, and the hall, which had no fire lighted in it, looked dark and gloomy; but we did not stay there a moment. The old servant, who had opened the door for us, bowed to Mr. Henry, and took us in through the door at the further side of the great organ, and led us through several smaller halls and passages into the west drawing-room, where he said that Miss Furnivall was sitting. Poor little Miss Rosamond held very tight to me, as if she were scared and lost in that great place; and as for myself, I was not much better. The west drawing-room was very cheerful-looking, with a warm fire in it, and plenty of good, comfortable furniture about. Miss Furnivall was an old lady not far from eighty, I should think, but I do not know. She was thin and tall, and had a face as full of fine wrinkles as if they had been drawn all over it with a needle's point. Her eyes were very watchful, to make up, I suppose, for her being so deaf as to be obliged to use a trumpet. Sitting with her, working at the same great piece of tapestry, was Mrs. Stark, her maid and companion, and almost as old as she was. She had lived with Miss Furnivall ever since they both were young, and now she seemed more like a friend than a servant; she looked so cold, and grey, and stony, as if she had never loved or cared for any one; and I don't suppose she did care for any one, except her mistress; and, owing to the great deafness of the latter, Mrs. Stark treated her very much as if she were a child. Mr. Henry gave some message from my lord, and then he bowed good-bye to us all--taking no notice of my sweet little Miss Rosamond's outstretched hand--and left us standing there, being looked at by the two old ladies through their spectacles.

I was right glad when they rung for the old footman who had shown us in at first, and told him to take us to our rooms. So we went out of that great drawing-room, and into another sitting-room, and out of that, and then up a great flight of stairs, and along a broad gallery--which was something like a library, having books all down one side, and windows and writing-tables all down the other--till we came to our rooms, which I was not sorry to hear were just over the kitchens; for I began to think I should be lost in that wilderness of a house. There was an old nursery, that had been used for all the little lords and ladies long ago, with a pleasant fire burning in the grate, and the kettle boiling on the hob, and tea-things spread out on the table; and out of that room was the night-nursery, with a little crib for Miss Rosamond close to my bed. And old James called up Dorothy, his wife, to bid us welcome; and both he and she were so hospitable and kind, that by-and-by Miss Rosamond and me felt quite at home; and by the time tea was over, she was sitting on Dorothy's knee, and chattering away as fast as her little tongue could go. I soon found out that Dorothy was from Westmoreland, and that bound her and me together, as it were; and I would never wish to meet with kinder people than were old James and his wife. James had lived pretty nearly all his life in my lord's family, and thought there was no one so grand as they. He even looked down a little on his wife; because, till he had married her, she had never lived in any but a farmer's household. But he was very fond of her, as well he might be. They had one servant under them, to do all the rough work. Agnes they called her; and she and me, and James and Dorothy, with Miss Furnivall and Mrs. Stark, made up the family; always remembering my sweet little Miss Rosamond! I used to wonder what they had done before she came, they thought so much of her now. Kitchen and drawing-room, it was all the same. The hard, sad Miss Furnivall, and the cold Mrs. Stark, looked pleased when she came fluttering in like a bird, playing and pranking hither and thither, with a continual murmur, and pretty prattle of gladness. I am sure, they were sorry many a time when she flitted away into the kitchen, though they were too proud to ask her to stay with them, and were a little surprised at her taste; though to be sure, as Mrs. Stark said, it was not to be wondered at, remembering what stock her father had come of. The great, old rambling house was a famous place for little Miss Rosamond. She made expeditions all over it, with me at her heels: all, except the east wing, which was never opened, and whither we never thought of going. But in the western and northern part was many a pleasant room; full of things that were curiosities to us, though they might not have been to people who had seen more. The windows were darkened by the sweeping boughs of the trees, and the ivy which had overgrown them; but, in the green gloom, we could manage to see old china jars and carved ivory boxes, and great heavy books, and, above all, the old pictures!

Once, I remember, my darling would have Dorothy go with us to tell us who they all were; for they were all portraits of some of my lord's family, though Dorothy could not tell us the names of every one. We had gone through most of the rooms, when we came to the old state drawing-room over the hall, and there was a picture of Miss Furnivall; or, as she was called in those days, Miss Grace, for she was the younger sister. Such a beauty she must have been! but with such a set, proud look, and such scorn looking out of her handsome eyes, with her eyebrows just a little raised, as if she wondered how any one could have the impertinence to look at her, and her lip curled at us, as we stood there gazing. She had a dress on, the like of which I had never seen before, but it was all the fashion when she was young: a hat of some soft white stuff like beaver, pulled a little over her brows, and a beautiful plume of feathers sweeping round it on one side; and her gown of blue satin was open in front to a quilted white stomacher.

"Well, to be sure!" said I, when I had gazed my fill. "Flesh is grass, they do say; but who would have thought that Miss Furnivall had been such an out-and-out beauty, to see her now?"

"Yes," said Dorothy. "Folks change sadly. But if what my master's father used to say was true, Miss Furnivall, the elder sister, was handsomer than Miss Grace. Her picture is here somewhere; but, if I show it you, you must never let on, even to James, that you have seen it Can the little lady hold her tongue, think you?" asked she.

I was not so sure, for she was such a little sweet, bold, open-spoken child, so I set her to hide herself; and then I helped Dorothy to turn a great picture, that leaned with its face towards the wall, and was not hung up as the others were. To be sure, it beat Miss Grace for beauty; and I think, for scornful pride, too, though in that matter it might be hard to choose. I could have looked at it an hour but Dorothy seemed half frightened at having shown it to me, and hurried it back again, and bade me run and find Miss Rosamond, for that there were some ugly places about the house, where she should like ill for the child to go. I was a brave, high-spirited girl, and thought little of what the old woman said, for I liked hide-and-seek as well as any child in the parish; so off I ran to find my little one.

As winter drew on, and the days grew shorter, I was sometimes almost certain that I heard a noise as if some one was playing on the great organ in the hall. I did not hear it every evening; but, certainly, I did very often, usually when I was sitting with Miss Rosamond, after I had put her to bed, and keeping quite still and silent in the bedroom. Then I used to hear it booming and swelling away in the distance. The first night, when I went down to my supper, I asked Dorothy who had been playing music, and James said very shortly that I was a gowk to take the wind soughing among the trees for music; but I saw Dorothy look at him very fearfully, and Bessy, the kitchen-maid, said something beneath her breath, and went quite white. I saw they did not like my question, so I held my peace till I was with Dorothy alone, when I knew I could get a good deal out of her. So, the next day, I watched my time, and I coaxed and asked her who it was that played the organ; for I knew that it was the organ and not the wind well enough, for all I had kept silence before James.

But Dorothy had had her lesson, I'll warrant, and never a word could I get from her. So then I tried Bessy, though I had always held my head rather above her, as I was evened to James and Dorothy, and she was little better than their servant So she said I must never, never tell; and if ever told, I was never to say she had told me; but it was a very strange noise, and she had heard it many a time, but most of all on winter nights, and before storms; and folks did say it was the old lord playing on the great organ in the hall, just as he used to do when he was alive; but who the old lord was, or why he played, and why he played on stormy winter evenings in particular, she either could not or would not tell me. Well! I told you I had a brave heart; and I thought it was rather pleasant to have that grand music rolling about the house, let who would be the player; for now it rose above the great gusts of wind, and wailed and triumphed just like a living creature, and then it fell to a softness most complete, only it was always music, and tunes, so it was nonsense to call it the wind. I thought at first, that it might be Miss Furnivall who played, unknown to Bessy; but one day, when I was in the hall by myself, I opened the organ and peeped all about it and around it, as I had done to the organ in Crosthwaite Church once before, and I saw it was all broken and destroyed inside, though it looked so brave and fine; and then, though it was noon-day, my flesh began to creep a little, and I shut it up, and run away pretty quickly to my own bright nursery; and I did not like hearing the music for some time after that, any more than James and Dorothy did. All this time Miss Rosamond was making herself more and more beloved. The old ladies liked her to dine with them at their early dinner James stood behind Miss Furnivall's chair, and I behind Miss Rosamond's all in state; and, after dinner, she would play about in a corner of the great drawing-room as still as any mouse, while Miss Furnivall slept, and I had my dinner in the kitchen. But she was glad enough to come to me in the nursery afterwards; for, as she said Miss Furnivall was so sad, and Mrs. Stark so dull; but she and were merry enough; and, by-and-by, I got not to care for that weird rolling music, which did one no harm, if we did not know where it came from.

That winter was very cold. In the middle of October the frosts began, and lasted many, many weeks. I remember one day, at dinner, Miss Furnivall lifted up her sad, heavy eyes, and said to Mrs. Stark, "I am afraid we shall have a terrible winter," in a strange kind of meaning way But Mrs. Stark pretended not to hear, and talked very loud of something else. My little lady and I did not care for the frost; not we! As long as it was dry, we climbed up the steep brows behind the house, and went up on the Fells which were bleak and bare enough, and there we ran races in the fresh, sharp air; and once we came down by a new path, that took us past the two old gnarled holly-trees, which grew about half-way down by the east side of the house. But the days grew shorter and shorter, and the old lord, if it was he, played away, more and more stormily and sadly, on the great organ. One Sunday afternoon--it must have been towards the end of November--I asked Dorothy to take charge of little missy when she came out of the drawing-room, after Miss Furnivall had had her nap; for it was too cold to take her with me to church, and yet I wanted to go, And Dorothy was glad enough to promise and was so fond of the child, that all seemed well; and Bessy and I set off very briskly, though the sky hung heavy and black over the white earth, as if the night had never fully gone away, and the air, though still, was very biting.

"We shall have a fall of snow," said Bessy to me. And sure enough, even while we were in church, it came down thick, in great large flakes--so thick, it almost darkened the windows. It had stopped snowing before we came out, but it lay soft, thick, and deep beneath our feet, as we tramped home. Before we got to the hall, the moon rose, and I think it was lighter then--what with the moon, and what with the white dazzling snow--than it had been when we went to church, between two and three o'clock. I have not told you that Miss Furnivall and Mrs. Stark never went to church; they used to read the prayers together, in their quiet, gloomy way; they seemed to feel the Sunday very long without their tapestry-work to be busy at. So when I went to Dorothy in the kitchen, to fetch Miss Rosamond and take her upstairs with me, I did not much wonder when the old woman told me that the ladies had kept the child with them, and that she had never come to the kitchen, as I had bidden her, when she was tired of behaving pretty in the drawing-room. So I took off my things and went to find her, and bring her to her supper in the nursery. But when I went into the best drawing-room, there sat the two old ladies, very still and quiet, dropping out a word now and then, but looking as if nothing so bright and merry as Miss Rosamond had ever been near them. Still I thought she might be hiding from me; it was one of her pretty ways,--and that she had persuaded them to look as if they knew nothing about her; so I went softly peeping under this sofa and behind that chair, making believe I was sadly frightened at not finding her.

"What's the matter, Hester?" said Mrs. Stark sharply. I don't know if Miss Furnivall had seen me for, as I told you, she was very deaf, and she sat quite still, idly staring into the fire, with her hopeless face. "I'm only looking for my little Rosy Posy," replied I, still thinking that the child was there, and near me, though I could not see her.

"Miss Rosamond is not here," said Mrs. Stark. "She went away, more than an hour ago, to find Dorothy." And she, too, turned and went on looking into the fire.

My heart sank at this, and I began to wish I had never left my darling. I went back to Dorothy and told her. James was gone out for the day, but she, and me, and Bessy took lights, and went up into the nursery first; and then we roamed over the great, large house, calling and entreating Miss Rosamond to come out of her hiding-place, and not frighten us to death in that way. But there was no answer; no sound.

"Oh!" said I, at last, "can she have got into the east wing and hidden there?"

But Dorothy said it was not possible, for that she herself had never been in there; that the doors were always locked, and my lord's steward had the keys, she believed; at any rate, neither she nor James had ever seen them: so I said I would go back, and see if, after all, she was not hidden in the drawing-room, unknown to the old ladies; and if I found her there, I said, I would whip her well for the fright she had given me; but I never meant to do it. Well, I went back to the west drawing-room, and I told Mrs. Stark we could not find her anywhere, and asked for leave to look all about the furniture there, for I thought now that she might have fallen asleep in some warm, hidden corner; but no! we looked--Miss Furnivall got up and looked, trembling all over--and she was nowhere there; then we set off again, every one in the house, and looked in all the places we had searched before, but we could not find her. Miss Furnivall shivered and shook so much, that Mrs. Stark took her back into the warm drawing-room; but not before they had made me promise to bring her to them when she was found. Well-a-day! I began to think she never would be found, when I bethought me to look into the great front court, all covered with snow. I was upstairs when I looked out; but, it was such clear moonlight, I could see, quite plain, two little footprints, which might be traced from the hall-door and round the corner of the east wing. I don't know how I got down, but I tugged open the great stiff hall-door, and, throwing the skirt of my gown over my head for a cloak, I ran out. I turned the east corner, and there a black shadow fell on the snow but when I came again into the moonlight, there were the little footmarks going up--up to the Fells. It was bitter cold; so cold, that the air almost took the skin off my face as I ran; but I ran on, crying to think how my poor little darling must be perished and frightened. I was within sight of the holly-trees, when I saw a shepherd coming down the hill, bearing something in his arms wrapped in his maud. He shouted to me, and asked me if I had lost a bairn; and, when I could not speak for crying, he bore towards me, and I saw my wee bairnie, lying still, and white, and stiff in his arms, as if she had been dead. He told me he had been up the Fells to gather in his sheep, before the deep cold of night came on, and that under the holly-trees (black marks on the hill-side, where no other bush was for miles around) he had found my little lady--my lamb--my queen--my darling--stiff and cold in the terrible sleep which is frost-begotten. Oh! the joy and the tears of having her in my arms once again I for I would not let him carry her; but took her, maud and all, into my own arms, and held her near my own warm neck and heart, and felt the life stealing slowly back again into her little gentle limbs. But she was still insensible when we reached the hall, and I had no breath for speech. We went in by the kitchen-door.

"Bring the warming-pan," said I; and I carried her upstairs, and began undressing her by the nursery fire, which Bessy had kept up. I called my little lammie all the sweet and playful names I could think of,--even while my eyes were blinded by my tears; and at last, oh! at length she opened her large blue eyes. Then I put her into her warm bed, and sent Dorothy down to tell Miss Furnivall that all was well; and I made up my mind to sit by my darling's bedside the live-long night. She fell away into a soft sleep as soon as her pretty head had touched the pillow, and I watched by her till morning light; when she wakened up bright and clear--or so I thought at first--and, my dears, so I think now.

She said, that she had fancied that she should like to go to Dorothy, for that both the old ladies were asleep, and it was very dull in the drawing-room; and that, as she was going through the west lobby, she saw the snow through the high window falling--falling--soft and steady; but she wanted to see it lying pretty and white on the ground; so she made her way into the great hall: and then, going to the window, she saw it bright and soft upon the drive; but while she stood there, she saw a little girl, not so old as she was, "but so pretty," said my darling; "and this little girl beckoned to me to come out; and oh, she was so pretty and so sweet, I could not choose but go." And then this other little girl had taken her by the hand, and side by side the two had gone round the east corner.

"Now you are a naughty little girl, and telling stories," said I. "What would your good mamma, that is in heaven, and never told a story in her life, say to her little Rosamond, if she heard her--and I dare say she does--telling stories!"

"Indeed, Hester," sobbed out my child, "I'm telling you true. Indeed I am."

"Don't tell me!" said I, very stern. "I tracked you by your foot-marks through the snow; there were only yours to be seen: and if you had had a little girl to go hand-in-hand with you up the hill, don't you think the footprints would have gone along with yours?"

"I can't help it, dear, dear Hester," said she, crying, "if they did not; I never looked at her feet, but she held my hand fast and tight in her little one, and it was very, very cold. She took me up the Fell-path, up to the holly-trees; and there I saw a lady weeping and crying; but when she saw me, she hushed her weeping, and smiled very proud and grand, and took me on her knee, and began to lull me to sleep, and that's all, Hester--but that is true; and my dear mamma knows it is," said she, crying. So I thought the child was in a fever, and pretended to believe her, as she went over her story--over and over again, and always the same. At last Dorothy knocked at the door with Miss Rosamond's breakfast; and she told me the old ladies were down in the eating parlour, and that they wanted to speak to me. They had both been into the night-nursery the evening before, but it was after Miss Rosamond was asleep; so they had only looked at her--not asked me any questions.

"I shall catch it," thought I to myself, as I went along the north gallery. "And yet," I thought, taking courage, "it was in their charge I left her; and it's they that's to blame for letting her steal away unknown and unwatched." So I went in boldly, and told my story. I told it all to Miss Furnivall, shouting it close to her ear; but when I came to the mention of the other little girl out in the snow, coaxing and tempting her out, and wiling her up to the grand and beautiful lady by the holly-tree, she threw her arms up--her old and withered arms--and cried aloud, "Oh! Heaven forgive! Have mercy!"

Mrs. Stark took hold of her; roughly enough, I thought; but she was past Mrs. Stark's management, and spoke to me, in a kind of wild warning and authority.

"Hester! keep her from that child! It will lure her to her death! That evil child! Tell her it is a wicked, naughty child." Then, Mrs. Stark hurried me out of the room; where, indeed, I was glad enough to go; but Miss Furnivall kept shrieking out, "Oh, have mercy! Wilt Thou never forgive! It is many a long year ago"--

I was very uneasy in my mind after that. I durst never leave Miss Rosamond, night or day, for fear lest she might slip off again, after some fancy or other; and all the more, because I thought I could make out that Miss Furnivall was crazy, from their odd ways about her; and I was afraid lest something of the same kind (which might be in the family, you know) hung over my darling. And the great frost never ceased all this time; and, whenever it was a more stormy night than usual, between the gusts, and through the wind we heard the old lord playing on the great organ. But, old lord, or not, wherever Miss Rosamond went, there I followed; for my love for her, pretty, helpless orphan, was stronger than my fear for the grand and terrible sound. Besides, it rested with me to keep her cheerful and merry, as beseemed her age. So we played together, and wandered together, here and there, and everywhere; for I never dared to lose sight of her again in that large and rambling house. And so it happened, that one afternoon, not long before Christmas-day, we were playing together on the billiard-table in the great hall (not that we knew the right way of playing, but she liked to roll the smooth ivory balls with her pretty hands, and I liked to do whatever she did); and, by-and-by, without our noticing it, it grew dusk indoors, though it was still light in the open air, and I was thinking of taking her back into the nursery, when, all of a sudden, she cried out--

"Look, Hester! look! there is my poor little girl out in the snow!"

I turned towards the long narrow windows, and there, sure enough, I saw a little girl, less than my Miss Rosamond--dressed all unfit to be out-of-doors such a bitter night--crying, and beating against the window panes, as if she wanted to be let in. She seemed to sob and wail, till Miss Rosamond could bear it no longer, and was flying to the door to open it, when, all of a sudden, and close upon us, the great organ pealed out so loud and thundering, it fairly made me tremble; and all the more, when I remembered me that, even in the stillness of that dead-cold weather, I had heard no sound of little battering hands upon the window-glass, although the phantom child had seemed to put forth all its force; and, although I had seen it wail and cry, no faintest touch of sound had fallen upon my ears. Whether I remembered all this at the very moment, I do not know; the great organ sound had so stunned me into terror; but this I know, I caught up Miss Rosamond before she got the hall-door opened, and clutched her, and carried her away, kicking and screaming, into the large, bright kitchen, where Dorothy and Agnes were busy with their mince-pies.

"What is the matter with my sweet one?" cried Dorothy, as I bore in Miss Rosamond, who was sobbing as if her heart would break.

"She won't let me open the door for my little girl to come in; and she'll die if she is out on the Fells all night. Cruel, naughty Hester," she said, slapping me; but she might have struck harder, for I had seen a look of ghastly terror on Dorothy's face, which made my very blood run cold.

"Shut the back-kitchen door fast, and bolt it well," said she to Agues. She said no more; she gave me raisins and almonds to quiet Miss Rosamond; but she sobbed about the little girl in the snow, and would not touch any of the good things. I was thankful when she cried herself to sleep in bed. Then I stole down to the kitchen, and told Dorothy I had made up my mind. I would carry my darling back to my father's house in Applethwaite; where, if we lived humbly, we lived at peace. I said I had been frightened enough with the old lord's organ-playing; but now that I had seen for myself this little moaning child, all decked out as no child in the neighbourhood could be, beating and battering to get in, yet always without any sound or noise--with the dark wound on its right shoulder; and that Miss Rosamond had known it again for the phantom that had nearly lured her to death (which Dorothy knew was true); I would stand it no longer.

I saw Dorothy change colour once or twice. When I had done, she told me she did not think I could take Miss Rosamond with me, for that she was my lord's ward, and I had no right over her; and she asked me would I leave the child that I was so fond of just for sounds and sights that could do me no harm; and that they had all had to get used to in their turns? I was all in a hot, trembling passion; and I said it was very well for her to talk, that knew what these sights and noises betokened, and that had, perhaps, had something to do with the spectre child while it was alive. And I taunted her so, that she told me all she knew at last; and then I wished I had never been told, for it only made me more afraid than ever.

She said she had heard the tale from old neighbours that were alive when she was first married; when folks used to come to the hall sometimes, before it had got such a bad name on the country side: it might not be true, or it might, what she had been told.

The old lord was Miss Furnivall's father--Miss Grace, as Dorothy called her, for Miss Maude was the elder, and Miss Furnivall by lights. The old lord was eaten up with pride. Such a proud man was never seen or heard of; and his daughters were like him. No one was good enough to wed them, although they had choice enough; for they were the great beauties of their day, as I had seen by their portraits, where they hung in the state drawing-room. But, as the old saying is, "Pride will have a fall;" and these two haughty beauties fell in love with the same man, and he no better than a foreign musician, whom their father had down from London to play music with him at the Manor House. For, above all things, next to his pride, the old lord loved music. He could play`on nearly every instrument that ever was heard of; and it was a strange thing it did not soften him; but he was a fierce, dour old man, and had broken his poor wife's heart with his cruelty, they said. He was mad after music, and would pay any money for it. So he got this foreigner to come; who made such beautiful music, that they said the very birds on the trees stopped their singing to listen. And, by degrees, this foreign gentleman got such a hold over the old lord, that nothing would serve him but that he must come every year; and it was he that had the great organ brought from Holland, and built up in the hall, where it stood now. He taught the old lord to play on it; but many and many a time, when Lord Furnivall was thinking of nothing but his fine organ, and his finer music, the dark foreigner was walking abroad in the woods, with one of the young ladies: now Miss Maude, and then Miss Grace.

Miss Maude won the day and carried off the prize, such as it was; and he and she were married, all unknown to any one; and, before he made his next yearly visit, she had been confined of a little girl at a farm-house on the Moors, while her father and Miss Grace thought she was away at Doncaster Races. But though she was a wife and a mother, she was not a bit softened, but as haughty and as passionate as ever; and perhaps more so, for she was jealous of Miss Grace, to whom her foreign husband paid a deal of court--by way of blinding her--as he told his wife. But Miss Grace triumphed over Miss Maude, and Miss Maude grew fiercer and fiercer, both with her husband and with her sister; and the former--who could easily shake off what was disagreeable, and hide himself in foreign countries--went away a month before his usual time that summer, and half-threatened that he would never come back again. Meanwhile, the little girl was left at the farm-house, and her mother used to have her horse saddled and gallop wildly over the hills to see her once every week, at the very least; for where she loved she loved, and where she hated she hated. And the old lord went on playing--playing on his organ; and the servants thought the sweet music he made had soothed down his awful temper, of which (Dorothy said) some terrible tales could be told. He grew infirm too, and had to walk with a crutch; and his son--that was the present

Lord Furnivall's father--was with the army in America, and the other son at sea; so Miss Maude had it pretty much her own way, and she and Miss Grace grew colder and bitterer to each other every day; till at last they hardly ever spoke, except when the old lord was by. The foreign musician came again the next summer, but it was for the last time; for they led him such a life with their jealousy and their passions, that he grew weary, and went away, and never was heard of again. And Miss Maude, who had always meant to have her marriage acknowledged when her father should be dead, was left now a deserted wife, whom nobody knew to have been married, with a child that she dared not own, although she loved it to distraction; living with a father whom she feared, and a sister whom she hated. When the next summer passed over, and the dark foreigner never came, both Miss Maude and Miss Grace grew gloomy and sad; they had a haggard look about them, though they looked handsome as ever. But, by-and-by, Miss Maude brightened; for her father grew more and more infirm, and more than ever carried away by his music, and she and Miss Grace lived almost entirely apart, having separate rooms, the one on the west side, Miss Maude on the east--those very rooms which were now shut up. So she thought she might have her little girl with her, and no one need ever know except those who dared not speak about it, and were bound to believe that it was, as she said, a cottager's child she had taken a fancy to. All this, Dorothy said, was pretty well known; but what came afterwards no one knew, except Miss Grace and Mrs. Stark, who was even then her maid, and much more of a friend to her than ever her sister had been. But the servants supposed, from words that were dropped, that Miss Maude had triumphed over Miss Grace, and told her that all the time the dark foreigner had been mocking her with pretended love--he was her own husband. The colour left Miss Grace's cheek and lips that very day for ever, and she was heard to say many a time that sooner or later she would have her revenge; and Mrs. Stark was for ever spying about the east rooms.

One fearful night, just after the New Year had come in, when the snow was lying thick and deep; and the flakes were still falling--fast enough to blind any one who might be out and abroad--there was a great and violent noise heard, and the old lord's voice above all, cursing and swearing awfully, and the cries of a little child, and the proud defiance of a fierce woman, and the sound of a blow, and a dead stillness, and moans and wailings, dying away on the hill-side! Then the old lord summoned all his servants, and told them, with terrible oaths, and words more terrible, that his daughter had disgraced herself, and that he had turned her out of doors--her, and her child--and that if ever they gave her help, or food, or shelter, he prayed that they might never enter heaven.

And, all the while, Miss Grace stood by him, white and still as any stone; and, when he had ended, she heaved a great sigh, as much as to say her work was done, and her end was accomplished. But the old lord never touched his organ again, and died within the year; and no wonder I for, on the morrow of that wild and fearful night, the shepherds, coming down the Fell side, found Miss Maude sitting, all crazy and smiling, under the holly-trees, nursing a dead child, with a terrible mark on its right shoulder. "But that was not what killed it," said Dorothy: "it was the frost and the cold. Every wild creature was in its hole, and every beast in its fold, while the child and its mother were turned out to wander on the Fells! And now you know all! and I wonder if you are less frightened now?"

I was more frightened than ever; but I said I was not. I wished Miss Rosamond and myself well out of that dreadful house for ever; but I would not leave her, and I dared not take her away. But oh, how I watched her, and guarded her! We bolted the doors, and shut the window-shutters fast, an hour or more before dark, rather than leave them open five minutes too late. But my little lady still heard the weird child crying and mourning; and not all we could do or say could keep her from wanting to go to her, and let her in from the cruel wind and snow. All this time I kept away from Miss Furnivall and Mrs. Stark, as much as ever I could; for I feared them--I knew no good could be about them, with their grey, hard faces, and their dreamy eyes, looking back into the ghastly years that were gone. But, even in my fear, I had a kind of pity for Miss Furnivall, at least. Those gone down to the pit can hardly have a more hopeless look than that which was ever on her face. At last I even got so sorry for her--who never said a word but what was quite forced from her--that I prayed for her; and I taught Miss Rosamond to pray for one who had done a deadly sin; but often, when she came to those words, she would listen, and start up from her knees, and say, "I hear my little girl plaining and crying, very sad,--oh, let her in, or she will die!"

One night--just after New Year's Day had come at last, and the long winter had taken a turn, as I hoped--I heard the west drawing-room bell ring three times, which was the signal for me. I would not leave Miss Rosamond alone, for all she was asleep--for the old lord had been playing wilder than ever--and I feared lest my darling should waken to hear the spectre child; see her I knew she could not. I had fastened the windows too well for that. So I took her out of her bed, and wrapped her up in such outer clothes as were most handy, and carried her down to the drawing-room, where the old ladies sat at their tapestry-work as usual. They looked up when I came in, and Mrs. Stark asked, quite astounded, "Why did I bring Miss Rosamond there, out of her warm bed?" I had begun to whisper, "Because I was afraid of her being tempted out while I was away, by the wild child in the snow," when she stopped me short (with a glance at Miss Furnivall), and said Miss Furnivall wanted me to undo some work she had done wrong, and which neither of them could see to unpick. So I laid my pretty dear on the sofa, and sat down on a stool by them, and hardened my heart against them, as I heard the wind rising and howling.

Miss Rosamond slept on sound, for all the wind blew so; and Miss Furnivall said never a word, nor looked round when the gusts shook the windows. All at once she started up to her full height, and put up one hand, as if to bid us listen.

"I hear voices!" said she. "I hear terrible screams--I hear my father's voice!"

Just at that moment my darling wakened with a sudden start: "My little girl is crying, oh, how she is crying!" and she tried to get up and go to her, but she got her feet entangled in the blanket, and I caught her up; for my flesh had begun to creep at these noises, which they heard while we could catch no sound. In a minute or two the noises came, and gathered fast, and filled our ears; we, too, heard voices and screams, and no longer heard the winter's wind that raged abroad. Mrs. Stark looked at me, and I at her, but we dared not speak. Suddenly Miss Furnivall, went towards the door, out into the ante-room, through the west lobby, and opened the door into the great hall. Mrs. Stark followed, and I durst not be left, though my heart almost stopped beating for fear. I wrapped my darling tight in my arms, and went out with them. In the hall the screams were louder than ever; they seemed to come from the east wing--nearer and nearer--close on the other side of the locked-up doors--close behind them. Then I noticed that the great bronze chandelier seemed all alight, though the hall was dim, and that a fire was blazing in the vast hearth-place, though it gave no heat; and I shuddered up with terror, and folded my darling closer to me. But as I did so the east door shook, and she, suddenly struggling to get free from me, cried, "Hester! I must go. My little girl is there I hear her; she is coming! Hester, I must go!"

I held her tight with all my strength; with a set will, I held her. If I had died, my hands would have grasped her still, I was so resolved in my mind. Miss Furnivall stood listening, and paid no regard to my darling, who had got down to the ground, and whom I, upon my knees now, was holding with both my arms clasped round her neck; she still striving and crying to get free.

All at once, the east door gave way with a thundering crash, as if torn open in a violent passion, and there came into that broad and mysterious light, the figure of a tall old man, with grey hair and gleaming eyes. He drove before him, with many a relentless gesture of abhorrence, a stern and beautiful woman, with a little child clinging to her dress.

"O Hester! Hester!" cried Miss Rosamond; "it's the lady! the lady below the holly-trees; and my little girl is with her. Hester! Hester! let me go to her; they are drawing me to them. I feel them--I feel them. I must go!"

Again she was almost convulsed by her efforts to get away; but I held her tighter and tighter, till I feared I should do her a hurt; but rather that than let her go towards those terrible phantoms. They passed along towards the great hall-door, where the winds howled and ravened for their prey; but before they reached that, the lady turned; and I could see that she defied the old man with a fierce and proud defiance; but then she quailed--and then she threw up her arms wildly and piteously to save her child--her little child--from a blow from his uplifted crutch.

And Miss Rosamond was torn as by a power stronger than mine, and writhed in my arms, and sobbed (for by this time the poor darling was growing faint).

"They want me to go with them on to the Fells--they are drawing me to them. Oh, my little girl! I would come, but cruel, wicked Hester holds me very tight." But when she saw the uplifted crutch, she swooned away, and I thanked God for it. Just at this moment--when the tall old man, his hair streaming as in the blast of a furnace, was going to strike the little shrinking child--Miss Furnivall, the old woman by my side, cried out, "O father! father! spare the little innocent child!" But just then I saw--we all saw--another phantom shape itself, and grow clear out of the blue and misty light that filled the hall; we had not seen her till now, for it was another lady who stood by the old man, with a look of relentless hate and triumphant scorn. That figure was very beautiful to look upon, with a soft, white hat drawn down over the proud brows, and a red and curling lip. It was dressed in an open robe of blue satin. I had seen that figure before. It was the likeness of Miss Furnivall in her youth; and the terrible phantoms moved on, regardless of old Miss Furnivall's wild entreaty,--and the uplifted crutch fell on the right shoulder of the little child, and the younger sister looked on, stony, and deadly serene. But at that moment, the dim lights, and the fire that gave no heat, went out of themselves, and Miss Furnivall lay at our feet stricken down by the palsy--death-stricken.

Yes! she was carried to her bed that night never to rise again. She lay with her face to the wall, muttering low, but muttering always: "Alas! alas! what is done in youth can never be undone in age! What is done in youth can never be undone in age!"

"OH, WHISTLE, AND I'LL COME TO YOU, MY LAD"

M. R. James, 1904

"I suppose you will be getting away pretty soon, now Full term is over, Professor," said a person not in the story to the Professor of Ontography, soon after they had sat down next to each other at a feast in the hospitable hall of St. James's College.

The Professor was young, neat, and precise in speech.

"Yes," he said; "my friends have been making me take up golf this term, and I mean to go to the East Coast—in point of fact to Burnstow—(I dare say you know it) for a week or ten days, to improve my game. I hope to get off to-morrow."

"Oh, Parkins," said his neighbour on the other side, "if you are going to Burnstow, I wish you would look at the site of the Templars' preceptory, and let me know if you think it would be any good to have a dig there in the summer."

It was, as you might suppose, a person of antiquarian pursuits who said this, but, since he merely appears in this prologue, there is no need to give his entitlements.

"Certainly," said Parkins, the Professor: "if you will describe to me whereabouts the site is, I will do my best to give you an idea of the lie of the land when I get back; or I could write to you about it, if you would tell me where you are likely to be."

"Don't trouble to do that, thanks. It's only that I'm thinking of taking my family in that direction in the Long, and it occurred to me that, as very few of the English preceptories have ever been properly planned, I might have an opportunity of doing something useful on off-days."

The Professor rather sniffed at the idea that planning out a preceptory could be described as useful. His neighbour continued:

"The site—I doubt if there is anything showing above ground—must be down quite close to the beach now. The sea has encroached tremendously, as you know, all along that bit of coast. I should think, from the map, that it must be about three-quarters of a mile from the Globe Inn, at the north end of the town. Where are you going to stay?"

"Well, at the Globe Inn, as a matter of fact," said Parkins; "I have engaged a room there. I couldn't get in anywhere else; most of the lodging-houses are shut up in winter, it seems; and, as it is, they tell me that the only room of any size I can have is really a double-bedded one, and that they haven't a corner in which to store the other bed, and so on. But I must have a fairly large room, for I am taking some books down, and mean to do a bit of work; and though I don't quite fancy having an empty bed—not to speak of two—in what I may call for the time being my study, I suppose I can manage to rough it for the short time I shall be there."

"Do you call having an extra bed in your room roughing it, Parkins?" said a bluff person opposite. "Look here, I shall come down and occupy it for a bit; it'll be company for you."

The Professor quivered, but managed to laugh in a courteous manner.

"By all means, Rogers; there's nothing I should like better. But I'm afraid you would find it rather dull; you don't play golf, do you?"

"No, thank Heaven!" said rude Mr. Rogers.

"Well, you see, when I'm not writing I shall most likely be out on the links, and that, as I say, would be rather dull for you, I'm afraid."

"Oh, I don't know! There's certain to be somebody I know in the place; but, of course, if you don't want me, speak the word, Parkins; I shan't be offended. Truth, as you always tell us, is never offensive."

Parkins was, indeed, scrupulously polite and strictly truthful. It is to be feared that Mr. Rogers sometimes practised upon his knowledge of these characteristics. In Parkins's breast there was a conflict now raging, which for a moment or two did not allow him to answer. That interval being over, he said:

"Well, if you want the exact truth, Rogers, I was considering whether the room I speak of would really be large enough to accommodate us both comfortably; and also whether (mind, I shouldn't have said this if you hadn't pressed me) you would not constitute something in the nature of a hindrance to my work."

Rogers laughed loudly.

"Well done, Parkins!" he said. "It's all right. I promise not to interrupt your work; don't you disturb yourself about that. No, I won't come if you don't want me; but I thought I should do so nicely to keep the ghosts off." Here he might have been seen to wink and to nudge his next neighbour. Parkins might also have been seen to become pink. "I beg pardon, Parkins," Rogers continued; "I oughtn't to have said that. I forgot you didn't like levity on these topics."

"Well," Parkins said, "as you have mentioned the matter, I freely own that I do not like careless talk about what you call ghosts. A man in my position," he went on, raising his voice a little, "cannot, I find, be too careful about appearing to sanction the current beliefs on such subjects. As you know, Rogers, or as you ought to know; for I think I have never concealed my views——"

"No, you certainly have not, old man," put in Rogers sotto voce.

"——I hold that any semblance, any appearance of concession to the view that such things might exist is equivalent to a renunciation of all that I hold most sacred. But I'm afraid I have not succeeded in securing your attention."

"Your undivided attention, was what Dr. Blimber actually said,"[1] Rogers interrupted, with every appearance of an earnest desire for accuracy. "But I beg your pardon, Parkins: I'm stopping you."

"No, not at all," said Parkins. "I don't remember Blimber; perhaps he was before my time. But I needn't go on. I'm sure you know what I mean."

"Yes, yes," said Rogers, rather hastily—"just so. We'll go into it fully at Burnstow, or somewhere."

In repeating the above dialogue I have tried to give the impression which it made on me, that Parkins was something of an old woman—rather hen-like, perhaps, in his little ways; totally destitute, alas! of the sense of humour, but at the same time dauntless and sincere in his convictions, and a man deserving of the greatest respect. Whether or not the reader has gathered so much, that was the character which Parkins had.

On the following day Parkins did, as he had hoped, succeed in getting away from his college, and in arriving at Burnstow. He was made welcome at the Globe Inn, was safely installed in the large double-bedded room of which we have heard, and was able before retiring to rest to arrange his materials for work in apple-pie order upon a commodious table which occupied the outer end of the room, and was surrounded on three sides by windows looking out seaward; that is to say, the central window looked straight out to sea, and those on the left and right commanded prospects along the shore to the north and south respectively. On the south you saw the village of Burnstow. On the north no houses were to be seen, but only the beach and the low cliff backing it. Immediately in front was a strip—not considerable—of rough grass, dotted with old anchors, capstans, and so forth; then a broad path; then the beach. Whatever may have been the original distance between the Globe Inn and the sea, not more than sixty yards now separated them.

The rest of the population of the inn was, of course, a golfing one, and included few elements that call for a special description. The most conspicuous figure was, perhaps, that of an ancient militaire, secretary of a London club, and possessed of a voice of incredible strength, and of views of a pronouncedly Protestant type. These were apt to find utterance after his attendance upon the ministrations of the Vicar, an estimable man with inclinations towards a picturesque ritual, which he gallantly kept down as far as he could out of deference to East Anglian tradition.

Professor Parkins, one of whose principal characteristics was pluck, spent the greater part of the day following his arrival at Burnstow in what he had called improving his game, in company with this Colonel Wilson: and during the afternoon—whether the process of improvement were to blame or not, I am not sure—the Colonel's demeanour assumed a colouring so lurid that even Parkins jibbed at the thought of walking home with him from the links. He determined, after a short and furtive look at that bristling moustache and those incarnadined features, that it would be wiser to allow the influences of tea and tobacco to do what they could with the Colonel before the dinner-hour should render a meeting inevitable.

"I might walk home to-night along the beach," he reflected—"yes, and take a look—there will be light enough for that—at the ruins of which Disney was talking. I don't exactly know where they are, by the way; but I expect I can hardly help stumbling on them."

This he accomplished, I may say, in the most literal sense, for in picking his way from the links to the shingle beach his foot caught, partly in a gorse-root and partly in a biggish stone, and over he went. When he got up and surveyed his surroundings, he found himself in a patch of somewhat broken ground covered with small depressions and mounds. These latter, when he came to examine them, proved to be simply masses of flints embedded in mortar and grown over with turf. He must, he quite rightly concluded, be on the site of the preceptory he had promised to look at. It seemed not unlikely to reward the spade of the explorer; enough of the foundations was probably left at no great depth to throw a good deal of light on the general plan. He remembered vaguely that the Templars, to whom this site had belonged, were in the habit of building round churches, and he thought a particular series of the humps or mounds near him did appear to be arranged in something of a circular form. Few people can resist the temptation to try a little amateur research in a department quite outside their own, if only for the satisfaction of showing how successful they would have been had they only taken it up seriously. Our Professor, however, if he felt something of this mean desire, was also truly anxious to oblige Mr. Disney. So he paced with care the circular area he had noticed, and wrote down its rough dimensions in his pocket-book. Then he proceeded to examine an oblong eminence which lay east of the centre of the circle, and seemed to his thinking likely to be the base of a platform or altar. At one end of it, the northern, a patch of the turf was gone—removed by some boy or other creature feræ naturæ. It might, he thought, be as well to probe the soil here for evidences of masonry, and he took out his knife and began scraping away the earth. And now followed another little discovery: a portion of soil fell inward as he scraped, and disclosed a small cavity. He lighted one match after another to help him to see of what nature the hole was, but the wind was too strong for them all. By tapping and scratching the sides with his knife, however, he was able to make out that it must be an artificial hole in masonry. It was rectangular, and the sides, top, and bottom, if not actually plastered, were smooth and regular. Of course it was empty. No! As he withdrew the knife he heard a metallic clink, and when he introduced his hand it met with a cylindrical object lying on the floor of the hole. Naturally enough, he picked it up, and when he brought it into the light, now fast fading, he could see that it, too, was of man's making—a metal tube about four inches long, and evidently of some considerable age.

By the time Parkins had made sure that there was nothing else in this odd receptacle, it was too late and too dark for him to think of undertaking any further search. What he had done had proved so unexpectedly interesting that he determined to sacrifice a little more of the daylight on the morrow to archæology. The object which he now had safe in his pocket was bound to be of some slight value at least, he felt sure.

Bleak and solemn was the view on which he took a last look before starting homeward. A faint yellow light in the west showed the links, on which a few figures moving towards the club-house were still visible, the squat martello tower, the lights of Aldsey village, the pale ribbon of sands intersected at intervals by black wooden groynes, the dim and murmuring sea. The wind was bitter from the north, but was at his back when he set out for the Globe. He quickly rattled and clashed through the shingle and gained the sand, upon which, but for the groynes which had to be got over every few yards, the going was both good and quiet. One last look behind, to measure the distance he had made since leaving the ruined Templars' church, showed him a prospect of company on his walk, in the shape of a rather indistinct personage, who seemed to be making great efforts to catch up with him, but made little, if any, progress. I mean that there was an appearance of running about his movements, but that the distance between him and Parkins did not seem materially to lessen. So, at least, Parkins thought, and decided that he almost certainly did not know him, and that it would be absurd to wait until he came up. For all that, company, he began to think, would really be very welcome on that lonely shore, if only you could choose your companion. In his unenlightened days he had read of meetings in such places which even now would hardly bear thinking of. He went on thinking of them, however, until he reached home, and particularly of one which catches most people's fancy at some time of their childhood. "Now I saw in my dream that Christian had gone but a very little way when he saw a foul fiend coming over the field to meet him." "What should I do now," he thought, "if I looked back and caught sight of a black figure sharply defined against the yellow sky, and saw that it had horns and wings? I wonder whether I should stand or run for it. Luckily, the gentleman behind is not of that kind, and he seems to be about as far off now as when I saw him first. Well, at this rate he won't get his dinner as soon as I shall; and, dear me! it's within a quarter of an hour of the time now. I must run!"

Parkins had, in fact, very little time for dressing. When he met the Colonel at dinner, Peace—or as much of her as that gentleman could manage—reigned once more in the military bosom; nor was she put to flight in the hours of bridge that followed dinner, for Parkins was a more than respectable player. When, therefore, he retired towards twelve o'clock, he felt that he had spent his evening in quite a satisfactory way, and that, even for so long as a fortnight or three weeks, life at the Globe would be supportable under similar conditions—"especially," thought he, "if I go on improving my game."

As he went along the passages he met the boots of the Globe, who stopped and said:

"Beg your pardon, sir, but as I was a-brushing your coat just now there was somethink fell out of the pocket. I put it on your chest of drawers, sir, in your room, sir—a piece of a pipe or somethink of that, sir. Thank you, sir. You'll find it on your chest of drawers, sir—yes, sir. Good night, sir."

The speech served to remind Parkins of his little discovery of that afternoon. It was with some considerable curiosity that he turned it over by the light of his candles. It was of bronze, he now saw, and was shaped very much after the manner of the modern dog-whistle; in fact it was—yes, certainly it was—actually no more nor less than a whistle. He put it to his lips, but it was quite full of a fine, caked-up sand or earth, which would not yield to knocking, but must be loosened with a knife. Tidy as ever in his habits, Parkins cleared out the earth on to a piece of paper, and took the latter to the window to empty it out. The night was clear and bright, as he saw when he had opened the casement, and he stopped for an instant to look at the sea and note a belated wanderer stationed on the shore in front of the inn. Then he shut the window, a little surprised at the late hours people kept at Burnstow, and took his whistle to the light again. Why, surely there were marks on it, and not merely marks, but letters! A very little rubbing rendered the deeply-cut inscription quite legible, but the Professor had to confess, after some earnest thought, that the meaning of it was as obscure to him as the writing on the wall to Belshazzar. There were legends both on the front and on the back of the whistle. The one read thus:

FLA
FUR BIS
FLE

The other:

"I ought to be able to make it out," he thought; "but I suppose I am a little rusty in my Latin. When I come to think of it, I don't believe I even know the word for a whistle. The long one does seem simple enough. It ought to mean, 'Who is this who is coming?' Well, the best way to find out is evidently to whistle for him."

He blew tentatively and stopped suddenly, startled and yet pleased at the note he had elicited. It had a quality of infinite distance in it, and, soft as it was, he somehow felt it must be audible for miles round. It was a sound, too, that seemed to have the power (which many scents possess) of forming pictures in the brain. He saw quite clearly for a moment a vision of a wide, dark expanse at night, with a fresh wind blowing, and in the midst a lonely figure—how employed, he could not tell. Perhaps he would have seen more had not the picture been broken by the sudden surge of a gust of wind against his casement, so sudden that it made him look up, just in time to see the white glint of a sea-bird's wing somewhere outside the dark panes.

The sound of the whistle had so fascinated him that he could not help trying it once more, this time more boldly. The note was little, if at all, louder than before, and repetition broke the illusion—no picture followed, as he had half hoped it might. "But what is this? Goodness! what force the wind can get up in a few minutes! What a tremendous gust! There! I knew that window-fastening was no use! Ah! I thought so—both candles out. It's enough to tear the room to pieces."

The first thing was to get the window shut. While you might count twenty Parkins was struggling with the small casement, and felt almost as if he were pushing back a sturdy burglar, so strong was the pressure. It slackened all at once, and the window banged to and latched itself. Now to relight the candles and see what damage, if any, had been done. No, nothing seemed amiss; no glass even was broken in the casement. But the noise had evidently roused at least one member of the household: the Colonel was to be heard stumping in his stockinged feet on the floor above, and growling.

Quickly as it had risen, the wind did not fall at once. On it went, moaning and rushing past the house, at times rising to a cry so desolate that, as Parkins disinterestedly said, it might have made fanciful people feel quite uncomfortable; even the unimaginative, he thought after a quarter of an hour, might be happier without it.

Whether it was the wind, or the excitement of golf, or of the researches in the preceptory that kept Parkins awake, he was not sure. Awake he remained, in any case, long enough to fancy (as I am afraid I often do myself under such conditions) that he was the victim of all manner of fatal disorders: he would lie counting the beats of his heart, convinced that it was going to stop work every moment, and would entertain grave suspicions of his lungs, brain, liver, etc.—suspicions which he was sure would be dispelled by the return of daylight, but which until then refused to be put aside. He found a little vicarious comfort in the idea that someone else was in the same boat. A near neighbour (in the darkness it was not easy to tell his direction) was tossing and rustling in his bed, too.

The next stage was that Parkins shut his eyes and determined to give sleep every chance. Here again over-excitement asserted itself in another form—that of making pictures. Experto crede, pictures do come to the closed eyes of one trying to sleep, and are often so little to his taste that he must open his eyes and disperse them.

Parkins's experience on this occasion was a very distressing one. He found that the picture which presented itself to him was continuous. When he opened his eyes, of course, it went; but when he shut them once more it framed itself afresh, and acted itself out again, neither quicker nor slower than before. What he saw was this:

A long stretch of shore—shingle edged by sand, and intersected at short intervals with black groynes running down to the water—a scene, in fact, so like that of his afternoon's walk that, in the absence of any landmark, it could not be distinguished therefrom. The light was obscure, conveying an impression of gathering storm, late winter evening, and slight cold rain. On this bleak stage at first no actor was visible. Then, in the distance, a bobbing black object appeared; a moment more, and it was a man running, jumping, clambering over the groynes, and every few seconds looking eagerly back. The nearer he came the more obvious it was that he was not only anxious, but even terribly frightened, though his face was not to be distinguished. He was, moreover, almost at the end of his strength. On he came; each successive obstacle seemed to cause him more difficulty than the last. "Will he get over this next one?" thought Parkins; "it seems a little higher than the others." Yes;

half climbing, half throwing himself, he did get over, and fell all in a heap on the other side (the side nearest to the spectator). There, as if really unable to get up again, he remained crouching under the groyne, looking up in an attitude of painful anxiety.

So far no cause whatever for the fear of the runner had been shown; but now there began to be seen, far up the shore, a little flicker of something light-coloured moving to and fro with great swiftness and irregularity. Rapidly growing larger, it, too, declared itself as a figure in pale, fluttering draperies, ill-defined. There was something about its motion which made Parkins very unwilling to see it at close quarters. It would stop, raise arms, bow itself toward the sand, then run stooping across the beach to the water-edge and back again; and then, rising upright, once more continue its course forward at a speed that was startling and terrifying. The moment came when the pursuer was hovering about from left to right only a few yards beyond the groyne where the runner lay in hiding. After two or three ineffectual castings hither and thither it came to a stop, stood upright, with arms raised high, and then darted straight forward towards the groyne.

It was at this point that Parkins always failed in his resolution to keep his eyes shut. With many misgivings as to incipient failure of eyesight, over-worked brain, excessive smoking, and so on, he finally resigned himself to light his candle, get out a book, and pass the night waking, rather than be tormented by this persistent panorama, which he saw clearly enough could only be a morbid reflection of his walk and his thoughts on that very day.

The scraping of match on box and the glare of light must have startled some creatures of the night—rats or what not—which he heard scurry across the floor from the side of his bed with much rustling. Dear, dear! the match is out! Fool that it is! But the second one burnt better, and a candle and book were duly procured, over which Parkins pored till sleep of a wholesome kind came upon him, and that in no long space. For about the first time in his orderly and prudent life he forgot to blow out the candle, and when he was called next morning at eight there was still a flicker in the socket and a sad mess of guttered grease on the top of the little table.

After breakfast he was in his room, putting the finishing touches to his golfing costume—fortune had again allotted the Colonel to him for a partner—when one of the maids came in.

"Oh, if you please," she said, "would you like any extra blankets on your bed, sir?"

"Ah! thank you," said Parkins. "Yes, I think I should like one. It seems likely to turn rather colder."

In a very short time the maid was back with the blanket.

"Which bed should I put it on, sir?" she asked.

"What? Why, that one—the one I slept in last night," he said, pointing to it.

"Oh yes! I beg your pardon, sir, but you seemed to have tried both of 'em; leastways, we had to make 'em both up this morning."

"Really? How very absurd!" said Parkins. "I certainly never touched the other, except to lay some things on it. Did it actually seem to have been slept in?"

"Oh yes, sir!" said the maid. "Why, all the things was crumpled and throwed about all ways, if you'll excuse me, sir—quite as if anyone 'adn't passed but a very poor night, sir."

"Dear me," said Parkins. "Well, I may have disordered it more than I thought when I unpacked my things. I'm very sorry to have given you the extra trouble, I'm sure. I expect a friend of mine soon, by the way—a gentleman from Cambridge—to come and occupy it for a night or two. That will be all right, I suppose, won't it?"

"Oh yes, to be sure, sir. Thank you, sir. It's no trouble, I'm sure," said the maid, and departed to giggle with her colleagues.

Parkins set forth, with a stern determination to improve his game.

I am glad to be able to report that he succeeded so far in this enterprise that the Colonel, who had been rather repining at the prospect of a second day's play in his company, became quite chatty as the morning advanced; and his voice boomed out over the flats, as certain also of our own minor poets have said, "like some great bourdon in a minster tower."

"Extraordinary wind, that, we had last night," he said. "In my old home we should have said someone had been whistling for it."

"Should you, indeed!" said Parkins. "Is there a superstition of that kind still current in your part of the country?"

"I don't know about superstition," said the Colonel. "They believe in it all over Denmark and Norway, as well as on the Yorkshire coast; and my experience is, mind you, that there's generally something at the bottom of what these country-folk hold to, and have held to for generations. But it's your drive" (or whatever it might have been: the golfing reader will have to imagine appropriate digressions at the proper intervals).

When conversation was resumed, Parkins said, with a slight hesitancy:

"Apropos of what you were saying just now, Colonel, I think I ought to tell you that my own views on such subjects are very strong. I am, in fact, a convinced disbeliever in what is called the 'supernatural.'"

"What!" said the Colonel, "do you mean to tell me you don't believe in second-sight, or ghosts, or anything of that kind?"

"In nothing whatever of that kind," returned Parkins firmly.

"Well," said the Colonel, "but it appears to me at that rate, sir, that you must be little better than a Sadducee."

Parkins was on the point of answering that, in his opinion, the Sadducees were the most sensible persons he had ever read of in the Old Testament; but, feeling some doubt as to whether much mention of them was to be found in that work, he preferred to laugh the accusation off.

"Perhaps I am," he said; "but— —Here, give me my cleek, boy!—Excuse me one moment, Colonel." A short interval. "Now, as to whistling for the wind, let me give you my theory about it. The laws which govern winds are really not at all perfectly known—to fisher-folk and such, of course, not known at all. A man or woman of eccentric habits, perhaps, or a stranger, is seen repeatedly on the beach at some unusual hour, and is heard whistling. Soon afterwards a violent wind rises; a man who could read the sky perfectly or who possessed a barometer could have foretold that it would. The simple people of a fishing-village have no barometers, and only a few rough rules for prophesying weather. What more natural than that the eccentric personage I postulated should be regarded as having raised the wind, or that he or she should clutch eagerly at the reputation of being able to do so? Now, take last night's wind: as it happens, I myself was whistling. I blew a whistle twice, and the wind seemed to come absolutely in answer to my call. If anyone had seen me— —"

The audience had been a little restive under this harangue, and Parkins had, I fear, fallen somewhat into the tone of a lecturer; but at the last sentence the Colonel stopped.

"Whistling, were you?" he said. "And what sort of whistle did you use? Play this stroke first." Interval.

"About that whistle you were asking, Colonel. It's rather a curious one. I have it in my— —No; I see I've left it in my room. As a matter of fact, I found it yesterday."

And then Parkins narrated the manner of his discovery of the whistle, upon hearing which the Colonel grunted, and opined that, in Parkins's place, he should himself be careful about using a thing that had belonged to a set of Papists, of whom, speaking generally, it might be affirmed that you never knew what they might not have been up to. From this topic he diverged to the enormities of the Vicar, who had given notice on the previous Sunday that Friday would be the Feast of St. Thomas the Apostle, and that there would be service at eleven o'clock in the church. This and other similar proceedings constituted in the Colonel's view a strong presumption that the Vicar was a concealed Papist, if not a Jesuit; and Parkins, who could not very readily follow the Colonel in this region, did not disagree with him. In fact, they got on so well together in the morning that there was no talk on either side of their separating after lunch.

Both continued to play well during the afternoon, or, at least, well enough to make them forget everything else until the light began to fail them. Not until then did Parkins remember that he had meant to do some more investigating at the preceptory; but it was of no great importance, he reflected. One day was as good as another; he might as well go home with the Colonel.

As they turned the corner of the house, the Colonel was almost knocked down by a boy who rushed into him at the very top of his speed, and then, instead of running away, remained hanging on to him and panting. The first words of the warrior were naturally those of reproof and objurgation, but he very quickly discerned that the boy was almost speechless with fright. Inquiries were useless at first. When the boy got his breath he began to howl, and still clung to the Colonel's legs. He was at last detached, but continued to howl.

"What in the world is the matter with you? What have you been up to? What have you seen?" said the two men.

"Ow, I seen it wive at me out of the winder," wailed the boy, "and I don't like it."

"What window?" said the irritated Colonel. "Come, pull yourself together, my boy."

"The front winder it was, at the 'otel," said the boy.

At this point Parkins was in favour of sending the boy home, but the Colonel refused; he wanted to get to the bottom of it, he said; it was most dangerous to give a boy such a fright as this one had had, and if it turned out that people had been playing jokes, they should suffer for it in some way. And by a series of questions he made out this story: The boy had been playing about on the grass in front of the Globe with some others; then they had gone home to their teas, and he was just going, when he happened to look up at the front winder and see it a-wiving at him. It seemed to be a figure of some sort, in white as far as he knew—couldn't see its face; but it wived at him, and it warn't a right thing—not to say not a right person. Was there a light in the room? No, he didn't think to look if there was a light. Which was the window? Was it the top one or the second one? The seckind one it was—the big winder what got two little uns at the sides.

"Very well, my boy," said the Colonel, after a few more questions. "You run away home now. I expect it was some person trying to give you a start. Another time, like a brave English boy, you just throw a stone—well, no, not that exactly, but you go and speak to the waiter, or to Mr. Simpson, the landlord, and—yes—and say that I advised you to do so."

The boy's face expressed some of the doubt he felt as to the likelihood of Mr. Simpson's lending a favourable ear to his complaint, but the Colonel did not appear to perceive this, and went on:

"And here's a sixpence—no, I see it's a shilling—and you be off home, and don't think any more about it."

The youth hurried off with agitated thanks, and the Colonel and Parkins went round to the front of the Globe and reconnoitred. There was only one window answering to the description they had been hearing.

"Well, that's curious," said Parkins; "it's evidently my window the lad was talking about. Will you come up for a moment, Colonel Wilson? We ought to be able to see if anyone has been taking liberties in my room."

They were soon in the passage, and Parkins made as if to open the door. Then he stopped and felt in his pockets.

"This is more serious than I thought," was his next remark. "I remember now that before I started this morning I locked the door. It is locked now, and, what is more, here is the key." And he held it up. "Now," he went on, "if the servants are in the habit of going into one's room during the day when one is away, I can only say that—well, that I don't approve of it at all." Conscious of a somewhat weak climax, he busied himself in opening the door (which was indeed locked) and in lighting candles. "No," he said, "nothing seems disturbed."

"Except your bed," put in the Colonel.

"Excuse me, that isn't my bed," said Parkins. "I don't use that one. But it does look as if someone had been playing tricks with it."

It certainly did: the clothes were bundled up and twisted together in a most tortuous confusion. Parkins pondered.

"That must be it," he said at last: "I disordered the clothes last night in unpacking, and they haven't made it since. Perhaps they came in to make it, and that boy saw them through the window; and then they were called away and locked the door after them. Yes, I think that must be it."

"Well, ring and ask," said the Colonel, and this appealed to Parkins as practical.

The maid appeared, and, to make a long story short, deposed that she had made the bed in the morning when the gentleman was in the room, and hadn't been there since. No, she hadn't no other key. Mr. Simpson he kep' the keys; he'd be able to tell the gentleman if anyone had been up.

This was a puzzle. Investigation showed that nothing of value had been taken, and Parkins remembered the disposition of the small objects on tables and so forth well enough to be pretty sure that no pranks had been played with them. Mr. and Mrs. Simpson furthermore agreed that neither of them had given the duplicate key of the room to any person whatever during the day. Nor could Parkins, fair-minded man as he was, detect anything in the demeanour of master, mistress, or maid that indicated guilt. He was much more inclined to think that the boy had been imposing on the Colonel.

The latter was unwontedly silent and pensive at dinner and throughout the evening. When he bade good night to Parkins, he murmured in a gruff undertone:

"You know where I am if you want me during the night."

"Why, yes, thank you, Colonel Wilson, I think I do; but there isn't much prospect of my disturbing you, I hope. By the way," he added, "did I show you that old whistle I spoke of? I think not. Well, here it is."

The Colonel turned it over gingerly in the light of the candle.

"Can you make anything of the inscription?" asked Parkins, as he took it back.

"No, not in this light. What do you mean to do with it?"

"Oh, well, when I get back to Cambridge I shall submit it to some of the archæologists there, and see what they think of it; and very likely, if they consider it worth having, I may present it to one of the museums."

"'M!" said the Colonel. "Well, you may be right. All I know is that, if it were mine, I should chuck it straight into the sea. It's no use talking, I'm well aware, but I expect that with you it's a case of live and learn. I hope so, I'm sure, and I wish you a good night."

He turned away, leaving Parkins in act to speak at the bottom of the stair, and soon each was in his own bedroom.

By some unfortunate accident, there were neither blinds nor curtains to the windows of the Professor's room. The previous night he had thought little of this, but to-night there seemed every prospect of a bright moon rising to shine directly on his bed, and probably wake him later on. When he noticed this he was a good deal annoyed, but, with an ingenuity which I can only envy, he succeeded in rigging up, with the help of a railway-rug, some safety-pins, and a stick and umbrella, a screen which, if it only held together, would completely keep the moonlight off his bed. And shortly afterwards he was comfortably in that bed. When he had read a somewhat solid work long enough to produce a decided wish for sleep, he cast a drowsy glance round the room, blew out the candle, and fell back upon the pillow.

He must have slept soundly for an hour or more, when a sudden clatter shook him up in a most unwelcome manner. In a moment he realized what had happened: his carefully-constructed screen had given way, and a very bright frosty moon was shining directly on his face. This was highly annoying. Could he possibly get up and reconstruct the screen? or could he manage to sleep if he did not?

For some minutes he lay and pondered over the possibilities; then he turned over sharply, and with all his eyes open lay breathlessly listening. There had been a movement, he was sure, in the empty bed on the opposite side of the room. To-morrow he would have it moved, for there must be rats or something playing about in it. It was quiet now. No! the commotion began again. There was a rustling and shaking: surely more than any rat could cause.

I can figure to myself something of the Professor's bewilderment and horror, for I have in a dream thirty years back seen the same thing happen; but the reader will hardly, perhaps, imagine how dreadful it was to him to see a figure suddenly sit up in what he had known was an empty bed. He was out of his own bed in one bound, and made a dash towards the window, where lay his only weapon, the stick with which he had propped his screen. This was, as it turned out, the worst thing he could have done, because the personage in the empty bed, with a sudden smooth motion, slipped from the bed and took up a position, with outspread arms, between the two beds, and in front of the door. Parkins watched it in a horrid perplexity. Somehow, the idea of getting past it and escaping through the door was intolerable to him; he could not have borne—he didn't know why—to touch it; and as for its touching him, he would sooner dash himself through the window than have that happen. It stood for the moment in a band of dark shadow, and he had not seen what its face was like. Now it began to move, in a stooping posture, and all at once the spectator realized, with some horror and some relief, that it must be blind, for it seemed to feel about it with its muffled arms in a groping and random fashion. Turning half away from him, it became suddenly conscious of the bed he had just left, and darted towards it, and bent over and felt the pillows in a way which made Parkins shudder as he had never in his life thought it possible. In a very few moments it seemed to know that the bed was empty, and then, moving forward into the area of light and facing the window, it showed for the first time what manner of thing it was.

Parkins, who very much dislikes being questioned about it, did once describe something of it in my hearing, and I gathered that what he chiefly remembers about it is a horrible, an intensely horrible, face of crumpled linen. What expression he read upon it he could not or would not tell, but that the fear of it went nigh to maddening him is certain.

But he was not at leisure to watch it for long. With formidable quickness it moved into the middle of the room, and, as it groped and waved, one corner of its draperies swept across Parkins's face. He could not—though he knew how perilous a sound was—he could not keep back a cry of disgust, and this gave the searcher an instant clue. It leapt towards him upon the instant, and the next moment he was half-way through the window backwards, uttering cry upon cry at the utmost pitch of his voice, and the linen face was thrust close into his own. At this, almost the last possible second, deliverance came, as you will have guessed: the Colonel burst the door open, and was just in time to see the dreadful group at the window. When he reached the figures only one was left. Parkins sank forward into the room in a faint, and before him on the floor lay a tumbled heap of bed-clothes.

Colonel Wilson asked no questions, but busied himself in keeping everyone else out of the room and in getting Parkins back to his bed; and himself, wrapped in a rug, occupied the other bed for the rest of the night. Early on the next day Rogers arrived, more welcome than he would have been a day before, and the three of them held a very long consultation in the Professor's room. At the end of it the Colonel left the hotel door carrying a small object between his finger and thumb, which he cast as far into the sea as a very brawny arm could send it. Later on the smoke of a burning ascended from the back premises of the Globe.

Exactly what explanation was patched up for the staff and visitors at the hotel I must confess I do not recollect. The Professor was somehow cleared of the ready suspicion of delirium tremens, and the hotel of the reputation of a troubled house.

There is not much question as to what would have happened to Parkins if the Colonel had not intervened when he did. He would either have fallen out of the window or else lost his wits. But it is not so evident what more the creature that came in answer to the whistle could have done than frighten. There seemed to be absolutely nothing material about it save the bed-clothes of which it had made itself a body. The Colonel, who remembered a not very dissimilar occurrence in India, was of opinion that if Parkins had closed with it it could really have done very little, and that its one power was that of frightening. The whole thing, he said, served to confirm his opinion of the Church of Rome.

There is really nothing more to tell, but, as you may imagine, the Professor's views on certain points are less clear cut than they used to be. His nerves, too, have suffered: he cannot even now see a surplice hanging on a door quite unmoved, and the spectacle of a scarecrow in a field late on a winter afternoon has cost him more than one sleepless night.

[1]Mr. Rogers was wrong, vide Dombey and Son, chapter xii.

THE SIGNAL-MAN

Charles Dickens

"Halloa! Below there!"

When he heard a voice thus calling to him, he was standing at the door of his box, with a flag in his hand, furled round its short pole. One would have thought, considering the nature of the ground, that he could not have doubted from what quarter the voice came; but instead of looking up to where I stood on the top of the steep cutting nearly over his head, he turned himself about, and looked down the Line. There was something remarkable in his manner of doing so, though I could not have said for my life what. But I know it was remarkable enough to attract my notice, even though his figure was foreshortened and shadowed, down in the deep trench, and mine was high above him, so steeped in the glow of an angry sunset, that I had shaded my eyes with my hand before I saw him at all.

"Halloa! Below!"

From looking down the Line, he turned himself about again, and, raising his eyes, saw my figure high above him.

"Is there any path by which I can come down and speak to you?"

He looked up at me without replying, and I looked down at him without pressing him too soon with a repetition of my idle question. Just then there came a vague vibration in the earth and air, quickly changing into a violent pulsation, and an oncoming rush that caused me to start back, as though it had force to draw me down. When such vapour as rose to my height from this rapid train had passed me, and was skimming away over the landscape, I looked down again, and saw him refurling the flag he had shown while the train went by.

I repeated my inquiry. After a pause, during which he seemed to regard me with fixed attention, he motioned with his rolled-up flag towards a point on my level, some two or three hundred yards distant. I called down to him, "All right!" and made for that point. There, by dint of looking closely about me, I found a rough zigzag descending path notched out, which I followed.

The cutting was extremely deep, and unusually precipitate. It was made through a clammy stone, that became oozier and wetter as I went down. For these reasons, I found the way long enough to give me time to recall a singular air of reluctance or compulsion with which he had pointed out the path.

When I came down low enough upon the zigzag descent to see him again, I saw that he was standing between the rails on the way by which the train had lately passed, in an attitude as if he were waiting for me to appear. He had his left hand at his chin, and that left elbow rested on his right hand, crossed over his breast. His attitude was one of such expectation and watchfulness that I stopped a moment, wondering at it.

I resumed my downward way, and stepping out upon the level of the railroad, and drawing nearer to him, saw that he was a dark, sallow man, with a dark beard and rather heavy eyebrows. His post was in as solitary and dismal a place as ever I saw. On either side, a dripping-wet wall of jagged stone, excluding all view but a strip of sky; the perspective one way only a crooked prolongation of this great dungeon; the shorter perspective in the other direction terminating in a gloomy red light, and the gloomier entrance to a black tunnel, in whose massive architecture there was a barbarous, depressing, and forbidding air. So little sunlight ever found its way to this spot, that it had an earthy, deadly smell; and so much cold wind rushed through it, that it struck chill to me, as if I had left the natural world.

Before he stirred, I was near enough to him to have touched him. Not even then removing his eyes from mine, he stepped back one step, and lifted his hand.

This was a lonesome post to occupy (I said), and it had riveted my attention when I looked down from up yonder. A visitor was a rarity, I should suppose; not an unwelcome rarity, I hoped? In me, he merely saw a man who had been shut up within narrow limits all his life, and who, being at last set free, had a newly-awakened interest in these great works. To such purpose I spoke to him; but I am far from sure of the terms I used; for, besides that I am not happy in opening any conversation, there was something in the man that daunted me.

He directed a most curious look towards the red light near the tunnel's mouth, and looked all about it, as if something were missing from it, and then looked at me.

That light was part of his charge? Was it not?

He answered in a low voice,—"Don't you know it is?"

The monstrous thought came into my mind, as I perused the fixed eyes and the saturnine face, that this was a spirit, not a man. I have speculated since, whether there may have been infection in his mind.

In my turn, I stepped back. But in making the action, I detected in his eyes some latent fear of me. This put the monstrous thought to flight.

"You look at me," I said, forcing a smile, "as if you had a dread of me."

"I was doubtful," he returned, "whether I had seen you before."

"Where?"

He pointed to the red light he had looked at.

"There?" I said.

Intently watchful of me, he replied (but without sound), "Yes."

"My good fellow, what should I do there? However, be that as it may, I never was there, you may swear."

"I think I may," he rejoined. "Yes; I am sure I may."

His manner cleared, like my own. He replied to my remarks with readiness, and in well-chosen words. Had he much to do there? Yes; that was to say, he had enough responsibility to bear; but exactness and watchfulness were what was required of him, and of actual work—manual labour—he had next to none. To change that signal, to trim those lights, and to turn this iron handle now and then, was all he had to do under that head. Regarding those many long and lonely hours of which I seemed to make so much, he could only say that the routine of his life had shaped itself into that form, and he had grown used to it. He had taught himself a language down here,—if only to know it by sight, and to have formed his own crude ideas of its pronunciation, could be called learning it. He had also worked at fractions and decimals, and tried a little algebra; but he was, and had been as a boy, a poor hand at figures. Was it necessary for him when on duty always to remain in that channel of damp air, and could he never rise into the sunshine from between those high stone walls? Why, that depended upon times and circumstances. Under some conditions there would be less upon the Line than under others, and the same held good as to certain hours of the day and night. In bright weather, he did choose occasions for getting a little above these lower shadows; but, being at all times liable to be called by his electric bell, and at such times listening for it with redoubled anxiety, the relief was less than I would suppose.

He took me into his box, where there was a fire, a desk for an official book in which he had to make certain entries, a telegraphic instrument with its dial, face, and needles, and the little bell of which he had spoken. On my trusting that he would excuse the remark that he had been well educated, and (I hoped I might say without offence) perhaps educated above that station, he observed that instances of slight incongruity in such wise would rarely be found wanting among large bodies of men; that he had heard it was so in workhouses, in the police force, even in that last desperate resource, the army; and that he knew it was so, more or less, in any great railway staff. He had been, when young (if I could believe it, sitting in that hut,—he scarcely could), a student of natural philosophy, and had attended lectures; but he had run wild, misused his opportunities, gone down, and never risen again. He had no complaint to offer about that. He had made his bed, and he lay upon it. It was far too late to make another.

All that I have here condensed he said in a quiet manner, with his grave, dark regards divided between me and the fire. He threw in the word, "Sir," from time to time, and especially when he referred to his youth,—as though to request me to understand that he claimed to be nothing but what I found him. He was several times interrupted by the little bell, and had to read off messages, and send replies. Once he had to stand without the door, and display a flag as a train passed, and make some verbal communication to the driver. In the discharge of his duties, I observed him to be remarkably exact and vigilant, breaking off his discourse at a syllable, and remaining silent until what he had to do was done.

In a word, I should have set this man down as one of the safest of men to be employed in that capacity, but for the circumstance that while he was speaking to me he twice broke off with a fallen colour, turned his face towards the little bell when it did NOT ring, opened the door of the hut (which was kept shut to exclude the unhealthy damp), and looked out towards the red light near the mouth of the tunnel. On both of those occasions, he came back to the fire with the inexplicable air upon him which I had remarked, without being able to define, when we were so far asunder.

Said I, when I rose to leave him, "You almost make me think that I have met with a contented man."

(I am afraid I must acknowledge that I said it to lead him on.)

"I believe I used to be so," he rejoined, in the low voice in which he had first spoken; "but I am troubled, sir, I am troubled."

He would have recalled the words if he could. He had said them, however, and I took them up quickly.

"With what? What is your trouble?"

"It is very difficult to impart, sir. It is very, very difficult to speak of. If ever you make me another visit, I will try to tell you."

"But I expressly intend to make you another visit. Say, when shall it be?"

"I go off early in the morning, and I shall be on again at ten to-morrow night, sir."

"I will come at eleven."

He thanked me, and went out at the door with me. "I'll show my white light, sir," he said, in his peculiar low voice, "till you have found the way up. When you have found it, don't call out! And when you are at the top, don't call out!"

His manner seemed to make the place strike colder to me, but I said no more than, "Very well."

"And when you come down to-morrow night, don't call out! Let me ask you a parting question. What made you cry, 'Halloa! Below there!' to-night?"

"Heaven knows," said I. "I cried something to that effect—"

"Not to that effect, sir. Those were the very words. I know them well."

"Admit those were the very words. I said them, no doubt, because I saw you below."

"For no other reason?"

"What other reason could I possibly have?"

"You had no feeling that they were conveyed to you in any supernatural way?"

"No."

He wished me good-night, and held up his light. I walked by the side of the down Line of rails (with a very disagreeable sensation of a train coming behind me) until I found the path. It was easier to mount than to descend, and I got back to my inn without any adventure.

Punctual to my appointment, I placed my foot on the first notch of the zigzag next night, as the distant clocks were striking eleven. He was waiting for me at the bottom, with his white light on. "I have not called out," I said, when we came close together; "may I speak now?" "By all means, sir." "Good-night, then, and here's my hand." "Good-night, sir, and here's mine." With that we walked side by side to his box, entered it, closed the door, and sat down by the fire.

"I have made up my mind, sir," he began, bending forward as soon as we were seated, and speaking in a tone but a little above a whisper, "that you shall not have to ask me twice what troubles me. I took you for some one else yesterday evening. That troubles me."

"That mistake?"

"No. That some one else."

"Who is it?"

"I don't know."

"Like me?"

"I don't know. I never saw the face. The left arm is across the face, and the right arm is waved,—violently waved. This way."

I followed his action with my eyes, and it was the action of an arm gesticulating, with the utmost passion and vehemence, "For God's sake, clear the way!"

"One moonlight night," said the man, "I was sitting here, when I heard a voice cry, 'Halloa! Below there!' I started up, looked from that door, and saw this Some one else standing by the red light near the tunnel, waving as I just now showed you. The voice seemed hoarse with shouting, and it cried, 'Look out! Look out!' And then again, 'Halloa! Below there! Look out!' I caught up my lamp, turned it on red, and ran towards the figure, calling, 'What's wrong? What has happened? Where?' It stood just outside the blackness of the tunnel. I advanced so close upon it that I wondered at its keeping the sleeve across its eyes. I ran right up at it, and had my hand stretched out to pull the sleeve away, when it was gone."

"Into the tunnel?" said I.

"No. I ran on into the tunnel, five hundred yards. I stopped, and held my lamp above my head, and saw the figures of the measured distance, and saw the wet stains stealing down the walls and trickling through the arch. I ran out again faster than I had run in (for I had a mortal abhorrence of the place upon me), and I looked all round the red light with my own red light, and I went up the iron ladder to the gallery atop of it, and I came down again, and ran back here. I telegraphed both ways, 'An alarm has been given. Is anything wrong?' The answer came back, both ways, 'All well.'"

Resisting the slow touch of a frozen finger tracing out my spine, I showed him how that this figure must be a deception of his sense of sight; and how that figures, originating in disease of the delicate nerves that minister to the functions of the eye, were known to have often troubled patients, some of whom had become conscious of the nature of their affliction, and had even proved it by experiments upon themselves. "As to an imaginary cry," said I, "do but listen for a moment to the wind in this unnatural valley while we speak so low, and to the wild harp it makes of the telegraph wires."

That was all very well, he returned, after we had sat listening for a while, and he ought to know something of the wind and the wires,—he who so often passed long winter nights there, alone and watching. But he would beg to remark that he had not finished.

I asked his pardon, and he slowly added these words, touching my arm,—

"Within six hours after the Appearance, the memorable accident on this Line happened, and within ten hours the dead and wounded were brought along through the tunnel over the spot where the figure had stood."

A disagreeable shudder crept over me, but I did my best against it. It was not to be denied, I rejoined, that this was a remarkable coincidence, calculated deeply to impress his mind. But it was unquestionable that remarkable coincidences did continually occur, and they must be taken into account in dealing with such a subject. Though to be sure I must admit, I added (for I thought I saw that he was going to bring the objection to bear upon me), men of common sense did not allow much for coincidences in making the ordinary calculations of life.

He again begged to remark that he had not finished.

I again begged his pardon for being betrayed into interruptions.

"This," he said, again laying his hand upon my arm, and glancing over his shoulder with hollow eyes, "was just a year ago. Six or seven months passed, and I had recovered from the surprise and shock, when one morning, as the day was breaking, I, standing at the door, looked towards the red light, and saw the spectre again." He stopped, with a fixed look at me.

"Did it cry out?"

"No. It was silent."

"Did it wave its arm?"

"No. It leaned against the shaft of the light, with both hands before the face. Like this."

Once more I followed his action with my eyes. It was an action of mourning. I have seen such an attitude in stone figures on tombs.

"Did you go up to it?"

"I came in and sat down, partly to collect my thoughts, partly because it had turned me faint. When I went to the door again, daylight was above me, and the ghost was gone."

"But nothing followed? Nothing came of this?"

He touched me on the arm with his forefinger twice or thrice giving a ghastly nod each time:—

"That very day, as a train came out of the tunnel, I noticed, at a carriage window on my side, what looked like a confusion of hands and heads, and something waved. I saw it just in time to signal the driver, Stop! He shut off, and put his brake on, but the train drifted past here a hundred and fifty yards or more. I ran after it, and, as I went along, heard terrible screams and cries. A beautiful young lady had died instantaneously in one of the compartments, and was brought in here, and laid down on this floor between us."

Involuntarily I pushed my chair back, as I looked from the boards at which he pointed to himself.

"True, sir. True. Precisely as it happened, so I tell it you."

I could think of nothing to say, to any purpose, and my mouth was very dry. The wind and the wires took up the story with a long lamenting wail.

He resumed. "Now, sir, mark this, and judge how my mind is troubled. The spectre came back a week ago. Ever since, it has been there, now and again, by fits and starts."

"At the light?"

"At the Danger-light."

"What does it seem to do?"

He repeated, if possible with increased passion and vehemence, that former gesticulation of, "For God's sake, clear the way!"

Then he went on. "I have no peace or rest for it. It calls to me, for many minutes together, in an agonised manner, 'Below there! Look out! Look out!' It stands waving to me. It rings my little bell—"

I caught at that. "Did it ring your bell yesterday evening when I was here, and you went to the door?"

"Twice."

"Why, see," said I, "how your imagination misleads you. My eyes were on the bell, and my ears were open to the bell, and if I am a living man, it did NOT ring at those times. No, nor at any other time, except when it was rung in the natural course of physical things by the station communicating with you."

He shook his head. "I have never made a mistake as to that yet, sir. I have never confused the spectre's ring with the man's. The ghost's ring is a strange vibration in the bell that it derives from nothing else, and I have not asserted that the bell stirs to the eye. I don't wonder that you failed to hear it. But I heard it."

"And did the spectre seem to be there, when you looked out?"

"It WAS there."

"Both times?"

He repeated firmly: "Both times."

"Will you come to the door with me, and look for it now?"

He bit his under lip as though he were somewhat unwilling, but arose. I opened the door, and stood on the step, while he stood in the doorway. There was the Danger-light. There was the dismal mouth of the tunnel. There were the high, wet stone walls of the cutting. There were the stars above them.

"Do you see it?" I asked him, taking particular note of his face. His eyes were prominent and strained, but not very much more so, perhaps, than my own had been when I had directed them earnestly towards the same spot.

"No," he answered. "It is not there."

"Agreed," said I.

We went in again, shut the door, and resumed our seats. I was thinking how best to improve this advantage, if it might be called one, when he took up the conversation in such a matter-of-course way, so assuming that there could be no serious question of fact between us, that I felt myself placed in the weakest of positions.

"By this time you will fully understand, sir," he said, "that what troubles me so dreadfully is the question, What does the spectre mean?"

I was not sure, I told him, that I did fully understand.

"What is its warning against?" he said, ruminating, with his eyes on the fire, and only by times turning them on me. "What is the danger? Where is the danger? There is danger overhanging somewhere on the Line. Some dreadful calamity will happen. It is not to be doubted this third time, after what has gone before. But surely this is a cruel haunting of me. What can I do?"

He pulled out his handkerchief, and wiped the drops from his heated forehead.

"If I telegraph Danger, on either side of me, or on both, I can give no reason for it," he went on, wiping the palms of his hands. "I should get into trouble, and do no good. They would think I was mad. This is the way it would work,—Message: 'Danger! Take care!' Answer: 'What Danger? Where?' Message: 'Don't know. But, for God's sake, take care!' They would displace me. What else could they do?"

His pain of mind was most pitiable to see. It was the mental torture of a conscientious man, oppressed beyond endurance by an unintelligible responsibility involving life.

"When it first stood under the Danger-light," he went on, putting his dark hair back from his head, and drawing his hands outward across and across his temples in an extremity of feverish distress, "why not tell me where that accident was to happen,—if it must happen? Why not tell me how it could be averted,—if it could have been averted? When on its second coming it hid its face, why not tell me, instead, 'She is going to die. Let them keep her at home'? If it came, on those two occasions, only to show me that its warnings were true, and so to prepare me for the third, why not warn me plainly now? And I, Lord help me! A mere poor signal-man on this solitary station! Why not go to somebody with credit to be believed, and power to act?"

When I saw him in this state, I saw that for the poor man's sake, as well as for the public safety, what I had to do for the time was to compose his mind. Therefore, setting aside all question of reality or unreality between us, I represented to him that whoever thoroughly discharged his duty must do well, and that at least it was his comfort that he understood his duty, though he did not understand these confounding Appearances. In this effort I succeeded far better than in the attempt to reason him out of his conviction. He became calm; the occupations incidental to his post as the night advanced began to make larger demands on his attention: and I left him at two in the morning. I had offered to stay through the night, but he would not hear of it.

That I more than once looked back at the red light as I ascended the pathway, that I did not like the red light, and that I should have slept but poorly if my bed had been under it, I see no reason to conceal. Nor did I like the two sequences of the accident and the dead girl. I see no reason to conceal that either.

But what ran most in my thoughts was the consideration how ought I to act, having become the recipient of this disclosure? I had proved the man to be intelligent, vigilant, painstaking, and exact; but how long might he remain so, in his state of mind? Though in a subordinate position, still he held a most important trust, and would I (for instance) like to stake my own life on the chances of his continuing to execute it with precision?

Unable to overcome a feeling that there would be something treacherous in my communicating what he had told me to his superiors in the Company, without first being plain with himself and proposing a middle course to him, I ultimately resolved to offer to accompany him (otherwise keeping his secret for the present) to the wisest medical practitioner we could hear of in those parts, and to take his opinion. A change in his time of duty would come round next night, he had apprised me, and he would be off an hour or two after sunrise, and on again soon after sunset. I had appointed to return accordingly.

Next evening was a lovely evening, and I walked out early to enjoy it. The sun was not yet quite down when I traversed the field-path near the top of the deep cutting. I would extend my walk for an hour, I said to myself, half an hour on and half an hour back, and it would then be time to go to my signal-man's box.

Before pursuing my stroll, I stepped to the brink, and mechanically looked down, from the point from which I had first seen him. I cannot describe the thrill that seized upon me, when, close at the mouth of the tunnel, I saw the appearance of a man, with his left sleeve across his eyes, passionately waving his right arm.

The nameless horror that oppressed me passed in a moment, for in a moment I saw that this appearance of a man was a man indeed, and that there was a little group of other men, standing at a short distance, to whom he seemed to be rehearsing the gesture he made. The Danger-light was not yet lighted. Against its shaft, a little low hut, entirely new to me, had been made of some wooden supports and tarpaulin. It looked no bigger than a bed.

With an irresistible sense that something was wrong,—with a flashing self-reproachful fear that fatal mischief had come of my leaving the man there, and causing no one to be sent to overlook or correct what he did,—I descended the notched path with all the speed I could make.

"What is the matter?" I asked the men.

"Signal-man killed this morning, sir."

"Not the man belonging to that box?"

"Yes, sir."

"Not the man I know?"

"You will recognise him, sir, if you knew him," said the man who spoke for the others, solemnly uncovering his own head, and raising an end of the tarpaulin, "for his face is quite composed."

"O, how did this happen, how did this happen?" I asked, turning from one to another as the hut closed in again.

"He was cut down by an engine, sir. No man in England knew his work better. But somehow he was not clear of the outer rail. It was just at broad day. He had struck the light, and had the lamp in his hand. As the engine came out of the tunnel, his back was towards her, and she cut him down. That man drove her, and was showing how it happened. Show the gentleman, Tom."

The man, who wore a rough dark dress, stepped back to his former place at the mouth of the tunnel.

"Coming round the curve in the tunnel, sir," he said, "I saw him at the end, like as if I saw him down a perspective-glass. There was no time to check speed, and I knew him to be very careful. As he didn't seem to take heed of the whistle, I shut it off when we were running down upon him, and called to him as loud as I could call."

"What did you say?"

"I said, 'Below there! Look out! Look out! For God's sake, clear the way!'"

I started.

"Ah! it was a dreadful time, sir. I never left off calling to him. I put this arm before my eyes not to see, and I waved this arm to the last; but it was no use."

Without prolonging the narrative to dwell on any one of its curious circumstances more than on any other, I may, in closing it, point out the coincidence that the warning of the Engine-Driver included, not only the words which the unfortunate Signal-man had repeated to me as haunting him, but also the words which I myself—not he—had attached, and that only in my own mind, to the gesticulation he had imitated.

THE SEARCHER OF THE END HOUSE

William Hope Hodgson, 1910

It was still evening, as I remember, and the four of us, Jessop, Arkright, Taylor and I, looked disappointedly at Carnacki, where he sat silent in his great chair.

We had come in response to the usual card of invitation, which—as you know—we have come to consider as a sure prelude to a good story; and now, after telling us the short incident of the Three Straw Platters, he had lapsed into a contented silence, and the night not half gone, as I have hinted.

However, as it chanced, some pitying fate jogged Carnacki's elbow, or his memory, and he began again, in his queer level way:—

"The 'Straw Platters' business reminds me of the 'Searcher' Case, which I have sometimes thought might interest you. It was some time ago, in fact a deuce of a long time ago, that the thing happened; and my experience of what I might term 'curious' things was very small at that time.

"I was living with my mother when it occurred, in a small house just outside of Appledorn, on the South Coast. The house was the last of a row of detached cottage villas, each house standing in its own garden; and very dainty little places they were, very old, and most of them smothered in roses; and all with those quaint old leaded windows, and doors of genuine oak. You must try to picture them for the sake of their complete niceness.

"Now I must remind you at the beginning that my mother and I had lived in that little house for two years; and in the whole of that time there had not been a single peculiar happening to worry us.

"And then, something happened.

"It was about two o'clock one morning, as I was finishing some letters, that I heard the door of my mother's bedroom open, and she came to the top of the stairs, and knocked on the banisters.

"'All right, dear,' I called; for I suppose she was merely reminding me that I should have been in bed long ago; then I heard her go back to her room, and I hurried my work, for fear she should lie awake, until she heard me safe up to my room.

"When I was finished, I lit my candle, put out the lamp, and went upstairs. As I came opposite the door of my mother's room, I saw that it was open, called good night to her, very softly, and asked whether I should close the door. As there was no answer, I knew that she had dropped off to sleep again, and I closed the door very gently, and turned into my room, just across the passage. As I did so, I experienced a momentary, half-aware sense of a faint, peculiar, disagreeable odor in the passage; but it was not until the following night that I realized I had noticed a smell that offended me. You follow me? It is so often like that—one suddenly knows a thing that really recorded itself on one's consciousness, perhaps a year before.

"The next morning at breakfast, I mentioned casually to my mother that she had 'dropped off,' and I had shut the door for her. To my surprise, she assured me she had never been out of her room. I reminded her about the two raps she had given upon the banister; but she still was certain I must be mistaken; and in the end I teased her, saying she had grown so accustomed to my bad habit of sitting up late, that she had come to call me in her sleep. Of course, she denied this, and I let the matter drop; but I was more than a little puzzled, and did not know whether to believe my own explanation, or to take the mater's, which was to put the noises down to the mice, and the open door to the fact that she couldn't have properly latched it, when she went to bed. I suppose, away in the subconscious part of me, I had a stirring of less reasonable thoughts; but certainly, I had no real uneasiness at that time.

"The next night there came a further development. About two thirty a.m., I heard my mother's door open, just as on the previous night, and immediately afterward she rapped sharply, on the banister, as it seemed to me. I stopped my work and called up that I would not be long. As she made no reply, and I did not hear her go back to bed, I had a quick sense of wonder whether she might not be doing it in her sleep, after all, just as I had said.

"With the thought, I stood up, and taking the lamp from the table, began to go toward the door, which was open into the passage. It was then I got a sudden nasty sort of thrill; for it came to me, all at once, that my mother never knocked, when I sat up too late; she always called. You will understand I was not really frightened in any way; only vaguely uneasy, and pretty sure she must really be doing the thing in her sleep.

"I went quickly up the stairs, and when I came to the top, my mother was not there; but her door was open. I had a bewildered sense though believing she must have gone quietly back to bed, without my hearing her. I entered her room and found her sleeping quietly and naturally; for the vague sense of trouble in me was sufficiently strong to make me go over to look at her.

"When I was sure that she was perfectly right in every way, I was still a little bothered; but much more inclined to think my suspicion correct and that she had gone quietly back to bed in her sleep, without knowing what she had been doing. This was the most reasonable thing to think, as you must see.

"And then it came to me, suddenly, that vague, queer, mildewy smell in the room; and it was in that instant I became aware I had smelt the same strange, uncertain smell the night before in the passage.

"I was definitely uneasy now, and began to search my mother's room; though with no aim or clear thought of anything, except to assure myself that there was nothing in the room. All the time, you know, I never expected really to find anything; only my uneasiness had to be assured.

"In the middle of my search my mother woke up, and of course I had to explain. I told her about her door opening, and the knocks on the banister, and that I had come up and found her asleep. I said nothing about the smell, which was not very distinct; but told her that the thing happening twice had made me a bit nervous, and possibly fanciful, and I thought I would take a look 'round, just to feel satisfied.

"I have thought since that the reason I made no mention of the smell, was not only that I did not want to frighten my mother, for I was scarcely that myself; but because I had only a vague half-knowledge that I associated the smell with fancies too indefinite and peculiar to bear talking about. You will understand that I am able now to analyze and put the thing into words; but then I did not even know my chief reason for saying nothing; let alone appreciate its possible significance.

"It was my mother, after all, who put part of my vague sensations into words:—

"'What a disagreeable smell!' she exclaimed, and was silent a moment, looking at me. Then:—'You feel there's something wrong?' still looking at me, very quietly but with a little, nervous note of questioning expectancy.

"'I don't know,' I said. 'I can't understand it, unless you've really been walking about in your sleep.'

"'The smell,' she said.

"'Yes,' I replied. 'That's what puzzles me too. I'll take a walk through the house; but I don't suppose it's anything.'

"I lit her candle, and taking the lamp, I went through the other bedrooms, and afterward all over the house, including the three underground cellars, which was a little trying to the nerves, seeing that I was more nervous than I would admit.

"Then I went back to my mother, and told her there was really nothing to bother about; and, you know, in the end, we talked ourselves into believing it was nothing. My mother would not agree that she might have been sleepwalking; but she was ready to put the door opening down to the fault of the latch, which certainly snicked very lightly. As for the knocks, they might be the old warped woodwork of the house cracking a bit, or a mouse rattling a piece of loose plaster. The smell was more difficult to explain; but finally we agreed that it might easily be the queer night smell of the moist earth, coming in through the open window of my mother's room, from the back garden, or—for that matter—from the little churchyard beyond the big wall at the bottom of the garden.

"And so we quietened down, and finally I went to bed, and to sleep.

"I think this is certainly a lesson on the way we humans can delude ourselves; for there was not one of these explanations that my reason could really accept. Try to imagine yourself in the same circumstances, and you will see how absurd our attempts to explain the happenings really were.

"In the morning, when I came down to breakfast, we talked it all over again, and whilst we agreed that it was strange, we also agreed that we had begun to imagine funny things in the backs of our minds, which now we felt half ashamed to admit. This is very strange when you come to look into it; but very human.

"And then that night again my mother's door was slammed once more just after midnight. I caught up the lamp, and when I reached her door, I found it shut. I opened it quickly, and went in, to find my mother lying with her eyes open, and rather nervous; having been waked by the bang of the door. But what upset me more than anything, was the fact that there was a disgusting smell in the passage and in her room.

"Whilst I was asking her whether she was all right, a door slammed twice downstairs; and you can imagine how it made me feel. My mother and I looked at one another; and then I lit her candle, and taking the poker from the fender, went downstairs with the lamp, beginning to feel really nervous. The cumulative effect of so many queer happenings was getting hold of me; and all the apparently reasonable explanations seemed futile.

"The horrible smell seemed to be very strong in the downstairs passage; also in the front room and the cellars; but chiefly in the passage. I made a very thorough search of the house, and when I had finished, I knew that all the lower windows and doors were properly shut and fastened, and that there was no living thing in the house, beyond our two selves. Then I went up to my mother's room again, and we talked the thing over for an hour or more, and in the end came to the conclusion that we might, after all, be reading too much into a number of little things; but, you know, inside of us, we did not believe this.

"Later, when we had talked ourselves into a more comfortable state of mind, I said good night, and went off to bed; and presently managed to get to sleep.

"In the early hours of the morning, whilst it was still dark, I was waked by a loud noise. I sat up in bed, and listened. And from downstairs, I heard:—bang, bang, bang, one door after another being slammed; at least, that is the impression the sounds gave to me.

"I jumped out of bed, with the tingle and shiver of sudden fright on me; and at the same moment, as I lit my candle, my door was pushed slowly open; I had left it unlatched, so as not to feel that my mother was quite shut off from me.

"'Who's there?' I shouted out, in a voice twice as deep as my natural one, and with a queer breathlessness, that sudden fright so often gives one. 'Who's there?'

"Then I heard my mother saying:—

"'It's me, Thomas. Whatever is happening downstairs?'

"She was in the room by this, and I saw she had her bedroom poker in one hand, and her candle in the other. I could have smiled at her, had it not been for the extraordinary sounds downstairs.

"I got into my slippers, and reached down an old sword bayonet from the wall; then I picked up my candle, and begged my mother not to come; but I knew it would be little use, if she had made up her mind; and she had, with the result that she acted as a sort of rearguard for me, during our search. I know, in some ways, I was very glad to have her with me, as you will understand.

"By this time, the door slamming had ceased, and there seemed, probably because of the contrast, to be an appalling silence in the house. However, I led the way, holding my candle high, and keeping the sword bayonet very handy. Downstairs we found all the doors wide open; although the outer doors and the windows were closed all right. I began to wonder whether the noises had been made by the doors after all. Of one thing only were we sure, and that was, there was no living thing in the house, beside ourselves, while everywhere throughout the house, there was the taint of that disgusting odor.

"Of course it was absurd to try to make believe any longer. There was something strange about the house; and as soon as it was daylight, I set my mother to packing; and soon after breakfast, I saw her off by train.

"Then I set to work to try to clear up the mystery. I went first to the landlord, and told him all the circumstances. From him, I found that twelve or fifteen years back, the house had got rather a curious name from three or four tenants; with the result that it had remained empty a long while; in the end he had let it at a low rent to a Captain Tobias, on the one condition that he should hold his tongue, if he saw anything peculiar. The landlord's idea—as he told me frankly—was to free the house from these tales of 'something queer,' by keeping a tenant in it, and then to sell it for the best price he could get.

"However, when Captain Tobias left, after a ten years' tenancy, there was no longer any talk about the house; so when I offered to take it on a five years' lease, he had jumped at the offer. This was the whole story; so he gave me to understand. When I pressed him for details of the supposed peculiar happenings in the house, all those years back, he said the tenants had talked about a woman who always moved about the house at night. Some tenants never saw anything; but others would not stay out the first month's tenancy.

"One thing the landlord was particular to point out, that no tenant had ever complained about knockings, or door slamming. As for the smell, he seemed positively indignant about it; but why, I don't suppose he knew himself, except that he probably had some vague feeling that it was an indirect accusation on my part that the drains were not right.

"In the end, I suggested that he should come down and spend the night with me. He agreed at once, especially as I told him I intended to keep the whole business quiet, and try to get to the bottom of the curious affair; for he was anxious to keep the rumor of the haunting from getting about.

"About three o'clock that afternoon, he came down, and we made a thorough search of the house, which, however, revealed nothing unusual. Afterward, the landlord made one or two tests, which showed him the drainage was in perfect order; after that we made our preparations for sitting up all night.

"First, we borrowed two policemen's dark lanterns from the station nearby, and where the superintendent and I were friendly, and as soon as it was really dusk, the landlord went up to his house for his gun. I had the sword bayonet I have told you about; and when the landlord got back, we sat talking in my study until nearly midnight.

"Then we lit the lanterns and went upstairs. We placed the lanterns, gun and bayonet handy on the table; then I shut and sealed the bedroom doors; afterward we took our seats, and turned off the lights.

"From then until two o'clock, nothing happened; but a little after two, as I found by holding my watch near the faint glow of the closed lanterns, I had a time of extraordinary nervousness; and I bent toward the landlord, and whispered to him that I had a queer feeling something was about to happen, and to be ready with his lantern; at the same time I reached out toward mine.

In the very instant I made this movement, the darkness which filled the passage seemed to become suddenly of a dull violet color; not, as if a light had been shone; but as if the natural blackness of the night had changed color. And then, coming through this violet night, through this violet-colored gloom, came a little naked Child, running. In an extraordinary way, the Child seemed not to be distinct from the surrounding gloom; but almost as if it were a concentration of that extraordinary atmosphere; as if that gloomy color which had changed the night, came from the Child. It seems impossible to make clear to you; but try to understand it.

"The Child went past me, running, with the natural movement of the legs of a chubby human child, but in an absolute and inconceivable silence. It was a very small Child, and must have passed under the table; but I saw the Child through the table, as if it had been only a slightly darker shadow than the colored gloom. In the same instant, I saw that a fluctuating glimmer of violet light outlined the metal of the gun-barrels and the blade of the sword bayonet, making them seem like faint shapes of glimmering light, floating unsupported where the tabletop should have shown solid.

"Now, curiously, as I saw these things, I was subconsciously aware that I heard the anxious breathing of the landlord, quite clear and labored, close to my elbow, where he waited nervously with his hands on the lantern. I realized in that moment that he saw nothing; but waited in the darkness, for my warning to come true.

"Even as I took heed of these minor things, I saw the Child jump to one side, and hide behind some half-seen object that was certainly nothing belonging to the passage. I stared, intently, with a most extraordinary thrill of expectant wonder, with fright making goose flesh of my back. And even as I stared, I solved for myself the less important problem of what the two black clouds were that hung over a part of the table. I think it very curious and interesting, the double working of the mind, often so much more apparent during times of stress. The two clouds came from two faintly shining shapes, which I knew must be the metal of the lanterns; and the things that looked black to the sight with which I was then seeing, could be nothing else but what to normal human sight is known as light. This phenomenon I have always remembered. I have twice seen a somewhat similar thing; in the Dark Light Case and in that trouble of Maetheson's, which you know about.

"Even as I understood this matter of the lights, I was looking to my left, to understand why the Child was hiding. And suddenly, I heard the landlord shout out:—'The Woman!' But I saw nothing. I had a disagreeable sense that something repugnant was near to me, and I was aware in the same moment that the landlord was gripping my arm in a hard, frightened grip. Then I was looking back to where the Child had hidden. I saw the Child peeping out from behind its hiding place, seeming to be looking up the passage; but whether in fear I could not tell. Then it came out, and ran headlong away, through the place where should have been the wall of my mother's bedroom; but the Sense with which I was seeing these things, showed me the wall only as a vague, upright shadow, unsubstantial. And immediately the child was lost to me, in the dull violet gloom. At the same time, I felt the landlord press back against me, as if something had passed close to him; and he called out again, a hoarse sort of cry:—'The Woman! The Woman!' and turned the shade clumsily from off his lantern. But I had seen no Woman; and the passage showed empty, as he shone the beam of his light jerkily to and fro; but chiefly in the direction of the doorway of my mother's room.

"He was still clutching my arm, and had risen to his feet; and now, mechanically and almost slowly, I picked up my lantern and turned on the light. I shone it, a little dazedly, at the seals upon the doors; but none were broken; then I sent the light to and fro, up and down the passage; but there was nothing; and I turned to the landlord, who was saying something in a rather incoherent fashion. As my light passed over his face, I noted, in a dull sort of way, that he was drenched with sweat.

"Then my wits became more handleable, and I began to catch the drift of his words:—'Did you see her? Did you see her?' he was saying, over and over again; and then I found myself telling him, in quite a level voice, that I had not seen any Woman. He became more coherent then, and I found that he had seen a Woman come from the end of the passage, and go past us; but he could not describe her, except that she kept stopping and looking about her, and had even peered at the wall, close beside him, as if looking for something. But what seemed to trouble him most, was that she had not seemed to see him at all. He repeated this so often, that in the end I told him, in an absurd sort of way, that he ought to be very glad she had not. What did it all mean? was the question; somehow I was not so frightened, as utterly bewildered. I had seen less then, than since; but what I had seen, had made me feel adrift from my anchorage of Reason.

"What did it mean? He had seen a Woman, searching for something. I had not seen this Woman. I had seen a Child, running away, and hiding from Something or Someone. He had not seen the Child, or the other things—only the Woman. And I had not seen her. What did it all mean?

"I had said nothing to the landlord about the Child. I had been too bewildered, and I realized that it would be futile to attempt an explanation. He was already stupid with the thing he had seen; and not the kind of man to understand. All this went through my mind as we stood there, shining the lanterns to and fro. All the time, intermingled with a streak of practical reasoning, I was questioning myself, what did it all mean? What was the Woman searching for; what was the Child running from?

"Suddenly, as I stood there, bewildered and nervous, making random answers to the landlord, a door below was violently slammed, and directly I caught the horrible reek of which I have told you.

"'There!' I said to the landlord, and caught his arm, in my turn. 'The Smell! Do you smell it?'

"He looked at me so stupidly that in a sort of nervous anger, I shook him.

"'Yes,' he said, in a queer voice, trying to shine the light from his shaking lantern at the stair head.

"'Come on!' I said, and picked up my bayonet; and he came, carrying his gun awkwardly. I think he came, more because he was afraid to be left alone, than because he had any pluck left, poor beggar. I never sneer at that kind of funk, at least very seldom; for when it takes hold of you, it makes rags of your courage.

"I led the way downstairs, shining my light into the lower passage, and afterward at the doors to see whether they were shut; for I had closed and latched them, placing a corner of a mat against each door, so I should know which had been opened.

"I saw at once that none of the doors had been opened; then I threw the beam of my light down alongside the stairway, in order to see the mat I had placed against the door at the top of the cellar stairs. I got a horrid thrill; for the mat was flat! I paused a couple of seconds, shining my light to and fro in the passage, and holding fast to my courage, I went down the stairs.

"As I came to the bottom step, I saw patches of wet all up and down the passage. I shone my lantern on them. It was the imprint of a wet foot on the oilcloth of the passage; not an ordinary footprint, but a queer, soft, flabby, spreading imprint, that gave me a feeling of extraordinary horror.

"Backward and forward I flashed the light over the impossible marks and saw them everywhere. Suddenly I noticed that they led to each of the closed doors. I felt something touch my back, and glanced 'round swiftly, to find the landlord had come close to me, almost pressing against me, in his fear.

"'It's all right,' I said, but in a rather breathless whisper, meaning to put a little courage into him; for I could feel that he was shaking through all his body. Even then as I tried to get him steadied enough to be of some use, his gun went off with a tremendous bang. He jumped, and yelled with sheer terror; and I swore because of the shock.

"'Give it to me, for God's sake!' I said, and slipped the gun from his hand; and in the same instant there was a sound of running steps up the garden path, and immediately the flash of a bull's-eye lantern upon the fan light over the front door. Then the door was tried, and directly afterward there came a thunderous knocking, which told me a policeman had heard the shot.

"I went to the door, and opened it. Fortunately the constable knew me, and when I had beckoned him in, I was able to explain matters in a very short time. While doing this, Inspector Johnstone came up the path, having missed the officer, and seeing lights and the open door. I told him as briefly as possible what had occurred, and did not mention the Child or the Woman; for it would have seem too fantastic for him to notice. I showed him the queer, wet footprints and how they went toward the closed doors. I explained quickly about the mats, and how that the one against the cellar door was flat, which showed the door had been opened.

"The inspector nodded, and told the constable to guard the door at the top of the cellar stairs. He then asked the hall lamp to be lit, after which he took the policeman's lantern, and led the way into the front room. He paused with the door wide open, and threw the light all 'round; then he jumped into the room, and looked behind the door; there was no one there; but all over the polished oak floor, between the scattered rugs, went the marks of those horrible spreading footprints; and the room permeated with the horrible odor.

"The inspector searched the room carefully, and then went into the middle room, using the same precautions. There was nothing in the middle room, or in the kitchen or pantry; but everywhere went the wet footmarks through all the rooms, showing plainly wherever there were woodwork or oilcloth; and always there was the smell.

"The inspector ceased from his search of the rooms, and spent a minute in trying whether the mats would really fall flat when the doors were open, or merely ruckle up in a way as to appear they had been untouched; but in each case, the mats fell flat, and remained so.

"'Extraordinary!' I heard Johnstone mutter to himself. And then he went toward the cellar door. He had inquired at first whether there were windows to the cellar, and when he learned there was no way out, except by the door, he had left this part of the search to the last.

"As Johnstone came up to the door, the policeman made a motion of salute, and said something in a low voice; and something in the tone made me flick my light across him. I saw then that the man was very white, and he looked strange and bewildered.

"'What?' said Johnstone impatiently. 'Speak up!'

"'A woman come along 'ere, sir, and went through this 'ere door,' said the constable, clearly, but with a curious monotonous intonation that is sometimes heard from an unintelligent man.

"'Speak up!' shouted the inspector.

"'A woman come along and went through this 'ere door,' repeated the man, monotonously.

"The inspector caught the man by the shoulder, and deliberately sniffed his breath.

"'No!' he said. And then sarcastically:—'I hope you held the door open politely for the lady.'

"'The door weren't opened, sir,' said the man, simply.

"'Are you mad—' began Johnstone.

"'No,' broke in the landlord's voice from the back. Speaking steadily enough. 'I saw the Woman upstairs.' It was evident that he had got back his control again.

"'I'm afraid, Inspector Johnstone,' I said, 'that there's more in this than you think. I certainly saw some very extraordinary things upstairs.'

"The inspector seemed about to say something; but instead, he turned again to the door, and flashed his light down and 'round about the mat. I saw then that the strange, horrible footmarks came straight up to the cellar door; and the last print showed under the door; yet the policeman said the door had not been opened.

"And suddenly, without any intention, or realization of what I was saying, I asked the landlord:—

"'What were the feet like?'

"I received no answer; for the inspector was ordering the constable to open the cellar door, and the man was not obeying. Johnstone repeated the order, and at last, in a queer automatic way, the man obeyed, and pushed the door open. The loathsome smell beat up at us, in a great wave of horror, and the inspector came backward a step.

"'My God!' he said, and went forward again, and shone his light down the steps; but there was nothing visible, only that on each step showed the unnatural footprints.

"The inspector brought the beam of the light vividly on the top step; and there, clear in the light, there was something small, moving. The inspector bent to look, and the policeman and I with him. I don't want to disgust you; but the thing we looked at was a maggot. The policeman backed suddenly out of the doorway:

"'The churchyard,' he said, '... at the back of the 'ouse.'

"'Silence!' said Johnstone, with a queer break in the word, and I knew that at last he was frightened. He put his lantern into the doorway, and shone it from step to step, following the footprints down into the darkness; then he stepped back from the open doorway, and we all gave back with him. He looked 'round, and I had a feeling that he was looking for a weapon of some kind.

"'Your gun,' I said to the landlord, and he brought it from the front hall, and passed it over to the inspector, who took it and ejected the empty shell from the right barrel. He held out his hand for a live cartridge, which the landlord brought from his pocket. He loaded the gun and snapped the breech. He turned to the constable:—

"'Come on,' he said, and moved toward the cellar doorway.

"'I ain't comin', sir,' said the policeman, very white in the face.

"With a sudden blaze of passion, the inspector took the man by the scruff and hove him bodily down into the darkness, and he went downward, screaming. The inspector followed him instantly, with his lantern and the gun; and I after the inspector, with the bayonet ready. Behind me, I heard the landlord.

"At the bottom of the stairs, the inspector was helping the policeman to his feet, where he stood swaying a moment, in a bewildered fashion; then the inspector went into the front cellar, and his man followed him in stupid fashion; but evidently no longer with any thought of running away from the horror.

"We all crowded into the front cellar, flashing our lights to and fro. Inspector Johnstone was examining the floor, and I saw that the footmarks went all 'round the cellar, into all the corners, and across the floor. I thought suddenly of the Child that was running away from Something. Do you see the thing that I was seeing vaguely?

"We went out of the cellar in a body, for there was nothing to be found. In the next cellar, the footprints went everywhere in that queer erratic fashion, as of someone searching for something, or following some blind scent.

"In the third cellar the prints ended at the shallow well that had been the old water supply of the house. The well was full to the brim, and the water so clear that the pebbly bottom was plainly to be seen, as we shone the lights into the water. The search came to an abrupt end, and we stood about the well, looking at one another, in an absolute, horrible silence.

"Johnstone made another examination of the footprints; then he shone his light again into the clear shallow water, searching each inch of the plainly seen bottom; but there was nothing there. The cellar was full of the dreadful smell; and everyone stood silent, except for the constant turning of the lamps to and fro around the cellar.

"The inspector looked up from his search of the well, and nodded quietly across at me, with his sudden acknowledgment that our belief was now his belief, the smell in the cellar seemed to grow more dreadful, and to be, as it were, a menace—the material expression that some monstrous thing was there with us, invisible.

"'I think—' began the inspector, and shone his light toward the stairway; and at this the constable's restraint went utterly, and he ran for the stairs, making a queer sound in his throat.

"The landlord followed, at a quick walk, and then the inspector and I. He waited a single instant for me, and we went up together, treading on the same steps, and with our lights held backward. At the top, I slammed and locked the stair door, and wiped my forehead, and my hands were shaking.

"The inspector asked me to give his man a glass of whisky, and then he sent him on his beat. He stayed a short while with the landlord and me, and it was arranged that he would join us again the following night and watch the Well with us from midnight until daylight. Then he left us, just as the dawn was coming in. The landlord and I locked up the house, and went over to his place for a sleep.

"In the afternoon, the landlord and I returned to the house, to make arrangements for the night. He was very quiet, and I felt he was to be relied on, now that he had been 'salted,' as it were, with his fright of the previous night.

"We opened all the doors and windows, and blew the house through very thoroughly; and in the meanwhile, we lit the lamps in the house, and took them into the cellars, where we set them all about, so as to have light everywhere. Then we carried down three chairs and a table, and set them in the cellar where the well was sunk. After that, we stretched thin piano wire across the cellar, about nine inches from the floor, at such a height that it should catch anything moving about in the dark.

"When this was done, I went through the house with the landlord, and sealed every window and door in the place, excepting only the front door and the door at the top of the cellar stairs.

"Meanwhile, a local wire-smith was making something to my order; and when the landlord and I had finished tea at his house, we went down to see how the smith was getting on. We found the thing complete. It looked rather like a huge parrot's cage, without any bottom, of very heavy gage wire, and stood about seven feet high and was four feet in diameter. Fortunately, I remembered to have it made longitudinally in two halves, or else we should never have got it through the doorways and down the cellar stairs.

"I told the wire-smith to bring the cage up to the house so he could fit the two halves rigidly together. As we returned, I called in at an ironmonger's, where I bought some thin hemp rope and an iron rack pulley, like those used in Lancashire for hauling up the ceiling clothes racks, which you will find in every cottage. I bought also a couple of pitchforks.

"'We shan't want to touch it," I said to the landlord; and he nodded, rather white all at once.

"As soon as the cage arrived and had been fitted together in the cellar, I sent away the smith; and the landlord and I suspended it over the well, into which it fitted easily. After a lot of trouble, we managed to hang it so perfectly central from the rope over the iron pulley, that when hoisted to the ceiling and dropped, it went every time plunk into the well, like a candle-extinguisher. When we had it finally arranged, I hoisted it up once more, to the ready position, and made the rope fast to a heavy wooden pillar, which stood in the middle of the cellar.

"By ten o'clock, I had everything arranged, with the two pitchforks and the two police lanterns; also some whisky and sandwiches. Underneath the table I had several buckets full of disinfectant.

"A little after eleven o'clock, there was a knock at the front door, and when I went, I found Inspector Johnstone had arrived, and brought with him one of his plainclothes men. You will understand how pleased I was to see there would be this addition to our watch; for he looked a tough, nerveless man, brainy and collected; and one I should have picked to help us with the horrible job I felt pretty sure we should have to do that night.

"When the inspector and the detective had entered, I shut and locked the front door; then, while the inspector held the light, I sealed the door carefully, with tape and wax. At the head of the cellar stairs, I shut and locked that door also, and sealed it in the same way.

"As we entered the cellar, I warned Johnstone and his man to be careful not to fall over the wires; and then, as I saw his surprise at my arrangements, I began to explain my ideas and intentions, to all of which he listened with strong approval. I was pleased to see also that the detective was nodding his head, as I talked, in a way that showed he appreciated all my precautions.

"As he put his lantern down, the inspector picked up one of the pitchforks, and balanced it in his hand; he looked at me, and nodded.

"'The best thing,' he said. 'I only wish you'd got two more.'

"Then we all took our seats, the detective getting a washing stool from the corner of the cellar. From then, until a quarter to twelve, we talked quietly, whilst we made a light supper of whisky and sandwiches; after which, we cleared everything off the table, excepting the lanterns and the pitchforks. One of the latter, I handed to the inspector; the other I took myself, and then, having set my chair so as to be handy to the rope which lowered the cage into the well, I went 'round the cellar and put out every lamp.

"I groped my way to my chair, and arranged the pitchfork and the dark lantern ready to my hand; after which I suggested that everyone should keep an absolute silence throughout the watch. I asked, also, that no lantern should be turned on, until I gave the word.

"I put my watch on the table, where a faint glow from my lantern made me able to see the time. For an hour nothing happened, and everyone kept an absolute silence, except for an occasional uneasy movement.

"About half-past one, however, I was conscious again of the same extraordinary and peculiar nervousness, which I had felt on the previous night. I put my hand out quickly, and eased the hitched rope from around the pillar. The inspector seemed aware of the movement; for I saw the faint light from his lantern, move a little, as if he had suddenly taken hold of it, in readiness.

"A minute later, I noticed there was a change in the color of the night in the cellar, and it grew slowly violet tinted upon my eyes. I glanced to and fro, quickly, in the new darkness, and even as I looked, I was conscious that the violet color deepened. In the direction of the well, but seeming to be at a great distance, there was, as it were, a nucleus to the change; and the nucleus came swiftly toward us, appearing to come from a great space, almost in a single moment. It came near, and I saw again that it was a little naked Child, running, and seeming to be of the violet night in which it ran.

"The Child came with a natural running movement, exactly as I described it before; but in a silence so peculiarly intense, that it was as if it brought the silence with it. About half-way between the well and the table, the Child turned swiftly, and looked back at something invisible to me; and suddenly it went down into a crouching attitude, and seemed to be hiding behind something that showed vaguely; but there was nothing there, except the bare floor of the cellar; nothing, I mean, of our world.

"I could hear the breathing of the three other men, with a wonderful distinctness; and also the tick of my watch upon the table seemed to sound as loud and as slow as the tick of an old grandfather's clock. Someway I knew that none of the others saw what I was seeing.

"Abruptly, the landlord, who was next to me, let out his breath with a little hissing sound; I knew then that something was visible to him. There came a creak from the table, and I had a feeling that the inspector was leaning forward, looking at something that I could not see. The landlord reached out his hand through the darkness, and fumbled a moment to catch my arm:—

"'The Woman!' he whispered, close to my ear. 'Over by the well.'

"I stared hard in that direction; but saw nothing, except that the violet color of the cellar seemed a little duller just there.

"I looked back quickly to the vague place where the Child was hiding. I saw it was peering back from its hiding place. Suddenly it rose and ran straight for the middle of the table, which showed only as vague shadow half-way between my eyes and the unseen floor. As the Child ran under the table, the steel prongs of my pitchfork glimmered with a violet, fluctuating light. A little way off, there showed high up in the gloom, the vaguely shining outline of the other fork, so I knew the inspector had it raised in his hand, ready. There was no doubt but that he saw something. On the table, the metal of the five lanterns shone with the same strange glow; and about each lantern there was a little cloud of absolute blackness, where the phenomenon that is light to our natural eyes, came through the fittings; and in this complete darkness, the metal of each lantern showed plain, as might a cat's-eye in a nest of black cotton wool.

"Just beyond the table, the Child paused again, and stood, seeming to oscillate a little upon its feet, which gave the impression that it was lighter and vaguer than a thistle-down; and yet, in the same moment, another part of me seemed to know that it was to me, as something that might be beyond thick, invisible glass, and subject to conditions and forces that I was unable to comprehend.

"The Child was looking back again, and my gaze went the same way. I stared across the cellar, and saw the cage hanging clear in the violet light, every wire and tie outlined with its glimmering; above it there was a little space of gloom, and then the dull shining of the iron pulley which I had screwed into the ceiling.

"I stared in a bewildered way 'round the cellar; there were thin lines of vague fire crossing the floor in all directions; and suddenly I remembered the piano wire that the landlord and I had stretched. But there was nothing else to be seen, except that near the table there were indistinct glimmerings of light, and at the far end the outline of a dull glowing revolver, evidently in the detective's pocket. I remember a sort of subconscious satisfaction, as I settled the point in a queer automatic fashion. On the table, near to me, there was a little shapeless collection of the light; and this I knew, after an instant's consideration, to be the steel portions of my watch.

"I had looked several times at the Child, and 'round at the cellar, whilst I was decided these trifles; and had found it still in that attitude of hiding from something. But now, suddenly, it ran clear away into the distance, and was nothing more than a slightly deeper colored nucleus far away in the strange colored atmosphere.

"The landlord gave out a queer little cry, and twisted over against me, as if to avoid something. From the inspector there came a sharp breathing sound, as if he had been suddenly drenched with cold water. Then suddenly the violet color went out of the night, and I was conscious of the nearness of something monstrous and repugnant.

"There was a tense silence, and the blackness of the cellar seemed absolute, with only the faint glow about each of the lanterns on the table. Then, in the darkness and the silence, there came a faint tinkle of water from the well, as if something were rising noiselessly out of it, and the water running back with a gentle tinkling. In the same instant, there came to me a sudden waft of the awful smell.

"I gave a sharp cry of warning to the inspector, and loosed the rope. There came instantly the sharp splash of the cage entering the water; and then, with a stiff, frightened movement, I opened the shutter of my lantern, and shone the light at the cage, shouting to the others to do the same.

"As my light struck the cage, I saw that about two feet of it projected from the top of the well, and there was something protruding up out of the water, into the cage. I stared, with a feeling that I recognized the thing; and then, as the other lanterns were opened, I saw that it was a leg of mutton. The thing was held by a brawny fist and arm, that rose out of the water. I stood utterly bewildered, watching to see what was coming. In a moment there rose into view a great bearded face, that I felt for one quick instant was the face of a drowned man, long dead. Then the face opened at the mouth part, and spluttered and coughed. Another big hand came into view, and wiped the water from the eyes, which blinked rapidly, and then fixed themselves into a stare at the lights.

"From the detective there came a sudden shout:—

"'Captain Tobias!' he shouted, and the inspector echoed him; and instantly burst into loud roars of laughter.

"The inspector and the detective ran across the cellar to the cage; and I followed, still bewildered. The man in the cage was holding the leg of mutton as far away from him, as possible, and holding his nose.

"'Lift thig dam trap, quig!' he shouted in a stifled voice; but the inspector and the detective simply doubled before him, and tried to hold their noses, whilst they laughed, and the light from their lanterns went dancing all over the place.

"'Quig! quig!' said the man in the cage, still holding his nose, and trying to speak plainly.

"Then Johnstone and the detective stopped laughing, and lifted the cage. The man in the well threw the leg across the cellar, and turned swiftly to go down into the well; but the officers were too quick for him, and had him out in a twinkling. Whilst they held him, dripping upon the floor, the inspector jerked his thumb in the direction of the offending leg, and the landlord, having harpooned it with one of the pitchforks, ran with it upstairs and so into the open air.

"Meanwhile, I had given the man from the well a stiff tot of whisky; for which he thanked me with a cheerful nod, and having emptied the glass at a draft, held his hand for the bottle, which he finished, as if it had been so much water.

"As you will remember, it was a Captain Tobias who had been the previous tenant; and this was the very man, who had appeared from the well. In the course of the talk that followed, I learned the reason for Captain Tobias leaving the house; he had been wanted by the police for smuggling. He had undergone imprisonment; and had been released only a couple of weeks earlier.

"He had returned to find new tenants in his old home. He had entered the house through the well, the walls of which were not continued to the bottom (this I will deal with later); and gone up by a little stairway in the cellar wall, which opened at the top through a panel beside my mother's bedroom. This panel was opened, by revolving the left doorpost of the bedroom door, with the result that the bedroom door always became unlatched, in the process of opening the panel.

"The captain complained, without any bitterness, that the panel had warped, and that each time he opened it, it made a cracking noise. This had been evidently what I mistook for raps. He would not give his reason for entering the house; but it was pretty obvious that he had hidden something, which he wanted to get. However, as he found it impossible to get into the house without the risk of being caught, he decided to try to drive us out, relying on the bad reputation of the house, and his own artistic efforts as a ghost. I must say he succeeded. He intended then to rent the house again, as before; and would then, of course have plenty of time to get whatever he had hidden. The house suited him admirably; for there was a passage—as he showed me afterward—connecting the dummy well with the crypt of the church beyond the garden wall; and these, in turn, were connected with certain caves in the cliffs, which went down to the beach beyond the church.

"In the course of his talk, Captain Tobias offered to take the house off my hands; and as this suited me perfectly, for I was about stalled with it, and the plan also suited the landlord, it was decided that no steps should be taken against him; and that the whole business should be hushed up.

"I asked the captain whether there was really anything queer about the house; whether he had ever seen anything. He said yes, that he had twice seen a Woman going about the house. We all looked at one another, when the captain said that. He told us she never bothered him, and that he had only seen her twice, and on each occasion it had followed a narrow escape from the Revenue people.

"Captain Tobias was an observant man; he had seen how I had placed the mats against the doors; and after entering the rooms, and walking all about them, so as to leave the foot-marks of an old pair of wet woollen slippers everywhere, he had deliberately put the mats back as he found them.

"The maggot which had dropped from his disgusting leg of mutton had been an accident, and beyond even his horrible planning. He was hugely delighted to learn how it had affected us.

"The moldy smell I had noticed was from the little closed stairway, when the captain opened the panel. The door slamming was also another of his contributions.

"I come now to the end of the captain's ghost play; and to the difficulty of trying to explain the other peculiar things. In the first place, it was obvious there was something genuinely strange in the house; which made itself manifest as a Woman. Many different people had seen this Woman, under differing circumstances, so it is impossible to put the thing down to fancy; at the same time it must seem extraordinary that I should have lived two years in the house, and seen nothing; whilst the policeman saw the Woman, before he had been there twenty minutes; the landlord, the detective, and the inspector all saw her.

"I can only surmise that fear was in every case the key, as I might say, which opened the senses to the presence of the Woman. The policeman was a highly-strung man, and when he became frightened, was able to see the Woman. The same reasoning applies all 'round. I saw nothing, until I became really frightened; then I saw, not the Woman; but a Child, running away from Something or Someone. However, I will touch on that later. In short, until a very strong degree of fear was present, no one was affected by the Force which made Itself evident, as a Woman. My theory explains why some tenants were never aware of anything strange in the house, whilst others left immediately. The more sensitive they were, the less would be the degree of fear necessary to make them aware of the Force present in the house.

"The peculiar shining of all the metal objects in the cellar, had been visible only to me. The cause, naturally I do not know; neither do I know why I, alone, was able to see the shining."

"The Child," I asked. "Can you explain that part at all? Why you didn't see the Woman, and why they didn't see the Child. Was it merely the same Force, appearing differently to different people?"

"No," said Carnacki, "I can't explain that. But I am quite sure that the Woman and the Child were not only two complete and different entities; but even they were each not in quite the same planes of existence.

"To give you a root idea, however, it is held in the Sigsand MS. that a child 'stillborn' is 'Snatyched back bye thee Haggs.' This is crude; but may yet contain an elemental truth. Yet, before I make this clearer, let me tell you a thought that has often been made. It may be that physical birth is but a secondary process; and that prior to the possibility, the Mother Spirit searches for, until it finds, the small Element—the primal Ego or child's soul. It may be that a certain waywardness would cause such to strive to evade capture by the Mother Spirit. It may have been such a thing as this, that I saw. I have always tried to think so; but it is impossible to ignore the sense of repulsion that I felt when the unseen Woman went past me. This repulsion carries forward the idea suggested in the Sigsand MS., that a stillborn child is thus, because its ego or spirit has been snatched back by the 'Hags.' In other words, by certain of the Monstrosities of the Outer Circle. The thought is inconceivably terrible, and probably the more so because it is so fragmentary. It leaves us with the conception of a child's soul adrift half-way between two lives, and running through Eternity from Something incredible and inconceivable (because not understood) to our senses.

"The thing is beyond further discussion; for it is futile to attempt to discuss a thing, to any purpose, of which one has a knowledge so fragmentary as this. There is one thought, which is often mine. Perhaps there is a Mother Spirit—"

"And the well?" said Arkwright. "How did the captain get in from the other side?"

"As I said before," answered Carnacki. "The side walls of the well did not reach to the bottom; so that you had only to dip down into the water, and come up again on the other side of the wall, under the cellar floor, and so climb into the passage. Of course, the water was the same height on both sides of the walls. Don't ask me who made the well entrance or the little stairway; for I don't know. The house was very old, as I have told you; and that sort of thing was useful in the old days."

"And the Child," I said, coming back to the thing which chiefly interested me. "You would say that the birth must have occurred in that house; and in this way, one might suppose that the house to have become en rapport, if I can use the word in that way, with the Forces that produced the tragedy?"

"Yes," replied Carnacki. "This is, supposing we take the suggestion of the Sigsand MS., to account for the phenomenon."

"There may be other houses—" I began.

"There are," said Carnacki; and stood up.

"Out you go," he said, genially, using the recognized formula. And in five minutes we were on the Embankment, going thoughtfully to our various homes.

THE EYES

Edith Wharton, 1910

WE had been put in the mood for ghosts, that evening, after an excellent dinner at our old friend Culwin's, by a tale of Fred Murchard's—the narrative of a strange personal visitation.

Seen through the haze of our cigars, and by the drowsy gleam of a coal fire, Culwin's library, with its oak walls and dark old bindings, made a good setting for such evocations; and ghostly experiences at first hand being, after Murchard's brilliant opening, the only kind acceptable to us, we proceeded to take stock of our group and tax each member for a contribution. There were eight of us, and seven contrived, in a manner more or less adequate, to fulfil the condition imposed. It surprised us all to find that we could muster such a show of supernatural impressions, for none of us, excepting Murchard himself and young Phil Frenham—whose story was the slightest of the lot—had the habit of sending our souls into the invisible. So that, on the whole, we had every reason to be proud of our seven "exhibits," and none of us would have dreamed of expecting an eighth from our host.

Our old friend, Mr. Andrew Culwin, who had sat back in his arm-chair, listening and blinking through the smoke circles with the cheerful tolerance of a wise old idol, was not the kind of man likely to be favoured with such contacts, though he had imagination enough to enjoy, without envying, the superior privileges of his guests. By age and by education he belonged to the stout Positivist tradition, and his habit of thought had been formed in the days of the epic struggle between physics and metaphysics. But he had been, then and always, essentially a spectator, a humorous detached observer of the immense muddled variety show of life, slipping out of his seat now and then for a brief dip into the convivialities at the back of the house, but never, as far as one knew, showing the least desire to jump on the stage and do a "turn."

Among his contemporaries there lingered a vague tradition of his having, at a remote period, and in a romantic clime, been wounded in a duel; but this legend no more tallied with what we younger men knew of his character than my mother's assertion that he had once been "a charming little man with nice eyes" corresponded to any possible reconstitution of his dry thwarted physiognomy.

"He never can have looked like anything but a bundle of sticks," Murchard had once said of him. "Or a phosphorescent log, rather," some one else amended; and we recognized the happiness of this description of his small squat trunk, with the red blink of the eyes in a face like mottled bark. He had always been possessed of a leisure which he had nursed and protected, instead of squandering it in vain activities. His carefully guarded hours had been devoted to the cultivation of a fine intelligence and a few judiciously chosen habits; and none of the disturbances common to human experience seemed to have crossed his sky. Nevertheless, his dispassionate survey of the universe had not raised his opinion of that costly experiment, and his study of the human race seemed to have resulted in the conclusion that all men were superfluous, and women necessary only because some one had to do the cooking. On the importance of this point his convictions were absolute, and gastronomy was the only science which he revered as dogma. It must be owned that his little dinners were a strong argument in favour of this view, besides being a reason—though not the main one—for the fidelity of his friends.

Mentally he exercised a hospitality less seductive but no less stimulating. His mind was like a forum, or some open meeting-place for the exchange of ideas: somewhat cold and draughty, but light, spacious and orderly—a kind of academic grove from which all the leaves had fallen. In this privileged area a dozen of us were wont to stretch our muscles and expand our lungs; and, as if to prolong as much as possible the tradition of what we felt to be a vanishing institution, one or two neophytes were now and then added to our band.

Young Phil Frenham was the last, and the most interesting, of these recruits, and a good example of Murchard's somewhat morbid assertion that our old friend "liked 'em juicy." It was indeed a fact that Culwin, for all his mental dryness, specially tasted the lyric qualities in youth. As he was far too good an Epicurean to nip the flowers of soul which he gathered for his garden, his friendship was not a disintegrating influence: on the contrary, it forced the young idea to robuster bloom. And in Phil Frenham he had a fine subject for experimentation. The boy was really intelligent, and the soundness of his nature was like the pure paste under a delicate glaze. Culwin had fished him out of a thick fog of family dulness, and pulled him up to a peak in Darien; and the adventure hadn't hurt him a bit. Indeed, the skill with which Culwin had contrived to stimulate his curiosities without robbing them of their young bloom of awe seemed to me a sufficient answer to Murchard's ogreish metaphor. There was nothing hectic in Frenham's efflorescence, and his old friend had not laid even a finger-tip on the sacred stupidities. One wanted no better proof of that than the fact that Frenham still reverenced them in Culwin.

"There's a side of him you fellows don't see. I believe that story about the duel!" he declared; and it was of the very essence of this belief that it should impel him—just as our little party was dispersing—to turn back to our host with the absurd demand: "And now you've got to tell us about your ghost!"

The outer door had closed on Murchard and the others; only Frenham and I remained; and the vigilant servant who presided over Culwin's destinies, having brought a fresh supply of soda-water, had been laconically ordered to bed.

Culwin's sociability was a night-blooming flower, and we knew that he expected the nucleus of his group to tighten around him after midnight. But Frenham's appeal seemed to disconcert him comically, and he rose from the chair in which he had just reseated himself after his farewells in the hall.

"My ghost? Do you suppose I'm fool enough to go to the expense of keeping one of my own, when there are so many charming ones in my friends' closets?—Take another cigar," he said, revolving toward me with a laugh.

Frenham laughed too, pulling up his slender height before the chimney-piece as he turned to face his short bristling friend.

"Oh," he said, "you'd never be content to share if you met one you really liked."

Culwin had dropped back into his armchair, his shock head embedded in its habitual hollow, his little eyes glimmering over a fresh cigar.

"Liked—liked? Good Lord!" he growled.

"Ah, you have, then!" Frenham pounced on him in the same instant, with a sidewise glance of victory at me; but Culwin cowered gnomelike among his cushions, dissembling himself in a protective cloud of smoke.

"What's the use of denying it? You've seen everything, so of course you've seen a ghost!" his young friend persisted, talking intrepidly into the cloud. "Or, if you haven't seen one, it's only because you've seen two!"

The form of the challenge seemed to strike our host. He shot his head out of the mist with a queer tortoise-like motion he sometimes had, and blinked approvingly at Frenham.

"Yes," he suddenly flung at us on a shrill jerk of laughter; "it's only because I've seen two!"

The words were so unexpected that they dropped down and down into a fathomless silence, while we continued to stare at each other over Culwin's head, and Culwin stared at his ghosts. At length Frenham, without speaking, threw himself into the chair on the other side of the hearth, and leaned forward with his listening smile ...

II

"OH, of course they're not show ghosts—a collector wouldn't think anything of them ... Don't let me raise your hopes ... their one merit is their numerical strength: the exceptional fact of their being two. But, as against this, I'm bound to admit that at any moment I could probably have exorcised them both by asking my doctor for a prescription, or my oculist for a pair of spectacles. Only, as I never could make up my mind whether to go to the doctor or the oculist—whether I was afflicted by an optical or a digestive delusion—I left them to pursue their interesting double life, though at times they made mine exceedingly comfortable ...

"Yes—uncomfortable; and you know how I hate to be uncomfortable! But it was part of my stupid pride, when the thing began, not to admit that I could be disturbed by the trifling matter of seeing two—

"And then I'd no reason, really, to suppose I was ill. As far as I knew I was simply bored—horribly bored. But it was part of my boredom—I remember—that I was feeling so uncommonly well, and didn't know how on earth to work off my surplus energy. I had come back from a long journey—down in South America and Mexico—and had settled down for the winter near New York, with an old aunt who had known Washington Irving and corresponded with N. P. Willis. She lived, not far from Irvington, in a damp Gothic villa, overhung by Norway spruces, and looking exactly like a memorial emblem done in hair. Her personal appearance was in keeping with this image, and her own hair—of which there was little left—might have been sacrificed to the manufacture of the emblem.

"I had just reached the end of an agitated year, with considerable arrears to make up in money and emotion; and theoretically it seemed as though my aunt's mild hospitality would be as beneficial to my nerves as to my purse. But the deuce of it was that as soon as I felt myself safe and sheltered my energy began to revive; and how was I to work it off inside of a memorial emblem? I had, at that time, the agreeable illusion that sustained intellectual effort could engage a man's whole activity; and I decided to write a great book—I forget about what. My aunt, impressed by my plan, gave up to me her Gothic library, filled with classics in black cloth and daguerrotypes of faded celebrities; and I sat down at my desk to make myself a place among their number. And to facilitate my task she lent me a cousin to copy my manuscript.

"The cousin was a nice girl, and I had an idea that a nice girl was just what I needed to restore my faith in human nature, and principally in myself. She was neither beautiful nor intelligent—poor Alice Nowell!—but it interested me to see any woman content to be so uninteresting, and I wanted to find out the secret of her content. In doing this I handled it rather rashly, and put it out of joint—oh, just for a moment! There's no fatuity in telling you this, for the poor girl had never seen any one but cousins ...

"Well, I was sorry for what I'd done, of course, and confoundedly bothered as to how I should put it straight. She was staying in the house, and one evening, after my aunt had gone to bed, she came down to the library to fetch a book she'd mislaid, like any artless heroine on the shelves behind us. She was pink-nosed and flustered, and it suddenly occurred to me that her hair, though it was fairly thick and pretty, would look exactly like my aunt's when she grew older. I was glad I had noticed this, for it made it easier for me to do what was right; and when I had found the book she hadn't lost I told her I was leaving for Europe that week.

"Europe was terribly far off in those days, and Alice knew at once what I meant. She didn't take it in the least as I'd expected—it would have been easier if she had. She held her book very tight, and turned away a moment to wind up the lamp on my desk—it had a ground glass shade with vine leaves, and glass drops around the edge, I remember. Then she came back, held out her hand, and said: 'Good-bye.' And as she said it she looked straight at me and kissed me. I had never felt anything as fresh and shy and brave as her kiss. It was worse than any reproach, and it made me ashamed to deserve a reproach from her. I said to myself: 'I'll marry her, and when my aunt dies she'll leave us this house, and I'll sit here at the desk and go on with my book; and Alice will sit over there with her embroidery and look at me as she's looking now. And life will go on like that for any number of years.' The prospect frightened me a little, but at the time it didn't frighten me as much as doing anything to hurt her; and ten minutes later she had my seal ring on my finger, and my promise that when I went abroad she should go with me.

"You'll wonder why I'm enlarging on this familiar incident. It's because the evening on which it took place was the very evening on which I first saw the queer sight I've spoken of. Being at that time an ardent believer in a necessary sequence between cause and effect I naturally tried to trace some kind of link between what had just happened to me in my aunt's library, and what was to happen a few hours later on the same night; and so the coincidence between the two events always remained in my mind.

"I went up to bed with rather a heavy heart, for I was bowed under the weight of the first good action I had ever consciously committed; and young as I was, I saw the gravity of my situation. Don't imagine from this that I had hitherto been an instrument of destruction. I had been merely a harmless young man, who had followed his bent and declined all collaboration with Providence. Now I had suddenly undertaken to promote the moral order of the world, and I felt a good deal like the trustful spectator who has given his gold watch to the conjurer, and doesn't know in what shape he'll get it back when the trick is over ... Still, a glow of self-righteousness tempered my fears, and I said to myself as I undressed that when I'd got used to being good it probably wouldn't make me as nervous as it did at the start. And by the time I was in bed, and had blown out my candle, I felt that I really was getting used to it, and that, as far as I'd got, it was not unlike sinking down into one of my aunt's very softest wool mattresses.

"I closed my eyes on this image, and when I opened them it must have been a good deal later, for my room had grown cold, and the night was intensely still. I was waked suddenly by the feeling we all know—the feeling that there was something near me that hadn't been there when I fell asleep. I sat up and strained my eyes into the darkness. The room was pitch black, and at first I saw nothing; but gradually a vague glimmer at the foot of the bed turned into two eyes staring back at me. I couldn't see the face attached to them—on account of the darkness, I imagined—but as I looked the eyes grew more and more distinct: they gave out a light of their own.

"The sensation of being thus gazed at was far from pleasant, and you might suppose that my first impulse would have been to jump out of bed and hurl myself on the invisible figure attached to the eyes. But it wasn't—my impulse was simply to lie still ... I can't say whether this was due to an immediate sense of the uncanny nature of the apparition—to the certainty that if I did jump out of bed I should hurl myself on nothing—or merely to the benumbing effect of the eyes themselves. They were the very worst eyes I've ever seen: a man's eyes—but what a man! My first thought was that he must be frightfully old. The orbits were sunk, and the thick red-lined lids hung over the eyeballs like blinds of which the cords are broken. One lid drooped a little lower than the other, with the effect of a crooked leer; and between these pulpy folds of flesh, with their scant bristle of lashes, the eyes themselves, small glassy disks with an agate-like rim about the pupils, looked like sea-pebbles in the grip of a starfish.

"But the age of the eyes was not the most unpleasant thing about them. What turned me sick was their expression of vicious security. I don't know how else to describe the fact that they seemed to belong to a man who had done a lot of harm in his life, but had always kept just inside the danger lines. They were not the eyes of a coward, but of some one much too clever to take risks; and my gorge rose at their look of base astuteness. Yet even that wasn't the worst; for as we continued to scan each other I saw in them a tinge of faint derision, and felt myself to be its object.

"At that I was seized by an impulse of rage that jerked me out of bed and pitched me straight on the unseen figure at its foot. But of course there wasn't any figure there, and my fists struck at emptiness. Ashamed and cold, I groped about for a match and lit the candles. The room looked just as usual—as I had known it would; and I crawled back to bed, and blew out the lights.

"As soon as the room was dark again the eyes reappeared; and I now applied myself to explaining them on scientific principles. At first I thought the illusion might have been caused by the glow of the last embers in the chimney; but the fire-place was on the other side of my bed, and so placed that the fire could not possibly be reflected in my toilet glass, which was the only mirror in the room. Then it occurred to me that I might have been tricked by the reflection of the embers in some polished bit of wood or metal; and though I couldn't discover any object of the sort in my line of vision, I got up again, groped my way to the hearth, and covered what was left of the fire. But as soon as I was back in bed the eyes were back at its foot.

"They were an hallucination, then: that was plain. But the fact that they were not due to any external dupery didn't make them a bit pleasanter to see. For if they were a projection of my inner consciousness, what the deuce was the matter with that organ? I had gone deeply enough into the mystery of morbid pathological states to picture the conditions under which an exploring mind might lay itself open to such a midnight admonition; but I couldn't fit it to my present case. I had never felt more normal, mentally and physically; and the only unusual fact in my situation—that of having assured the happiness of an amiable girl—did not seem of a kind to summon unclean spirits about my pillow. But there were the eyes still looking at me ...

"I shut mine, and tried to evoke a vision of Alice Nowell's. They were not remarkable eyes, but they were as wholesome as fresh water, and if she had had more imagination—or longer lashes—their expression might have been interesting. As it was, they did not prove very efficacious, and in a few moments I perceived that they had mysteriously changed into the eyes at the foot of the bed. It exasperated me more to feel these glaring at me through my shut lids than to see them, and I opened my eyes again and looked straight into their hateful stare ...

"And so it went on all night. I can't tell you what that night was, nor how long it lasted. Have you ever lain in bed, hopelessly wide awake, and tried to keep your eyes shut, knowing that if you opened 'em you'd see something you dreaded and loathed? It sounds easy, but it's devilish hard. Those eyes hung there and drew me. I had the vertige de l'abime, and their red lids were the edge of my abyss. ... I had known nervous hours before: hours when I'd felt the wind of danger in my neck; but never this kind of strain. It wasn't that the eyes were so awful; they hadn't the majesty of the powers of darkness. But they had—how shall I say?—a physical effect that was the equivalent of a bad smell: their look left a smear like a snail's. And I didn't see what business they had with me, anyhow—and I stared and stared, trying to find out ...

"I don't know what effect they were trying to produce; but the effect they did produce was that of making me pack my portmanteau and bolt to town early the next morning. I left a note for my aunt, explaining that I was ill and had gone to see my doctor; and as a matter of fact I did feel uncommonly ill—the night seemed to have pumped all the blood out of me. But when I reached town I didn't go to the doctor's. I went to a friend's rooms, and threw myself on a bed, and slept for ten heavenly hours. When I woke it was the middle of the night, and I turned cold at the thought of what might be waiting for me. I sat up, shaking, and stared into the darkness; but there wasn't a break in its blessed surface, and when I saw that the eyes were not there I dropped back into another long sleep.

"I had left no word for Alice when I fled, because I meant to go back the next morning. But the next morning I was too exhausted to stir. As the day went on the exhaustion increased, instead of wearing off like the lassitude left by an ordinary night of insomnia: the effect of the eyes seemed to be cumulative, and the thought of seeing them again grew intolerable. For two days I struggled with my dread; but on the third evening I pulled myself together and decided to go back the next morning. I felt a good deal happier as soon as I'd decided, for I knew that my abrupt disappearance, and the strangeness of my not writing, must have been very painful for poor Alice. That night I went to bed with an easy mind, and fell asleep at once; but in the middle of the night I woke, and there were the eyes ...

"Well, I simply couldn't face them; and instead of going back to my aunt's I bundled a few things into a trunk and jumped onto the first steamer for England. I was so dead tired when I got on board that I crawled straight into my berth, and slept most of the way over; and I can't tell you the bliss it was to wake from those long stretches of dreamless sleep and look fearlessly into the darkness, knowing that I shouldn't see the eyes ...

"I stayed abroad for a year, and then I stayed for another; and during that time I never had a glimpse of them. That was enough reason for prolonging my stay if I'd been on a desert island. Another was, of course, that I had perfectly come to see, on the voyage over, the folly, complete impossibility, of my marrying Alice Nowell. The fact that I had been so slow in making this discovery annoyed me, and made me want to avoid explanations. The bliss of escaping at one stroke from the eyes, and from this other embarrassment, gave my freedom an extraordinary zest; and the longer I savoured it the better I liked its taste.

"The eyes had burned such a hole in my consciousness that for a long time I went on puzzling over the nature of the apparition, and wondering nervously if it would ever come back. But as time passed I lost this dread, and retained only the precision of the image. Then that faded in its turn.

"The second year found me settled in Rome, where I was planning, I believe, to write another great book—a definitive work on Etruscan influences in Italian art. At any rate, I'd found some pretext of the kind for taking a sunny apartment in the Piazza di Spagna and dabbling about indefinitely in the Forum; and there, one morning, a charming youth came to me. As he stood there in the warm light, slender and smooth and hyacinthine, he might have stepped from a ruined altar—one to Antinous, say—but he'd come instead from New York, with a letter (of all people) from Alice Nowell. The letter—the first I'd had from her since our break—was simply a line introducing her young cousin, Gilbert Noyes, and appealing to me to befriend him. It appeared, poor lad, that he 'had talent,' and 'wanted to write'; and, an obdurate family having insisted that his calligraphy should take the form of double entry, Alice had intervened to win him six months' respite, during which he was to travel on a meagre pittance, and somehow prove his ultimate ability to increase it by his pen. The quaint conditions of the test struck me first: it seemed about as conclusive as a mediaeval 'ordeal.' Then I was touched by her having sent him to me. I had always wanted to do her some service, to justify myself in my own eyes rather than hers; and here was a beautiful embodiment of my chance.

"Well, I imagine it's safe to lay down the general principle that predestined geniuses don't, as a rule, appear before one in the spring sunshine of the Forum looking like one of its banished gods. At any rate, poor Noyes wasn't a predestined genius. But he was beautiful to see, and charming as a comrade too. It was only when he began to talk literature that my heart failed me. I knew all the symptoms so well—the things he had 'in him,' and the things outside him that impinged! There's the real test, after all. It was always—punctually, inevitably, with the inexorableness of a mechanical law—it was always the wrong thing that struck him. I grew to find a certain grim fascination in deciding in advance exactly which wrong thing he'd select; and I acquired an astonishing skill at the game ...

"The worst of it was that his betise wasn't of the too obvious sort. Ladies who met him at picnics thought him intellectual; and even at dinners he passed for clever. I, who had him under the microscope, fancied now and then that he might develop some kind of a slim talent, something that he could make 'do' and be happy on; and wasn't that, after all, what I was concerned with? He was so charming—he continued to be so charming—that he called forth all my charity in support of this argument; and for the first few months I really believed there was a chance for him ...

"Those months were delightful. Noyes was constantly with me, and the more I saw of him the better I liked him. His stupidity was a natural grace—it was as beautiful, really, as his eye-lashes. And he was so gay, so affectionate, and so happy with me, that telling him the truth would have been about as pleasant as slitting the throat of some artless animal. At first I used to wonder what had put into that radiant head the detestable delusion that it held a brain. Then I began to see that it was simply protective mimicry—an instinctive ruse to get away from family life and an office desk. Not that Gilbert didn't—dear lad!—believe in himself. There wasn't a trace of hypocrisy in his composition. He was sure that his 'call' was irresistible, while to me it was the saving grace of his situation that it wasn't, and that a little money, a little leisure, a little pleasure would have turned him into an inoffensive idler. Unluckily, however, there was no hope of money, and with the grim alternative of the office desk before him he couldn't postpone his attempt at literature. The stuff he turned out was deplorable, and I see now that I knew it from the first. Still, the absurdity of deciding a man's whole future on a first trial seemed to justify me in withholding my verdict, and perhaps even in encouraging him a little, on the ground that the human plant generally needs warmth to flower.

"At any rate, I proceeded on that principle, and carried it to the point of getting his term of probation extended. When I left Rome he went with me, and we idled away a delicious summer between Capri and Venice. I said to myself: 'If he has anything in him, it will come out now; and it did. He was never more enchanting and enchanted. There were moments of our pilgrimage when beauty born of murmuring sound seemed actually to pass into his face—but only to issue forth in a shallow flood of the palest ink ...

"Well the time came to turn off the tap; and I knew there was no hand but mine to do it. We were back in Rome, and I had taken him to stay with me, not wanting him to be alone in his dismal pension when he had to face the necessity of renouncing his ambition. I hadn't, of course, relied solely on my own judgment in deciding to advise him to drop literature. I had sent his stuff to various people—editors and critics—and they had always sent it back with the same chilling lack of comment. Really there was nothing on earth to say about it—

"I confess I never felt more shabbily than I did on the day when I decided to have it out with Gilbert. It was well enough to tell myself that it was my duty to knock the poor boy's hopes into splinters—but I'd like to know what act of gratuitous cruelty hasn't been justified on that plea? I've always shrunk from usurping the functions of Providence, and when I have to exercise them I decidedly prefer that it shouldn't be on an errand of destruction. Besides, in the last issue, who was I to decide, even after a year's trial, if poor Gilbert had it in him or not?

"The more I looked at the part I'd resolved to play, the less I liked it; and I liked it still less when Gilbert sat opposite me, with his head thrown back in the lamplight, just as Phil's is now ... I'd been going over his last manuscript, and he knew it, and he knew that his future hung on my verdict—we'd tacitly agreed to that. The manuscript lay between us, on my table—a novel, his first novel, if you please!—and he reached over and laid his hand on it, and looked up at me with all his life in the look.

"I stood up and cleared my throat, trying to keep my eyes away from his face and on the manuscript.

"'The fact is, my dear Gilbert,' I began—

"I saw him turn pale, but he was up and facing me in an instant.

"'Oh, look here, don't take on so, my dear fellow! I'm not so awfully cut up as all that!' His hands were on my shoulders, and he was laughing down on me from his full height, with a kind of mortally-stricken gaiety that drove the knife into my side.

"He was too beautifully brave for me to keep up any humbug about my duty. And it came over me suddenly how I should hurt others in hurting him: myself first, since sending him home meant losing him; but more particularly poor Alice Nowell, to whom I had so uneasily longed to prove my good faith and my immense desire to serve her. It really seemed like failing her twice to fail Gilbert—

"But my intuition was like one of those lightning flashes that encircle the whole horizon, and in the same instant I saw what I might be letting myself in for if I didn't tell the truth. I said to myself: 'I shall have him for life'—and I'd never yet seen any one, man or woman, whom I was quite sure of wanting on those terms. Well, this impulse of egotism decided me. I was ashamed of it, and to get away from it I took a leap that landed me straight in Gilbert's arms.

"'The thing's all right, and you're all wrong!' I shouted up at him; and as he hugged me, and I laughed and shook in his incredulous clutch, I had for a minute the sense of self-complacency that is supposed to attend the footsteps of the just. Hang it all, making people happy has its charms—

"Gilbert, of course, was for celebrating his emancipation in some spectacular manner; but I sent him away alone to explode his emotions, and went to bed to sleep off mine. As I undressed I began to wonder what their after-taste would be—so many of the finest don't keep! Still, I wasn't sorry, and I meant to empty the bottle, even if it did turn a trifle flat.

"After I got into bed I lay for a long time smiling at the memory of his eyes—his blissful eyes... Then I fell asleep, and when I woke the room was deathly cold, and I sat up with a jerk—and there were the other eyes ...

"It was three years since I'd seen them, but I'd thought of them so often that I fancied they could never take me unawares again. Now, with their red sneer on me, I knew that I had never really believed they would come back, and that I was as defenceless as ever against them ... As before, it was the insane irrelevance of their coming that made it so horrible. What the deuce were they after, to leap out at me at such a time? I had lived more or less carelessly in the years since I'd seen them, though my worst indiscretions were not dark enough to invite the searchings of their infernal glare; but at this particular moment I was really in what might have been called a state of grace; and I can't tell you how the fact added to their horror ...

"But it's not enough to say they were as bad as before: they were worse. Worse by just so much as I'd learned of life in the interval; by all the damnable implications my wider experience read into them. I saw now what I hadn't seen before: that they were eyes which had grown hideous gradually, which had built up their baseness coral-wise, bit by bit, out of a series of small turpitudes slowly accumulated through the industrious years. Yes—it came to me that what made them so bad was that they'd grown bad so slowly ...

"There they hung in the darkness, their swollen lids dropped across the little watery bulbs rolling loose in the orbits, and the puff of fat flesh making a muddy shadow underneath—and as their filmy stare moved with my movements, there came over me a sense of their tacit complicity, of a deep hidden understanding between us that was worse than the first shock of their strangeness. Not that I understood them; but that they made it so clear that some day I should ... Yes, that was the worst part of it, decidedly; and it was the feeling that became stronger each time they came back to me ...

"For they got into the damnable habit of coming back. They reminded me of vampires with a taste for young flesh, they seemed so to gloat over the taste of a good conscience. Every night for a month they came to claim their morsel of mine: since I'd made Gilbert happy they simply wouldn't loosen their fangs. The coincidence almost made me hate him, poor lad, fortuitous as I felt it to be. I puzzled over it a good deal, but couldn't find any hint of an explanation except in the chance of his association with Alice Nowell. But then the eyes had let up on me the moment I had abandoned her, so they could hardly be the emissaries of a woman scorned, even if one could have pictured poor Alice charging such spirits to avenge her. That set me thinking, and I began to wonder if they would let up on me if I abandoned Gilbert. The temptation was insidious, and I had to stiffen myself against it; but really, dear boy! he was too charming to be sacrificed to such demons. And so, after all, I never found out what they wanted ..."

III

THE fire crumbled, sending up a flash which threw into relief the narrator's gnarled red face under its grey-black stubble. Pressed into the hollow of the dark leather armchair, it stood out an instant like an intaglio of yellowish red-veined stone, with spots of enamel for the eyes; then the fire sank and in the shaded lamp-light it became once more a dim Rembrandtish blur.

Phil Frenham, sitting in a low chair on the opposite side of the hearth, one long arm propped on the table behind him, one hand supporting his thrown-back head, and his eyes steadily fixed on his old friend's face, had not moved since the tale began. He continued to maintain his silent immobility after Culwin had ceased to speak, and it was I who, with a vague sense of disappointment at the sudden drop of the story, finally asked: "But how long did you keep on seeing them?"

Culwin, so sunk into his chair that he seemed like a heap of his own empty clothes, stirred a little, as if in surprise at my question. He appeared to have half-forgotten what he had been telling us.

"How long? Oh, off and on all that winter. It was infernal. I never got used to them. I grew really ill."

Frenham shifted his attitude silently, and as he did so his elbow struck against a small mirror in a bronze frame standing on the table behind him. He turned and changed its angle slightly; then he resumed his former attitude, his dark head thrown back on his lifted palm, his eyes intent on Culwin's face. Something in his stare embarrassed me, and as if to divert attention from it I pressed on with another question:

"And you never tried sacrificing Noyes?"

"Oh, no. The fact is I didn't have to. He did it for me, poor infatuated boy!"

"Did it for you? How do you mean?"

"He wore me out—wore everybody out. He kept on pouring out his lamentable twaddle, and hawking it up and down the place till he became a thing of terror. I tried to wean him from writing—oh, ever so gently, you understand, by throwing him with agreeable people, giving him a chance to make himself felt, to come to a sense of what he really had to give. I'd foreseen this solution from the beginning—felt sure that, once the first ardour of authorship was quenched, he'd drop into his place as a charming parasitic thing, the kind of chronic Cherubino for whom, in old societies, there's always a seat at table, and a shelter behind the ladies' skirts. I saw him take his place as 'the poet': the poet who doesn't write. One knows the type in every drawing-room. Living in that way doesn't cost much—I'd worked it all out in my mind, and felt sure that, with a little help, he could manage it for the next few years; and meanwhile he'd be sure to marry. I saw him married to a widow, rather older, with a good cook and a well-run house. And I actually had my eye on the widow ... Meanwhile I did everything to facilitate the transition—lent him money to ease his conscience, introduced him to pretty women to make him forget his vows. But nothing would do him: he had but one idea in his beautiful obstinate head. He wanted the laurel and not the rose, and he kept on repeating Gautier's axiom, and battering and filing at his limp prose till he'd spread it out over Lord knows how many thousand sloppy pages. Now and then he would send a pailful to a publisher, and of course it would always come back.

"At first it didn't matter—he thought he was 'misunderstood.' He took the attitudes of genius, and whenever an opus came home he wrote another to keep it company. Then he had a reaction of despair, and accused me of deceiving him, and Lord knows what. I got angry at that, and told him it was he who had deceived himself. He'd come to me determined to write, and I'd done my best to help him. That was the extent of my offence, and I'd done it for his cousin's sake, not his.

"That seemed to strike home, and he didn't answer for a minute. Then he said: 'My time's up and my money's up. What do you think I'd better do?'

"'I think you'd better not be an ass,' I said.

"He turned red, and asked: 'What do you mean by being an ass?'

"I took a letter from my desk and held it out to him.

"'I mean refusing this offer of Mrs. Ellinger's: to be her secretary at a salary of five thousand dollars. There may be a lot more in it than that.'

"He flung out his hand with a violence that struck the letter from mine. 'Oh, I know well enough what's in it!' he said, scarlet to the roots of his hair.

"'And what's your answer, if you know?' I asked.

"He made none at the minute, but turned away slowly to the door. There, with his hand on the threshold, he stopped to ask, almost under his breath: 'Then you really think my stuff's no good?'

"I was tired and exasperated, and I laughed. I don't defend my laugh—it was in wretched taste. But I must plead in extenuation that the boy was a fool, and that I'd done my best for him—I really had.

"He went out of the room, shutting the door quietly after him. That afternoon I left for Frascati, where I'd promised to spend the Sunday with some friends. I was glad to escape from Gilbert, and by the same token, as I learned that night, I had also escaped from the eyes. I dropped into the same lethargic sleep that had come to me before when their visitations ceased; and when I woke the next morning, in my peaceful painted room above the ilexes, I felt the utter weariness and deep relief that always followed on that repairing slumber. I put in two blessed nights at Frascati, and when I got back to my rooms in Rome I found that Gilbert had gone ... Oh, nothing tragic had happened—the episode never rose to that. He'd simply packed his manuscripts and left for America—for his family and the Wall Street desk. He left a decent little note to tell me of his decision, and behaved altogether, in the circumstances, as little like a fool as it's possible for a fool to behave ..."

IV

CULWIN paused again, and again Frenham sat motionless, the dusky contour of his young head reflected in the mirror at his back.

"And what became of Noyes afterward?" I finally asked, still disquieted by a sense of incompleteness, by the need of some connecting thread between the parallel lines of the tale.

Culwin twitched his shoulders. "Oh, nothing became of him—because he became nothing. There could be no question of 'becoming' about it. He vegetated in an office, I believe, and finally got a clerkship in a consulate, and married drearily in China. I saw him once in Hong Kong, years afterward. He was fat and hadn't shaved. I was told he drank. He didn't recognize me."

"And the eyes?" I asked, after another pause which Frenham's continued silence made oppressive.

Culwin, stroking his chin, blinked at me meditatively through the shadows. "I never saw them after my last talk with Gilbert. Put two and two together if you can. For my part, I haven't found the link."

He rose stiffly, his hands in his pockets, and walked over to the table on which reviving drinks had been set out.

"You must be parched after this dry tale. Here, help yourself, my dear fellow. Here, Phil—" He turned back to the hearth.

Frenham still sat in his low chair, making no response to his host's hospitable summons. But as Culwin advanced toward him, their eyes met in a long look; after which, to my intense surprise, the young man, turning suddenly in his seat, flung his arms across the table, and dropped his face upon them.

Culwin, at the unexpected gesture, stopped short, a flush on his face.

"Phil—what the deuce? Why, have the eyes scared you? My dear boy—my dear fellow—I never had such a tribute to my literary ability, never!"

He broke into a chuckle at the thought, and halted on the hearth-rug, his hands still in his pockets, gazing down in honest perplexity at the youth's bowed head. Then, as Frenham still made no answer, he moved a step or two nearer.

"Cheer up, my dear Phil! It's years since I've seen them—apparently I've done nothing lately bad enough to call them out of chaos. Unless my present evocation of them has made you see them; which would be their worst stroke yet!"

His bantering appeal quivered off into an uneasy laugh, and he moved still nearer, bending over Frenham, and laying his gouty hands on the lad's shoulders.

"Phil, my dear boy, really—what's the matter? Why don't you answer? Have you seen the eyes?"

Frenham's face was still pressed against his arms, and from where I stood behind Culwin I saw the latter, as if under the rebuff of this unaccountable attitude, draw back slowly from his friend. As he did so, the light of the lamp on the table fell full on his perplexed congested face, and I caught its sudden reflection in the mirror behind Frenham's head.

Culwin saw the reflection also. He paused, his face level with the mirror, as if scarcely recognizing the countenance in it as his own. But as he looked his expression gradually changed, and for an appreciable space of time he and the image in the glass confronted each other with a glare of slowly gathering hate. Then Culwin let go of Frenham's shoulders, and drew back a step, covering his eyes with his hands ...

Frenham, his face still hidden, did not stir.

CHRISTMAS EVE ON A HAUNTED HULK

Frank Cowper, 1889

I shall never forget that night as long as I live.

It was during the Christmas vacation 187-. I was staying with an old college friend who had lately been appointed the curate of a country parish, and had asked me to come and cheer him up, since he could not get away at that time.

As we drove along the straight country lane from the little wayside station, it forcibly struck me that a life in such a place must be dreary indeed. I have always been much influenced by local colour; above all things, I am depressed by a dead level, and here was monotony with a vengeance. On each side of the low hedges, lichen-covered and wind-cropped, stretched bare fields, the absolute level of the horizon being only broken at intervals by some mournful tree that pointed like a decrepit finger-post towards the east, for all its western growth was nipped and blasted by the roaring south-west winds. An occasional black spot, dotted against the grey distance, marked a hay-rick or labourer's cottage, while some two miles ahead of us the stunted spire of my friend's church stood out against the wintry sky, amid the withered branches of a few ragged trees. On our right hand stretched dreary wastes of mud, interspersed here and there with firmer patches of land, but desolate and forlorn, cut off from all communication with the mainland by acres of mud and thin streaks of brown water.

A few sea-birds were piping over the waste, and this was the only sound, except the grit of our own wheels and the steady step of the horse, which broke the silence.

"Not lively is it?" said Jones; and I couldn't say it was. As we drove "up street," as the inhabitants fondly called the small array of low houses which bordered the highroad, I noticed the lack-lustre expression of the few children and untidy women who were loitering about the doors of their houses.

There was an old tumble-down inn, with a dilapidated sign-board, scarcely held up by its rickety ironwork. A daub of yellow and red paint, with a dingy streak of blue, was supposed to represent the Duke's head, although what exalted member of the aristocracy was thus distinguished it would be hard to say. Jones inclined to think it was the Duke of Wellington; but I upheld the theory that it was the Duke of Marlborough, chiefly basing my arguments on the fact that no artist who desired to convey a striking likeness would fail to show the Great Duke in profile, whereas this personage was evidently depicted full face, and wearing a three-cornered hat.

At the end of the village was the church, standing in an untidy churchyard, and opposite it was a neat little house, quite new, and of that utilitarian order of architecture which will stamp the Victorian age as one of the least imaginative of eras. Two windows flanked the front door, and three narrow windows looked out overhead from under a slate roof; variety and distinction being given to the façade by the brilliant blending of the yellow bricks with red, so bright as to suggest the idea of their having been painted. A scrupulously clean stone at the front door, together with the bright green of the little palings and woodwork, told me what sort of landlady to expect, and I was not disappointed. A kindly featured woman, thin, cheery, and active, received us, speaking in that encouraging tone of halfcompassionate, half-proprietary patronage, which I have observed so many women adopt towards lone beings of the opposite sex.

"You will find it precious dull, old man," said Jones, as we were eating our frugal dinner. "There's nothing for you to do, unless you care to try a shot at the duck over the mud-flats. I shall be busy on and off nearly all to-morrow."

As we talked, I could not help admiring the cheerful pluck with which Jones endured the terrible monotony of his life in this dreary place. His rector was said to be delicate, and in order to prolong a life, which no doubt he considered valuable to the Church, he lived with his family either at Torquay or Cannes in elegant idleness, quite unable to do any duty, but fully equal to enjoying the pleasant society of those charming places, and quite satisfied that he had done his duty when he sacrificed a tenth of his income to provide for the spiritual needs of his parish. There was no squire in the place; no "gentlefolk," as the rustics called them, lived nearer than five miles; and there was not a single being of his own class with whom poor Jones could associate. And yet he made no complaint. The nearest approach to one being the remark that the worst of it was, it was so difficult, if not impossible, to be really understood. "The poor being so suspicious and ignorant, they look at everything from such a low standpoint, enthusiasm and freshness sink so easily into formalism and listlessness."

The next day, finding that I really could be of no use, and feeling awkward and bored, as a man always is when another is actively doing his duty, I went off to the marshes to see if I could get any sport.

I took some sandwiches and a flask with me, not intending to return until dinner. After wandering about for some time, crossing dyke after dyke by treacherous rails more or less rotten, I found myself on the edge of a wide mere. I could see some duck out in the middle, and standing far out in the shallow water was a heron. They were all out of shot, and I saw I should do no good without a duck-punt.

I sat down on an old pile left on the top of the sea-wall, which had been lately repaired. The duck looked very tempting; but I doubted if I should do much good in broad daylight, even if I had a duck-punt, without a duck-gun. After sitting disconsolately for some time, I got up and wandered on.

The dreariness of the scene was most depressing: everything was brown and grey. Nothing broke the monotony of the wide-stretching mere; the whole scene gave me the impression of a straight line of interminable length, with a speck in the centre of it. That speck was myself.

At last, as I turned an angle in the sea-wall, I saw something lying above highwater mark, which looked like a boat.

Rejoiced to see any signs of humanity, I quickened my pace. It was a boat, and, better still, a duck-punt. As I came nearer I could see that she was old and very likely leaky; but here was a prospect of adventure, and I was not going to be readily daunted. On examination, the old craft seemed more water-tight than I expected. At least she held water very well, and if she kept it in, she must equally well keep it out. I turned her over to run the water out, and then dragging the crazy old boat over the line of seaweed, launched her. But now a real difficulty met me. The paddles were nowhere to be seen. They had doubtless been taken away by the owner, and it would be little use searching for them. But a stout stick would do to punt her over the shallow water; and after some little search. I found an old stake which would answer well.

This was real luck. I had now some hope of bagging a few duck; at any rate, I was afloat, and could explore the little islets, which barely rose above the brown water. I might at least find some rabbits on them. I cautiously poled myself towards the black dots; but before I came within range, up rose first one, then another and another, like a string of beads, and the whole flight went, with outstretched necks and rapidly beating wings, away to my right, and seemed to pitch again beyond a low island some half-mile away. The heron had long ago taken himself off; so there was nothing to be done but pole across the mud in pursuit of the duck. I had not gone many yards when I found that I was going much faster than I expected, and soon saw the cause. The tide was falling, and I was being carried along with it. This would bring me nearer to my ducks, and I lazily guided the punt with the stake.

On rounding the island I found a new source of interest. The mere opened out to a much larger extent, and away towards my right I could see a break in the low land, as if a wide ditch had been cut through; while in this opening ever and anon dark objects rose up and disappeared again in a way I could not account for. The water seemed to be running off the mud-flats, and I saw that if I did not wish to be left high, but not dry, on the long slimy wastes, I must be careful to keep in the little channels or "lakes," which acted as natural drains to the acres of greasy mud.

A conspicuous object attracted my attention some mile or more towards the opening in the land. It was a vessel lying high up on the mud, and looking as if she was abandoned.

The ducks had pitched a hundred yards or so beyond the island, and I approached as cautiously as I could; but just as I was putting down the stake to take up my gun, there was a swift sound of beating wings and splashing water, and away my birds flew, low over the mud, towards the old hulk.

Here was a chance, I thought. If I could get on board and remain hidden, I might, by patiently waiting, get a shot. I looked at my watch; there was still plenty of daylight left, and the tide was only just beginning to leave the mud. I punted away, therefore, with renewed hope, and was not long in getting up to the old ship.

There was just sufficient water over the mud to allow me to approach within ten or twelve feet, but further I could not push the punt. This was disappointing; however, I noticed a deep lake ran round the other side, and determined to try my luck there. So with a slosh and a heave I got the flat afloat again, and made for the deeper water. It turned out quite successful, and I was enabled to get right under the square overhanging counter, while a little lane of water led alongside her starboard quarter. I pushed the nose of the punt into this, and was not long in clambering on board by the rusty irons of her fore-chains.

The old vessel lay nearly upright in the soft mud, and a glance soon told she would never be used again. Her gear and rigging were all rotten, and everything valuable had been removed. She was a brig of some two hundred tons, and had been a fine vessel, no doubt. To me there is always a world of romance in a deserted ship. The places she has been to, the scenes she has witnessed, the possibilities of crime, of adventure — all these thoughts crowd upon me when I see an old hulk lying deserted and forgotten — left to rot upon the mud of some lonely creek.

In order to keep my punt afloat as long as possible, I towed her round and moored her under the stern, and then looked over the bulwarks for the duck. There they were, swimming not more than a hundred and fifty yards away, and they were coming towards me. I remained perfectly concealed under the high bulwark, and could see them paddling and feeding in the greasy weed. Their approach was slow, but I could afford to wait. Nearer and nearer they came; another minute, and they would be well within shot. I was already congratulating myself upon the success of my adventure, and thinking of the joy of Jones at this large accession to his larder, when suddenly there was a heavy splash, and with a wild spluttering rush the whole pack rose out of the water, and went skimming over the mud towards the distant sea. I let off both barrels after them, and tried to console myself by thinking that I saw the feathers fly from one; but not a bird dropped, and I was left alone in my chagrin.

What could have caused the splash, that luckless splash, I wondered. There was surely no one else on board the ship, and certainly no one could get out here without mud-pattens or a boat. I looked round. All was perfectly still. Nothing broke the monotony of the grey scene — sodden and damp and lifeless. A chill breeze came up from the southwest, bringing with it a raw mist, which was blotting out the dark distance, and fast limiting my horizon. The day was drawing in, and I must be thinking of going home. As I turned round, my attention was arrested by seeing a duck-punt glide past me in the now rapidly falling water, which was swirling by the mud-bank on which the vessel lay. But there was no one in her. A dreadful thought struck me. It must be my boat, and how shall I get home? I ran to the stern and looked over. The duck-punt was gone.

The frayed and stranded end of the painter told me how it had happened. I had not allowed for the fall of the tide, and the strain of the punt, as the water fell away, had snapped the line, old and rotten as it was.

I hurried to the bows, and jumping on to the bitts, saw my punt peacefully drifting away, some quarter of a mile off. It was perfectly evident I could not hope to get her again.

It was beginning to rain steadily. I could see that I was in for dirty weather, and became a little anxious about how I was to get back, especially as it was now rapidly growing dark. So thick was it that I could not see the low land anywhere, and could only judge of its position by remembering that the stern of the vessel pointed that way.

The conviction grew upon me that I could not possibly get away from this doleful old hulk without assistance, and how to get it, I could not for the life of me see. I had not seen a sign of a human being the whole day. It was not likely any more would be about at night. However, I shouted as loud as I could, and then waited to hear if there were any response. There was not a sound, only the wind moaned slightly through the stumps of the masts, and something creaked in the cabin.

Well, I thought, at least it might be worse. I shall have shelter for the night; while had I been left on one of these islands, I should have had to spend the night exposed to the pelting rain. Happy thought! Go below before it gets too dark, and see what sort of a berth can be got, if the worst comes to the worst. So thinking, I went to the booby-hatch, and found as I expected that it was half broken open, and anyone could go below who liked.

As I stepped down the rotting companion, the air smelt foul and dank. I went below very cautiously, for I was not at all sure that the boards would bear me. It was fortunate I did so, for as I stepped off the lowest step the floor gave way under my foot, and had I not been holding on to the stair-rail, I should have fallen through. Before going any further, I took a look round.

The prospect was not inviting. The light was dim; I could scarcely make out objects near me, all else was obscurity. I could see that the whole of the inside of the vessel was completely gutted. What little light there was came through the stern ports. A small round speck of light looked at me out of the darkness ahead, and I could see that the flooring had either all given way or been taken out of her. At my feet a gleam of water showed me what to expect if I should slip through the floorjoists. Altogether, a more desolate, gloomy, ghostly place it would be difficult to find.

I could not see any bunk or locker where I could sit down, and everything movable had been taken out of the hulk. Groping my way with increasing caution, I stepped across the joists, and felt along the side of the cabin. I soon came to a bulkhead. Continuing to grope, I came to an opening. If the cabin was dim, here was blackness itself. I felt it would be useless to attempt to go further, especially as a very damp foul odour came up from the bilge-water in her hold. As I stood looking into the darkness, a creepy, chilly shudder passed over me, and with a shiver I turned round to look at the cabin. My eyes had now become used to the gloom. A deeper patch of darkness on my right suggested the possibility of a berth, and groping my way over to it, I found the lower bunk was still entire. Here at least I could rest, if I found it impossible to get to shore. Having some wax vestas in my pocket, I struck a light and examined the bunk. It was better than I expected. If I could only find something to burn, I should be comparatively cheerful.

Before reconciling myself to my uncomfortable position, I resolved to see whether I could not get to the shore, and went up the rickety stairs again. It was raining hard, and the wind had got up. Nothing could be more dismal. I looked over the side and lowered myself down from the main-chains, to see if it were possible to walk over the mud. I found I could not reach the mud at all; and fearful of being unable to climb back if I let go, I clambered up the side again and got on board.

It was quite clear I must pass the night here. Before going below I once more shouted at the top of my voice, more to keep up my own spirits than with any hope of being heard, and then paused to listen. Not a sound of any sort replied. I now prepared to make myself as comfortable as I could.

It was a dreary prospect. I would rather have spent the night on deck than down below in that foul cabin; but the drenching driving rain, as well as the cold, drove me to seek shelter below. It seemed so absurd to be in the position of a shipwrecked sailor, within two or three miles of a prosy country hamlet, and in a landlocked harbour while actually on land, if the slimy deep mud could be called land. I had not many matches left, but I had my gun and cartridges. The idea occurred to me to fire off minute-guns. "That's what I ought to do, of course. The red flash will be seen in this dark night," for it was dark now and no mistake. Getting up on to the highest part of the vessel, I blazed away. The noise sounded to me deafening; surely the whole countryside would be aroused. After firing off a dozen cartridges, I waited. But the silence only seemed the more oppressive, and the blackness all the darker. "It's no good; I'll turn in," I thought, dejectedly.

With great difficulty I groped my way to the top of the companion-ladder, and bumped dismally down the steps. If only I had a light I should be fairly comfortable, I thought. "Happy thought, make a 'spit-devil!'" as we used when boys to call a little cone of damp gunpowder.

I got out my last two cartridges, and emptying the powder carefully into my hand, I moistened it, and worked it up to a paste. I then placed it on the smooth end of the rail, and lighted it. This was brilliant: at least so it seemed by contrast with the absolute blackness around me. By its light I was able to find my way to the bunk, and it lasted just long enough for me to arrange myself fairly comfortably for the night. By contriving a succession of matches, I was enabled to have enough light to see to eat my frugal supper; for I had kept a little sherry and a few sandwiches to meet emergencies, and it was a fortunate thing I had. The light and the food made me feel more cheery, and by the time the last match had gone out, I felt worse might have happened to me by a long way.

As I lay still, waiting for sleep to come, the absurdity of the situation forced itself upon me. Here was I, to all intents and purposes as much cut off from all communication with the rest of the world as if I were cast away upon a desert island. The chances were that I should make some one see or hear me the next day. Jones would be certain to have the country searched, and at the longest I should only endure the discomfort of one night, and get well laughed at for my pains; but meanwhile I was absolutely severed from all human contact, and was as isolated as Robinson Crusoe, only "more so," for I had no other living thing whatever to share my solitude. The silence of the place was perfect; and if silence can woo sleep, sleep ought very soon to have come. But when one is hungry and wet, and in a strange uncanny kind of place, besides being in one's clothes, it is a very difficult thing to go to sleep. First, my head was too low; then, after resting it on my arms, I got cramp in them. My back seemed all over bumps; when I turned on my side, I appeared to have got a rather serious enlargement of the hip-joint; and I found my damp clothes smell very musty. After sighing and groaning for some time, I sat up for change of position, and nearly fractured my skull in so doing, against the remains of what had once been a berth above me. I didn't dare to move in the inky blackness, for I had seen sufficient to know that I might very easily break my leg or my neck in the floorless cabin.

There was nothing for it but to sit still, or lie down and wait for daylight. I had no means of telling the time. When I had last looked at my watch, before the last match had gone out, it was not more than six o'clock; it might be now about eight, or perhaps not so late. Fancy twelve long hours spent in that doleful black place, with nothing in the world to do to pass away the time! I must go to sleep; and so, full of this resolve, I lay down again.

I suppose I went to sleep. All I can recollect, after lying down, is keeping my mind resolutely turned inwards, as it were, and fixed upon the arduous business of counting an imaginary and interminable flock of sheep pass one by one through an ideal gate. This meritorious method of compelling sleep had, no doubt, been rewarded; but I have no means of knowing how long I slept, and I cannot tell at what hour of the night the following strange circumstances occurred — for occur they certainly did — and I am as perfectly convinced that I was the oral witness to some ghastly crime, as I am that I am writing these lines. I have little doubt I shall be laughed at, as Jones laughed at me — be told that I was dreaming, that I was overtired and nervous. In fact, so accustomed have I become to this sort of thing, that I now hardly ever tell my tale; or, if I do, I put it in the third person, and then I find people believe it, or at least take much more interest in it. I suppose the reason is, that people cannot bring themselves to think so strange a thing could have happened to such a prosy everyday sort of man as myself, and they cannot divest their minds of the idea that I am — well, to put it mildly — "drawing on my imagination for facts." Perhaps, if the tale appears in print, it will be believed, as a facetious friend of mine once said to a newly married couple, who had just seen the announcement of their marriage in the 'Times,' "Ah, didn't know you were married till you saw it in print!"

Well, be the time what it may have been, all I know is that the next thing I can remember after getting my five-hundredth sheep through the gate is, that I heard two most horrible yells ring through the darkness. I sat bolt-upright; and as a proof that my senses were "all there," I did not bring my head this time against the berth overhead, remembering to bend it outwards so as to clear it.

There was not another sound. The silence was as absolute as the darkness. "I must have been dreaming," I thought; but the sounds were ringing in my ears, and my heart was beating with excitement. There must have been some reason for this. I never was "taken this way" before. I could not make it out, and felt very uncomfortable. I sat there listening for some time. No other sound breaking the deathly stillness, and becoming tired of sitting, I lay down again. Once more I set myself to get my interminable flocks through that gate, but I could not help myself listening.

There seemed to me a sound growing in the darkness, a something gathering in the particles of the air, as if molecules of the atmosphere were rustling together, and with stilly movement were whispering something. The wind had died down, and I would have gone on deck if I could move; but it was hazardous enough moving about in the light: it would have been madness to attempt to move in that blackness. And so I lay still and tried to sleep.

But now there was a sound, indistinct, but no mere fancy; a muffled sound, as of some movement in the forepart of the ship.

I listened intently and gazed into the darkness.

What was the sound? It did not seem like rats. It was a dull, shuffling kind of noise, very indistinct, and conveying no clue whatever as to its cause. It lasted only for a short time. But now the cold damp air seemed to have become more piercingly chilly. The raw iciness seemed to strike into the very marrow of my bones, and my teeth chattered. At the same time a new sense seemed to be assailed: the foul odour which I had noticed arising from the stagnant water in the bilge appeared to rise into more objectionable prominence, as if it had been stirred.

"I cannot stand this," I muttered, shivering in horrible aversion at the disgusting odour; "I will go on deck at all hazards."

Rising to put this resolve in execution, I was arrested by the noise beginning again. I listened. This time I distinctly distinguished two separate sounds: one, like a heavy soft weight being dragged along with difficulty; the other like the hard sound of boots on boards. Could there be others on board after all? If so, why had they made no sound when I clambered on deck, or afterwards, when I shouted and fired my gun?

Clearly, if there were people, they wished to remain concealed, and my presence was inconvenient to them. But how absolutely still and quiet they had kept! It appeared incredible that there should be anyone. I listened intently. The sound had ceased again, and once more the most absolute stillness reigned around. A gentle swishing, wobbling, lapping noise seemed to form itself in the darkness. It increased, until I recognised the chattering and bubbling of water. "It must be the tide which is rising," I thought; "it has reached the rudder, and is eddying round the stern-post." This also accounted, in my mind, for the other noises, because, as the tide surrounded the vessel, and she thus became water-borne, all kinds of sounds might be produced in the old hulk as she resumed her upright position.

However, I could not get rid of the chilly horrid feeling those two screams had produced, combined with the disgusting smell, which was getting more and more obtrusive. It was foul, horrible, revolting, like some carrion, putrid and noxious. I prepared to take my chances of damage, and rose up to grope my way to the companion-ladder.

It was a more difficult job than I had any idea of. I had my gun, it was true, and with it I could feel for the joists; but when once I let go of the edge of the bunk I had nothing to steady me, and nearly went headlong at the first step. Fortunately I reached back in time to prevent my fall; but this attempt convinced me that I had better endure the strange horrors of the unknown, than the certain miseries of a broken leg or neck.

I sat down, therefore, on the bunk.

Now that my own movements had ceased, I became aware that the shuffling noise was going on all the time. "Well," thought I, "they may shuffle. They won't hurt me, and I shall go to sleep again." So reflecting, I lay down, holding my gun, ready to use as a club if necessary.

Now it is all very well to laugh at superstitious terrors. Nothing is easier than to obtain a cheap reputation for brilliancy, independence of thought, and courage, by deriding the fear of the supernatural when comfortably seated in a drawing-room well lighted, and with company. But put those scoffers in a like situation with mine, and I don't believe they would have been any more free from a feeling the reverse of bold, mocking, and comfortable, than I was.

I had read that most powerful ghost-story, 'The Haunted and the Haunters,' by the late Lord Lytton, and the vividness of that weird tale had always impressed me greatly. Was I actually now to experience in my own person, and with no possibility of escape, the trying ordeal that bold ghost-hunter went through, under much more favourable circumstances? He at least had his servant with him. He had fuel and a light, and above all, he could get away when he wanted to. I felt I could face any number of spiritual manifestations, if only I had warmth and light. But the icy coldness of the air was eating into my bones, and I shivered until my teeth chattered.

I could not get to sleep. I could not prevent myself listening, and at last I gave up the contest, and let myself listen. But there seemed now nothing to listen to. All the time I had been refusing to let my ears do their office, by putting my handkerchief over one ear, and lying on my arm with the other, a confused noise appeared to reach me, but the moment I turned round and lay on my back, everything seemed quiet. "It's only my fancy after all; the result of cold and want of a good dinner. I will go to sleep." But in spite of this I lay still, listening a little longer. There was the sound of trickling water against the broad bilge of the old hulk, and I knew the tide was rising fast: my thoughts turned to the lost canoe, and to reproaching myself with my stupidity in not allowing enough rope, or looking at it more carefully. Suddenly I became all attention again. An entirely different sound now arrested me. It was distinctly a low groan, and followed almost immediately by heavy blows — blows which fell on a soft substance, and then more groans, and again those sickening blows.

"There must be men here. Where are they? and what is it?" I sat up, and strained my eyes towards where the sound came from. The sounds had ceased again. Should I call out, and let the man or men know that I was here? What puzzled me was the absolute darkness. How could anyone see to hit an object; or do anything else in this dense obscurity? It appalled me. Anything might pass at an inch's distance, and I could not tell who or what it was. But how could anything human find its way about, any more than I could? Perhaps there was a solid bulkhead dividing the forecastle from me. But it would have to be very sound, and with no chink whatever, to prevent a gleam or ray of light finding its way out somewhere. I could not help feeling convinced that the whole hull was open from one end to the other. Was I really dreaming after all? To convince myself that I was wide awake, I felt in my pockets for my notebook, and pulling out my pencil, I opened the book, and holding it in my left hand, wrote as well as I could, by feel alone: "I am wide awake; it is about midnight — Christmas eve, 187-." I found I had got to the bottom of the page, so I shut the book up, resolving to look at it the next morning. I felt curious to see what the writing looked like by daylight.

But all further speculation was cut short by the shuffling and dragging noise beginning again. There was no doubt the sounds were louder, and were coming my way.

I never in all my life felt so uncomfortable — I may as well at once confess it — so frightened. There, in that empty hull, over that boardless floor, over these rotting joists, somebody or something was dragging some heavy weight. What, I could not imagine; only the shrieks, the blows, the groans, the dull thumping sounds, compelled me to suspect the worst, — to feel convinced that I was actually within some few feet of a horrible murder then being committed. I could form no idea of who the victim was, or who was the assassin. That I actually heard the sounds I had no doubt; that they were growing louder and more distinct I felt painfully aware. The horror of the situation was intense. If only I could strike a light, and see what was passing close there — but I had no matches. I could hear a sound as of some one breathing slowly, stertorously, then a dull groan. And once more the cruel sodden blows fell again, followed by a drip, drip, and heavy drop in the dank water below, from which the sickening smell rose, pungent, reeking, horrible.

The dragging shuffling noise now began again. It came quite close to me, so close that I felt I had only to put out my hand to touch, the thing. Good heavens! was it coming to my bunk? The thing passed, and all the time the dull drip, as of some heavy drops, fell into the water below. It was awful. All this time I was sitting up, and holding my gun by its barrel, ready to use it if I were attacked. As the sound passed me at the closest, I put out the gun involuntarily; but it touched nothing, and I shuddered at the thought that there was no floor over which the weight could be drawn.

I must be dreaming some terribly vivid dream. It could not be real. I pinched myself. I felt I was pinching myself. It was no dream. The sweat poured off my brow, my teeth chattered with the cold. It was terrific in its dreadful mystery.

And now the sounds altered. The noises had reached the companion-ladder. Something was climbing them with difficulty. The old stairs creaked. Bump, thump, the thing was dragged up the steps with many pauses, and at last it seemed to have reached the deck. A long pause now followed. The silence grew dense around. I dreaded the stillness — the silence that made itself be heard almost more than the sounds. What new horror would that awful quiet bring forth? What terror was still brooding in the depths of that clinging darkness — darkness that could be felt?

The absolute silence was broken, — horribly broken, — by a dull drip from the stairs, and then the dragging began again. Distant and less distinct, but the steps were louder. They came nearer — over my head — the old boards creaked, and the weight was dragged right over me. I could hear it above my head: for the steps stopped, and two distinct raps, followed by a third heavier one, sounded so clearly above me, that it seemed almost as if it was something striking the rotten woodwork of the berth over my head. The sounds were horribly suggestive of the elbows and head of a body being dropped on the deck.

And now, as if the horrors had not been enough, a fresh ghastliness was added. So close were the raps above me that I involuntarily moved, as if I had been struck by what caused them. As I did so, I felt something drop on to my head and slowly trickle over my forehead: it was too horrible! I sprang up in my disgust, and with a wild cry I stepped forward, and instantly fell between the joists into the rank water below.

The shock was acute. Had I been asleep and dreaming before, this must inevitably have roused me up. I found myself completely immersed in water, and, for a moment, was absolutely incapable of thinking. As it was pitch-dark and my head had gone under, I could not tell whether I was above water or not, as I felt the bottom and struggled and splashed on to my legs. It was only by degrees I knew I must be standing with my head out of the foul mixture, because I was able to breathe easily, although the wet running down from my hair dribbled into my mouth as I stood shivering and gasping.

It was astonishing how a physical discomfort overcame a mental terror. Nothing could be more miserable than my present position, and my efforts were at once directed to getting out of this dreadful place. But let anyone who has ever had the ill-luck to fall out of bed in his boyhood try and recollect his sensations. The bewildering realisation that he is not in bed, that he does not know where he is, which way to go, or what to do to get back again; everything he touches seems strange, and one piece of furniture much the same as any other. I well remember such an accident, and how, having rolled under the bed before I was wide awake, I could not for the life of me understand why I could not get up, what it was that kept me down. I had not the least idea which way to get out, and kept going round and round in a circle under my bed for a long time, and should probably have been doing it until daylight, had not my sighs and groans awoke my brother, who slept in the same room, and who came to my help.

If, then, one is so utterly at fault in a room every inch of which one knows intimately, how much more hopeless was my position at the bottom of this old vessel, half immersed in water, and totally without any clue which could help me to get out! I had not the least idea which was the ship's stern or which her stem, and every movement I made with my feet only served to unsteady me, as the bottom was all covered with slime, and uneven with the great timbers of the vessel.

My first thought on recovering my wits was to stretch my arms up over my head, and I was relieved to find that I could easily reach the joists above me. I was always fairly good at gymnastics, and I had not much difficulty in drawing myself up and sitting on the joist, although the weight of my wet clothes added to my exertions considerably. Having so far succeeded, I sat and drained, as it were, into the water below. The smell was abominable. I never disliked myself so much, and I shivered with cold.

As I could not get any wetter, I determined to go on deck somehow, but where was the companion-ladder? I had nothing to guide me. Strange to say, the reality of my struggles had almost made me forget the mysterious phenomena I had been listening to. But now, as I looked round, my attention was caught by a luminous patch which quivered and flickered on my right, at what distance from me I could not tell. It was like the light from a glow-worm, only larger and changing in shape; sometimes elongated like a lambent oval, and then it would sway one way or another, as if caught in a draught of air. While I was looking at it and wondering what could cause it, I heard the steps over my head; they passed above me, and then seemed to grow louder on my left. A creeping dread again came over me. If only I could get out of this horrible place — but where were the stairs? I listened. The footfall seemed to be coming down some steps; then the companion-ladder must be on my left. But if I moved that way I should meet the Thing, whatever it was, that was coming down. I shuddered at the thought. However, I made up my mind. Stretching out my hand very carefully, I felt for the next joist, reached it, and crawled across. I stopped to listen. The steps were coming nearer. My hearing had now become acute; I could almost tell the exact place of each footfall. It came closer — closer, — quite close, surely — on the very joist on which I was sitting. I thought I could feel the joist quiver, and involuntarily moved my hand to prevent the heavy tread falling on it. The steps passed on, grew fainter, and ceased, as they drew near the pale lambent light. One thing I noticed with curious horror, and that was, that although the thing must have passed between me and the light, yet it was never for a moment obscured, which it must have been had any body or substance passed between, and yet I was certain that the steps went directly from me to it.

It was all horribly mysterious; and what had become of the other sound — the thing that was being dragged? An irresistible shudder passed over me; but I determined to pursue my way until I came to something. It would never do to sit still and shiver there.

After many narrow escapes of falling again, I reached a bulkhead, and cautiously feeling along it, I came to an opening. It was the companion-ladder. By this time my hands, by feeling over the joists, had become dry again. I felt along the step to be quite sure that it was the stairs, and in so doing I touched something wet, sticky, clammy. Oh, horror! what was it? A cold shiver shook me nearly off the joist, and I felt an unutterable sense of repulsion to going on. However, the fresher air which came down the companion revived me, and, conquering my dread, I clambered on to the step. It did not take long to get upstairs and stand on the deck again.

I think I never in all my life experienced such a sense of joy as I did on being out of that disgusting hole. It was true I was soaking wet, and the night wind cut through me like a knife; but these were things I could understand, and were matter of common experience. What I had gone through might only be a question of nerves, and had no tangible or visible terror; but it was none the less very dreadful, and I would not go through such an experience again for worlds. As I stood cowering under the lee of the bulwark, I looked round at the sky. There was a pale light as if of daybreak away in the east, and it seemed as if all my troubles would be over with the dawn. It was bitterly cold. The wind had got round to the north, and I could faintly make out the low shore astern.

While I stood shivering there, a cry came down the wind. At first I thought it was a sea-bird, but it sounded again. I felt sure it was a human voice. I sprang up on to the taffrail, and shouted at the top of my lungs, then paused. The cry came down clearer and distinct. It was Jones's voice — had he heard me? I waved my draggled pocket-handkerchief and shouted again. In the silence which followed, I caught the words, "We are coming." What joyful words!

Never did shipwrecked mariner on a lonely isle feel greater delight. My misery would soon be over. Anyhow, I should not have to wait long.

Unfortunately the tide was low, and was still falling. Nothing but a boat could reach me, I thought, and to get a boat would take some time. I therefore stamped up and down the deck to get warm; but I had an instinctive aversion for the companion-ladder, and the deep shadows of the forepart of the vessel.

As I turned round in my walk, I thought I saw something moving over the mud. I stopped. It was undoubtedly a figure coming towards me. A voice hailed me in gruff accents –

"Lily, ahoy! Be anyone aboard?"

Was anyone aboard? What an absurd question! and here had I been shouting myself hoarse. However, I quickly reassured him, and then understood why my rescuer did not sink in the soft mud. He had mud-pattens on. Coming up as close as he could, he shouted to me to keep clear, and then threw first one, then the other, clattering wooden board on to the deck. I found them, and under the instructions of my friend, I did not take long in putting them on. The man was giving me directions as to how to manage; but I did not care how much wetter I got, and dropped over the side into the slime. Sliding and straddling, I managed to get up to my friend, and then together we skated, as it were, to the shore – although skating very little represents the awkward splashes and slips I made on my way to land. I found quite a little crowd awaiting me on the bank; but Jones, with ready consideration, hurried me off to a cart he had in a lane near, and drove me home.

I told him the chief points of the adventure on our way; but did not say anything of the curious noises. It is odd how shy a man feels at telling what he knows people will never believe. It was not until the evening of the next day that I began to tell him, and then only after I was fortified by an excellent dinner, and some very good claret. Jones listened attentively. He was far too kindly and well bred to laugh at me; but I could see he did not believe one word as to the reality of the occurrence. "Very strange!" "How remarkable!" "Quite extraordinary!" he kept saying, with evident interest. But I was sure he put it all down to my fatigue and disordered imagination. And so, to do him justice, has everybody else to whom I have told the tale since.

The fact is, we cannot, in this prosaic age, believe in anything the least approaching the supernatural. Nor do I. But nevertheless I am as certain as I am that I am writing these words, that the thing did really happen, and will happen again, may happen every night for all I know, only I don't intend to try and put my belief to the test. I have a theory which of course will be laughed at, and as I am not in the least scientific, I cannot bolster it up by scientific arguments. It is this: As Mr. Edison has now discovered that by certain simple processes human sounds can be reproduced at any future date, so accidentally, and owing to the combination of most curious coincidences, it might happen that the agonised cries of some suffering being, or the sounds made by one at a time when all other emotions are as nothing compared to the supreme sensations of one committing some awful crime, could be impressed on the atmosphere or surface of an enclosed building, which could be reproduced by a current of air passing into that building under the same atmospheric conditions. This is the vague explanation I have given to myself.

However, be the explanation what it may, the facts are as I have stated them. Let those laugh who did not experience them. To return to the end of the story. There were two things I pointed out to Jones as conclusive that I was not dreaming. One was my pocket-book. I showed it him, and the words were quite clear — only, of course, very straggling. This is a facsimile of the writing, but I cannot account for the date being 1837 —

I AM WIDE A WAKE IT IS ABOUT MIDNIGHT
CHRISTMAS EVE 1837

The other point was the horrible stains on my hands and clothes. A foulsmelling dark chocolate stain was on my hair, hands, and clothes. Jones said, of course, this was from the rust off the mouldering iron-work, some of which no doubt had trickled down, owing to the heavy rain, through the defective caulking of the deck. The fact is, there is nothing that an ingenious mind cannot explain; but the question is, Is the explanation the right one?

I could easily account for the phosphorescent light. The water was foul and stagnant, and it was no doubt caused by the same gases which produce the well known ignis-fatuus or Will-o'-the-wisp.

We visited the ship, and I recovered my gun. There were the same stains on the deck as there were on my clothes; and curiously enough they went in a nearly straight line over the place where I lay, from the top of the companion to the starboard bulwark. We carefully examined the forepart of the ship: it was as completely gutted as the rest of her. Jones was glad to get on deck again, as the atmosphere was very unpleasant, and I had no wish to stay.

At my request Jones made every inquiry he could about the old hulk. Not much was elicited. It bore an evil name, and no one would go on board who could help it. So far it looked as if it were credited with being haunted. The owner, who had been the captain of her, had died about three years before. His character did not seem amiable; but as he had left his money to the most influential farmer in the district, the country-people were unwilling to talk against him.

I went with Jones to call on the farmer, and asked him point-blank if he had ever heard whether a murder had been committed on board the Lily. He stared at me, and then laughed. "Not as I know of" was all his answer — and I never got any nearer than that.

I feel that this is all very unsatisfactory. I wish I could give some thrilling and sensational explanation. I am sorry I cannot. My imagination suggests many, as no doubt it will to each of my readers who possesses that faculty; but I have only written this to tell the actual facts, not to add to our superabundant fiction.

If ever I come across any details bearing upon the subject, I will not fail to communicate them at once.

The vessel I found was the Lily of Goole, owned by one Master Gad Earwaker, and built in 1801.

THEY

Rudyard Kipling, 1904

THE RETURN OF THE CHILDREN

Neither the harps nor the crowns amused, nor the cherubs' dove-winged
  races—
Holding hands forlornly the Children wandered beneath the Dome;
Plucking the radiant robes of the passers by, and with pitiful faces
Begging what Princes and Powers refused:—"Ah, please will you let us
  go home?"

Over the jewelled floor, nigh weeping, ran to them Mary the Mother,
Kneeled and caressed and made promise with kisses, and drew them along
  to the gateway—
Yea, the all-iron unbribable Door which Peter must guard and none other.
Straightway She took the Keys from his keeping, and opened and freed
  them straightway.

Then to Her Son, Who had seen and smiled, She said: "On the night that
  I bore Thee
What didst Thou care for a love beyond mine or a heaven that was not my
  arm?
Didst Thou push from the nipple O Child, to hear the angels adore Thee?
When we two lay in the breath of the kine?" And He said:—"Thou hast
  done no harm."

So through the Void the Children ran homeward merrily hand in hand,
Looking neither to left nor right where the breathless Heavens stood
  still;
And the Guards of the Void resheathed their swords, for they heard the
  Command.
"Shall I that have suffered the children to come to me hold them against
  their will?"

"THEY" One view called me to another; one hill top to its fellow, half across the county, and since I could answer at no more trouble than the snapping forward of a lever, I let the country flow under my wheels. The orchid- studded flats of the East gave way to the thyme, ilex, and grey grass of the Downs; these again to the rich cornland and fig-trees of the lower coast, where you carry the beat of the tide on your left hand for fifteen level miles; and when at last I turned inland through a huddle of rounded hills and woods I had run myself clean out of my known marks. Beyond that precise hamlet which stands godmother to the capital of the United States, I found hidden villages where bees, the only things awake, boomed in eighty-foot lindens that overhung grey Norman churches; miraculous brooks diving under stone bridges built for heavier traffic than would ever vex them again; tithe-barns larger than their churches, and an old smithy that cried out aloud how it had once been a hall of the Knights of the Temple. Gipsies I found on a common where the gorse, bracken, and heath fought it out together up a mile of Roman road; and a little farther on I disturbed a red fox rolling dog-fashion in the naked sunlight.

As the wooded hills closed about me I stood up in the car to take the bearings of that great Down whose ringed head is a landmark for fifty miles across the low countries. I judged that the lie of the country would bring me across some westward running road that went to his feet, but I did not allow for the confusing veils of the woods. A quick turn plunged me first into a green cutting brimful of liquid sunshine, next into a gloomy tunnel where last year's dead leaves whispered and scuffled about my tyres. The strong hazel stuff meeting overhead had not been cut for a couple of generations at least, nor had any axe helped the moss-cankered oak and beech to spring above them. Here the road changed frankly into a carpetted ride on whose brown velvet spent primrose-clumps showed like jade, and a few sickly, white-stalked bluebells nodded together. As the slope favoured I shut off the power and slid over the whirled leaves, expecting every moment to meet a keeper; but I only heard a jay, far off, arguing against the silence under the twilight of the trees.

Still the track descended. I was on the point of reversing and working my way back on the second speed ere I ended in some swamp, when I saw sunshine through the tangle ahead and lifted the brake.

It was down again at once. As the light beat across my face my fore-wheels took the turf of a great still lawn from which sprang horsemen ten feet high with levelled lances, monstrous peacocks, and sleek round-headed maids of honour—blue, black, and glistening—all of clipped yew. Across the lawn—the marshalled woods besieged it on three sides—stood an ancient house of lichened and weather-worn stone, with mullioned windows and roofs of rose-red tile. It was flanked by semi-circular walls, also rose-red, that closed the lawn on the fourth side, and at their feet a box hedge grew man-high. There were doves on the roof about the slim brick chimneys, and I caught a glimpse of an octagonal dove-house behind the screening wall.

Here, then, I stayed; a horseman's green spear laid at my breast; held by the exceeding beauty of that jewel in that setting.

"If I am not packed off for a trespasser, or if this knight does not ride a wallop at me," thought I, "Shakespeare and Queen Elizabeth at least must come out of that half-open garden door and ask me to tea."

A child appeared at an upper window, and I thought the little thing waved a friendly hand. But it was to call a companion, for presently another bright head showed. Then I heard a laugh among the yew-peacocks, and turning to make sure (till then I had been watching the house only) I saw the silver of a fountain behind a hedge thrown up against the sun. The doves on the roof cooed to the cooing water; but between the two notes I caught the utterly happy chuckle of a child absorbed in some light mischief.

The garden door—heavy oak sunk deep in the thickness of the wall—opened further: a woman in a big garden hat set her foot slowly on the time-hollowed stone step and as slowly walked across the turf. I was forming some apology when she lifted up her head and I saw that she was blind.

"I heard you," she said. "Isn't that a motor car?"

"I'm afraid I've made a mistake in my road. I should have turned off up above—I never dreamed"—I began.

"But I'm very glad. Fancy a motor car coming into the garden! It will be such a treat——" She turned and made as though looking about her. "You— you haven't seen any one have you—perhaps?"

"No one to speak to, but the children seemed interested at a distance."

"Which?"

"I saw a couple up at the window just now, and I think I heard a little chap in the grounds."

"Oh, lucky you!" she cried, and her face brightened. "I hear them, of course, but that's all. You've seen them and heard them?"

"Yes," I answered. "And if I know anything of children one of them's having a beautiful time by the fountain yonder. Escaped, I should imagine."

"You're fond of children?"

I gave her one or two reasons why I did not altogether hate them.

"Of course, of course," she said. "Then you understand. Then you won't think it foolish if I ask you to take your car through the gardens, once or twice—quite slowly. I'm sure they'd like to see it. They see so little, poor things. One tries to make their life pleasant, but— —" she threw out her hands towards the woods. "We're so out of the world here."

"That will be splendid," I said. "But I can't cut up your grass."

She faced to the right. "Wait a minute," she said. "We're at the South gate, aren't we? Behind those peacocks there's a flagged path. We call it the Peacock's Walk. You can't see it from here, they tell me, but if you squeeze along by the edge of the wood you can turn at the first peacock and get on to the flags."

It was sacrilege to wake that dreaming house-front with the clatter of machinery, but I swung the car to clear the turf, brushed along the edge of the wood and turned in on the broad stone path where the fountain-basin lay like one star-sapphire.

"May I come too?" she cried. "No, please don't help me. They'll like it better if they see me."

She felt her way lightly to the front of the car, and with one foot on the step she called: "Children, oh, children! Look and see what's going to happen!"

The voice would have drawn lost souls from the Pit, for the yearning that underlay its sweetness, and I was not surprised to hear an answering shout behind the yews. It must have been the child by the fountain, but he fled at our approach, leaving a little toy boat in the water. I saw the glint of his blue blouse among the still horsemen.

Very disposedly we paraded the length of the walk and at her request backed again. This time the child had got the better of his panic, but stood far off and doubting.

"The little fellow's watching us," I said. "I wonder if he'd like a ride."

"They're very shy still. Very shy. But, oh, lucky you to be able to see them! Let's listen."

I stopped the machine at once, and the humid stillness, heavy with the scent of box, cloaked us deep. Shears I could hear where some gardener was clipping; a mumble of bees and broken voices that might have been the doves.

"Oh, unkind!" she said weariedly.

"Perhaps they're only shy of the motor. The little maid at the window looks tremendously interested."

"Yes?" She raised her head. "It was wrong of me to say that. They are really fond of me. It's the only thing that makes life worth living—when they're fond of you, isn't it? I daren't think what the place would be without them. By the way, is it beautiful?"

"I think it is the most beautiful place I have ever seen."

"So they all tell me. I can feel it, of course, but that isn't quite the same thing."

"Then have you never—-?" I began, but stopped abashed.

"Not since I can remember. It happened when I was only a few months old, they tell me. And yet I must remember something, else how could I dream about colours. I see light in my dreams, and colours, but I never see them. I only hear them just as I do when I'm awake."

"It's difficult to see faces in dreams. Some people can, but most of us haven't the gift," I went on, looking up at the window where the child stood all but hidden.

"I've heard that too," she said. "And they tell me that one never sees a dead person's face in a dream. Is that true?"

"I believe it is—now I come to think of it."

"But how is it with yourself—yourself?" The blind eyes turned towards me.

"I have never seen the faces of my dead in any dream," I answered.

"Then it must be as bad as being blind."

The sun had dipped behind the woods and the long shades were possessing the insolent horsemen one by one. I saw the light die from off the top of a glossy-leaved lance and all the brave hard green turn to soft black. The house, accepting another day at end, as it had accepted an hundred thousand gone, seemed to settle deeper into its rest among the shadows.

"Have you ever wanted to?" she said after the silence.

"Very much sometimes," I replied. The child had left the window as the shadows closed upon it.

"Ah! So've I, but I don't suppose it's allowed. ... Where d'you live?"

"Quite the other side of the county—sixty miles and more, and I must be going back. I've come without my big lamp."

"But it's not dark yet. I can feel it."

"I'm afraid it will be by the time I get home. Could you lend me someone to set me on my road at first? I've utterly lost myself."

"I'll send Madden with you to the cross-roads. We are so out of the world, I don't wonder you were lost! I'll guide you round to the front of the house; but you will go slowly, won't you, till you're out of the grounds? It isn't foolish, do you think?"

"I promise you I'll go like this," I said, and let the car start herself down the flagged path.

We skirted the left wing of the house, whose elaborately cast lead guttering alone was worth a day's journey; passed under a great rose-grown gate in the red wall, and so round to the high front of the house which in beauty and stateliness as much excelled the back as that all others I had seen.

"Is it so very beautiful?" she said wistfully when she heard my raptures. "And you like the lead-figures too? There's the old azalea garden behind. They say that this place must have been made for children. Will you help me out, please? I should like to come with you as far as the cross-roads, but I mustn't leave them. Is that you, Madden? I want you to show this gentleman the way to the cross-roads. He has lost his way but—he has seen them."

A butler appeared noiselessly at the miracle of old oak that must be called the front door, and slipped aside to put on his hat. She stood looking at me with open blue eyes in which no sight lay, and I saw for the first time that she was beautiful.

"Remember," she said quietly, "if you are fond of them you will come again," and disappeared within the house.

The butler in the car said nothing till we were nearly at the lodge gates, where catching a glimpse of a blue blouse in a shrubbery I swerved amply lest the devil that leads little boys to play should drag me into child- murder.

"Excuse me," he asked of a sudden, "but why did you do that, Sir?"

"The child yonder."

"Our young gentleman in blue?"

"Of course."

"He runs about a good deal. Did you see him by the fountain, Sir?"

"Oh, yes, several times. Do we turn here?"

"Yes, Sir. And did you 'appen to see them upstairs too?"

"At the upper window? Yes."

"Was that before the mistress come out to speak to you, Sir?"

"A little before that. Why d'you want to know?"

He paused a little. "Only to make sure that—that they had seen the car, Sir, because with children running about, though I'm sure you're driving particularly careful, there might be an accident. That was all, Sir. Here are the cross-roads. You can't miss your way from now on. Thank you, Sir, but that isn't our custom, not with— —"

"I beg your pardon," I said, and thrust away the British silver.

"Oh, it's quite right with the rest of 'em as a rule. Goodbye, Sir."

He retired into the armour-plated conning tower of his caste and walked away. Evidently a butler solicitous for the honour of his house, and interested, probably through a maid, in the nursery.

Once beyond the signposts at the cross-roads I looked back, but the crumpled hills interlaced so jealously that I could not see where the house had lain. When I asked its name at a cottage along the road, the fat woman who sold sweetmeats there gave me to understand that people with motor cars had small right to live—much less to "go about talking like carriage folk." They were not a pleasant-mannered community.

When I retraced my route on the map that evening I was little wiser. Hawkin's Old Farm appeared to be the survey title of the place, and the old County Gazetteer, generally so ample, did not allude to it. The big house of those parts was Hodnington Hall, Georgian with early Victorian embellishments, as an atrocious steel engraving attested. I carried my difficulty to a neighbour—a deep-rooted tree of that soil—and he gave me a name of a family which conveyed no meaning.

A month or so later—I went again, or it may have been that my car took the road of her own volition. She over-ran the fruitless Downs, threaded every turn of the maze of lanes below the hills, drew through the high- walled woods, impenetrable in their full leaf, came out at the cross roads where the butler had left me, and a little further on developed an internal trouble which forced me to turn her in on a grass way-waste that cut into a summer-silent hazel wood. So far as I could make sure by the sun and a six-inch Ordnance map, this should be the road flank of that wood which I had first explored from the heights above. I made a mighty serious business of my repairs and a glittering shop of my repair kit, spanners, pump, and the like, which I spread out orderly upon a rug. It was a trap to catch all childhood, for on such a day, I argued, the children would not be far off. When I paused in my work I listened, but the wood was so full of the noises of summer (though the birds had mated) that I could not at first distinguish these from the tread of small cautious feet stealing across the dead leaves. I rang my bell in an alluring manner, but the feet fled, and I repented, for to a child a sudden noise is very real terror. I must have been at work half an hour when I heard in the wood the voice of the blind woman crying: "Children, oh children, where are you?" and the stillness made slow to close on the perfection of that cry. She came towards me, half feeling her way between the tree boles, and though a child it seemed clung to her skirt, it swerved into the leafage like a rabbit as she drew nearer.

"Is that you?" she said, "from the other side of the county?"

"Yes, it's me from the other side of the county."

"Then why didn't you come through the upper woods? They were there just now."

"They were here a few minutes ago. I expect they knew my car had broken down, and came to see the fun."

"Nothing serious, I hope? How do cars break down?"

"In fifty different ways. Only mine has chosen the fifty first."

She laughed merrily at the tiny joke, cooed with delicious laughter, and pushed her hat back.

"Let me hear," she said.

"Wait a moment," I cried, "and I'll get you a cushion."

She set her foot on the rug all covered with spare parts, and stooped above it eagerly. "What delightful things!" The hands through which she saw glanced in the chequered sunlight. "A box here—another box! Why you've arranged them like playing shop!"

"I confess now that I put it out to attract them. I don't need half those things really."

"How nice of you! I heard your bell in the upper wood. You say they were here before that?"

"I'm sure of it. Why are they so shy? That little fellow in blue who was with you just now ought to have got over his fright. He's been watching me like a Red Indian."

"It must have been your bell," she said. "I heard one of them go past me in trouble when I was coming down. They're shy—so shy even with me." She turned her face over her shoulder and cried again: "Children! Oh, children! Look and see!"

"They must have gone off together on their own affairs,"

I suggested, for there was a murmur behind us of lowered voices broken by the sudden squeaking giggles of childhood. I returned to my tinkerings and she leaned forward, her chin on her hand, listening interestedly.

"How many are they?" I said at last. The work was finished, but I saw no reason to go.

Her forehead puckered a little in thought. "I don't quite know," she said simply. "Sometimes more—sometimes less. They come and stay with me because I love them, you see."

"That must be very jolly," I said, replacing a drawer, and as I spoke I heard the inanity of my answer.

"You—you aren't laughing at me," she cried. "I—I haven't any of my own. I never married. People laugh at me sometimes about them because— because— — —"

"Because they're savages," I returned. "It's nothing to fret for. That sort laugh at everything that isn't in their own fat lives."

"I don't know. How should I? I only don't like being laughed at about them. It hurts; and when one can't see.... I don't want to seem silly," her chin quivered like a child's as she spoke, "but we blindies have only one skin, I think. Everything outside hits straight at our souls. It's different with you. You've such good defences in your eyes—looking out— before anyone can really pain you in your soul. People forget that with us."

I was silent reviewing that inexhaustible matter—the more than inherited (since it is also carefully taught) brutality of the Christian peoples, beside which the mere heathendom of the West Coast nigger is clean and restrained. It led me a long distance into myself.

"Don't do that!" she said of a sudden, putting her hands before her eyes.

"What?"

She made a gesture with her hand.

"That! It's—it's all purple and black. Don't! That colour hurts."

"But, how in the world do you know about colours?" I exclaimed, for here was a revelation indeed.

"Colours as colours?" she asked.

"No. Those Colours which you saw just now."

"You know as well as I do," she laughed, "else you wouldn't have asked that question. They aren't in the world at all. They're in you—when you went so angry."

"D'you mean a dull purplish patch, like port-wine mixed with ink?" I said.

"I've never seen ink or port-wine, but the colours aren't mixed. They are separate—all separate."

"Do you mean black streaks and jags across the purple?"

She nodded. "Yes—if they are like this," and zigzagged her finger again, "but it's more red than purple—that bad colour."

"And what are the colours at the top of the—whatever you see?"

Slowly she leaned forward and traced on the rug the figure of the Egg itself.

"I see them so," she said, pointing with a grass stem, "white, green, yellow, red, purple, and when people are angry or bad, black across the red—as you were just now."

"Who told you anything about it—in the beginning?" I demanded.

"About the colours? No one. I used to ask what colours were when I was little—in table-covers and curtains and carpets, you see—because some colours hurt me and some made me happy. People told me; and when I got older that was how I saw people." Again she traced the outline of the Egg which it is given to very few of us to see.

"All by yourself?" I repeated.

"All by myself. There wasn't anyone else. I only found out afterwards that other people did not see the Colours."

She leaned against the tree-hole plaiting and unplaiting chance-plucked grass stems. The children in the wood had drawn nearer. I could see them with the tail of my eye frolicking like squirrels.

"Now I am sure you will never laugh at me," she went on after a long silence. "Nor at them."

"Goodness! No!" I cried, jolted out of my train of thought. "A man who laughs at a child—unless the child is laughing too—is a heathen!"

"I didn't mean that of course. You'd never laugh at children, but I thought—I used to think—that perhaps you might laugh about them. So now I beg your pardon.... What are you going to laugh at?"

I had made no sound, but she knew.

"At the notion of your begging my pardon. If you had done your duty as a pillar of the state and a landed proprietress you ought to have summoned me for trespass when I barged through your woods the other day. It was disgraceful of me—inexcusable."

She looked at me, her head against the tree trunk—long and steadfastly—this woman who could see the naked soul.

"How curious," she half whispered. "How very curious."

"Why, what have I done?"

"You don't understand ... and yet you understood about the Colours. Don't you understand?"

She spoke with a passion that nothing had justified, and I faced her bewilderedly as she rose. The children had gathered themselves in a roundel behind a bramble bush. One sleek head bent over something smaller, and the set of the little shoulders told me that fingers were on lips. They, too, had some child's tremendous secret. I alone was hopelessly astray there in the broad sunlight.

"No," I said, and shook my head as though the dead eyes could note. "Whatever it is, I don't understand yet. Perhaps I shall later—if you'll let me come again."

"You will come again," she answered. "You will surely come again and walk in the wood."

"Perhaps the children will know me well enough by that time to let me play with them—as a favour. You know what children are like."

"It isn't a matter of favour but of right," she replied, and while I wondered what she meant, a dishevelled woman plunged round the bend of the road, loose-haired, purple, almost lowing with agony as she ran. It was my rude, fat friend of the sweetmeat shop. The blind woman heard and stepped forward. "What is it, Mrs. Madehurst?" she asked.

The woman flung her apron over her head and literally grovelled in the dust, crying that her grandchild was sick to death, that the local doctor was away fishing, that Jenny the mother was at her wits end, and so forth, with repetitions and bellowings.

"Where's the next nearest doctor?" I asked between paroxysms.

"Madden will tell you. Go round to the house and take him with you. I'll attend to this. Be quick!" She half-supported the fat woman into the shade. In two minutes I was blowing all the horns of Jericho under the front of the House Beautiful, and Madden, in the pantry, rose to the crisis like a butler and a man.

A quarter of an hour at illegal speeds caught us a doctor five miles away. Within the half-hour we had decanted him, much interested in motors, at the door of the sweetmeat shop, and drew up the road to await the verdict.

"Useful things cars," said Madden, all man and no butler. "If I'd had one when mine took sick she wouldn't have died."

"How was it?" I asked.

"Croup. Mrs. Madden was away. No one knew what to do. I drove eight miles in a tax cart for the doctor. She was choked when we came back. This car 'd ha' saved her. She'd have been close on ten now."

"I'm sorry," I said. "I thought you were rather fond of children from what you told me going to the cross-roads the other day."

"Have you seen 'em again, Sir—this mornin'?"

"Yes, but they're well broke to cars. I couldn't get any of them within twenty yards of it."

He looked at me carefully as a scout considers a stranger—not as a menial should lift his eyes to his divinely appointed superior.

"I wonder why," he said just above the breath that he drew.

We waited on. A light wind from the sea wandered up and down the long lines of the woods, and the wayside grasses, whitened already with summer dust, rose and bowed in sallow waves.

A woman, wiping the suds off her arms, came out of the cottage next the sweetmeat shop.

"I've be'n listenin' in de back-yard," she said cheerily. "He says Arthur's unaccountable bad. Did ye hear him shruck just now? Unaccountable bad. I reckon t'will come Jenny's turn to walk in de wood nex' week along, Mr. Madden." "Excuse me, Sir, but your lap-robe is slipping," said Madden deferentially. The woman started, dropped a curtsey, and hurried away.

"What does she mean by 'walking in the wood'?" I asked.

"It must be some saying they use hereabouts. I'm from Norfolk myself," said Madden. "They're an independent lot in this county. She took you for a chauffeur, Sir."

I saw the Doctor come out of the cottage followed by a draggle-tailed wench who clung to his arm as though he could make treaty for her with Death. "Dat sort," she wailed—"dey're just as much to us dat has 'em as if dey was lawful born. Just as much—just as much! An' God he'd be just as pleased if you saved 'un, Doctor. Don't take it from me. Miss Florence will tell ye de very same. Don't leave 'im, Doctor!"

"I know. I know," said the man, "but he'll be quiet for a while now. We'll get the nurse and the medicine as fast as we can." He signalled me to come forward with the car, and I strove not to be privy to what followed; but I saw the girl's face, blotched and frozen with grief, and I felt the hand without a ring clutching at my knees when we moved away.

The Doctor was a man of some humour, for I remember he claimed my car under the Oath of Æsculapius, and used it and me without mercy. First we convoyed Mrs. Madehurst and the blind woman to wait by the sick bed till the nurse should come. Next we invaded a neat county town for prescriptions (the Doctor said the trouble was cerebro-spinal meningitis), and when the County Institute, banked and flanked with scared market cattle, reported itself out of nurses for the moment we literally flung ourselves loose upon the county. We conferred with the owners of great houses—magnates at the ends of overarching avenues whose big-boned womenfolk strode away from their tea-tables to listen to the imperious Doctor. At last a white-haired lady sitting under a cedar of Lebanon and surrounded by a court of magnificent Borzois—all hostile to motors—gave the Doctor, who received them as from a princess, written orders which we bore many miles at top speed, through a park, to a French nunnery, where we took over in exchange a pallid-faced and trembling Sister. She knelt at the bottom of the tonneau telling her beads without pause till, by short cuts of the Doctor's invention, we had her to the sweetmeat shop once more. It was a long afternoon crowded with mad episodes that rose and dissolved like the dust of our wheels; cross-sections of remote and incomprehensible lives through which we raced at right angles; and I went home in the dusk, wearied out, to dream of the clashing horns of cattle; round-eyed nuns walking in a garden of graves; pleasant tea-parties beneath shaded trees; the carbolic-scented, grey-painted corridors of the County Institute; the steps of shy children in the wood, and the hands that clung to my knees as the motor began to move.

* * * * *

I had intended to return in a day or two, but it pleased Fate to hold me from that side of the county, on many pretexts, till the elder and the wild rose had fruited. There came at last a brilliant day, swept clear from the south-west, that brought the hills within hand's reach—a day of unstable airs and high filmy clouds. Through no merit of my own I was free, and set the car for the third time on that known road. As I reached the crest of the Downs I felt the soft air change, saw it glaze under the sun; and, looking down at the sea, in that instant beheld the blue of the Channel turn through polished silver and dulled steel to dingy pewter. A laden collier hugging the coast steered outward for deeper water and, across copper-coloured haze, I saw sails rise one by one on the anchored fishing-fleet. In a deep dene behind me an eddy of sudden wind drummed through sheltered oaks, and spun aloft the first day sample of autumn leaves. When I reached the beach road the sea-fog fumed over the brickfields, and the tide was telling all the groins of the gale beyond Ushant. In less than an hour summer England vanished in chill grey. We were again the shut island of the North, all the ships of the world bellowing at our perilous gates; and between their outcries ran the piping of bewildered gulls. My cap dripped moisture, the folds of the rug held it in pools or sluiced it away in runnels, and the salt-rime stuck to my lips.

Inland the smell of autumn loaded the thickened fog among the trees, and the drip became a continuous shower. Yet the late flowers—mallow of the wayside, scabious of the field, and dahlia of the garden—showed gay in the mist, and beyond the sea's breath there was little sign of decay in the leaf. Yet in the villages the house doors were all open, and bare- legged, bare-headed children sat at ease on the damp doorsteps to shout "pip-pip" at the stranger.

I made bold to call at the sweetmeat shop, where Mrs. Madehurst met me with a fat woman's hospitable tears. Jenny's child, she said, had died two days after the nun had come. It was, she felt, best out of the way, even though insurance offices, for reasons which she did not pretend to follow, would not willingly insure such stray lives. "Not but what Jenny didn't tend to Arthur as though he'd come all proper at de end of de first year— like Jenny herself." Thanks to Miss Florence, the child had been buried with a pomp which, in Mrs. Madehurst's opinion, more than covered the small irregularity of its birth. She described the coffin, within and without, the glass hearse, and the evergreen lining of the grave.

"But how's the mother?" I asked.

"Jenny? Oh, she'll get over it. I've felt dat way with one or two o' my own. She'll get over. She's walkin' in de wood now."

"In this weather?"

Mrs. Madehurst looked at me with narrowed eyes across the counter.

"I dunno but it opens de 'eart like. Yes, it opens de 'eart. Dat's where losin' and bearin' comes so alike in de long run, we do say."

Now the wisdom of the old wives is greater than that of all the Fathers, and this last oracle sent me thinking so extendedly as I went up the road, that I nearly ran over a woman and a child at the wooded corner by the lodge gates of the House Beautiful.

"Awful weather!" I cried, as I slowed dead for the turn.

"Not so bad," she answered placidly out of the fog. "Mine's used to 'un. You'll find yours indoors, I reckon."

Indoors, Madden received me with professional courtesy, and kind inquiries for the health of the motor, which he would put under cover.

I waited in a still, nut-brown hall, pleasant with late flowers and warmed with a delicious wood fire—a place of good influence and great peace. (Men and women may sometimes, after great effort, achieve a creditable lie; but the house, which is their temple, cannot say anything save the truth of those who have lived in it.) A child's cart and a doll lay on the black-and-white floor, where a rug had been kicked back. I felt that the children had only just hurried away—to hide themselves, most like—in the many turns of the great adzed staircase that climbed statelily out of the hall, or to crouch at gaze behind the lions and roses of the carven gallery above. Then I heard her voice above me, singing as the blind sing —from the soul:—

In the pleasant orchard-closes.

And all my early summer came back at the call.

In the pleasant orchard-closes,
God bless all our gains say we—
But may God bless all our losses,
Better suits with our degree,

She dropped the marring fifth line, and repeated—

Better suits with our degree!

I saw her lean over the gallery, her linked hands white as pearl against the oak.

"Is that you—from the other side of the county?" she called.

"Yes, me—from the other side of the county," I answered laughing.

"What a long time before you had to come here again." She ran down the stairs, one hand lightly touching the broad rail. "It's two months and four days. Summer's gone!"

"I meant to come before, but Fate prevented."

"I knew it. Please do something to that fire. They won't let me play with it, but I can feel it's behaving badly. Hit it!"

I looked on either side of the deep fireplace, and found but a half-charred hedge-stake with which I punched a black log into flame.

"It never goes out, day or night," she said, as though explaining. "In case any one conies in with cold toes, you see."

"It's even lovelier inside than it was out," I murmured. The red light poured itself along the age-polished dusky panels till the Tudor roses and lions of the gallery took colour and motion. An old eagle-topped convex mirror gathered the picture into its mysterious heart, distorting afresh the distorted shadows, and curving the gallery lines into the curves of a ship. The day was shutting down in half a gale as the fog turned to stringy scud. Through the uncurtained mullions of the broad window I could see valiant horsemen of the lawn rear and recover against the wind that taunted them with legions of dead leaves. "Yes, it must be beautiful," she said. "Would you like to go over it? There's still light enough upstairs."

I followed her up the unflinching, wagon-wide staircase to the gallery whence opened the thin fluted Elizabethan doors.

"Feel how they put the latch low down for the sake of the children." She swung a light door inward.

"By the way, where are they?" I asked. "I haven't even heard them to-day."

She did not answer at once. Then, "I can only hear them," she replied softly. "This is one of their rooms—everything ready, you see."

She pointed into a heavily-timbered room. There were little low gate tables and children's chairs. A doll's house, its hooked front half open, faced a great dappled rocking-horse, from whose padded saddle it was but a child's scramble to the broad window-seat overlooking the lawn. A toy gun lay in a corner beside a gilt wooden cannon.

"Surely they've only just gone," I whispered. In the failing light a door creaked cautiously. I heard the rustle of a frock and the patter of feet— quick feet through a room beyond.

"I heard that," she cried triumphantly. "Did you? Children, O children, where are you?"

The voice filled the walls that held it lovingly to the last perfect note, but there came no answering shout such as I had heard in the garden. We hurried on from room to oak-floored room; up a step here, down three steps there; among a maze of passages; always mocked by our quarry. One might as well have tried to work an unstopped warren with a single ferret. There were bolt-holes innumerable—recesses in walls, embrasures of deep slitten windows now darkened, whence they could start up behind us; and abandoned fireplaces, six feet deep in the masonry, as well as the tangle of communicating doors. Above all, they had the twilight for their helper in our game. I had caught one or two joyous chuckles of evasion, and once or twice had seen the silhouette of a child's frock against some darkening window at the end of a passage; but we returned empty-handed to the gallery, just as a middle-aged woman was setting a lamp in its niche.

"No, I haven't seen her either this evening, Miss Florence," I heard her say, "but that Turpin he says he wants to see you about his shed."

"Oh, Mr. Turpin must want to see me very badly. Tell him to come to the hall, Mrs. Madden."

I looked down into the hall whose only light was the dulled fire, and deep in the shadow I saw them at last. They must have slipped down while we were in the passages, and now thought themselves perfectly hidden behind an old gilt leather screen. By child's law, my fruitless chase was as good as an introduction, but since I had taken so much trouble I resolved to force them to come forward later by the simple trick, which children detest, of pretending not to notice them. They lay close, in a little huddle, no more than shadows except when a quick flame betrayed an outline.

"And now we'll have some tea," she said. "I believe I ought to have offered it you at first, but one doesn't arrive at manners somehow when one lives alone and is considered—h'm—peculiar." Then with very pretty scorn, "would you like a lamp to see to eat by?" "The firelight's much pleasanter, I think." We descended into that delicious gloom and Madden brought tea.

I took my chair in the direction of the screen ready to surprise or be surprised as the game should go, and at her permission, since a hearth is always sacred, bent forward to play with the fire.

"Where do you get these beautiful short faggots from?" I asked idly. "Why, they are tallies!"

"Of course," she said. "As I can't read or write I'm driven back on the early English tally for my accounts. Give me one and I'll tell you what it meant."

I passed her an unburned hazel-tally, about a foot long, and she ran her thumb down the nicks.

"This is the milk-record for the home farm for the month of April last year, in gallons," said she. "I don't know what I should have done without tallies. An old forester of mine taught me the system. It's out of date now for every one else; but my tenants respect it. One of them's coming now to see me. Oh, it doesn't matter. He has no business here out of office hours. He's a greedy, ignorant man—very greedy or—he wouldn't come here after dark."

"Have you much land then?"

"Only a couple of hundred acres in hand, thank goodness. The other six hundred are nearly all let to folk who knew my folk before me, but this Turpin is quite a new man—and a highway robber."

"But are you sure I sha'n't be——?"

"Certainly not. You have the right. He hasn't any children."

"Ah, the children!" I said, and slid my low chair back till it nearly touched the screen that hid them. "I wonder whether they'll come out for me."

There was a murmur of voices—Madden's and a deeper note—at the low, dark side door, and a ginger-headed, canvas-gaitered giant of the unmistakable tenant farmer type stumbled or was pushed in.

"Come to the fire, Mr. Turpin," she said.

"If—if you please, Miss, I'll—I'll be quite as well by the door." He clung to the latch as he spoke like a frightened child. Of a sudden I realised that he was in the grip of some almost overpowering fear.

"Well?"

"About that new shed for the young stock—that was all. These first autumn storms settin' in ... but I'll come again, Miss." His teeth did not chatter much more than the door latch.

"I think not," she answered levelly. "The new shed—m'm. What did my agent write you on the 15th?"

"I—fancied p'raps that if I came to see you—ma—man to man like, Miss.

But— —"

His eyes rolled into every corner of the room wide with horror. He half opened the door through which he had entered, but I noticed it shut again — from without and firmly.

"He wrote what I told him," she went on. "You are overstocked already. Dunnett's Farm never carried more than fifty bullocks—even in Mr. Wright's time. And he used cake. You've sixty-seven and you don't cake. You've broken the lease in that respect. You're dragging the heart out of the farm."

"I'm—I'm getting some minerals—superphosphates—next week. I've as good as ordered a truck-load already. I'll go down to the station to-morrow about 'em. Then I can come and see you man to man like, Miss, in the daylight.... That gentleman's not going away, is he?" He almost shrieked.

I had only slid the chair a little further back, reaching behind me to tap on the leather of the screen, but he jumped like a rat.

"No. Please attend to me, Mr. Turpin." She turned in her chair and faced him with his back to the door. It was an old and sordid little piece of scheming that she forced from him—his plea for the new cowshed at his landlady's expense, that he might with the covered manure pay his next year's rent out of the valuation after, as she made clear, he had bled the enriched pastures to the bone. I could not but admire the intensity of his greed, when I saw him out-facing for its sake whatever terror it was that ran wet on his forehead.

I ceased to tap the leather—was, indeed, calculating the cost of the shed—when I felt my relaxed hand taken and turned softly between the soft hands of a child. So at last I had triumphed. In a moment I would turn and acquaint myself with those quick-footed wanderers....

The little brushing kiss fell in the centre of my palm—as a gift on which the fingers were, once, expected to close: as the all faithful half- reproachful signal of a waiting child not used to neglect even when grown-ups were busiest—a fragment of the mute code devised very long ago.

Then I knew. And it was as though I had known from the first day when I looked across the lawn at the high window.

I heard the door shut. The woman turned to me in silence, and I felt that she knew.

What time passed after this I cannot say. I was roused by the fall of a log, and mechanically rose to put it back. Then I returned to my place in the chair very close to the screen.

"Now you understand," she whispered, across the packed shadows.

"Yes, I understand—now. Thank you."

"I—I only hear them." She bowed her head in her hands. "I have no right, you know—no other right. I have neither borne nor lost—neither borne nor lost!"

"Be very glad then," said I, for my soul was torn open within me.

"Forgive me!"

She was still, and I went back to my sorrow and my joy.

"It was because I loved them so," she said at last, brokenly. "That was why it was, even from the first—even before I knew that they—they were all I should ever have. And I loved them so!"

She stretched out her arms to the shadows and the shadows within the shadow.

"They came because I loved them—because I needed them. I—I must have made them come. Was that wrong, think you?"

"No—no."

"I—I grant you that the toys and—and all that sort of thing were nonsense, but—but I used to so hate empty rooms myself when I was little." She pointed to the gallery. "And the passages all empty. ... And how could I ever bear the garden door shut? Suppose——"

"Don't! For pity's sake, don't!" I cried. The twilight had brought a cold rain with gusty squalls that plucked at the leaded windows.

"And the same thing with keeping the fire in all night. I don't think it so foolish—do you?"

I looked at the broad brick hearth, saw, through tears I believe, that there was no unpassable iron on or near it, and bowed my head.

"I did all that and lots of other things—just to make believe. Then they came. I heard them, but I didn't know that they were not mine by right till Mrs. Madden told me——"

"The butler's wife? What?"

"One of them—I heard—she saw. And knew. Hers! Not for me. I didn't know at first. Perhaps I was jealous. Afterwards, I began to understand that it was only because I loved them, not because——... Oh, you must bear or lose," she said piteously. "There is no other way—and yet they love me. They must! Don't they?"

There was no sound in the room except the lapping voices of the fire, but we two listened intently, and she at least took comfort from what she heard. She recovered herself and half rose. I sat still in my chair by the screen.

"Don't think me a wretch to whine about myself like this, but—but I'm all in the dark, you know, and you can see."

In truth I could see, and my vision confirmed me in my resolve, though that was like the very parting of spirit and flesh. Yet a little longer I would stay since it was the last time.

"You think it is wrong, then?" she cried sharply, though I had said nothing.

"Not for you. A thousand times no. For you it is right.... I am grateful to you beyond words. For me it would be wrong. For me only...."

"Why?" she said, but passed her hand before her face as she had done at our second meeting in the wood. "Oh, I see," she went on simply as a child. "For you it would be wrong." Then with a little indrawn laugh, "and, d'you remember, I called you lucky—once—at first. You who must never come here again!"

She left me to sit a little longer by the screen, and I heard the sound of her feet die out along the gallery above.

A DEAD MAN'S FACE

Hugh Conway, 1884

IMAGINATIVE beings who invent marvelous tales may take what license they please, but a simple narrator is nothing if not accurate ; so, before beginning this, I looked up old correspondences and various memoranda made at the time when the following things occurred. The first paper upon which I put my hand was a letter. I may as well open with a copy of it:

" Dear Old Boy. — I have met her at last— my fate — the one woman in the world for me. Nothing is settled as yet; but I should not write this unless hope were a certainty. You must wish me joy, although she is a widow and an American — two qualifications which I know you will find fault with. No matter; when you see her you will recant and be envious. Yours ever,

"Claud Morton."

The writer was my brother — I was going to say my only brother, but I had another once, although the less said about him the better. Nearly every family has its black sheep. Ours had been a peculiarly sable one. When he died, some years ago, I passed a sponge over his long list of delinquencies, and tried to think of him as kindly as possible. He died a disgraced man, far away from home.

I call this black sheep, Stephen, my brother, not Claud's, the fact being that Claud can scarcely be said to have known him. I stood in age midway between the two. Claud was sixteen years younger than Stephen, so that when the latter was shipped off as irreclaimable, the former was a little golden-haired fellow of seven.

The above letter made me feel both glad and sorry. I was glad that the boy — he was still the boy to me, although his age was seven-and-twenty — was going to be married; but I was sorry that his choice had not fallen on one of his own countrywomen, and one who could have given him her first love. Still, all this was his own peculiar business. No doubt he had made a suitable choice, and the only thing left for me to do was to write him a cheerful letter of congratulation, and hope that his love affairs would soon be happily settled.

A week went by; then came a long letter from him. He had proposed in orthodox form, and had been duly accepted. His letter lies before me at this moment, and I feel sad as I read again the two pages covered with the lover's usual raptures.

I am not a mercenary man, but I own I felt somewhat disappointed on learning that she was poor. Somehow one associates wealth with an American widow who is sojourning in England. But, so far as I could gather from Claud's letter, Mrs. Despard, or Judith, as he called her, was not well off. He spoke of her as being all alone in London, which fact, he added, would necessarily hasten his marriage. It would take place, he hoped, in a week or two. In conclusion he pressed me to run up to town in order to make the acquaintance of my future sister-in-law.

I was very busy at the time — I may say, in passing, that my business is to cure people's ailments, not to tell stories — nevertheless! managed to pay a flying visit to town, and was duly presented to Claud's betrothed.

Yes, she was handsome — strikingly handsome. Her whole appearance was much out of the common. She was tall, superbly built, on a large scale, perhaps, yet graceful as a panther in every movement. Her face gave evidence of much character, power, and determination, and of passion also, I decided. Her rich dark beauty was at that time in full bloom, and although I saw at a glance that she was some years older than my brother, I was not at all inclined to blame Claud for his rapturous expressions. So far as personal charms went, I could find no fault with Judith Despard. For the rest it was easy to see that she was passionately in love with Claud, and for the sake of this I gladly overlooked all my fanciful objections to his choice, and congratulated him heartily on having won so beautiful a creature.

Yet, strange to say, in the midst of his newfound happiness my brother seemed any thing but his usual cheerful self. He, the merriest and most talkative of men, seemed taciturn, moody and preoccupied. The curious thing was that his changed manner struck me particularly while we were in Mrs. Despard's company. He spoke and behaved in the most affectionate and lover-like way, but there was in his general bearing something which puzzled me altogether. It seemed to me that he might perhaps be nervous as to what impression his fair friend might make upon the elder brother whom he so reverenced and respected.

This theory of mine was strengthened by the fact that when, at night, we found ourselves alone and I was able to freely express my admiration of Mrs. Despard's good looks, he brightened up considerably, and we sat until a very late hour, and talked over the past, the present and the future.

"When do you mean to be married?" I asked.

"In a fortnight or three weeks. There is nothing to wait for. Judith is living alone in lodgings. She has no friends to consult, so we shall just walk to church some morning and get it over."

" Well, let me walk with you. I should like to see the last of you."

" All right, old fellow. But you'll be the only one — unless Mary likes to honor us."

Mary was my wife; but as her time was just then fully occupied by a very young baby, I did not think it at all likely she would be able to make the long journey to town.

"I shall fix the earliest day I can," added Claud. "The fact is, I have been feeling rather queer lately. I want a change."

Thereupon I questioned him as to what ailed him. So far as I could ascertain, all that was the matter was his having worked too hard, and being a little below par. I prescribed a tonic, and quite agreed with him as to the benefit which he would derive from change of air.

When I reached home my wife scolded me for my stupidity. It seems that it was my duty to have found out all about Mrs. Despard's antecedents, relations, connections, circumstances, habits and disposition, whereas all I could say was that she was a beautiful widow with a small income and that she and Claud were devoted to each other.

"Yes," said Mrs. Morton, scornfully, " like all other men, the moment you see a pretty face you inquire no further. I quite tremble for Claud." When I reflected how little I really knew about Mrs. Despard, I felt abashed and guilty. However, Claud was a full-grown man, and no fraternal counsel was likely to turn him aside from his desire.

In the course of a few days he wrote me that he was to be married on the 5th of the next month. I made arrangements which would enable me to go to the wedding; but three days before the date named I heard again from him. The wedding was postponed for a fortnight. He gave no reason for the delay ; but he said he was anxious to see me, and to-morrow he should run down to my home.

He came as promised. I was aghast when I saw him. He looked worn, haggard, wretched. My first thought was that business had gone wrong with him. His looks might well be those of a man on the brink of ruin. After the first greeting I at once took him to my study in order to be put out of suspense. Just as I was about to begin my anxious questions he turned to me.

"Frank, old fellow," he said, imploringly, and with a faint attempt at a smile, " don't laugh at me.

Laugh! That was the last thing I was likely to do. I pressed his hand in silence.

"You won't believe me, I know," he continued.
"I can't believe it myself. Frank, I am haunted."

"Haunted I" I was bound to smile, not from any disposition toward merriment, but in order to show the poor boy the absurdity of his idea.

"Yes, haunted. The word sounds ridiculous, but I can use no other. Haunted."

"What haunts you ?"

He came close to me and grasped my arm. His voice sank to a hoarse whisper.

"A horrible, ghastly, grewsome thing. It is killing me. It comes between me and my happiness. I have fought and struggled against this phantom terror. I have reasoned calmly with myself. I have laughed my own folly to scorn. In vain — in vain. It goes, but it comes again."

"Overwork," I said, "insomnia, too many cigars, late hours ; and had you been a drinking man I should add, too much stimulant, too little food, anxiety, perhaps. Have you any thing on your mind — any special worry?"

" Of course I have," he said, pettishly. " Did I not tell you it is killing me?"

"What is killing you?"

He rose and paced the room excitedly; then suddenly he stopped short, and once more clutched my arm.

"A face," he said, wildly — "a man's face; a fearful white face that comes to me; a horrible mask, with features drawn as in agony — ghastly, pale, hideous! Death or approaching death, violent death, written in every line. Every feature distorted. Eyes starting from the head. Every cord in the throat standing out, strained as by mortal struggle. Long dark hair lying flat and wet. Thin lips moving and working — lips that are cursing, although I hear no sound. Why should this come to me — why to me? Who is this dead man whose face wrecks my life? Frank, my brother, if this is disease or madness, cure me; if not, let me die."

His words, his gestures, sent a cold thrill through me. He was worse, far worse, than I had feared.

"Claud," I said, "you are talking nonsense. Cure you! of course I mean to cure you. Now sit down, collect yourself, and tell me how this hallucination comes."

"Comes! How does it come? It gathers in corners of the room; it forms and takes shape; it glares at me out of the wall; it looks up at me from the floor. Ever the same fearful white dying face, threatening, cursing, sometimes mocking. Why does it come?"

I had already told the poor fellow why it came, but it was no use repeating my words. "Tell me when you see it, "I asked; "at night — in darkness?"

He hesitated, and seemed troubled. " No, never at night. In broad daylight only. That to me IS the crowning terror, the ghastliness of it. At night I could call it a dream. Frank, believe me, I am no weak fool. For weeks I have borne with this. At last it has conquered me. Send it away, or I shall go mad!"

"I'll send it away, old boy, never fear. Tell me: can you see it now?"

" No; thank God, not now."

"Have you seen it to-day?"

"No; today I have been free from it."

"Well, you'll be free from it to-morrow, and the next day, and the next. It will be gone forever before you leave me. Now come and see Mary and the babies. I haven't even asked you how Mrs. Despard is."

A curious look crossed his face. " I think she grows more beautiful every day," he said. Then he seized my hand. " Oh, Frank," he exclaimed, "rid me of this horror, and I shall be the happiest man in the world."

"All right," I answered, perhaps with more confidence than I felt.

Although I made light of it to my patient, his state greatly alarmed me. I hastened to put him under the strictest and most approved treatment. I enforced the most rigid sumptuary laws, made him live on plain food, and docked his consumption of tobacco unmercifully. In a few days I was delighted to find that my diagnosis of the case was correct. Claud was rapidly recovering tone. In a week's time he seemed restored to health.

The days went by. As yet Claud had said nothing about leaving me; yet, unless the date was once more adjourned, he was to be married on the 19th. I did not counsel him to postpone the happy day. He was by now so well that I thought he could not do better than adhere to his arrangement. A month's holiday, spent in the society of the woman he loved, would, I felt certain, complete his cure, and banish forever that grisly intruder begotten of disorganized nerves.

From the monotonous regularity and voluminous nature of their correspondence it was evident, delay and separation notwithstanding, that matters were going on quite smoothly between Claud and Judith Despard. Every day he received and wrote a long letter. Nevertheless, it was not until the 16th of the month that I knew exactly what he meant to do about his marriage.

"Frank," he said, " you have been wonderfully kind to me. I believe you have saved my life, or at least my reason. Will you do something more for me?"

" Even unto half my kingdom," I answered.

"Look here: I am ashamed of the feeling, but I absolutely dread returning to town. At any rate I wish to stay there no longer than is needful. Thursday morning I must, of course, be there, to be married. You think me cured, Frank?" he added, abruptly.

"Honestly, yes. If you take care of yourself you will be troubled no more."

"Yet why do I dread London so? Well, nevermind. I will go up by the night mail on Wednesday — then I need only be there for a few hours. Will you do this for me — go up on Wednesday morning, see Judith, and explain how it is that I shall not see her until we meet in the church?"

"Certainly, if you wish it. But you had better write as well."

"Yes, I shall do that. There are several other little things you must see to for me. The license I have, but you must let the clergyman know. You had better go and see my partners. They may think it strange if I marry and go away without a word."

Thinking it better that he should have his own way, I promised to do as he wished. Upon my arrival in town on Wednesday afternoon I went straight to Mrs. Despard's. I was not sorry to have this opportunity of seeing her alone. I wished to urge upon her the necessity of being careful that Claud did not again get into that highly wrought nervous state, from which my treatment had so happily extricated him.

She was not looking so well as when last I saw her. At times her manner was restless, and she seemed striving to suppress agitation. She made no adverse comments on her lover's strange whim of reaching town to-morrow only in time for the ceremony. Her inquiries as to his health were most solicitous, and when 1 told her that I no longer feared any thing on his account, her heartfelt sigh of relief told me how deeply she loved him.

Presently she looked me full in the face. Her eyes were half closed, but I could see an anxious, eager look in them. "He saw a face," she said. "Has it left him?"

"He told you of his queer hallucination, then?"

"No; but once or twice when sitting with me he sprang to his feet and muttered: "0h, that face! that ghastly, horrible face! I can bear it no longer!" Then he rushed wildly from the room. What face did he see, Dr. Morton?"

To set her mind at rest, I gave her a little scientific discourse, which explained to her how such mental phenomena were brought about. She listened attentively, and seemed satisfied. Then I bade her adieu until to-morrow.

The marriage was to be of the quiet kind. I found that Mrs. Despard had made no arrangement for any friend to accompany her; so, setting all rules of etiquette at defiance, I suggested that, although the bridegroom's brother, I should call for her in the morning and conduct her to the church. To this she readily consented.

Somehow that evening I did not carry away such a pleasing impression of my brother's bride as I did when first I met her. I can give no reason for this, except that I was not forgetful of my wife's accusation, that when first I met Judith Despard I had been carried away by the glamour of her beauty, and thought of nothing else. As I walked to Claud's rooms, which I occupied for the night, I almost regretted that he had been so hasty — certainly I wished that we knew more of his bride. But it was now too late for regrets or wishes.

I called for Mrs. Despard at the appointed hour, and found her quite ready to start. Her dress was plain and simple — I cannot describe it; but I saw that in spite of her excessive pallor she looked very beautiful. In the carriage on our way to the church she was very silent, answering my remarks with monosyllables. I left her in peace, supposing that at such a moment every woman must be more or less agitated.

When the carriage drew up at the church door, the bride laid her hand upon my arm. I could feel that she was trembling. "Claud will be here?" she asked. "Nothing will stop him?"

"Nothing. But I may as well step out and see that he is waiting."

Yes, Claud was in the church waiting for us. We exchanged greetings. The old sexton summoned the curate; and Judith Despard, my brother, and myself walked up to the altar rails.

Claud looked very well that morning ; a little fagged perhaps, but the long night journey would account for that. He certainly looked proud and happy as he stood on the altar step side by side with the woman who in a few minutes would be his wife.

But before the curate had finished reading the opening address a great change came over him. From where I was standing I could see only his side face, but that was enough to show me that he was suffering from some agitation — something far above the nervousness so often displayed by a bridegroom. A deadly pallor came over his face, small beads of perspiration sprang to his brow, and I noticed that those tell-tales of mental disturbance, the hands, were so tightly clinched that the knuckles grew white. It was evident that he was suffering anguish of some kind, and for a moment I thought of stopping the service. But the rite is but a short one, and from whatever cause Claud's agitation might proceed, it was perhaps better to trust to him to curb it for a few moments than to make a scene. Nevertheless I watched him intently and anxiously.

Then came the charge to declare any impediment. As the curate made the conventional pause, Claud, to my surprise, glanced round in a startled way, as if fearing that his marriage would at the last moment be forbidden. The look on his face was now one of actual terror.

Both bride and bridegroom said their "I wills" in such low tones that I could scarcely hear their voices. Then, in pursuance of my duty, I gave the woman to the priest. He joined the hands of Claud and Judith.

After having played my little part I had not moved back to my former station. I was now close to the bride, and as Claud turned to her, could see his face to advantage. It was positively distorted with suppressed emotion of some kind. His mouth was set, and I could see that his teeth were closed on his under lip. He did not look at his fair bride. His gaze passed over her shoulder. In fact, he seemed almost oblivious to her presence. I was dreadfully frightened.

The clergyman's voice rang out: "I, Claud, take thee, Judith, to my wedded wife." Then, hearing no echo of his words, he paused.

"Repeat after me," he prompted. Again he began, " I, Claud—"

But his voice was drowned in a louder one, which rang through the empty church. With a fierce cry, as of inexpressible rage, Claud had thrown the bride's hand from him, and was pointing and gesticulating toward the wall, upon which his eyes had been riveted.

"Here! — even here!" he almost shrieked. "That cursed, white, wicked, dying face! Whose is it! Why does it come between me and my love! Mad! Mad! I am going mad!"

I heeded not the clergyman's look of dismay, or the bride's cry of distress. I thought of nothing but my unfortunate brother. Here, at the moment which should be the happiest he had yet known, the grewsome hallucination had come back to him. I threw my arm round him and tried to calm him.

"It is fancy, dear boy," I said. "In a moment
it will be gone."

"Gone! Why does it come? What have I to do with this dying man? Look, Frank, look! Something tells me if you look you will see it. There! there! Look there!

His eyes were ever fixed on the same point. He grasped my arm convulsively. I am ashamed to say that I yielded, and looked in the direction of his gaze.

"There is nothing there," I said, soothingly.

"Look!" he exclaimed. "It will come to you as to me."

It may have been the hope of convincing Claud of the illusionary nature of the sight which tormented him, it may have been some strange fascination, wrought by his words and manner, which made me for some moments gaze with him. God of heaven! I saw gradually forming out of nothing, gathering on the blank wall in front of me, a face, or the semblance of a face, white, ghastly, horrible! Long, dank, wet-looking dark hair, eyes starting from their sockets, lips working — the whole appearance that of the face of a man who is struggling with death : in every detail as Claud had described it. And yet to me that face was more terrible than ever it could be to Claud.

I gazed in horror. I felt my eyes growing riveted to the sight as his own. I felt my whole frame trembling. I knew that in another moment I should be raving as wildly as he raved. Only his hoarse whisper recalled me to my senses.

"You see?" he asked, or rather asserted.

Horror forced the truth from me. "I see, or fancy I see," I answered.

With a wild laugh Claud broke from me. He rushed down the church and disappeared. As he left me, the face, thank Heaven! faded from the wall, or from my imagination.

I turned to my companions. Judith Despard was lying in a dead swoon on the altar steps; the curate with trembling hands was loosening the throat of her dress. I called for water. The sexton brought it. I bathed the poor woman's temples, and in a few minutes she sighed, opened her eyes, and then shuddered. I took her in my arms and staggered to the church door. The curate removed his surplice and followed me. I placed my almost senseless burden in the carriage.

"For Heaven's sake, see her home," I said to the curate. " I must go and look after my brother. As soon as I have seen him I will come round to Mrs. Despard's. Get her home quickly. The coachman knows where to go."

The brougham drove off. I threw myself into a cab, and drove toward Claud's rooms. I hoped he might have gone straight there.

To my great relief, when I reached his house he was on the door-step. We entered his room together ; he sank wearily into a chair, and buried his face in his hands. I was scarcely less agitated than himself, and my face, as I caught its reflection in the mirror, was as white as his own. I waited for him to speak.

Presently he raised his head. "Go to her," he said. " Ask her why that face comes between us. You saw it — even you. It can be no fancy of mine. Tell her we can meet no more."

" I will wait until you are calmer before I go."

"Calm! I am myself now. The thing has left me, as it always does. Frank, I have hidden from you one peculiarity of my state. That awful face never shows itself to me unless I am in her company. Even at the altar it came between us. Go to her; ask her why it comes."

I left him, but did not quit the house for some time. I went into an adjoining room and tried to collect my thoughts; for, as I said, my mind was more troubled than even Claud's could be.

I am ashamed to re-assert it; I am willing to own that excitement, my brother's impressive manner, superstition which I did not know I possessed — any thing that may bear a natural explanation — may have raised that vision. But why should that phantom, gathering and growing from nothing until it attained to form, or at least semblance, have been the face of one I had known? Why should the features distorted in deadly- agony have been those of my brother Stephen? For his was the dreadful face which Claud's prompting or my own imagination had raised.

Almost like one in a dream I went to do Claud's bidding. I was thankful, upon reaching Mrs. Despard's, to find that she had gone to her room, and left word that she could see no one to-day. This gave me time to consider the position.

Acting on a sudden impulse, I went to the telegraph office, and sent instructions to my wife to forward to me, by passenger train, a small box in which I kept old letters and papers. Then I went back to Claud, and after some persuasion induced him to leave town at once. I told him I would arrange every thing on the morrow. He was better away.

In the morning my box arrived. In it I found what I wanted. After the calming effects of a night's rest I felt ashamed of my weakness as I drew from old letters a photograph of my brother Stephen — one taken about two years before the report of his death reached us. Nevertheless I put the portrait in my pocket, and about noon went to Mrs. Despard's.

I was at once admitted, and in a few minutes she came to me. She looked worn and haggard, as if sleep had not visited her for nights. Dark circles had formed round her fine eyes; lines seemed to have deepened round her firm, passionate mouth. She advanced eagerly toward me and held out her hand. I took it in silence. Indeed, I scarcely knew what to say or how to act.

"Where is Claud?" she asked., in a quick voice, but scarcely above a whisper.

"He has left town for a few days."

She pressed her hand to her heart. "Does that mean I shall see him no more?"

"I am afraid I must say it does. He thinks it better you should part."

She gave a sharp cry, and walked up and down the room wringing her hands. Her lips moved rapidly, and I knew she was muttering many words, but in so low a key that I could not catch their meaning. Suddenly she stopped, and turned upon me fiercely.

"Is this by your council and advice?" she demanded.

"No. It is his own unbiassed decision."

"Why? — tell me why? He loved me — I love him. Why does he leave me?"

The passionate entreaty of her voice is indescribable. What could I say to her? Words stuck in my throat. It seemed the height of absurdity for a sane man to give a sane woman the true reason for Claud's broken faith. I stammered out something about his bad state of health.

"If he is ill, I will nurse him," she cried. "I will wait for years if he will give me hope. Dr. Morton, I love Claud as I never before loved a man."

She clasped her hands and looked imploringly into my face. In a mechanical way I drew the portrait of my dead brother from my breast. She saw the action.

"His likeness!" she cried, joyfully. "He sends it to me! Ah, he loves me!"

I handed her the photograph. "Mrs. Despard," I asked, " do you know — "

I did not finish the question, yet it was fully answered. Never, I believe, save then did a human face undergo such a sudden, frightful change. The woman's very lips grew ashen, her eyes glared into mine, and I saw them full of dread. She staggered — all but fell.

"Why is it here — who is it?" she gasped out.

I was a prey to the wildest excitement. To what revelation was this tending? what awful thing had I to learn?

"Listen," I said, sternly. "Woman, it is for you to answer the question. It is the face of this man, his dying face, that comes between you and your lover."

"Tell me his name." I read rather than heard the words her dry lips formed.

"The name he was once known by was Stanley."

A quick, sharp shudder ran through her. For a moment I thought she was going to faint.

"He is dead," she said. "Why does he come between my love and me? Others have loved or said they loved me since then. They saw no dead faces. Had I loved them I might have married and been happy. Claud I love. Why does the dead man trouble him?"

"That man," I replied, "was my brother — Claud's brother."

She threw out her arms with a gesture of utter despair. "Your brother — Claud's brother!" she repeated. Then she fixed her eyes on mine as if she would read the secrets of my soul.

"You are lying," she said.

"I am not. He was our eldest brother. He left England years ago. He passed under a false name. He died. When and how did he die?"

She sank, a dead weight, into a chair; but still she looked at me like one under a spell. I seized her wrist.

"Tell me, woman," I cried — "tell me what this man was to you ; why his dying face comes to us? The truth — speak the truth."

She seemed to cower beneath my words, but her eyes were still on my face. " Speak!" I cried, fiercely, and tightening my grasp upon her wrist. At last she found words.

"He was my husband; I killed him," she said in a strange voice, low yet perfectly distinct.

I recoiled in horror. This woman, the widow and self-confessed murderess of one brother, within an ace of being the wife of the other!

"You murdered him?" I said, turning to the woman.

“I murdered him. He made my life a hell upon earth. He beat me, cursed me, ruined me. He was the foulest-hearted fiend that ever lived. I killed him."

No remorse, no regret in her words. Quite overcome, I leaned against the chimney-piece. Bad as I knew Stephen Morton to have been, I could at that moment only think of him as a gay, light-hearted school-boy, my elder brother, and in those days a perfect hero in my eyes. No wonder my heart was full of vengeance.

Yet even in the first flush of my rage I knew that I could do nothing. No human justice could be meted out to this woman. There was nothing to prove the truth of her self-accusation. She would escape scot-free.

"Would that I could avenge his death!" I said, sullenly.

She sprang to her feet. Her dark eyes blazed. "Avenged!" she cried. " Is it not doubly, trebly avenged? Has he not taken all I care for in life from me? Has he not taken my love from my side? Coward in life, coward in death. When I killed him I knew he would try to come back to me. He has tried for years. Ah, I was too strong for him. I could banish the face with which he strove to haunt me. I could forget. I could love. I could have been happy. Yet he has conquered at last. Not me — he could not conquer me — but the one I love. Oh, the coward is avenged!"

In spite of my feeling of abhorrence, I gazed on the speaker in amazement. Her words were not those of one who had committed a black crime, but of one who had suffered wrong. The strange, fanciful idea that the dead man had been trying to haunt her, but had been kept at bay by her strong will, was in my experience unprecedented. As I saw the agony of mind under which she was laboring, the thought came to me that perhaps her words were true, that my brother's death was this day avenged. I resolved to leave her. I could gain no good by prolonging the painful scene.

She was still pacing the room in fierce passion. Suddenly she stopped short, and in thrilling accents began to speak. It seemed as if she had forgotten my presence.

"See," she cried, "the river-bank — the dark rushing stream. Ah, we are all alone, side by side, far away from every one. Fool! if you could read my heart, would you walk so near to the giddy brink? Do you think the memory of the old love will stay my hand when the chance comes? Old love is dead: you beat it, cursed it to death ! How fast does the stream run? Can a strong man swim against it? Oh, if I could be sure — sure that one push would end it all and give me freedom! Once I longed for love — your love. Now I long for death — your death. Oh, brave, swift tide, are you strong enough to free me forever? Hark! I can hear the roar of the rapids in the distance. There is a deep fall from the river cliff; there are rocks. Fool! you stand at the very edge and look down. The moment is come. Ah!"

With her last exclamation she used a violent gesture, as if pushing something fiercely from her. She was, I knew, in her excitement, re-acting the tragedy.

"Free! free! free! " she cried, with a delirious, almost rapturous laugh, and clasped her hands. "Hold him, brave stream! Sweep him away. See! he swims; but he dare not swim with you. You are hurrying down to the rapids. He must face you, and wrestle with you for his life. Bear him down; keep him from me. If he masters you, he will land and kill me. Hold him fast, brave stream! Ha! his strength fails. He is swept away; he is under. No, I see him again. He turns his face to me. He knows I did it. With his last breath he is cursing me. His last breath! He is gone, gone forever! I am free!"

The changes in her voice, ranging from dread to tearful joy, her passionate words, her eloquent gestures, all these combined to bring the very scene before my eyes. I stood spell-bound, and even, as she described it, seemed to see the unfortunate man battling for dear life in the rushing stream, growing every moment weaker and weaker. As the woman's last wild exclamation — "Gone forever! I am free! " — rang through the room, I seemed to hear the cry of despair drowned as the waves closed over the wretched man's head. I knew every detail of my brother's fate.

I turned to leave the room. I longed to get away, and if possible to banish the events of the day from my mind. It was not given to me to be Stephen Morton's avenger.

My hand was on the door, when the woman sprang to my side. She grasped my arm and drew me back into the room.

"Look!" she whispered. "Do you see it! There! The face — that awful face! It has come at last to me. The dead man has conquered. There! look! His eyes glaring, his mouth mocking. Now it has once come, I shall see it always — always. Look!"

No, I was not doomed again to see or to fancy I saw that face. Its mission, so far as I was concerned, was at an end. But the look of concentrated horror which Judith Despard cast at the wall of the room beggars description. Then with a piteous cry she fell at my feet, and seemed to strive to make me shield her from something she dreaded. I raised her. She broke from my grasp, and again fell upon the floor, this time in paroxysms of madness.

My tale is ended. That night she was removed to a private lunatic asylum, where for three years she was kept at my expense. She died raving mad, and from inquiries I made I know that from the moment when it first appeared to her to the hour of her death the face of the man she had killed was ever with Judith Despard.

THE SCREAMING SKULL

F. Marion Crawford, 1911

I have often heard it scream. No, I am not nervous, I am not imaginative, and I never believed in ghosts, unless that thing is one. Whatever it is, it hates me almost as much as it hated Luke Pratt, and it screams at me.

If I were you, I would never tell ugly stories about ingenious ways of killing people, for you never can tell but that some one at the table may be tired of his or her nearest and dearest. I have always blamed myself for Mrs. Pratt's death, and I suppose I was responsible for it in a way, though heaven knows I never wished her anything but long life and happiness. If I had not told that story she might be alive yet. That is why the thing screams at me, I fancy.

She was a good little woman, with a sweet temper, all things considered, and a nice gentle voice; but I remember hearing her shriek once when she thought her little boy was killed by a pistol that went off, though every one was sure that it was not loaded. It was the same scream; exactly the same, with a sort of rising quaver at the end; do you know what I mean? Unmistakable.

The truth is, I had not realised that the doctor and his wife were not on good terms. They used to bicker a bit now and then when I was here, and I often noticed that little Mrs. Pratt got very red and bit her lip hard to keep her temper, while Luke grew pale and said the most offensive things. He was that sort when he was in the nursery, I remember, and afterward at school. He was my cousin, you know; that is how I came by this house; after he died, and his boy Charley was killed in South Africa, there were no relations left. Yes, it's a pretty little property, just the sort of thing for an old sailor like me who has taken to gardening.

One always remembers one's mistakes much more vividly than one's cleverest things, doesn't one? I've often noticed it. I was dining with the Pratts one night, when I told them the story that afterwards made so much difference. It was a wet night in November, and the sea was moaning. Hush!—if you don't speak you will hear it now....

Do you hear the tide? Gloomy sound, isn't it? Sometimes, about this time of year—hallo!—there it is! Don't be frightened, man—it won't eat you—it's only a noise, after all! But I'm glad you've heard it, because there are always people who think it's the wind, or my imagination, or something. You won't hear it again to-night, I fancy, for it doesn't often come more than once. Yes—that's right. Put another stick on the fire, and a little more stuff into that weak mixture you're so fond of. Do you remember old Blauklot the carpenter, on that German ship that picked us up when the Clontarf went to the bottom? We were hove to in a howling gale one night, as snug as you please, with no land within five hundred miles, and the ship coming up and falling off as regularly as clockwork—"Biddy te boor beebles ashore tis night, poys!" old Blauklot sang out, as he went off to his quarters with the sail-maker. I often think of that, now that I'm ashore for good and all.

Yes, it was on a night like this, when I was at home for a spell, waiting to take the Olympia out on her first trip—it was on the next voyage that she broke the record, you remember—but that dates it. Ninety-two was the year, early in November.

The weather was dirty, Pratt was out of temper, and the dinner was bad, very bad indeed, which didn't improve matters, and cold, which made it worse. The poor little lady was very unhappy about it, and insisted on making a Welsh rarebit on the table to counteract the raw turnips and the half-boiled mutton. Pratt must have had a hard day. Perhaps he had lost a patient. At all events, he was in a nasty temper.

"My wife is trying to poison me, you see!" he said. "She'll succeed some day." I saw that she was hurt, and I made believe to laugh, and said that Mrs. Pratt was much too clever to get rid of her husband in such a simple way; and then I began to tell them about Japanese tricks with spun glass and chopped horsehair and the like.

Pratt was a doctor, and knew a lot more than I did about such things, but that only put me on my mettle, and I told a story about a woman in Ireland who did for three husbands before any one suspected foul play.

Did you never hear that tale? The fourth husband managed to keep awake and caught her, and she was hanged. How did she do it? She drugged them, and poured melted lead into their ears through a little horn funnel when they were asleep.... No—that's the wind whistling. It's backing up to the southward again. I can tell by the sound. Besides, the other thing doesn't often come more than once in an evening even at this time of year—when it happened. Yes, it was in November. Poor Mrs. Pratt died suddenly in her bed not long after I dined here. I can fix the date, because I got the news in New York by the steamer that followed the Olympia when I took her out on her first trip. You had the Leofric the same year? Yes, I remember. What a pair of old buffers we are coming to be, you and I. Nearly fifty years since we were apprentices together on the Clontarf. Shall you ever forget old Blauklot? "Biddy te boor beebles ashore, poys!" Ha, ha! Take a little more, with all that water. It's the old Hulstkamp I found in the cellar when this house came to me, the same I brought Luke from Amsterdam five-and-twenty years ago. He had never touched a drop of it. Perhaps he's sorry now, poor fellow.

Where did I leave off? I told you that Mrs. Pratt died suddenly—yes. Luke must have been lonely here after she was dead, I should think; I came to see him now and then, and he looked worn and nervous, and told me that his practice was growing too heavy for him, though he wouldn't take an assistant on any account. Years went on, and his son was killed in South Africa, and after that he began to be queer. There was something about him not like other people. I believe he kept his senses in his profession to the end; there was no complaint of his having made bad mistakes in cases, or anything of that sort, but he had a look about him——

Luke was a red-headed man with a pale face when he was young, and he was never stout; in middle age he turned a sandy grey, and after his son died he grew thinner and thinner, till his head looked like a skull with parchment stretched over it very tight, and his eyes had a sort of glare in them that was very disagreeable to look at.

He had an old dog that poor Mrs. Pratt had been fond of, and that used to follow her everywhere. He was a bull-dog, and the sweetest tempered beast you ever saw, though he had a way of hitching his upper lip behind one of his fangs that frightened strangers a good deal. Sometimes, of an evening, Pratt and Bumble—that was the dog's name—used to sit and look at each other a long time, thinking about old times, I suppose, when Luke's wife used to sit in that chair you've got. That was always her place, and this was the doctor's, where I'm sitting. Bumble used to climb up by the footstool—he was old and fat by that time, and could not jump much, and his teeth were getting shaky. He would look steadily at Luke, and Luke looked steadily at the dog, his face growing more and more like a skull with two little coals for eyes; and after about five minutes or so, though it may have been less, old Bumble would suddenly begin to shake all over, and all on a sudden he would set up an awful howl, as if he had been shot, and tumble out of the easy-chair and trot away, and hide himself under the sideboard, and lie there making odd noises.

Considering Pratt's looks in those last months, the thing is not surprising, you know. I'm not nervous or imaginative, but I can quite believe he might have sent a sensitive woman into hysterics—his head looked so much like a skull in parchment.

At last I came down one day before Christmas, when my ship was in dock and I had three weeks off. Bumble was not about, and I said casually that I supposed the old dog was dead.

"Yes," Pratt answered, and I thought there was something odd in his tone even before he went on after a little pause. "I killed him," he said presently. "I could not stand it any longer."

I asked what it was that Luke could not stand, though I guessed well enough.

"He had a way of sitting in her chair and glaring at me, and then howling." Luke shivered a little. "He didn't suffer at all, poor old Bumble," he went on in a hurry, as if he thought I might imagine he had been cruel. "I put dionine into his drink to make him sleep soundly, and then I chloroformed him gradually, so that he could not have felt suffocated even if he was dreaming. It's been quieter since then."

I wondered what he meant, for the words slipped out as if he could not help saying them. I've understood since. He meant that he did not hear that noise so often after the dog was out of the way. Perhaps he thought at first that it was old Bumble in the yard howling at the moon, though it's not that kind of noise, is it? Besides, I know what it is, if Luke didn't. It's only a noise, after all, and a noise never hurt anybody yet. But he was much more imaginative than I am. No doubt there really is something about this place that I don't understand; but when I don't understand a thing, I call it a phenomenon, and I don't take it for granted that it's going to kill me, as he did. I don't understand everything, by long odds, nor do you, nor does any man who has been to sea. We used to talk of tidal waves, for instance, and we could not account for them; now we account for them by calling them submarine earthquakes, and we branch off into fifty theories, any one of which might make earthquakes quite comprehensible if we only knew what they are. I fell in with one of them once, and the inkstand flew straight up from the table against the ceiling of my cabin. The same thing happened to Captain Lecky—I dare say you've read about it in his "Wrinkles." Very good. If that sort of thing took place ashore, in this room for instance, a nervous person would talk about spirits and levitation and fifty things that mean nothing, instead of just quietly setting it down as a "phenomenon" that has not been explained yet. My view of that voice, you see.

Besides, what is there to prove that Luke killed his wife? I would not even suggest such a thing to any one but you. After all, there was nothing but the coincidence that poor little Mrs. Pratt died suddenly in her bed a few days after I told that story at dinner. She was not the only woman who ever died like that. Luke got the doctor over from the next parish, and they agreed that she had died of something the matter with her heart. Why not? It's common enough.

Of course, there was the ladle. I never told anybody about that, and it made me start when I found it in the cupboard in the bedroom. It was new, too—a little tinned iron ladle that had not been in the fire more than once or twice, and there was some lead in it that had been melted, and stuck to the bottom of the bowl, all grey, with hardened dross on it. But that proves nothing. A country doctor is generally a handy man, who does everything for himself, and Luke may have had a dozen reasons for melting a little lead in a ladle. He was fond of sea-fishing, for instance, and he may have cast a sinker for a night-line; perhaps it was a weight for the hall clock, or something like that. All the same, when I found it I had a rather queer sensation, because it looked so much like the thing I had described when I told them the story. Do you understand? It affected me unpleasantly, and I threw it away; it's at the bottom of the sea a mile from the Spit, and it will be jolly well rusted beyond recognising if it's ever washed up by the tide.

You see, Luke must have bought it in the village, years ago, for the man sells just such ladles still. I suppose they are used in cooking. In any case, there was no reason why an inquisitive housemaid should find such a thing lying about, with lead in it, and wonder what it was, and perhaps talk to the maid who heard me tell the story at dinner—for that girl married the plumber's son in the village, and may remember the whole thing.

You understand me, don't you? Now that Luke Pratt is dead and gone, and lies buried beside his wife, with an honest man's tombstone at his head, I should not care to stir up anything that could hurt his memory. They are both dead, and their son, too. There was trouble enough about Luke's death, as it was.

How? He was found dead on the beach one morning, and there was a coroner's inquest. There were marks on his throat, but he had not been robbed. The verdict was that he had come to his end "by the hands or teeth of some person or animal unknown," for half the jury thought it might have been a big dog that had thrown him down and gripped his windpipe, though the skin of his throat was not broken. No one knew at what time he had gone out, nor where he had been. He was found lying on his back above high-water mark, and an old cardboard bandbox that had belonged to his wife lay under his hand, open. The lid had fallen off. He seemed to have been carrying home a skull in the box—doctors are fond of collecting such things. It had rolled out and lay near his head, and it was a remarkably fine skull, rather small, beautifully shaped and very white, with perfect teeth. That is to say, the upper jaw was perfect, but there was no lower one at all, when I first saw it.

Yes, I found it here when I came. You see, it was very white and polished, like a thing meant to be kept under a glass case, and the people did not know where it came from, nor what to do with it; so they put it back into the bandbox and set it on the shelf of the cupboard in the best bedroom, and of course they showed it to me when I took possession. I was taken down to the beach, too, to be shown the place where Luke was found, and the old fisherman explained just how he was lying, and the skull beside him. The only point he could not explain was why the skull had rolled up the sloping sand toward Luke's head instead of rolling downhill to his feet. It did not seem odd to me at the time, but I have often thought of it since, for the place is rather steep. I'll take you there to-morrow if you like—I made a sort of cairn of stones there afterward.

When he fell down, or was thrown down—whichever happened—the bandbox struck the sand, and the lid came off, and the thing came out and ought to have rolled down. But it didn't. It was close to his head, almost touching it, and turned with the face toward it. I say it didn't strike me as odd when the man told me; but I could not help thinking about it afterward, again and again, till I saw a picture of it all when I closed my eyes; and then I began to ask myself why the plaguey thing had rolled up instead of down, and why it had stopped near Luke's head instead of anywhere else, a yard away, for instance.

You naturally want to know what conclusion I reached, don't you? None that at all explained the rolling, at all events. But I got something else into my head, after a time, that made me feel downright uncomfortable.

Oh, I don't mean as to anything supernatural! There may be ghosts, or there may not be. If there are, I'm not inclined to believe that they can hurt living people except by frightening them, and, for my part, I would rather face any shape of ghost than a fog in the Channel when it's crowded. No. What bothered me was just a foolish idea, that's all, and I cannot tell how it began, nor what made it grow till it turned into a certainty.

I was thinking about Luke and his poor wife one evening over my pipe and a dull book, when it occurred to me that the skull might possibly be hers, and I have never got rid of the thought since. You'll tell me there's no sense in it, no doubt; that Mrs. Pratt was buried like a Christian and is lying in the churchyard where they put her, and that it's perfectly monstrous to suppose her husband kept her skull in her old bandbox in his bedroom. All the same, in the face of reason, and common sense, and probability, I'm convinced that he did. Doctors do all sorts of queer things that would make men like you and me feel creepy, and those are just the things that don't seem probable, nor logical, nor sensible to us.

Then, don't you see?—if it really was her skull, poor woman, the only way of accounting for his having it is that he really killed her, and did it in that way, as the woman killed her husbands in the story, and that he was afraid there might be an examination some day which would betray him. You see, I told that too, and I believe it had really happened some fifty or sixty years ago. They dug up the three skulls, you know, and there was a small lump of lead rattling about in each one. That was what hanged the woman. Luke remembered that, I'm sure. I don't want to know what he did when he thought of it; my taste never ran in the direction of horrors, and I don't fancy you care for them either, do you? No. If you did, you might supply what is wanting to the story.

It must have been rather grim, eh? I wish I did not see the whole thing so distinctly, just as everything must have happened. He took it the night before she was buried, I'm sure, after the coffin had been shut, and when the servant girl was asleep. I would bet anything, that when he'd got it, he put something under the sheet in its place, to fill up and look like it. What do you suppose he put there, under the sheet?

I don't wonder you take me up on what I'm saying! First I tell you that I don't want to know what happened, and that I hate to think about horrors, and then I describe the whole thing to you as if I had seen it. I'm quite sure that it was her work-bag that he put there. I remember the bag very well, for she always used it of an evening; it was made of brown plush, and when it was stuffed full it was about the size of—you understand. Yes, there I am, at it again! You may laugh at me, but you don't live here alone, where it was done, and you didn't tell Luke the story about the melted lead. I'm not nervous, I tell you, but sometimes I begin to feel that I understand why some people are. I dwell on all this when I'm alone, and I dream of it, and when that thing screams—well, frankly, I don't like the noise any more than you do, though I should be used to it by this time.

I ought not to be nervous. I've sailed in a haunted ship. There was a Man in the Top, and two-thirds of the crew died of the West Coast fever inside of ten days after we anchored; but I was all right, then and afterward. I have seen some ugly sights, too, just as you have, and all the rest of us. But nothing ever stuck in my head in the way this does.

You see, I've tried to get rid of the thing, but it doesn't like that. It wants to be there in its place, in Mrs. Pratt's bandbox in the cupboard in the best bedroom. It's not happy anywhere else. How do I know that? Because I've tried it. You don't suppose that I've not tried, do you? As long as it's there it only screams now and then, generally at this time of year, but if I put it out of the house it goes on all night, and no servant will stay here twenty-four hours. As it is, I've often been left alone and have been obliged to shift for myself for a fortnight at a time. No one from the village would ever pass a night under the roof now, and as for selling the place, or even letting it, that's out of the question. The old women say that if I stay here I shall come to a bad end myself before long.

I'm not afraid of that. You smile at the mere idea that any one could take such nonsense seriously. Quite right. It's utterly blatant nonsense, I agree with you. Didn't I tell you that it's only a noise after all when you started and looked round as if you expected to see a ghost standing behind your chair?

I may be all wrong about the skull, and I like to think that I am—when I can. It may be just a fine specimen which Luke got somewhere long ago, and what rattles about inside when you shake it may be nothing but a pebble, or a bit of hard clay, or anything. Skulls that have lain long in the ground generally have something inside them that rattles, don't they? No, I've never tried to get it out, whatever it is; I'm afraid it might be lead, don't you see? And if it is, I don't want to know the fact, for I'd much rather not be sure. If it really is lead, I killed her quite as much as if I had done the deed myself. Anybody must see that, I should think. As long as I don't know for certain, I have the consolation of saying that it's all utterly ridiculous nonsense, that Mrs. Pratt died a natural death and that the beautiful skull belonged to Luke when he was a student in London. But if I were quite sure, I believe I should have to leave the house; indeed I do, most certainly. As it is, I had to give up trying to sleep in the best bedroom where the cupboard is.

You ask me why I don't throw it into the pond—yes, but please don't call it a "confounded bugbear"—it doesn't like being called names.

There! Lord, what a shriek! I told you so! You're quite pale, man. Fill up your pipe and draw your chair nearer to the fire, and take some more drink. Old Hollands never hurt anybody yet. I've seen a Dutchman in Java drink half a jug of Hulstkamp in a morning without turning a hair. I don't take much rum myself, because it doesn't agree with my rheumatism, but you are not rheumatic and it won't damage you. Besides, it's a very damp night outside. The wind is howling again, and it will soon be in the southwest; do you hear how the windows rattle? The tide must have turned too, by the moaning.

We should not have heard the thing again if you had not said that. I'm pretty sure we should not. Oh yes, if you choose to describe it as a coincidence, you are quite welcome, but I would rather that you should not call the thing names again, if you don't mind. It may be that the poor little woman hears, and perhaps it hurts her, don't you know? Ghost? No! You don't call anything a ghost that you can take in your hands and look at in broad daylight, and that rattles when you shake it. Do you, now? But it's something that hears and understands; there's no doubt about that.

I tried sleeping in the best bedroom when I first came to the house, just because it was the best and the most comfortable, but I had to give it up. It was their room, and there's the big bed she died in, and the cupboard is in the thickness of the wall, near the head, on the left. That's where it likes to be kept, in its bandbox. I only used the room for a fortnight after I came, and then I turned out and took the little room downstairs, next to the surgery, where Luke used to sleep when he expected to be called to a patient during the night.

I was always a good sleeper ashore; eight hours is my dose, eleven to seven when I'm alone, twelve to eight when I have a friend with me. But I could not sleep after three o'clock in the morning in that room—a quarter past, to be accurate—as a matter of fact, I timed it with my old pocket chronometer, which still keeps good time, and it was always at exactly seventeen minutes past three. I wonder whether that was the hour when she died?

It was not what you have heard. If it had been that I could not have stood it two nights. It was just a start and a moan and hard breathing for a few seconds in the cupboard, and it could never have waked me under ordinary circumstances, I'm sure. I suppose you are like me in that, and we are just like other people who have been to sea. No natural sounds disturb us at all, not all the racket of a square-rigger hove to in a heavy gale, or rolling on her beam ends before the wind. But if a lead pencil gets adrift and rattles in the drawer of your cabin table you are awake in a moment. Just so—you always understand. Very well, the noise in the cupboard was no louder than that, but it waked me instantly.

I said it was like a "start." I know what I mean, but it's hard to explain without seeming to talk nonsense. Of course you cannot exactly "hear" a person "start"; at the most, you might hear the quick drawing of the breath between the parted lips and closed teeth, and the almost imperceptible sound of clothing that moved suddenly though very slightly. It was like that.

You know how one feels what a sailing vessel is going to do, two or three seconds before she does it, when one has the wheel. Riders say the same of a horse, but that's less strange, because the horse is a live animal with feelings of its own, and only poets and landsmen talk about a ship being alive, and all that. But I have always felt somehow that besides being a steaming machine or a sailing machine for carrying weights, a vessel at sea is a sensitive instrument, and a means of communication between nature and man, and most particularly the man at the wheel, if she is steered by hand. She takes her impressions directly from wind and sea, tide and stream, and transmits them to the man's hand, just as the wireless telegraph picks up the interrupted currents aloft and turns them out below in the form of a message.

You see what I am driving at; I felt that something started in the cupboard, and I felt it so vividly that I heard it, though there may have been nothing to hear, and the sound inside my head waked me suddenly. But I really heard the other noise. It was as if it were muffled inside a box, as far away as if it came through a long-distance telephone; and yet I knew that it was inside the cupboard near the head of my bed. My hair did not bristle and my blood did not run cold that time. I simply resented being waked up by something that had no business to make a noise, any more than a pencil should rattle in the drawer of my cabin table on board ship. For I did not understand; I just supposed that the cupboard had some communication with the outside air, and that the wind had got in and was moaning through it with a sort of very faint screech. I struck a light and looked at my watch, and it was seventeen minutes past three. Then I turned over and went to sleep on my right ear. That's my good one; I'm pretty deaf with the other, for I struck the water with it when I was a lad in diving from the foretopsail yard. Silly thing to do, it was, but the result is very convenient when I want to go to sleep when there's a noise.

That was the first night, and the same thing happened again and several times afterward, but not regularly, though it was always at the same time, to a second; perhaps I was sometimes sleeping on my good ear, and sometimes not. I overhauled the cupboard and there was no way by which the wind could get in, or anything else, for the door makes a good fit, having been meant to keep out moths, I suppose; Mrs. Pratt must have kept her winter things in it, for it still smells of camphor and turpentine.

After about a fortnight I had had enough of the noises. So far I had said to myself that it would be silly to yield to it and take the skull out of the room. Things always look differently by daylight, don't they? But the voice grew louder—I suppose one may call it a voice—and it got inside my deaf ear, too, one night. I realised that when I was wide awake, for my good ear was jammed down on the pillow, and I ought not to have heard a fog-horn in that position. But I heard that, and it made me lose my temper, unless it scared me, for sometimes the two are not far apart. I struck a light and got up, and I opened the cupboard, grabbed the bandbox and threw it out of the window, as far as I could.

Then my hair stood on end. The thing screamed in the air, like a shell from a twelve-inch gun. It fell on the other side of the road. The night was very dark, and I could not see it fall, but I know it fell beyond the road. The window is just over the front door, it's fifteen yards to the fence, more or less, and the road is ten yards wide. There's a quickset hedge beyond, along the glebe that belongs to the vicarage.

I did not sleep much more that night. It was not more than half an hour after I had thrown the bandbox out when I heard a shriek outside—like what we've had to-night, but worse, more despairing, I should call it; and it may have been my imagination, but I could have sworn that the screams came nearer and nearer each time. I lit a pipe, and walked up and down for a bit, and then took a book and sat up reading, but I'll be hanged if I can remember what I read nor even what the book was, for every now and then a shriek came up that would have made a dead man turn in his coffin.

A little before dawn some one knocked at the front door. There was no mistaking that for anything else, and I opened my window and looked down, for I guessed that some one wanted the doctor, supposing that the new man had taken Luke's house. It was rather a relief to hear a human knock after that awful noise.

You cannot see the door from above, owing to the little porch. The knocking came again, and I called out, asking who was there, but nobody answered, though the knock was repeated. I sang out again, and said that the doctor did not live here any longer. There was no answer, but it occurred to me that it might be some old countryman who was stone deaf. So I took my candle and went down to open the door. Upon my word, I was not thinking of the thing yet, and I had almost forgotten the other noises. I went down convinced that I should find somebody outside, on the doorstep, with a message. I set the candle on the hall table, so that the wind should not blow it out when I opened. While I was drawing the old-fashioned bolt I heard the knocking again. It was not loud, and it had a queer, hollow sound, now that I was close to it, I remember, but I certainly thought it was made by some person who wanted to get in.

It wasn't. There was nobody there, but as I opened the door inward, standing a little on one side, so as to see out at once, something rolled across the threshold and stopped against my foot.

I drew back as I felt it, for I knew what it was before I looked down. I cannot tell you how I knew, and it seemed unreasonable, for I am still quite sure that I had thrown it across the road. It's a French window, that opens wide, and I got a good swing when I flung it out. Besides, when I went out early in the morning, I found the bandbox beyond the thickset hedge.

You may think it opened when I threw it, and that the skull dropped out; but that's impossible, for nobody could throw an empty cardboard box so far.

It's out of the question; you might as well try to fling a ball of paper twenty-five yards, or a blown bird's egg.

To go back, I shut and bolted the hall door, picked the thing up carefully, and put it on the table beside the candle. I did that mechanically, as one instinctively does the right thing in danger without thinking at all—unless one does the opposite. It may seem odd, but I believe my first thought had been that somebody might come and find me there on the threshold while it was resting against my foot, lying a little on its side, and turning one hollow eye up at my face, as if it meant to accuse me. And the light and shadow from the candle played in the hollows of the eyes as it stood on the table, so that they seemed to open and shut at me. Then the candle went out quite unexpectedly, though the door was fastened and there was not the least draught; and I used up at least half a dozen matches before it would burn again.

I sat down rather suddenly, without quite knowing why. Probably I had been badly frightened, and perhaps you will admit there was no great shame in being scared. The thing had come home, and it wanted to go upstairs, back to its cupboard. I sat still and stared at it for a bit, till I began to feel very cold; then I took it and carried it up and set it in its place, and I remember that I spoke to it, and promised that it should have its bandbox again in the morning.

You want to know whether I stayed in the room till daybreak? Yes, but I kept a light burning, and sat up smoking and reading, most likely out of fright; plain, undeniable fear, and you need not call it cowardice either, for that's not the same thing. I could not have stayed alone with that thing in the cupboard; I should have been scared to death, though I'm not more timid than other people. Confound it all, man, it had crossed the road alone, and had got up the doorstep and had knocked to be let in.

When the dawn came, I put on my boots and went out to find the bandbox. I had to go a good way round, by the gate near the highroad, and I found the box open and hanging on the other side of the hedge. It had caught on the twigs by the string, and the lid had fallen off and was lying on the ground below it. That shows that it did not open till it was well over; and if it had not opened as soon as it left my hand, what was inside it must have gone beyond the road too.

That's all. I took the box upstairs to the cupboard, and put the skull back and locked it up. When the girl brought me my breakfast she said she was sorry, but that she must go, and she did not care if she lost her month's wages. I looked at her, and her face was a sort of greenish, yellowish white. I pretended to be surprised, and asked what was the matter; but that was of no use, for she just turned on me and wanted to know whether I meant to stay in a haunted house, and how long I expected to live if I did, for though she noticed I was sometimes a little hard of hearing, she did not believe that even I could sleep through those screams again—and if I could, why had I been moving about the house and opening and shutting the front door, between three and four in the morning? There was no answering that, since she had heard me, so off she went, and I was left to myself. I went down to the village during the morning and found a woman who was willing to come and do the little work there is and cook my dinner, on condition that she might go home every night. As for me, I moved downstairs that day, and I have never tried to sleep in the best bedroom since. After a little while I got a brace of middle-aged Scotch servants from London, and things were quiet enough for a long time. I began by telling them that the house was in a very exposed position, and that the wind whistled round it a good deal in the autumn and winter, which had given it a bad name in the village, the Cornish people being inclined to superstition and telling ghost stories. The two hard-faced, sandy-haired sisters almost smiled, and they answered with great contempt that they had no great opinion of any Southern bogey whatever, having been in service in two English haunted houses, where they had never seen so much as the Boy in Gray, whom they reckoned no very particular rarity in Forfarshire.

They stayed with me several months, and while they were in the house we had peace and quiet. One of them is here again now, but she went away with her sister within the year. This one—she was the cook—married the sexton, who works in my garden. That's the way of it. It's a small village and he has not much to do, and he knows enough about flowers to help me nicely, besides doing most of the hard work; for though I'm fond of exercise, I'm getting a little stiff in the hinges. He's a sober, silent sort of fellow, who minds his own business, and he was a widower when I came here—Trehearn is his name, James Trehearn. The Scotch sisters would not admit that there was anything wrong about the house, but when November came they gave me warning that they were going, on the ground that the chapel was such a long walk from here, being in the next parish, and that they could not possibly go to our church. But the younger one came back in the spring, and as soon as the banns could be published she was married to James Trehearn by the vicar, and she seems to have had no scruples about hearing him preach since then. I'm quite satisfied, if she is! The couple live in a small cottage that looks over the churchyard.

I suppose you are wondering what all this has to do with what I was talking about. I'm alone so much that when an old friend comes to see me, I sometimes go on talking just for the sake of hearing my own voice. But in this case there is really a connection of ideas. It was James Trehearn who buried poor Mrs. Pratt, and her husband after her in the same grave, and it's not far from the back of his cottage. That's the connection in my mind, you see. It's plain enough. He knows something; I'm quite sure that he does, by his manner, though he's such a reticent beggar.

Yes, I'm alone in the house at night now, for Mrs. Trehearn does everything herself, and when I have a friend the sexton's niece comes in to wait on the table. He takes his wife home every evening in winter, but in summer, when there's light, she goes by herself. She's not a nervous woman, but she's less sure than she used to be that there are no bogies in England worth a Scotchwoman's notice. Isn't it amusing, the idea that Scotland has a monopoly of the supernatural? Odd sort of national pride, I call that, don't you?

That's a good fire, isn't it? When driftwood gets started at last there's nothing like it, I think. Yes, we get lots of it, for I'm sorry to say there are still a great many wrecks about here. It's a lonely coast, and you may have all the wood you want for the trouble of bringing it in. Trehearn and I borrow a cart now and then, and load it between here and the Spit. I hate a coal fire when I can get wood of any sort. A log is company, even if it's only a piece of a deck-beam or timber sawn off, and the salt in it makes pretty sparks. See how they fly, like Japanese hand-fireworks! Upon my word, with an old friend and a good fire and a pipe, one forgets all about that thing upstairs, especially now that the wind has moderated. It's only a lull, though, and it will blow a gale before morning.

You think you would like to see the skull? I've no objection. There's no reason why you shouldn't have a look at it, and you never saw a more perfect one in your life, except that there are two front teeth missing in the lower jaw.

Oh yes—I had not told you about the jaw yet. Trehearn found it in the garden last spring when he was digging a pit for a new asparagus bed. You know we make asparagus beds six or eight feet deep here. Yes, yes—I had forgotten to tell you that. He was digging straight down, just as he digs a grave; if you want a good asparagus bed made, I advise you to get a sexton to make it for you. Those fellows have a wonderful knack at that sort of digging.

Trehearn had got down about three feet when he cut into a mass of white lime in the side of the trench. He had noticed that the earth was a little looser there, though he says it had not been disturbed for a number of years. I suppose he thought that even old lime might not be good for asparagus, so he broke it out and threw it up. It was pretty hard, he says, in biggish lumps, and out of sheer force of habit he cracked the lumps with his spade as they lay outside the pit beside him; the jawbone of a skull dropped out of one of the pieces. He thinks he must have knocked out the two front teeth in breaking up the lime, but he did not see them anywhere. He's a very experienced man in such things, as you may imagine, and he said at once that the jaw had probably belonged to a young woman, and that the teeth had been complete when she died. He brought it to me, and asked me if I wanted to keep it; if I did not, he said he would drop it into the next grave he made in the churchyard, as he supposed it was a Christian jaw, and ought to have decent burial, wherever the rest of the body might be. I told him that doctors often put bones into quicklime to whiten them nicely, and that I supposed Dr. Pratt had once had a little lime pit in the garden for that purpose, and had forgotten the jaw. Trehearn looked at me quietly.

"Maybe it fitted that skull that used to be in the cupboard upstairs, sir," he said. "Maybe Dr. Pratt had put the skull into the lime to clean it, or something, and when he took it out he left the lower jaw behind. There's some human hair sticking in the lime, sir."

I saw there was, and that was what Trehearn said. If he did not suspect something, why in the world should he have suggested that the jaw might fit the skull? Besides, it did. That's proof that he knows more than he cares to tell. Do you suppose he looked before she was buried? Or perhaps—when he buried Luke in the same grave——

Well, well, it's of no use to go over that, is it? I said I would keep the jaw with the skull, and I took it upstairs and fitted it into its place. There's not the slightest doubt about the two belonging together, and together they are.

Trehearn knows several things. We were talking about plastering the kitchen a while ago, and he happened to remember that it had not been done since the very week when Mrs. Pratt died. He did not say that the mason must have left some lime on the place, but he thought it, and that it was the very same lime he had found in the asparagus pit. He knows a lot. Trehearn is one of your silent beggars who can put two and two together. That grave is very near the back of his cottage, too, and he's one of the quickest men with a spade I ever saw. If he wanted to know the truth, he could, and no one else would ever be the wiser unless he chose to tell. In a quiet village like ours, people don't go and spend the night in the churchyard to see whether the sexton potters about by himself between ten o'clock and daylight.

What is awful to think of, is Luke's deliberation, if he did it; his cool certainty that no one would find him out; above all, his nerve, for that must have been extraordinary. I sometimes think it's bad enough to live in the place where it was done, if it really was done. I always put in the condition, you see, for the sake of his memory, and a little bit for my own sake, too.

I'll go upstairs and fetch the box in a minute. Let me light my pipe; there's no hurry! We had supper early, and it's only half-past nine o'clock. I never let a friend go to bed before twelve, or with less than three glasses—you may have as many more as you like, but you shan't have less, for the sake of old times.

It's breezing up again, do you hear? That was only a lull just now, and we are going to have a bad night.

A thing happened that made me start a little when I found that the jaw fitted exactly. I'm not very easily startled in that way myself, but I have seen people make a quick movement, drawing their breath sharply, when they had thought they were alone and suddenly turned and saw some one very near them. Nobody can call that fear. You wouldn't, would you? No. Well, just when I had set the jaw in its place under the skull, the teeth closed sharply on my finger. It felt exactly as if it were biting me hard, and I confess that I jumped before I realised that I had been pressing the jaw and the skull together with my other hand. I assure you I was not at all nervous. It was broad daylight, too, and a fine day, and the sun was streaming into the best bedroom. It would have been absurd to be nervous, and it was only a quick mistaken impression, but it really made me feel queer. Somehow it made me think of the funny verdict of the coroner's jury on Luke's death, "by the hand or teeth of some person or animal unknown." Ever since that I've wished I had seen those marks on his throat, though the lower jaw was missing then.

I have often seen a man do insane things with his hands that he does not realise at all. I once saw a man hanging on by an old awning stop with one hand, leaning backward, outboard, with all his weight on it, and he was just cutting the stop with the knife in his other hand when I got my arms round him. We were in mid-ocean, going twenty knots. He had not the smallest idea what he was doing; neither had I when I managed to pinch my finger between the teeth of that thing. I can feel it now. It was exactly as if it were alive and were trying to bite me. It would if it could, for I know it hates me, poor thing! Do you suppose that what rattles about inside is really a bit of lead? Well, I'll get the box down presently, and if whatever it is happens to drop out into your hands that's your affair. If it's only a clod of earth or a pebble, the whole matter would be off my mind, and I don't believe I should ever think of the skull again; but somehow I cannot bring myself to shake out the bit of hard stuff myself. The mere idea that it may be lead makes me confoundedly uncomfortable, yet I've got the conviction that I shall know before long. I shall certainly know. I'm sure Trehearn knows, but he's such a silent beggar.

I'll go upstairs now and get it. What? You had better go with me? Ha, ha! do you think I'm afraid of a bandbox and a noise? Nonsense!

Bother the candle, it won't light! As if the ridiculous thing understood what it's wanted for! Look at that—the third match. They light fast enough for my pipe. There, do you see? It's a fresh box, just out of the tin safe where I keep the supply on account of the dampness. Oh, you think the wick of the candle may be damp, do you? All right, I'll light the beastly thing in the fire. That won't go out, at all events. Yes, it sputters a bit, but it will keep lighted now. It burns just like any other candle, doesn't it? The fact is, candles are not very good about here. I don't know where they come from, but they have a way of burning low occasionally, with a greenish flame that spits tiny sparks, and I'm often annoyed by their going out of themselves. It cannot be helped, for it will be long before we have electricity in our village. It really is rather a poor light, isn't it?

You think I had better leave you the candle and take the lamp, do you? I don't like to carry lamps about, that's the truth. I never dropped one in my life, but I have always thought I might, and it's so confoundedly dangerous if you do. Besides, I am pretty well used to these rotten candles by this time.

You may as well finish that glass while I'm getting it, for I don't mean to let you off with less than three before you go to bed. You won't have to go upstairs, either, for I've put you in the old study next to the surgery—that's where I live myself. The fact is, I never ask a friend to sleep upstairs now. The last man who did was Crackenthorpe, and he said he was kept awake all night. You remember old Crack, don't you? He stuck to the Service, and they've just made him an admiral. Yes, I'm off now—unless the candle goes out. I couldn't help asking if you remembered Crackenthorpe. If any one had told us that the skinny little idiot he used to be was to turn out the most successful of the lot of us, we should have laughed at the idea, shouldn't we? You and I did not do badly, it's true—but I'm really going now. I don't mean to let you think that I've been putting it off by talking! As if there were anything to be afraid of! If I were scared, I should tell you so quite frankly, and get you to go upstairs with me.

* * * * * * * *

Here's the box. I brought it down very carefully, so as not to disturb it, poor thing. You see, if it were shaken, the jaw might get separated from it again, and I'm sure it wouldn't like that. Yes, the candle went out as I was coming downstairs, but that was the draught from the leaky window on the landing. Did you hear anything? Yes, there was another scream. Am I pale, do you say? That's nothing. My heart is a little queer sometimes, and I went upstairs too fast. In fact, that's one reason why I really prefer to live altogether on the ground floor.

Wherever that shriek came from, it was not from the skull, for I had the box in my hand when I heard the noise, and here it is now; so we have proved definitely that the screams are produced by something else. I've no doubt I shall find out some day what makes them. Some crevice in the wall, of course, or a crack in a chimney, or a chink in the frame of a window. That's the way all ghost stories end in real life. Do you know, I'm jolly glad I thought of going up and bringing it down for you to see, for that last shriek settles the question. To think that I should have been so weak as to fancy that the poor skull could really cry out like a living thing!

Now I'll open the box, and we'll take it out and look at it under the bright light. It's rather awful to think that the poor lady used to sit there, in your chair, evening after evening, in just the same light, isn't it? But then—I've made up my mind that it's all rubbish from beginning to end, and that it's just an old skull that Luke had when he was a student; and perhaps he put it into the lime merely to whiten it, and could not find the jaw.

I made a seal on the string, you see, after I had put the jaw in its place, and I wrote on the cover. There's the old white label on it still, from the milliner's, addressed to Mrs. Pratt when the hat was sent to her, and as there was room I wrote on the edge: "A skull, once the property of the late Luke Pratt, M.D." I don't quite know why I wrote that, unless it was with the idea of explaining how the thing happened to be in my possession. I cannot help wondering sometimes what sort of hat it was that came in the bandbox. What colour was it, do you think? Was it a gay spring hat with a bobbing feather and pretty ribands? Strange that the very same box should hold the head that wore the finery—perhaps. No—we made up our minds that it just came from the hospital in London where Luke did his time. It's far better to look at it in that light, isn't it? There's no more connection between that skull and poor Mrs. Pratt than there was between my story about the lead and——

Good Lord! Take the lamp—don't let it go out, if you can help it—I'll have the window fastened again in a second—I say, what a gale! There, it's out! I told you so! Never mind, there's the firelight—I've got the window shut—the bolt was only half down. Was the box blown off the table? Where the deuce is it? There! That won't open again, for I've put up the bar. Good dodge, an old-fashioned bar—there's nothing like it. Now, you find the bandbox while I light the lamp. Confound those wretched matches! Yes, a pipe spill is better—it must light in the fire—I hadn't thought of it—thank you—there we are again. Now, where's the box? Yes, put it back on the table, and we'll open it.

That's the first time I have ever known the wind to burst that window open; but it was partly carelessness on my part when I last shut it. Yes, of course I heard the scream. It seemed to go all round the house before it broke in at the window. That proves that it's always been the wind and nothing else, doesn't it? When it was not the wind, it was my imagination. I've always been a very imaginative man: I must have been, though I did not know it. As we grow older we understand ourselves better, don't you know?

I'll have a drop of the Hulstkamp neat, by way of an exception, since you are filling up your glass. That damp gust chilled me, and with my rheumatic tendency I'm very much afraid of a chill, for the cold sometimes seems to stick in my joints all winter when it once gets in.

By George, that's good stuff! I'll just light a fresh pipe, now that everything is snug again, and then we'll open the box. I'm so glad we heard that last scream together, with the skull here on the table between us, for a thing cannot possibly be in two places at the same time, and the noise most certainly came from outside, as any noise the wind makes must. You thought you heard it scream through the room after the window was burst open? Oh yes, so did I, but that was natural enough when everything was open. Of course we heard the wind. What could one expect?

Look here, please. I want you to see that the seal is intact before we open the box together. Will you take my glasses? No, you have your own. All right. The seal is sound, you see, and you can read the words of the motto easily. "Sweet and low"—that's it—because the poem goes on "Wind of the Western sea," and says, "blow him again to me," and all that. Here is the seal on my watch-chain, where it's hung for more than forty years. My poor little wife gave it to me when I was courting, and I never had any other. It was just like her to think of those words—she was always fond of Tennyson.

It's of no use to cut the string, for it's fastened to the box, so I'll just break the wax and untie the knot, and afterward we'll seal it up again. You see, I like to feel that the thing is safe in its place, and that nobody can take it out. Not that I should suspect Trehearn of meddling with it, but I always feel that he knows a lot more than he tells.

You see, I've managed it without breaking the string, though when I fastened it I never expected to open the bandbox again. The lid comes off easily enough. There! Now look!

What? Nothing in it? Empty? It's gone, man, the skull is gone!

* * * * * * * *

No, there's nothing the matter with me. I'm only trying to collect my thoughts. It's so strange. I'm positively certain that it was inside when I put on the seal last spring. I can't have imagined that: it's utterly impossible. If I ever took a stiff glass with a friend now and then, I would admit that I might have made some idiotic mistake when I had taken too much. But I don't, and I never did. A pint of ale at supper and half a go of rum at bedtime was the most I ever took in my good days. I believe it's always we sober fellows who get rheumatism and gout! Yet there was my seal, and there is the empty bandbox. That's plain enough.

I say, I don't half like this. It's not right. There's something wrong about it, in my opinion. You needn't talk to me about supernatural manifestations, for I don't believe in them, not a little bit! Somebody must have tampered with the seal and stolen the skull. Sometimes, when I go out to work in the garden in summer, I leave my watch and chain, on the table. Trehearn must have taken the seal then, and used it, for he would be quite sure that I should not come in for at least an hour.

If it was not Trehearn—oh, don't talk to me about the possibility that the thing has got out by itself! If it has, it must be somewhere about the house, in some out-of-the-way corner, waiting. We may come upon it anywhere, waiting for us, don't you know?—just waiting in the dark. Then it will scream at me; it will shriek at me in the dark, for it hates me, I tell you!

The bandbox is quite empty. We are not dreaming, either of us. There, I turn it upside down.

What's that? Something fell out as I turned it over. It's on the floor, it's near your feet, I know it is, and we must find it. Help me to find it, man. Have you got it? For God's sake, give it to me, quickly!

Lead! I knew it when I heard it fall. I knew it couldn't be anything else by the little thud it made on the hearth-rug. So it was lead after all, and Luke did it.

I feel a little bit shaken up—not exactly nervous, you know, but badly shaken up, that's the fact. Anybody would, I should think. After all, you cannot say that it's fear of the thing, for I went up and brought it down—at least, I believed I was bringing it down, and that's the same thing, and by George, rather than give in to such silly nonsense, I'll take the box upstairs again and put it back in its place. It's not that. It's the certainty that the poor little woman came to her end in that way, by my fault, because I told the story. That's what is so dreadful. Somehow, I had always hoped that I should never be quite sure of it, but there is no doubting it now. Look at that!

Look at it! That little lump of lead with no particular shape. Think of what it did, man! Doesn't it make you shiver? He gave her something to make her sleep, of course, but there must have been one moment of awful agony. Think of having boiling lead poured into your brain. Think of it. She was dead before she could scream, but only think of—oh! there it is again—it's just outside—I know it's just outside—I can't keep it out of my head!—oh!—oh!

* * * * * * * *

You thought I had fainted? No, I wish I had, for it would have stopped sooner. It's all very well to say that it's only a noise, and that a noise never hurt anybody—you're as white as a shroud yourself. There's only one thing to be done, if we hope to close an eye to-night. We must find it and put it back into its bandbox and shut it up in the cupboard, where it likes to be. I don't know how it got out, but it wants to get in again. That's why it screams so awfully to-night—it was never so bad as this—never since I first— —

Bury it? Yes, if we can find it, we'll bury it, if it takes us all night. We'll bury it six feet deep and ram down the earth over it, so that it shall never get out again, and if it screams, we shall hardly hear it so deep down. Quick, we'll get the lantern and look for it. It cannot be far away; I'm sure it's just outside—it was coming in when I shut the window, I know it.

Yes, you're quite right. I'm losing my senses, and I must get hold of myself. Don't speak to me for a minute or two; I'll sit quite still and keep my eyes shut and repeat something I know. That's the best way.

"Add together the altitude, the latitude, and the polar distance, divide by two and subtract the altitude from the half-sum; then add the logarithm of the secant of the latitude, the cosecant of the polar distance, the cosine of the half-sum and the sine of the half-sum minus the altitude"—there! Don't say that I'm out of my senses, for my memory is all right, isn't it?

Of course, you may say that it's mechanical, and that we never forget the things we learned when we were boys and have used almost every day for a lifetime. But that's the very point. When a man is going crazy, it's the mechanical part of his mind that gets out of order and won't work right; he remembers things that never happened, or he sees things that aren't real, or he hears noises when there is perfect silence. That's not what is the matter with either of us, is it?

Come, we'll get the lantern and go round the house. It's not raining—only blowing like old boots, as we used to say. The lantern is in the cupboard under the stairs in the hall, and I always keep it trimmed in case of a wreck.

No use to look for the thing? I don't see how you can say that. It was nonsense to talk of burying it, of course, for it doesn't want to be buried; it wants to go back into its bandbox and be taken upstairs, poor thing! Trehearn took it out, I know, and made the seal over again. Perhaps he took it to the churchyard, and he may have meant well. I daresay he thought that it would not scream any more if it were quietly laid in consecrated ground, near where it belongs. But it has come home. Yes, that's it. He's not half a bad fellow, Trehearn, and rather religiously inclined, I think. Does not that sound natural, and reasonable, and well meant? He supposed it screamed because it was not decently buried—with the rest. But he was wrong. How should he know that it screams at me because it hates me, and because it's my fault that there was that little lump of lead in it?

No use to look for it, anyhow? Nonsense! I tell you it wants to be found—Hark! what's that knocking? Do you hear it? Knock—knock—knock—three times, then a pause, and then again. It has a hollow sound, hasn't it?

It has come home. I've heard that knock before. It wants to come in and be taken upstairs, in its box. It's at the front door.

Will you come with me? We'll take it in. Yes, I own that I don't like to go alone and open the door. The thing will roll in and stop against my foot, just as it did before, and the light will go out. I'm a good deal shaken by finding that bit of lead, and, besides, my heart isn't quite right—too much strong tobacco, perhaps. Besides, I'm quite willing to own that I'm a bit nervous to-night, if I never was before in my life.

That's right, come along! I'll take the box with me, so as not to come back. Do you hear the knocking? It's not like any other knocking I ever heard. If you will hold this door open, I can find the lantern under the stairs by the light from this room without bringing the lamp into the hall—it would only go out.

The thing knows we are coming—hark! It's impatient to get in. Don't shut the door till the lantern is ready, whatever you do. There will be the usual trouble with the matches, I suppose—no, the first one, by Jove! I tell you it wants to get in, so there's no trouble. All right with that door now; shut it, please. Now come and hold the lantern, for it's blowing so hard outside that I shall have to use both hands. That's it, hold the light low. Do you hear the knocking still? Here goes—I'll open just enough with my foot against the bottom of the door—now!

Catch it! it's only the wind that blows it across the floor, that's all—there's half a hurricane outside, I tell you! Have you got it? The bandbox is on the table. One minute, and I'll have the bar up. There!

Why did you throw it into the box so roughly? It doesn't like that, you know.

What do you say? Bitten your hand? Nonsense, man! You did just what I did. You pressed the jaws together with your other hand and pinched yourself. Let me see. You don't mean to say you have drawn blood? You must have squeezed hard, by Jove, for the skin is certainly torn. I'll give you some carbolic solution for it before we go to bed, for they say a scratch from a skull's tooth may go bad and give trouble.

Come inside again and let me see it by the lamp. I'll bring the bandbox—never mind the lantern, it may just as well burn in the hall, for I shall need it presently when I go up the stairs. Yes, shut the door if you will; it makes it more cheerful and bright. Is your finger still bleeding? I'll get you the carbolic in an instant; just let me see the thing.

Ugh! There's a drop of blood on the upper jaw. It's on the eye-tooth. Ghastly, isn't it? When I saw it running along the floor of the hall, the strength almost went out of my hands, and I felt my knees bending; then I understood that it was the gale, driving it over the smooth boards. You don't blame me? No, I should think not! We were boys together, and we've seen a thing or two, and we may just as well own to each other that we were both in a beastly funk when it slid across the floor at you. No wonder you pinched your finger picking it up, after that, if I did the same thing out of sheer nervousness, in broad daylight, with the sun streaming in on me.

Strange that the jaw should stick to it so closely, isn't it? I suppose it's the dampness, for it shuts like a vice—I have wiped off the drop of blood, for it was not nice to look at. I'm not going to try to open the jaws, don't be afraid! I shall not play any tricks with the poor thing, but I'll just seal the box again, and we'll take it upstairs and put it away where it wants to be. The wax is on the writing-table by the window. Thank you. It will be long before I leave my seal lying about again, for Trehearn to use, I can tell you. Explain? I don't explain natural phenomena, but if you choose to think that Trehearn had hidden it somewhere in the bushes, and that the gale blew it to the house against the door, and made it knock, as if it wanted to be let in, you're not thinking the impossible, and I'm quite ready to agree with you.

Do you see that? You can swear that you've actually seen me seal it this time, in case anything of the kind should occur again. The wax fastens the strings to the lid, which cannot possibly be lifted, even enough to get in one finger. You're quite satisfied, aren't you? Yes. Besides, I shall lock the cupboard and keep the key in my pocket hereafter.

Now we can take the lantern and go upstairs. Do you know? I'm very much inclined to agree with your theory that the wind blew it against the house. I'll go ahead, for I know the stairs; just hold the lantern near my feet as we go up. How the wind howls and whistles! Did you feel the sand on the floor under your shoes as we crossed the hall?

Yes—this is the door of the best bedroom. Hold up the lantern, please. This side, by the head of the bed. I left the cupboard open when I got the box. Isn't it queer how the faint odour of women's dresses will hang about an old closet for years? This is the shelf. You've seen me set the box there, and now you see me turn the key and put it into my pocket. So that's done!

* * * * * * *

Good-night. Are you sure you're quite comfortable? It's not much of a room, but I daresay you would as soon sleep here as upstairs to-night. If you want anything, sing out; there's only a lath and plaster partition between us. There's not so much wind on this side by half. There's the Hollands on the table, if you'll have one more nightcap. No? Well, do as you please. Good-night again, and don't dream about that thing, if you can.

* * * * * * *

The following paragraph appeared in the Penraddon News, 23rd November, 1906:

"Mysterious Death of a Retired Sea Captain

"The village of Tredcombe is much disturbed by the strange death of Captain Charles Braddock, and all sorts of impossible stories are circulating with regard to the circumstances, which certainly seem difficult of explanation. The retired captain, who had successfully commanded in his time the largest and fastest liners belonging to one of the principal transatlantic steamship companies, was found dead in his bed on Tuesday morning in his own cottage, a quarter of a mile from the village. An examination was made at once by the local practitioner, which revealed the horrible fact that the deceased had been bitten in the throat by a human assailant, with such amazing force as to crush the windpipe and cause death. The marks of the teeth of both jaws were so plainly visible on the skin that they could be counted, but the perpetrator of the deed had evidently lost the two lower middle incisors. It is hoped that this peculiarity may help to identify the murderer, who can only be a dangerous escaped maniac. The deceased, though over sixty-five years of age, is said to have been a hale man of considerable physical strength, and it is remarkable that no signs of any struggle were visible in the room, nor could it be ascertained how the murderer had entered the house. Warning has been sent to all the insane asylums in the United Kingdom, but as yet no information has been received regarding the escape of any dangerous patient.

"The coroner's jury returned the somewhat singular verdict that Captain Braddock came to his death 'by the hands or teeth of some person unknown.' The local surgeon is said to have expressed privately the opinion that the maniac is a woman, a view he deduces from the small size of the jaws, as shown by the marks of the teeth. The whole affair is shrouded in mystery. Captain Braddock was a widower, and lived alone. He leaves no children."

[Note.—Students of ghost lore and haunted houses will find the foundation of the foregoing story in the legends about a skull which is still preserved in the farm-house called Bettiscombe Manor, situated, I believe, on the Dorsetshire coast.]

A STRANGE CHRISTMAS GAME

Charlotte Riddell, 1868

WHEN, through the death of a distant relative, I, John Lester, succeeded to the Martingdale Estate, there could not have been found in the length and breadth of England a happier pair than myself and my only sister Clare.

We were not such utter hypocrites as to affect sorrow for the loss of our kinsman, Paul Lester, a man whom we had never seen, of whom we had heard but little, and that little unfavourable, at whose hands we had never received a single benefit - who was, in short, as great a stranger to us as the then Prime Minister, the Emperor of Russia, or any other human being utterly removed from our extremely humble sphere of life.

His loss was very certainly our gain. His death represented to us, not a dreary parting from one long loved and highly honoured, but the accession of lands, houses, consideration, wealth, to myself - John Lester, Esquire, Martingdale, Bedfordshire, whilom John Lester, artist and second-floor lodger at 32, Great Smith Street, Bloomsbury.

Not that Martingdale was much of an estate as country properties go. The Lesters who had succeeded to that domain from time to time during the course of a few hundred years, could by no stretch of courtesy have been called prudent men. In regard of their posterity they were, indeed, scarcely honest, for they parted with manors and farms, with common rights and advowsons, in a manner at once so baronial and so unbusiness-like, that Martingdale at length in the hands of Jeremy Lester, the last resident owner, melted to a mere little dot in the map of Bedfordshire.

Concerning this Jeremy Lester there was a mystery. No man could say what had become of him. He was in the oak parlour at Martingdale one Christmas Eve, and before the next morning he had disappeared - to reappear in the flesh no more.

Over night, one Mr Wharley, a great friend and boon companion of Jeremy's, had sat playing cards with him until after twelve o'clock chimes, then he took leave of his host and rode home under the moonlight. After that no person, as far as could be ascertained, ever saw Jeremy Lester alive.

His ways of life had not been either the most regular, or the most respectable, and it was not until a new year had come in without any tidings of his whereabouts reaching the house, that his servants became seriously alarmed concerning his absence.

Then enquiries were set on foot concerning him - enquiries which grew more urgent as weeks and months passed by without the slightest clue being obtained as to his whereabouts. Rewards were offered, advertisements inserted, but still Jeremy made no sign; and so in course of time the heir-at-law, Paul Lester, took possession of the house, and went down to spend the summer months at Martingdale with his rich wife, and her four children by a first husband. Paul Lester was a barrister – an over-worked barrister, who everyone supposed would be glad enough to leave the bar and settle at Martingdale, where his wife's money and the fortune he had accumulated could not have failed to give him a good standing even among the neighbouring country families; and perhaps it was with such intention that he went down into Bedfordshire.

If this were so, however, he speedily changed his mind, for with the January snows he returned to London, let off the land surrounding the house, shut up the Hall, put in a caretaker, and never troubled himself further about his ancestral seat.

Time went on, and people began to say the house was haunted, that Paul Lester had 'seen something', and so forth - all which stories were duly repeated for our benefit when, forty-one years after the disappearance of Jeremy Lester, Clare and I went down to inspect our inheritance.

I say 'our', because Clare had stuck bravely to me in poverty – grinding poverty, and prosperity was not going to part us now. What was mine was hers, and that she knew, God bless her, without my needing to tell her so.

The transition from rigid economy to comparative wealth was in our case the more delightful also, because we had not in the least degree anticipated it. We never expected Paul Lester's shoes to come to us, and accordingly it was not upon our consciences that we had ever in our dreariest moods wished him dead.

Had he made a will, no doubt we never should have gone to Martingdale, and I, consequently, never written this story; but, luckily for us, he died intestate, and the Bedfordshire property came to me.

As for the fortune, he had spent it in travelling, and in giving great entertainments at his grand house in Portman Square. Concerning his effects, Mrs Lester and I came to a very amicable arrangement, and she did me the honour of inviting me to call upon her occasionally, and, as I heard, spoke of me as a very worthy and presentable young man 'for my station', which, of course, coming from so good an authority, was gratifying. Moreover, she asked me if I intended residing at Martingdale, and on my replying in the affirmative, hoped I should like it.

It struck me at the time that there was a certain significance in her tone, and when I went down to Martingdale and heard the absurd stories which were afloat concerning the house being haunted, I felt confident that if Mrs Lester had hoped much, she had feared more.

People said Mr Jeremy 'walked' at Martingdale. He had been seen, it was averred, by poachers, by gamekeepers, by children who had come to use the park as a near cut to school, by lovers who kept their tryst under the elms and beeches.

As for the caretaker and his wife, the third in residence since Jeremy Lester's disappearance, the man gravely shook his head when questioned, while the woman stated that wild horses, or even wealth untold, should not draw her into the red bedroom, nor into the oak parlour, after dark.

'I have heard my mother tell, sir - it was her as followed old Mrs Reynolds, the first caretaker - how there were things went on in these self same rooms as might make any Christian's hair stand on end. Such stamping, and swearing, and knocking about on furniture; and then tramp, tramp, up the great staircase; and along the corridor and so into the red bedroom, and then bang, and tramp, tramp again. They do say, sir, Mr Paul Lester met him once, and from that time the oak parlour has never been opened. I never was inside it myself.'

Upon hearing which fact, the first thing I did was to proceed to the oak parlour, open the shutters, and let the August sun stream in upon the haunted chamber. It was an old-fashioned, plainly furnished apartment, with a large table in the centre, a smaller in a recess by the fire-place, chairs ranged against the walls, and a dusty moth-eaten carpet upon the floor. There were dogs on the hearth, broken and rusty; there was a brass fender, tarnished and battered; a picture of some sea-fight over the mantel-piece, while another work of art about equal in merit hung between the windows. Altogether, an utterly prosaic and yet not uncheerful apartment, from out of which the ghosts flitted as soon as daylight was let into it, and which I proposed, as soon as I 'felt my feet', to redecorate, refurnish, and convert into a pleasant morning-room. I was still under thirty, but I had learned prudence in that very good school, Necessity; and it was not my intention to spend much money until I had ascertained for certain what were the actual revenues derivable from the lands still belonging to the Martingdale estates, and the charges upon them. In fact, I wanted to know what I was worth before committing myself to any great extravagances, and the place had for so long been neglected, that I experienced some difficulty in arriving at the state of my real income.

But in the meanwhile, Clare and I found great enjoyment in exploring every nook and corner of our domain, in turning over the contents of old chests and cupboards, in examining the faces of our ancestors looking down on us from the walls, in walking through the neglected gardens, full of weeds, overgrown with shrubs and birdweed, where the boxwood was eighteen feet high, and the shoots of the rosetrees yards long. I have put the place in order since then; there is no grass on the paths, there are no trailing brambles over the ground, the hedges have been cut and trimmed, and the trees pruned and the boxwood clipped. But I often say nowadays that in spite of all my improvements, or rather, in consequence of them, Martingdale does not look one half so pretty as it did in its pristine state of uncivilised picturesqueness.

Although I determined not to commence repairing and decorating the house till better informed concerning the rental of Martingdale, still the state of my finances was so far satisfactory that Clare and I decided on going abroad to take our long-talked-of holiday before the fine weather was past. We could not tell what a year might bring forth, as Clare sagely remarked; it was wise to take our pleasure while we could; and accordingly, before the end of August arrived we were wandering about the continent, loitering at Rouen, visiting the galleries at Paris, and talking of extending our one month of enjoyment into three. What decided me on this course was the circumstance of our becoming acquainted with an English family who intended wintering in Rome. We met accidentally, but discovering that we were near neighbours in England - in fact that Mr Cronson's property lay close beside Martingdale - the slight acquaintance soon ripened into intimacy, and ere long we were travelling in company.

From the first, Clare did not much like this arrangement. There was 'a little girl' in England she wanted me to marry, and Mr Cronson had a daughter who certainly was both handsome and attractive. The little girl had not despised John Lester, artist, while Miss Cronson indisputably set her cap at John Lester of Martingdale, and would have turned away her pretty face from a poor man's admiring glance – all this I can see plainly enough now, but I was blind then and should have proposed for Maybel - that was her name - before the winter was over, had news not suddenly arrived of the illness of Mrs Cronson, senior. In a moment the programme was changed; our pleasant days of foreign travel were at an end. The Cronsons packed up and departed, while Clare and I returned more slowly to England, a little out of humour, it must be confessed, with each other.

It was the middle of November when we arrived at Martingdale, and found the place anything but romantic or pleasant. The walks were wet and sodden, the trees were leafless, there were no flowers save a few late pink roses blooming in the garden. It had been a wet season, and the place looked miserable. Clare would not ask Alice down to keep her company in the winter months, as she had intended; and for myself, the Cronsons were still absent in Norfolk, where they meant to spend Christmas with old Mrs. Cronson, now recovered.

Altogether, Martingdale seemed dreary enough, and the ghost stories we had laughed at while sunshine flooded the room, became less unreal,when we had nothing but blazing fires and wax candles to dispel the gloom. They became more real also when servant after servant left us to seek situations elsewhere; when "noises" grew frequent in the house; when we ourselves, Clare and I, with our own ears heard the tramp, tramp, the banging and the chattering which had been described to us.

My dear reader, you doubtless are free from superstitious fancies. You poohpooh the existence of ghosts, and "only wish you could find a haunted house in which to spend a night," which is all very brave and praiseworthy, but wait till you are left in a dreary, desolate old country mansion, filled with the most unaccountable sounds, without a servant, with none save an old caretaker and his wife, who, living at the extremest end of the building, heard nothing of the tramp, tramp, bang, bang, going on at all hours of the night.

At first I imagined the noises were produced by some evil-disposed persons, who wished, for purposes of their own, to keep the house uninhabited; but by degrees Clare and I came to the conclusion the visitation must be supernatural, and Martingdale by consequence untenantable.

Still being practical people, and unlike our predecessors, not having money to live where and how we liked, we decided to watch and see whether we could trace any human influence in the matter. If not, it was agreed we were to pull down the right wing of the house and the principal staircase.

For nights and nights we sat up till two or three o'clock in the morning, Clare engaged in needlework, I reading, with a revolver lying on the table beside me; but nothing, neither sound nor appearance rewarded our vigil. This confirmed my first ideas that the sounds were not supernatural; but just to test the matter, I determined on Christmas-eve, the anniversary of Mr. Jeremy Lester's disappearance, to keep watch myself in the red bed-chamber. Even to Clare I never mentioned my intention.

About ten, tired out with our previous vigils, we each retired to rest. Somewhat ostentatiously, perhaps, I noisily shut the door of my room, and when I opened it half an hour afterwards, no mouse could have pursued its way along the corridor with greater silence and caution than myself. Quite in the dark I sat in the red room. For over an hour I might as well have been in my grave for anything I could see in the apartment; but at the end of that time the moon rose and cast strange lights across the floor and upon the wall of the haunted chamber.

Hitherto I had kept my watch opposite the window; now I changed my place to a corner near the door, where I was shaded from observation by the heavy hangings of the bed, and an antique wardrobe.

Still I sat on, but still no sound broke the silence. I was weary with many nights' watching; and tired of my solitary vigil, I dropped at last into a slumber from which I wakened by hearing the door softly opened.

"John," said my sister, almost in a whisper; "John, are you here?"

"Yes, Clare," I answered; "but what are you doing up at this hour?"

"Come downstairs," she replied; "they are in the oak parlor."

I did not need any explanation as to whom she meant, but crept downstairs after her, warned by an uplifted hand of the necessity for silence and caution.

By the door—by the open door of the oak parlor, she paused, and we both looked in.

There was the room we left in darkness overnight, with a bright wood fire blazing on the hearth, candles on the chimney-piece, the small table pulled out from its accustomed corner, and two men seated beside it, playing at cribbage.

We could see the face of the younger player; it was that of a man about five and-twenty, of a man who had lived hard and wickedly; who had wasted his substance and his health; who had been while in the flesh Jeremy Lester. It would be difficult for me to say how I knew this, how in a moment I identified the features of the player with those of the man who had been missing for forty-one years— forty-one years that very night. He was dressed in the costume of a bygone period; his hair was powdered, and round his wrists there were ruffles of lace.

He looked like one who, having come from some great party, had sat down after his return home to play cards with an intimate friend. On his little finger there sparkled a ring, in the front of his shirt there gleamed a valuable diamond. There were diamond buckles in his shoes, and, according to the fashion of his time, he wore knee breeches and silk stockings, which showed off advantageously the shape of a remarkably good leg and ankle.

He sat opposite the door, but never once lifted his eyes to it. His attention seemed concentrated on the cards.

For a time there was utter silence in the room, broken only by the momentous counting of the game. In the doorway we stood, holding our breath, terrified and yet fascinated by the scene which was being acted before us.

The ashes dropped on the hearth softly and like the snow; we could hear the rustle of the cards as they were dealt out and fell upon the table; we listened to the count—fifteen-one, fifteen-two, and so forth—but there was no other word spoken till at length the player whose face we could not see, exclaimed, "I win; the game is mine."

Then his opponent took up the cards, sorted them over negligently in his hand, put them close together, and flung the whole pack in his guest's face, exclaiming, "Cheat; liar; take that!"

There was a bustle and confusion—a flinging over of chairs, and fierce gesticulation, and such a noise of passionate voices mingling, that we could not hear a sentence which was uttered. All at once, however, Jeremy Lester strode out of the room in so great a hurry that he almost touched us where we stood; out of the room, and tramp, tramp up the staircase to the red room, whence he descended in a few minutes with a couple of rapiers under his arm.

When he re-entered the room he gave, as it seemed to us, the other man his choice of the weapons, and then he flung open the window, and after ceremoniously giving place for his opponent to pass out first, he walked forth into the night air, Clare and I following.

We went through the garden and down a narrow winding walk to a smooth piece of turf, sheltered from the north by a plantation of young fir trees. It was a bright moonlight night by this time, and we could distinctly see Jeremy Lester measuring off the ground.

"When you say 'three,'" he said at last to the man whose back was still towards us. They had drawn lots for the ground, and the lot had fallen against Mr. Lester. He stood thus with the moonbeams falling upon him, and a handsomer fellow I would never desire to behold.

"One," began the other; "two," and before our kinsman had the slightest suspicion of his design, he was upon him, and his rapier through Jeremy Lester's breast.

At the sight of that cowardly treachery, Clare screamed aloud. In a moment the combatants had disappeared, the moon was obscured behind a cloud, and we were standing in the shadow of the fir-plantation, shivering with cold and terror.

But we knew at last what had become of the late owner of Martingdale, that he had fallen, not in fair fight, but foully murdered by a false friend.

When late on Christmas morning I awoke, it was to see a white world, to behold the ground, and trees, and shrubs all laden and covered with snow.

There was snow everywhere, such snow as no person could remember having fallen for forty-one years.

"It was on just such a Christmas as this that Mr. Jeremy disappeared," remarked the old sexton to my sister, who had insisted on dragging me through the snow to church, whereupon Clare fainted away and was carried into the vestry, where I made a full confession to the Vicar of all we had beheld the previous night.

At first that worthy individual rather inclined to treat the matter lightly, but when a fortnight after, the snow melted away and the fir-plantation came to be examined, he confessed there might be more things in heaven and earth than his limited philosophy had dreamed of.

In a little clear space just within the plantation, Jeremy Lester's body was found. We knew it by the ring and the diamond buckles, and the sparklin breastpin; and Mr. Cronson, who in his capacity as magistrate came over t inspect these relics, was visibly perturbed at my narrative.

"Pray, Mr. Lester, did you in your dream see the face of—of the gentleman— your kinsman's opponent?"

"No," I answered, "he sat and stood with his back to us all the time."

"There is nothing more, of course, to be done in the matter," observed Mr. Cronson.

"Nothing," I replied; and there the affair would doubtless have terminated, but that a few days afterwards, when we were dining at Cronson Park, Clare all of a sudden dropped the glass of water she was carrying to her lips, and exclaiming, "Look, John, there he is!" rose from her seat, and with a face as white as the table cloth, pointed to a portrait hanging on the wall. "I saw him for an instant when he turned his head towards the door as Jeremy Lester left it," she explained; "that is he."

Of what followed after this identification I have only the vaguest recollection.

Servants rushed hither and thither; Mrs. Cronson dropped off her chair into hysterics; the young ladies gathered round their mamma; Mr. Cronson, trembling like one in an ague fit, attempted some kind of an explanation, while Clare kept praying to be taken away—only to be taken away.

I took her away, not merely from Cronson Park but from Martingdale. Before we left the latter place, however, I had an interview with Mr. Cronson, who said the portrait Clare had identified was that of his wife's father, the last person who saw Jeremy Lester alive.

"He is an old man now," finished Mr. Cronson, "a man of over eighty, who has confessed everything to me. You won't bring further sorrow and disgrace upon us by making this matter public?"

I promised him I would keep silence, but the story gradually oozed out, and the Cronsons left the country.

My sister never returned to Martingdale; she married and is living in London.

Though I assure her there are no strange noises in my house, she will not visit Bedfordshire, where the "little girl" she wanted me so long ago to "think of seriously," is now my wife and the mother of my children.

Printed in Great Britain
by Amazon

51357235R00158